The Consciousness, the Rosette entity, the Alien Intelligence . . . all of those were names for something Humankind had never truly encountered and might never be able to understand.

Limpy was here to try to learn more.

"Hey, Limp?"

"Yes, Captain Mosely?"

"What's all that stuff over there? Opposite the Rosette opening?"

He knew exactly what Mosely was referring to. He'd been watching the phenomenon grow and develop for several minutes now . . . a huge cloud of what looked like smoke, white and gray-silver in the massed starlight.

"Unknown, Captain. It appears to be clouds of micromachines similar to those you call fireflies, numbering in the trillions."

"What are they doing?"

"Coming in this general direction."

"Shit . . ."

The *Olympia* AI continued watching for several moments.

"Captain, I would suggest you sound general quarters."

"I was just arriving at the same conclusion."

By Ian Douglas

Star Carrier
EARTH STRIKE
CENTER OF GRAVITY
SINGULARITY
DEEP SPACE
DARK MATTER
DEEP TIME
DARK MIND
BRIGHT LIGHT

Andromedan Dark
ALTERED STARSCAPE
DARKNESS FALLING

Star Corpsman
BLOODSTAR
ABYSS DEEP

The Galactic Marines Saga

The Heritage Trilogy
SEMPER MARS
LUNA MARINE
EUROPA STRIKE

The Legacy Trilogy
STAR CORPS
BATTLESPACE
STAR MARINES

The Inheritance Trilogy
STAR STRIKE
GALACTIC CORPS
SEMPER HUMAN

BRIGHT LIGHT
STAR CARRIER

BOOK EIGHT

IAN DOUGLAS

HARPER
Voyager

Harper*Voyager*
An imprint of HarperCollins*Publishers* Ltd
1 London Bridge Street
London SE1 9GF

www.harpercollins.co.uk

First published by HarperCollins*Publishers* 2018
This paperback original edition 2018

A catalogue record for this book is available from the British Library

ISBN: 978-0-00-812112-9

Printed and bound in the UK by CPI Group (UK) Ltd, Croydon CR0 4YY

MIX
Paper from
responsible sources
FSC
www.fsc.org   FSC® C007454

This book is produced from independently certified FSC™ paper
to ensure responsible forest management.
For more information visit: **www.harpercollins.co.uk/green**

As always . . .
for Brea

Prologue

The Consciousness had known of Earth and of the star-faring civilization centered there for a long time. Indeed, given that it spanned vast gulfs of time as well as space, it was as if it had *always* known.

In the heart of the teeming sphere of 10 million ancient suns known to the humans as Omega Centauri, at the central rosette of six massive black holes orbiting their common center in a patently artificial arrangement, the Consciousness brooded on the intelligent beings it had found in this new, painfully young universe.

Intelligent was such a relative concept.

This was bolstered by the fact that the Consciousness had . . . *tasted* a number of them, sampling the minute ships and other structures within this volume of space.

Most of the minds it had sampled were of pathetically slow and limited capabilities. A few—a very few—were of higher orders of intelligence, though none came close to the Consciousness in terms of depth or scope of Mind.

Methodically, the Consciousness consumed those worth the effort.

The rest it deleted.

And with a slowly increasing vigor, it explored more

deeply into this corner of the new universe. It had identified a sullen red ember of a star, called Kapteyn's Star by the minds it had assimilated, with a world engineered by beings uploaded into digital form, extremely ancient beings called the Baondyeddi, the Adjugredudhra, and the Groth Hoj. These species, parts of a corporate polity referred to by various sources as the Sh'daar, were in hiding from some unknown threat . . . quite possibly from the Consciousness itself, though the digital refugees didn't seem to know exactly what it was they feared.

Despite their attempts to make themselves undetectable—including the slowing of their awareness of time down to seconds on each century, the Consciousness had found them . . . and it had devoured them, absorbing trillions of minds into its own teeming hive, giving them order and a sense of purpose that had been lacking before.

And in the process it learned of the N'gai Cluster . . . and of the human presence much closer at hand.

And on the human homeworld, just twelve light years distant from Kapteyn's Star, the watching beings of that planet anticipated the arrival of the Consciousness over Earth with an increasing and existential dread.

Chapter One

Battery Park
New York City
1545 hours, EST

"Get the hell out of my head!"

"I submit that we will have to talk at some point," the voice in his head told him. It sounded faintly amused.

Trevor Gray, formerly of the USNA Navy, scowled. "Why?" he replied, blunt and challenging. "Damn it, Konstantin, you've wrecked my life. You know that, don't you?"

"It was necessary for you to leave naval service. Vital, in fact."

"Bullshit. You no longer own me. And I don't think we have a thing to say to one another."

Gray prowled the transparent observation deck extending out over the choppy waters of New York Harbor. At his back, the newly grown towers of what once had been the Manhatt Ruins stabbed skyward, gleaming glass and silver in the winter sun. The place had . . . changed during the past year, changed more than he'd ever imagined possible. The spot where he was standing had been underwater a few months ago. Now it was clean and shiny, with a scattering of civilians who looked like tourists.

He could sense Konstantin, the powerful AI entity based at Tsiolkovsky, on the far side of the moon, watching him closely from the vantage point of his own in-head circuitry. That took a little getting used to. Konstantin's principal hardware might be on the moon, but its—*his*—consciousness could be anywhere within the Global Net on Earth, in low earth orbit—LEO—or in cislunar space. And for sure, a tiny fraction of the super-AI was here in Manhatt, interacting with Gray through his in-head circuitry.

"I need you," Konstantin told him, "to meet with Elena Vasilyeva . . ."

"Damn it, Konstantin, you know how I feel about the Pan-Europeans."

"The war is over, Captain," Konstantin told him, as though explaining *why* to a four-year-old. "In any case, Ms. Vasilyeva is Russian. They were on *our* side, remember?"

"Sorry," Gray said, his mental voice sharp. "It's kind of hard to just forget about Columbus, y'know?"

"Which the Russians had nothing to do with, you may recall," Konstantin said. "In any case, no one is asking you to forget about Columbus."

Gray turned and scowled up at the new towers of Manhattan, his shoulders hunched against the chill, late-January wind off the water. He did not, in fact, hate the Europeans . . . not exactly. The destruction of the USNA capital at Columbus had almost certainly been an act by rogue elements within the Genevan military. Pan-European attempts to seize territory along the USNA east coast had been strategic opportunism, pure and simple, and the true *causus belli* had been their conviction that Humankind had to accept Sh'daar demands and restrict their fast-developing technologies.

And Konstantin was right. With the signing of the Treaty of London, the war was over. Even the alien Sh'daar were friends, now . . . of a sort. The recent discovery that they'd been under the influence of intelligent colonies of bacteria had finally enabled Humankind to begin to understand just what they wanted . . . and what they truly were.

No, Gray might not trust the Pan-Euros, but neither did he hate them. His anger right now was reserved for the AI that had arranged to have him drummed out of the Navy. At Konstantin's urging, he'd taken the star carrier *America* to the long-time stellar mystery of KIC 8462852—a distant, F3V sun better known as "Tabby's Star." What *America* had brought back, an alien e-virus called the Omega Code, had been of tremendous importance . . . but his fourteen-hundred-light-year detour had been in direct and blatant disregard of orders. Naval officers, even admirals, could not simply ignore the dictates of military command procedure, even when ordered to do so by super-AIs. The court-martial board had directed that Gray be reduced in rank to captain, and that he retire from the Navy.

Only recently had Gray learned that it had been Konstantin who'd recommended to the board that he be summarily cashiered.

With friends like that . . .

"I'm bringing in a robot shuttle," Konstantin told him. "Will you meet with Ms. Vasilyeva?"

"Why? More to the point, why *me*?"

"The Pan-Euros want to meet you face-to-face. Ms. Vasilyeva has requested that her team get to speak with you first. You are . . . something of a legend, Captain. Even among those who once were the enemy. You have the reputation of a brilliant tactician, and some of them, I believe, are a bit in awe of you."

Gray made a sour face at the obvious attempt at flattery. "Sure. Whatever. . . ."

"Ms. Vasilyeva's xeno team has some new assets that should make first contact with the Denebans more immediately productive."

"If you say so." A new thought occurred to him. "But why do we have to use the Pan-Euros at all? What's wrong with Doc Truitt? When it comes to understanding alien civilizations, he's the best. He's told me that on several occasions."

George Truitt had been the senior xenosophontological expert on board the *America*. He was testy, rude, and difficult to work with, but he *did* know his stuff.

"Dr. Truitt has returned to Crisium Base, where he will be working on interpreting the data from the Tabby's Star Dyson swarm. His work there is absolutely essential. I assure you that Dr. Vasilyeva is as qualified as he is in the field . . . and considerably easier to work with."

Gray cocked an eyebrow at that. How did the AI know whether or not it was easy for one set of humans to work with another?

"There's something more."

"What's that?"

"The identity of the ship you will be using. It may be of interest to you."

"Not *America*," Gray said. And stifled the sharp pang at the thought of her. *America*, along with her sister ship, *Lexington*, had been badly savaged a month ago out at Kapteyn's Star. Both carriers had made it back to Earth orbit, but they were in bad, bad shape.

"That is correct. *America* will be undergoing extensive repairs at the SupraQuito yards. Your vessel will be the *Republic*."

His eyes widened at that. "The . . . *Republic*?"

People always talked about how damned small the Navy was. If you served long enough, you kept running into the same shipmates, the same vessels, the same commanding officers. This seemed to prove that ancient adage.

"Yes. She's being taken out of mothballs and provisioned for the expedition. I believe you know her?"

"Hell, I was her CAG! I was her ACAG from oh-nine to eleven . . . then CAG from eleven to fourteen!"

"I know. Might that help you feel better about this assignment?"

"You know, I damn near cried when they retired her."

"She was obsolete and overdue for retirement. As the Sh'daar War and the Confederation Civil War both wound down, she was taken off the line. However, the upgrades she will be receiving should again make her quite a formidable vessel."

"Damn you, Konstantin." But he relented. "Okay. But I still don't know what you expect me to do or say."

"I'll be there to guide you, Captain."

That wasn't exactly an encouraging thought.

He was about to retort in kind when a bright star appeared in the dusk over the water of New York Harbor, rapidly approaching. Dropping lower, it resolved itself into a red-and-silver Sentinel 5000 autonomous flier. Its low-level AI pilot settled it gently on the observation deck and lifted the gull-wing door.

"So where are we going?" Gray asked as he ducked through into the passenger compartment. It was roomy and tastefully sleek inside—the luxury model. The robot pilot was invisibly tucked away somewhere forward. The dome roof gave him a full three-sixty view, and a thoughtclick would turn parts of the deck underfoot transparent as well.

"Geneva," Konstantin told him.

Of course.

The door closed silently and the robotic transport rose into the sky on quietly humming grav-impellers. To the southwest he could see Lady Liberty, still on her pedestal after 540 years. Her right arm, which had broken off and fallen into the harbor at some point during the city's decay, was back in place, the copper flame of her torch gleaming with the last touch of the setting sun. After centuries of neglect she once again represented the spirit of freedom and democracy in the North-American union.

But for how long that might ensue was anybody's guess. North America had dodged two nasty bullets in the Sh'daar War and in the conflict with Pan-Europe.

As bad as they had been, though, Gray seriously wondered if it could survive the quiet rise of its own super-AI minds.

The flier swung about, still gaining altitude, and passed above the tallest towers of Lower Manhatt. As it did, the nagging question finally surfaced for Gray.

"I still don't understand," he told the super-AI partially resident within his head, "why you wanted me out of the Navy. It was my whole *life*. . . ."

"I understand your feelings, Captain," Konstantin said, using his honorary retirement rank—which felt like a needle digging into the wound. "But I—and you—encountered certain limitations in what we could do when you were part of the military hierarchy. In order to make contact with the Denebans, you will need a degree of freedom and free will impossible for a naval flag officer."

"Bullshit. The president—"

"President Koenig has his own problems," Konstantin explained, "and his own agendas. His decisions are closely circumscribed by those around him, and by the requirements of his office. I require a true free agent. Why are you, of all people, so wedded to your position within the military line of command?"

"Maybe because I *belonged*."

Still, it was a good question, and one Gray had been wrestling with for a long time.

Gray had grown up in the Manhatt Ruins, a Prim making a marginal living working a small rooftop farm right over *there* . . . perched within the crumbling rooftop wreckage of the TriBeCa Tower, a couple of hundred meters above the flooded avenues of the city.

Damn . . . he couldn't even locate the labyrinthine tower any longer. With nano-engineering, new buildings could be grown, and old ones completely made over into new structures in a matter of hours.

Made it easier to forget the past, he supposed.

More than three centuries ago, rising sea levels and the resultant social unrest had led to large swaths of what had been the coastal areas of the former United States of

America being abandoned. The so-called Peripheries had been cut off from the technologies and from the social and governmental services of the new United States of North America. They'd become lawless frontiers too expensive to maintain, too difficult to control.

When Angela, his wife, had had a stroke, he'd been forced to get her to a medical center within the USNA proper. Angela had been healed . . . though either the treatment or the stroke itself had . . . changed her, dissolving her part of the emotional bond between them.

Gray had gotten over it . . . well, for the most part, at any rate. It had taken a long time and blossoming relationships with other people, but he'd finally done it. Sometimes he went for *days* now without even thinking of Angela.

And it had only taken him twenty-six years to get there. . . .

In a world of such rapid changes, Gray was an outlier.

Overall, though, Gray had approved the unexpected course change in his life. In a quarter of a century, he'd worked his way up the ladder of rank, eventually commanding the star carrier *America*, and then serving as flag officer for the entire *America* battlegroup. He'd found a place for himself. He'd found *respect*—no mean feat for a former Prim in the Risty-dominated ranks of naval officers. Risties, derived from *aristocrats*, represented the worldview of a majority of USNA citizens and especially of naval officers. Primitives, lacking the high-tech cerebral implants and social e-connections of full citizens, were seen somehow as less than fully human.

It made Gray feel good that—even if it was just a possibility—his rise through the ranks, his accomplishments as a naval officer, even his victory over the aliens at Kapteyn's Star all had been due to his fighting that old social stigma of *Prim*.

But now Konstantin had arranged to make him a civilian again. Of a sort, that is. Because he was still being swept up into bigger schemes.

It wasn't like he could go back to the TriBeCa farm,

though. No, the North-American government was taking the Peripheries back. Washington, D.C., had been fought over, drained, and rebuilt; swamplands from the Virginia Piedmont to Savannah were being reclaimed; here in Old New York City the Locust Point and Verrazano Narrows dams had been completed, and the water levels encroaching on Manhattan were slowly dropping.

Under steady assault by swarms of architectural nano-assemblers, the Ruins were ruins no more, as white towers grew from the sea's retreating caress. For the past year, teams of neurobiotechnicians had been moving through the city, offering the inhabitants the chance to shed their status as Prims; soon, the very idea of Prims would be a thing of the past.

Just like me.

He studied the white towers from the sky . . . their lack of vegetation and obvious decay. Their clean sterility. Their bright newness in the lights of the city coming on to dispel the dark of early evening in winter.

He shook his head. There was no place for him any longer in the Navy and there certainly wasn't a place for him down there among those newly grown skyscrapers. He felt out of place . . . and out of touch.

"Konstantin?" He still didn't want to talk to the artificial intelligence, but he'd become too reliant on having his questions answered. Usually, that was handled by his own in-head RAM, but he was genuinely curious about what the AI would say.

"Yes?"

"What's happening to them? The people like I was, down there in the Ruins?"

"Most have already been relocated."

"Where?"

"New New York. Atlantica and Oceana. The New City around the Columbus Crater. Wherever they want to go, really. Quite a few have volunteered for off-world colonies. Mars. Chiron. New Earth."

"'Volunteered?' No relocation camps?" He'd heard stories. . . .

"There *are* relocation camps for the Refusers. However, I assure you that they lack for nothing."

Refusers.

It was actually the translation of a Sh'daar term for those who'd refused to accept the Sh'daar Transcendence—their long-ago version of the Technological Singularity. It was also used, sometimes, to describe certain humans or human groups who rejected some aspects of modern technology. There were human religions, Gray knew, that rejected manipulation of the human genome, or medical life-extension technology.

In this case, Konstantin's use of the word referred to those Prims who would not take cerebral implants, for whatever reason, preferring what they thought of as "living naturally." Some would be afraid of change . . . or simply wanted to hang on to what they already had in the face of the unknown.

Gray didn't agree with so extreme an ideology, but, having been there, he certainly understood where it came from. And it rankled him to hear about them so easily dismissed.

"Why do you ask?" Konstantin wanted to know.

"Sometimes I still identify more strongly with the other Prims than I do with full citizens."

"*Full citizen* is an archaic term, Captain. They all are being happily and productively assimilated into the overall culture."

Yeah, right. Happily assimilated *was a contradiction in terms.*

The phrasing wasn't what truly bothered him, though. What Gray carefully guarded from the voice in his head was the fear that AIs, like Konstantin itself, were increasingly herding Humankind along narrowing paths that led to the gods alone knew where, paths understood and shaped by the AIs and utterly beyond the intellectual or emotional ken of organic humans. Beyond what made a human, well, human. Gray had worked with Konstantin many times and still didn't fully trust a machine intelligence that, almost by definition, he was unable to fully understand.

He was only now realizing that he trusted Konstantin far less than he trusted the Pan-Europeans. And the realization bothered him.

"Flight time to Geneva," the robot announced in Gray's head, "fifteen minutes."

The flier accelerated, leaving the gleaming towers of the new Manhattan vanishing below the horizon astern.

New White House
Washington, D.C.
1602 hours, EST

"Captain Gray is on his way," Konstantin said quietly in President Alexander Koenig's thoughts. "As you directed."

Koenig was seated at his desk in the newly grown White House, located approximately on the site of the original. For several centuries, Washington, D.C., had been submerged, its buildings and monuments in ruins, its grounds flooded and engulfed by mangrove swamps. As with the Manhatt Ruins, dams and flood walls had been nanotechnically grown across the tidal estuary to the southeast so that the swamps could be drained. The reclamation was far enough along that the seat of the USNA government had only weeks before been moved from Toronto back to its historic seat in the District of Columbia.

Koenig sat back in his chair, looking over the reconstruction. The work was ongoing and expensive . . . but progress was being made.

Now, other kinds of progress needed to be made.

"Good. Did he put up much of a fuss?"

"Not really. He is suspicious of the Pan-Europeans, of course, and, as expected, he trusts neither my motives nor yours. He does not like being manipulated."

"Hardly surprising. You pulled a damned dirty trick on him, you know."

"Yes, I do. But if the threat to Earth is as severe as I believe it now is, we cannot afford to have him tied down by the traditional chain of command."

"Maybe not. But at least we could have *told* the poor son-of-a-bitch. . . ."

"Mr. President, this is something we must not leave to chance . . . or to human will and fallibility."

Koenig scowled. "Sometimes, Konstantin," he said slowly, "I get the feeling that you don't trust humans."

Geneva
Pan-European Union
2217 hours, GMT+1

It was raining and dark as the flier shrieked in over Burgundy, dropping swiftly from its cruising altitude of forty thousand meters, its outer surface reconfiguring from hypersonic mode to landing. "Going from sperm mode to turkey mode" was how fighter pilots described it, as the ship morphed from a sleek teardrop to a flattened, domed box with wings for landing. A former Navy pilot, Gray wondered if he would have to edit those memories sometime soon. They were a part of him, sure . . . but they were of damned little use now beyond pure nostalgia.

The lights of Geneva Spaceport glared up ahead, with the European capital's urban sprawl delineating the black emptiness of Lake Geneva beyond. They touched down on a commercial pad, where an embarkation tube attached itself to the flier as the gravs were still spooling down.

Elena Vasilyeva, a tall woman in black with colorful abstract animations writhing over her face and hands, was there on the passenger concourse to meet him. "Captain Gray?" she said, extending a hand. "It was good of you to come on such short notice."

It's not like I had a whole lot of choice, he thought, but he kept it to himself and shook her hand. She was speaking Russian, but he heard the words in English as his in-head software translated them in real time.

"No problem," he replied. "A pleasure. I'm sorry you had to stay at work so late in order to meet me."

"It . . . what is the expression? It goes with the territory. This way, if you please."

They traveled by mag-tube to the Ad Astra Confederation Government Complex, and a large meeting room a couple of hundred meters up, near the top of the tower. The space's floor-to-ceiling windows looked out over the aptly named Plaza of Light and its titanic monument, Popolopolis's statue *Ascent of Man*.

A number of other people were already present in the room, including several European military officers. Gray stopped at the threshold. "I was given to understand that this would be a civilian operation, Ms. Vasilyeva."

"It is, Captain Gray," a European Spaceforce admiral told him. "Operation Cygni, a joint European-American scientific and first-contact expedition to the star Deneb. However, as you must be aware, there are serious military and governmental implications to this mission."

"Admiral Duchamp is correct," an AI voice said in Gray's thoughts. "In any event, we all wished to meet the man who would be commanding the expedition."

"You could have done *that* in virtual reality," he said.

In fact, the real reason for his transatlantic jaunt this afternoon had been bothering him quite a bit. With VR, people could meet in cyberspace, within AI-created realms with such resolution and fidelity to detail that it was quite impossible to tell illusion from reality.

"Perhaps," the AI told him, "but we would not have known whether we were meeting the avatar or the actual person."

"Nikolai is quite protective of us," Duchamp told him. "He wanted us to get a good feel for the man who will be leading Operation Cygni."

" 'Nikolai?' "

"For Nikolai Copernicus," Vasilyeva explained. "An artificial intelligence housed here in Geneva analogous to your Konstantin."

"A pleasure to meet you, Nikolai."

"I am delighted to make your acquaintance. Until now I knew you only through back channels with Konstantin, and through intelligence reports and strategic analyses. To be frank, some of our people feared that you are a . . . I believe the Americanism is 'cowboy.' Shooting first, asking questions later."

"And is that how you see me now?"

"Oh, most certainly not, Captain," Duchamp told him. "We have all seen the reports of your encounters at Tabby's Star. And many of us have been wondering why your senior staff would have retired you. It seems a poor use of a valuable asset."

"Having met you, Captain," Nikolai said, "and having spoken with you directly, I can unreservedly recommend that Operation Cygni proceed as it is currently organized, with our xenosophontological team under Captain Gray's direct command."

"So how about it, Konstantin?" Gray used a private channel to communicate with the AI without being overheard by the others. "I haven't heard of this AI before."

"Nikolai has only come on-line in the past few weeks," Konstantin told him.

"A baby, huh? Can he be trusted?"

"As much as *I* can be trusted."

Had that been sarcasm, Gray wondered? Or humor? Or a subtle rebuke? He found it difficult to understand what a super-AI was feeling—if *feeling* was the proper term—when he spoke with one.

"That's not saying a great deal."

Konstantin ignored the jibe. Gray wasn't even certain that it was possible to insult the AI. "Nikolai," Konstantin told him, "is several orders of magnitude faster, more powerful, and more compact than I. The Europeans wish to include a copy of him on the expedition to Deneb."

"I'm not sure that's such a good idea," Gray said, transmitting on the group's shared channel again. "The Omega virus, remember?"

"Nikolai was designed in part to be immune to Omega," a sophontologist told him, "as well as to other potential e-threats."

Gray wondered how any of them could be so certain of that, though. The Omega virus had been an alien software packet smuggled from Deneb back to Tabby's Star . . . and it had apparently been responsible for the destruction of the Tabby's Star civilization. Brought back to human space, it had been employed against the Rosette Aliens at Kapteyn's Star, and evidently had been responsible for stopping the monumentally powerful invaders. . . .

. . . at least for now. The Rosetters hadn't been destroyed in the encounter by any means. As far as the xenosophontologists were concerned, they'd simply been forced to halt their advance toward Earth and actually notice the humans defiantly standing in their way.

"A copy," Gray repeated. "Where? I mean, the *Republic* is going to have pretty limited running space for a full AI."

"In this," one of the civilian sophontologists said. She moved her hand in the air, summoning a hologram. "We call this the *Helleslicht Modul Eins*."

Gray's translator software told him the meaning of the German phrase: Bright Light Module One. The 3-D diagram floating in front of the woman was egg-shaped and, according to the listed dimensions, some three meters long and massing five metric tons.

"Dr. Marsh is a member of our xenosophontological team," Vasilyeva told him. "But her specialty is advanced AI."

"I see."

"The HM-1's internal matrix," Marsh explained, "is essentially computronium—solid computing matter—with quantum circuitry of sufficient complexity and power to support Nikolai with plenty of room to spare."

She sounded quite proud . . . and if she was even partly responsible for this device, she had every right to be. Artificial intelligences like Konstantin—in particular super-AIs, or "SAIs"—were resident within large computer complexes, usually underground and anything but mobile. Konstantin, for instance, had begun his existence in a subselene facility beneath Tsiolkovsky Crater, on the far side of the moon.

Using the far-flung Global Net, they could send independent parts of themselves anywhere within cislunar space. Pared-down copies of them, subsets of the larger and more powerful original software, could be resident within the electronic networks of starships or orbital stations. A sub-clone of Konstantin had made the passage to Tabby's Star on board the star carrier *America*, and even smaller copies had been used to remotely contact the alien Dyson-swarm intelligence there, and the uploaded minds called the Satori.

But that had been a fraction of what the original was capable of.

Gray wasn't certain how massive the Tsiolkovsky complex was, but he knew it was *big*. If the Europeans had managed to build a computer that could run a similar SAI in a volume amounting to a few cubic meters, that was more than impressive.

It was a giant step forward for SAIs.

"So why does Nikolai want to go to Deneb?" Gray asked. He hesitated, then looked up at the ceiling. "I assume you *do* want to go, Nikolai?"

"Very much, Captain Gray," Nikolai said.

"We cannot stress the importance of this expedition too much, Captain," Duchamp added. "It is vital—*vital*—that we engage the Deneban civilization peacefully, to learn about them and their abilities, and perhaps to secure their aid in our confrontation with the Rosette Aliens."

Gray shook his head. "I have to be honest with you, Admiral," he said. "The Denebans may not be a good prospect for contact, let alone military aid. As best as we can determine, they utterly destroyed a technologically advanced culture at Tabby's Star without even attempting to negotiate or open lines of communication."

"We know that, Captain," Duchamp said. "It was for that reason that we approached your President Koenig to request that we be included in Project Cygni. A copy of Nikolai, working with a copy of your Konstantin, offers, we believe, our best hope of establishing peaceful contact and technological help. It is unlikely that organic humans will be able to communicate in a meaningful way with such an advanced civilization."

"But human oversight of the expedition is necessary," Vasilyeva told him. "And when we learned that President Koenig was considering *you* as the expedition commander, we knew that there was hope."

"Why?" Gray asked, genuinely baffled.

"Captain . . . we know too well that you can win battles, even wars. But what interests us is your ability to win *peace*."

Chapter Two

VFA-96, Black Demons
SupraQuito Yards
Earth Synchorbit
1018 hours, TFT

Through the vista opened by his fighter's AI in his mind, Lieutenant Donald Gregory stared out into the tangle of orbital structures spread out before him. The SupraQuito Synchorbital was the largest of the human facilities in orbit over Earth, consisting of some hundreds of major stations and facilities strung together in a long, brilliantly lit arc.

The collection of structures was balanced on the Quito space elevator at an altitude of 37,786 kilometers, and a single orbit of the Earth took precisely twenty-four hours, which meant that the complex kept pace with the same spot on the turning Earth. From there, a slender tower reached down to its anchor point atop a mountain on Earth's equator, and up into the black of space to the tethered asteroid that kept the whole assembly in dynamic tension. Four centuries earlier, synchorbit had been the parking zone for a swarm of unmanned communications satellites. Now it was one of three major communities in Earth orbit, with a permanent population of over sixty thousand and some thousands more each day traveling up or down the "E," or arriving or departing on fleets of both interplanetary and interstellar ships.

The local sky, Gregory saw, was crowded with activity. The two badly damaged star carriers, *Lexington* and his own—or what used to be his own—*America* had been towed into position off the Navy yard, along with a couple of small asteroids. The two battered carriers were now almost obscured by swarming nanorepair 'bots busily eating away at the damaged hull surfaces, while simultaneously stripping the asteroids of raw material and bringing it across to the ships in steady streams.

We can rebuild our ships on the fly, Gregory thought. *We can give them new life with this tech. But we can't do anything for my squad mates.*

Like Meg. . . .

Lieutenant Meg Connor had been killed at Invictus, a frigid, ice-clad world out beyond the rim of the galaxy and 12 million years in the future. Gregory had lost his legs in that action. They'd grown those back for him . . . but nothing could bring back Megan.

Or Cynthia DeHaviland, killed in the hellfire of Kapteyn's Star just a month ago.

"Tighten up, Demon Four!" the squadron's CO snapped at him. "Belay the rubbernecking." Commander Mackey sounded stressed.

What the hell do you *have to be worried about?* he thought, a bit petulantly, but he bit down on the words. "Copy," was all he said. A moment's inattention had let his Starblade fighter drift almost imperceptibly within the seven-ship formation, and with a thought he brought himself back into line. The spacelanes above and around the SupraQuito orbital facility were indeed crowded with ships large and small, construction tugs, intrastation transports, ship's gigs, liberty boats, space-suited personnel on EVA, mobile repair shacks, and provisioning vessels. Theoretically, a lane had been cleared for the fighter squadron, but there was near-infinite opportunity here for a mistake.

And in space any mistake was likely to be expensive, fatal, or both.

At least Don Gregory was no longer suicidal. For a time after Invictus he'd been thinking about that a lot. The depression, at times, was overwhelming. His own in-head circuitry had urged him more than once to seek help, but he'd managed to put it off . . . and to avoid a mandatory checkup with the psych department. A down-grudge on his mental health would ground him . . . and might even get him kicked out of the Navy.

And now he thought he might see a better answer.

The seven fighters were moving at only eighty meters per second, a crawl against the scale of the titanic structures around them. They'd launched moments before from the *America*, followed a twisting route to stay clear of the nano-swarms and the small asteroid providing raw materials for the carrier's repairs, and dropped into a long, slow approach to the main naval base dead ahead.

"There she is," Lieutenant Gerald Ruxton called over the squadron channel. "Our new home!"

USNA CVL *Republic* was six hundred meters long, just over half the length of their former ship. Like *America*, though, she looked like an open umbrella, with a long, slender spine behind a dome-shaped shieldcap filled with water. In the shieldcap's shadow, two modules rotated about the central keel, providing artificial gravity for the crew. A CVL, or light carrier, she had facilities to carry three combat squadrons of twelve fighters each, plus a number of auxiliary vessels, including a search-and-rescue squadron. VFA-90, a strike squadron called the Star Reapers, was also being transferred from *America* to the smaller carrier. In addition to VFA-96, the fresh-minted VFA-198, the Hellfuries, would be coming up from Earth later in the day.

After Kapteyn's Star, the Black Demons could only muster seven fighters. They were supposed to be getting replacements up from Oceana, on Earth, but frankly, Gregory would believe *that* when he sat down with them in the ready room. Fighter losses during the past six months had been ungodly heavy, and they were having trouble recruiting and training replacements planetside fast enough to keep up with demand.

"VFA-96, this is *Republic* Primary Flight Control. You are cleared for final on Bay One, six-zero mps on approach."

"Copy, *Republic* PriFly," Commander Luther Mackey replied. "Bay One, sixty mps."

Slowing sharply, the Starblade fighters fell into line ahead, moving in on the *Republic* from dead astern. Gregory was second in line, behind Bruce Caswell. He let his fighter's AI cut his velocity and adjust his angle of approach; the landing bays on a star carrier were moving targets, rotating about the ship's spine to create the illusion of gravity. Docking required more-than-human precision, and a slight upward bump of the thrusters just as the Starblade swept across the bay's threshold. A feeling of gravity surged through Gregory's body as the bay's magnetic capture fields snagged his ship and brought him to a relative halt at the end of the deck.

"Demon Four," a voice said in his head. "Trap complete. Welcome aboard, Lieutenant."

Automated machinery grappled with his fighter, lifting it smoothly up through the overhead, making room for the next fighter in line behind him. The deck matrix molded about his Starblade for a moment, maintaining the vacuum in the landing bay as his fighter transitioned into pressure and the orchestrated bustle of deck personnel tending the incoming Starblades. Gregory's cockpit melted open and released him, and he stepped out into the open.

"Welcome to the *Republic*, Lieutenant," a woman with a commander's insignia on her utilities said. Gregory felt ̶ ping him as she accessed his in-head RAM and downloaded his personnel records and orders. "The ship will show you to your quarters. Debriefing at eleven hundred, Ready One."

"Thank you, Commander." Her name, he read through his in-head, was Sandra Dillon, and she was *Republic*'s ACAG, the assistant commander Aerospace Group. He opened a channel to the *Republic*'s AI and requested directions into the labyrinthine interior of the ship.

A light star carrier was considerably smaller than a monster like the *America*, but she still was an enormous vessel, with kilometers of internal passageways and compartments and a crew of more than two thousand. Junior officers quartered four to a stateroom; he found his berthing compartment and claimed a rack. Then he followed the ship's directions to take him up to one of the ready rooms.

Gregory had been in the Navy for four years, now, and was an old hand at this. They would be getting the standard welcome-aboard talk, get to meet the ship's CAG, and if they were lucky, find out something about the expedition to which they'd been assigned. That said, the setup for this mission was unusual: a Navy ship, with Navy personnel and three fighter squadrons . . . but with a civilian skipper and a load of double-dome civilian xenosophs. So that meant they were pulling first-contact duty.

Gregory didn't much care one way or the other. He'd been there, done that, and been issued a brand-new pair of legs. At the moment he had only one question.

When the hell was he going to be able to get liberty? There was some very important business he needed to conduct ashore.

USNA CVE Guadalcanal
Orbiting Heimdall
Kapteyn's Star
1213 hours, GMT

Captain Laurie Taggart floated into the bridge compartment of the escort star carrier *Guadalcanal* and pulled herself down into her command chair. "Captain on the bridge!" Commander Franklin Simmons, her XO, announced as her seat enclosed her lower body, gently restraining her in the ambient microgravity. In front of her, Lieutenant Rodriguez, the ship's combat information officer, intently studied the repeater screens that partially surrounded him, and Taggart's eyes widened as she glanced at them.

"What the hell is that?" she demanded. She'd received a "captain to the bridge" call moments earlier, but they hadn't told her what the call was about.

"Don't know for sure, Captain," Rodriguez told her. "But it's got to be the Rosies. Nothing else could work on that grand a scale!"

"Does the rest of the fleet see this?"

"They will when the signal reaches them, Captain. Transmission time . . . ten more minutes."

Taggart stared into the screens a moment longer, then linked in with Nelly, the ship's AI, opening the same channel in her mind.

She gazed into wonder. . . .

Not for the first time Taggart questioned if these beings truly were the Stargods of her religion. She'd drifted away from the old beliefs lately, but it was impossible to feel that inner stirring of awe and not at least wonder.

They were in orbit over an Earth-sized moon of the gas giant Bifrost. Heimdall was a barren, desolate world now, though it had given rise to intelligent life billions of years in the past. For the past 800 million years or so, it had been the site of the so-called Etched Cliffs, a super-computer network carved into solid rock and spanning the world. Several alien species had vanished into that network, living digital lives within a virtual universe of their own making.

Those uploaded minds, uncounted trillions of them, were gone now, devoured by the Rosette entity—"the Rosies," as Rodriguez had called them. For weeks the world had been utterly dead and empty. But now . . .

It looked like aurorae, slow-moving bars and circles of pale blue-green light, but the patterns were far too regular and organized to be natural emissions within the local magnetic field. They were emerging, it looked like, from the primary Etched Cliffs site, but expanding second by second with bewildering speed and complexity to engulf the world of Heimdall.

The Rosette entity had created large numbers of geometric constructs in open space, but the structures had vanished after the Battle of Heimdall. Navy xenosophontologists had assumed that the aliens had withdrawn.

Evidently, Taggart thought as she studied the phenomenon, they had not.

"Helm," she said.

"Helm, aye, Captain."

"Take us out of orbit. Come to one-one-five minus one eight, five-zero kps."

"Come to course one-one-five minus one eight at fifty kps, aye, aye."

She didn't know what was going on down there, but she wanted her ship well clear of it, whatever it was.

Her ship. Laurie Taggart's military career had taken some sudden and unexpected shifts in vector over the past few months. She'd started off as senior weapons officer on board the star carrier *America* . . . but then she'd received a new assignment as Exec on board *America*'s sister ship, the *Lexington*. From there, she'd volunteered for TAD— temporary attached duty—as skipper of the *Lucas*, a Marine transport and stealth lander, and then had returned to take command of the *Lady Lex* when Captain Bigelow had been killed.

She'd been the one who'd brought the crippled *Lexington* home.

Of course, there was no way the Navy Department was going to let her keep *that* billet. She was far too junior, too low on the Navy's rank hierarchy to skipper the *Lexington*. Upon reaching SupraQuito, though, she'd received a field promotion to the rank of captain and been given command of the light carrier *Guadalcanal*.

She suspected that Trev—her lover, Captain Trevor Gray—had made the recommendation for her promotion, but he'd refused to confirm or deny her accusation. Instead, he'd snuggled her in close and merely whispered, "Hush. You've earned it."

Now she just hoped she could keep what she'd earned. The light show was engulfing the entire globe of Heimdall now and reaching far out into space as well.

"Captain?" Lieutenant Peters, on sensor watch, called. "We're getting solid returns now. Fireflies."

"Shit . . ."

Fireflies referred to small, autonomous objects, ranging from dust specks to a few meters across in size, that seemed to be associated with the Rosette Alien structures. They flew in unimaginably vast swarms, could fit themselves together into solid components, or they could destroy a starship simply by ramming into it at high velocity. Fireflies were believed to be part of an enormous swarm intelligence numbering in the hundreds of trillions and providing the underlying computronium matrix for the Rosette intelligence.

What, she wondered, was the best call, here? Stay put and observe? Rejoin the rest of the Kapteyn's Star flotilla out at Thrymheim, the system's outermost planet some twelve light-minutes distant? Probe the bewildering tangle of light structures now unfolding across local space? Launch *Guadalcanal*'s fighters?

Her orders, the standing orders for the five-ship flotilla here, were simply to patrol the Kapteyn's Star system and alert Earth if the Rosies showed up again. Judging by what was unfolding out of Heimdall, they'd never left in the first place, and Earth was going to want to know about that.

"Get us back to the others," she told the helm officer.

"Aye, Captain."

"Exec? Go to general quarters."

. This was *not* looking good.

USNA FME Olympia
Rosette
Omega Centauri
1214 hours, GMT

Some 15,800 light years removed from Earth, an AI called Limpy by the humans working with it stared into strangeness as well. Although he did not think in the same way that humans did, and did not make the same value judgments, it knew that something was going on . . . and that it did not look good.

Omega Centauri was the largest globular star cluster in the Milky Way galaxy—10 million stars with a total mass some 4 million times that of Sol, packed into a sphere 150 light years across. At its gravitational center, deep within that teeming swarm of stars filling an impossibly crowded sky, six black holes, each the size of a world, orbited, in a patently artificial manner—a Klemperer rosette.

Centuries before, Terran astronomers had demonstrated that Omega Centauri was not, in fact, a typical globular cluster, but rather that it was the stripped-down core of a small galaxy that had been sucked in and devoured by the much larger Milky Way more than half a billion years before. Large galaxies, it was known, were cannibals, shredding smaller galaxies and slurping up the remains. Several stars—among them the red dwarf Kapteyn's Star, only 12.7 light years from Sol, had been proven by their spectral fingerprints to be escaped members of that ancient galaxy.

Much more recently, human warships engaging the so-called Sh'daar Empire had traveled back through time and discovered that galaxy, called the N'gai Cluster by its myriad inhabitants, during an epoch when it was still just above the Milky Way. At the heart of N'gai, they'd found what was almost certainly the precursor of the Rosette—six hyper-giant blue stars serving as a kind of beacon or monument for the Sh'daar.

Here within Omega Centauri, however, those hyperstars had long ago exploded, turning into black holes whirling around a tortured volume of space not much larger than Earth. And there was more. The enigmatic being known as the Consciousness had been busily building . . . something. Titanic structures apparently constructed of pure light hung suspended around the hexagon of rotating singularities and extended in all directions to impossible infinities.

The monitor *Olympia*, a high-tech listening post disguised as an innocuous chunk of rock the size of Mt. Everest—crewed by 150 humans and a late-model AI with some very special programming—had slipped into orbit around the Rosette only weeks before. With downloads based on data snatched from the Consciousness at Kapteyn's Star, Limpy could eavesdrop on the Consciousness by linking in to back channels and sidebands to tap into conversations between a few of the far-flung individual devices making up the whole.

So far, the effort had not been particularly productive. One xenosophontologist had declared that the eavesdropping effort was akin to finding out what a human was thinking by analyzing the waste emissions of a couple of the bacteria in his gut. Limpy felt that the chances of getting something useful were better than *that*, but he understood the problem. The Consciousness was very, very large and complex, and even the very best human-directed SAIs had little chance of understanding the entity in more than an extremely basic way.

To Limpy, it was a chance worth taking.

Right now, the AI on *Olympia* was drifting across the face of the Rosette, its orbit taking it cross the opening between the six whirling singularities. In the space at the center, stars were visible . . . but not the thronging, massed stars of Omega Centauri. *Olympia*'s bridge crew was looking, quite literally, through a hole punched in spacetime. They were looking into somewhere—and some*when*—else.

Clearly, the Rosette was a stargate of some kind. The high-velocity rotation of those black holes around their common center twisted the normal, sane dimensions of spacetime out of all reason, opening numerous gateways into the unknown. The starscapes glimpsed within that whirling gateway might be other regions of the galaxy, other times, or even other universes entirely.

The being called the Consciousness had come through from one of those elsewheres. The Consciousness, the Rosette entity, the Alien Intelligence . . . all of those were names for something Humankind had never truly encountered and might never be able to understand.

Limpy was here to try to learn more.

"Hey, Limp?"

"Yes, Captain Mosely?"

"What's all that stuff over there? Opposite the Rosette opening?"

He knew exactly what Mosely was referring to. He'd been watching the phenomenon grow and develop for several minutes now . . . a huge cloud of what looked like smoke, white and gray-silver in the massed starlight.

"Unknown, Captain. It appears to be clouds of micromachines similar to those you call fireflies, numbering in the trillions."

"What are they doing?"

"Coming in this general direction."

"Shit. . . ."

The *Olympia* AI continued watching for several moments. "Captain, I would suggest you sound general quarters."

"I was just arriving at the same conclusion."

A second later, *Olympia*'s internal passageways rang with the shrill clanging of the alarm. Not that it much mattered—the swarm was on them before most of the crew was able to take their positions. Yet the lead elements of the cloud swept past the ship at a range of several hundred kilometers, and it soon became clear that the cloud's target was not the *Olympia*.

"So where are they going in such a damned hurry?" Mosely wondered aloud, thinking the danger had passed.

And then a shudder ran through the drifting mountain, followed by several savage shocks.

"Limpy!" Mosely called. "We've been hit!" The starfield outside began drifting. "We're rotating!"

"We haven't been hit, Captain. We have been caught in an extremely powerful gravitational stream."

"What the hell is a 'gravitational stream'?"

"A narrow, tubular volume of space has been distorted in such a way as to create rapid movement toward the Rosette. We have been caught by the fringes of the effect and are being swept along."

"Toward the Rosette . . ."

"That is correct, Captain. Unless we can break free, we will pass through the central lumen of the hexagon in another forty-three seconds."

The *Olympia* possessed gravitational drive engines, but the ship was slow and underpowered for a vessel of its size and mass. Mosely was shouting orders, trying to engage the drive and bring the ship clear, but the AI had already determined that there simply was not enough power for the ship to break free, not in the time remaining.

Olympia's capture did not appear to be a hostile act; indeed, it seemed to be completely accidental. The column of gravitationally warped space enveloped the vast swarm streaming through space toward the Rosette. It seemed likely that the devices themselves were generating the warp as a means of propulsion, and that their destination was somewhere on the other side of the Rosette gateway through spacetime.

Regardless of the reason, *Olympia* was being dragged along with it.

With emotionless efficiency, Limpy compressed a complete record of recent events into a laser comm message and fired it into space. There were other vessels drifting in the heart of Omega Centauri that would get the record back to Earth.

Ahead, the blurred ring of distortion created by the rapidly circling singularities expanded, filling the sky. Brilliant hues of light—light trapped within the gravitational anomaly—created a radiant halo effect that resembled a titanic, unblinking eye. At the very center of the distortion, within the eye's pupil, a starfield had appeared. Limpy did a rapid scan and assessment and discovered that the starfield matched nothing in his own memory.

And then *Olympia* fell through the eye and vanished from local spacetime.

SupraQuito Space Elevator
In Transit
1635 hours, TFT

Gray was glad that he always traveled light. After his interview in Geneva, he'd been taken to a hotel for an uncomfortable night's sleep, and then he attended a six-hour briefing covering things of which he was already well aware: the wrecked high-technic civilization at Tabby's Star, the discovery of the Omega Code, and the fact . . . no, the *presumption* that a highly advanced civilization existed at the brilliant blue-white star Deneb some 173 light years from Tabby's Star.

Because he'd been the one to uncover most of this information, Gray sat bored and cross-armed through most of it. He was able to correct a presenter at one point, however. There *was* a possible motive for the Denebans to attack the Satori, the civilization at Tabby's Star. The Satori had encircled their sun with gravitational thrusters and been accelerating their entire civilization, star, Dyson swarm, and all, in the direction of Deneb. Why was still unknown . . .

but the Denebans evidently hadn't taken kindly to pushy neighbors.

It would be well, he told the large audience gathered in the Ad Astra center's amphitheater, to keep that in mind when they approached Deneb for the first time.

Later that afternoon, he, Vasilyeva, and a dozen of her xenosoph people had boarded another, considerably larger, grav flier for the very nearly 10,000-kilometer flight to Quito, in the Unión de América del Sur.

From there, a brief tube ride had taken them to the base of the first of Earth's three space elevators, anchored to a mountaintop perched directly astride Earth's equator. The group had then boarded a special express skycar for the trip up to SupraQuito.

Express meant an acceleration of one G—which, added to the one G of Earth's surface gravity, meant that the passengers were under *two* gravities for the first part of their trip. The magnetic skycar was impeccably appointed, however, with luxurious reclining seats designed to keep the passengers as comfortable as possible despite the sensation of another person sitting on their chests. Decks, bulkheads, and overhead projected views of their surroundings—in particular the gloriously beautiful vista of the cloud-wrapped Earth falling away below them.

Not that any of them had any particular interest in watching the Earth. Gray was focused on his breathing as they shot faster and faster into the sky above Quito, magnetically accelerated along the taut Earth-to-heaven cable.

The sensation of crushing weight lessened bit by bit as the skycar rose higher. Thirty-two minutes after leaving the elevator port, they were traveling at 19.5 kilometers per second and they were at the halfway point, almost 19,000 kilometers above the mountaintop. Acceleration ceased, and the passenger compartment rotated through 180 degrees, until the vast blue-and-white expanse of the Earth below swung around and took up a new position *above* them. They were now decelerating at one gravity, though it felt like considerably less because the Earth now was working against that acceleration rather than adding to it.

"I thought we would be in zero-G once we were in space!" one of the scientists grumbled. His name was Dr. Liu and Gray had been told he was on loan from the Shanghai Institute of Advanced Technology.

"Only if you're in orbit," Gray told him. "If you're in free fall, you're basically falling around the Earth . . . but you're never outside of the reach of its gravity. This part of the space elevator isn't in orbit, and if you were to open a hatch and step outside right now you'd fall all the way back down to Ecuador."

"It's different up at geosynch," Vasilyeva added gently. "We'll be in free fall there."

Liu grunted, and Gray fell silent, feeling a small disquiet. He would have thought that any scientifically literate person would know that, and not make such a rookie goof.

Expertise in one scientific area, evidently, didn't qualify the person as an expert in others. Space, however, was a place where ignorance could get you killed.

He wondered how savvy the rest of this crowd was when it came to basic orbital mechanics.

One hour and five minutes after leaving Earth, the skycar decelerated into SupraQuito Synchorbital Station, and a five-minute tube run brought them to the yards.

Gray sat in the tube capsule looking up through the overhead transparency at a labyrinth of struts and railguides, and orbital structures, gantries, and dockyard facilities slowly moving past against the backdrop of space. Ahead, docked within her gantry, the USNA CVL *Republic* looked just as Gray remembered her.

He was coming back on board her, he knew, with decidedly mixed feelings. He was eager to get back on board a ship—any ship—once again, and the sooner the better. There was little enough on Earth to hold him there now, he knew. Each time he returned to explore his roots within

Manhatt, he found more and more change, less and less a sense of home or belonging.

But his interview with the Pan-Euros had shaken him. They seemed to have a nearly apocalyptic prescience about this mission, a feeling that failure might well spell disaster for all of Humankind.

And knowing that so much was riding on his decisions, his experience, filled Gray with a deep and angry foreboding.

Chapter Three

Lieutenant Gregory
SupraQuito Synchorbital
1218 hours, TFT

The offices of Paradise, Inc. were located in a rotating wheel attached to the synchorbital complex just outside of the naval yards. Gregory had checked himself off of the *Republic* and taken a mag-tube to the office structure's microgravity hub, from which he caught an elevator "down" to the wheel's one-G rim. The reception office was luxuriously appointed, with viewalls set to peaceful mood-abstract animations, and with hauntingly ethereal music piped through from hidden speakers.

An android robot took Gregory's personal stats, and he was ushered through to an inner space where he met Kazuko Marukawa, seemingly adrift in swirls of colored light. "So, Lieutenant Gregory," she said with a dazzling smile as he took a chair opposite her desk. "What brings you to Paradise?"

"I've . . . lost someone," he told her. "Someone very important to me. I've been wondering about the eschatoverse."

"*An* eschatoverse," she said, gently correcting him. "We build one exactly to your specifications. We have, quite literally, billions of available models to choose from."

The thought of his own private heaven felt uncomfortably claustrophobic. "Isn't that . . . I don't know . . . kind of lonely? A virtual universe just for me and whoever I bring along?"

"Not at all. Think of your 'verse as a bubble . . . but one that is constantly merging and interacting with others, with *many* others. You would have access to the entire virtual multiverse of billions of distinct realities. We offer ready-made realities representing the afterlives of hundreds of distinct religions and belief sets. We offer realities tailor-made to your specifications, where you can fly with a thought, enjoy superhuman powers, *anything* that is possible for you to imagine . . . and much, much more! Your new reality, I assure you, will be far, *far* more intricate, more interesting, and more fulfilling than the so-called real world is for you now!"

Gregory knew about virtual uploads. It was the same trick, more or less, used by the Baondyeddi and other technically advanced alien species to vanish down a virtual rabbit hole out at Heimdall. Human technology had been moving toward this goal for centuries, but virtual uploads had become practical only within the past few decades and on a much smaller scale.

But that scale was growing fast.

"So . . . I know it's possible to make a copy of the human brain," he told her. "And that copy can be uploaded into a computer that's running a virtual simulation of a world . . . of an entire universe, even. But if I uploaded myself into one of your bubbles . . . would that really be me? I mean . . . even a perfect copy of my mental state is still a copy. What happens to the . . . uh . . . *real* me?"

She laughed and shook her head. "Lieutenant, you would be amazed at how many times we hear that exact question!"

"You would be amazed, Ms. Marukawa, how much I would hate to wake up and find that I was the version of myself that didn't get uploaded."

"Do you believe in the soul, Lieutenant?"

"I'm . . . not sure. I don't think so. . . ."

"Well, let's concentrate on your conscious awareness, your sense of self. You have one, I assume?"

He was becoming annoyed with her perky assertiveness. "Of course I do."

"Your brain is a network of interconnecting neurons . . . about one hundred billion of them linked with one another in complex structures through up to eleven topological dimensions, yes?"

"Uh . . . yeah. . . ."

"The interactions of all of those neurons give rise to memory, to decisions, to what we call consciousness."

He nodded.

"Okay. If I were to take just one of your neurons and replace it with a microscopic nanocomputer, maintaining all of those synaptic linkages . . . would you notice the difference?"

"Probably not."

"Would you still be you?"

"Yes. . . ." He saw where this was going. He'd heard the argument before, but still wasn't sure he bought it.

"And if I replaced ten of your neurons . . . ten out of one hundred billion. Would you still be you?"

"I know what you're saying, Ms. Marukawa. If you could magically replace my neurons one at a time, eventually, my brain would be all machine instead of organic jelly and my mind could be transferred to a robot body . . . or uploaded to a supercomputer. If all of the connections are the same, I shouldn't notice any difference."

"Your consciousness would be preserved, identical to what you think of as *you* in every way."

"I understand all of that. What I don't understand is how you can move my conscious mind from here"—he tapped his forehead—"into a machine. That's different than just swapping out parts."

"All I can tell you, Lieutenant, is that we've had no complaints."

"What happens to the organic body once the consciousness leaves it?" He realized as soon as the words were out that it was a damned silly question.

"The organic brain is destroyed in the scanning process, Lieutenant. The body is disposed of in a manner determined by the client. We offer a number of mortuary—"

He held up his hand. "I don't think I want to hear that part. Listen . . . about my friend . . ."

"This was someone you loved?" He nodded. "A woman?"

"Her name was Megan."

"Do you have a recording? Or is she already in an eschatoverse?"

He sighed. "I have her avatar."

"Ah." Marukawa's face fell. "We can offer you an extremely lifelike simulation, of course. A dedicated AI recreates her appearance, her emotions, her thoughts and mannerisms based on the available data. It's not—"

"It's not really her. I know."

Gregory leaned back in the chair, fingers drumming on an armrest. The flow of soft light and random shapes around him was distracting, even hypnotic. He needed to think this through.

Meg's avatar had been the electronic version of her she used to communicate with others virtually, a kind of personal assistant and secretary that could seamlessly stand in for her electronically. He thought of it as a kind of sketch of the real person, though that hadn't stopped him from having long conversations with it since Meg's death. Everyone had one—everyone except Prims, of course, or religious fanatics who didn't believe in using such things.

Gregory had been considering suicide for some time, now, a simple and painless way out of the pain of a world without Meg. Paradise, Inc. offered him an option: even if the mind—not the *real* Don Gregory—was transferred to a simulated universe, the Gregory left behind would end, and that in and of itself would be a form of heaven.

And if this company was able to transfer the conscious mind, the self, the sense of ego and being and self-awareness that was Don Gregory, he would wake up in a better, richer, more vibrant universe with at least the illusion of Megan with him again.

Maybe in time he could forget that she was an illusion wrapped around a packet of AI software.

Marukawa seemed to be reading his thoughts. "We can edit your memories during processing, Lieutenant," she told him. "You could be unaware that she was a copy. If you wished, you would be unaware that you were living in a simulated universe."

He chuckled. "I've heard it suggested that we're already in such a simulation. And how would we know?"

"An untestable hypothesis," she said, "but a fascinating one."

"If we *are* living in a simulation, someone up there programmed a piss-poor reality for us."

"And that, Lieutenant," she said cheerfully, "is why Paradise, Inc. is here. Now . . . you're currently on active duty?"

"I am. Two more years before I can resign my commission."

"That is not a problem, Lieutenant. We can make a reservation for you, and even begin designing your ideal universe for you before you process."

"I'll need to think about it, ma'am," he told her. He stood up. "One more question?"

"Of course."

"How do I pay for all this if I'm dead?"

"You turn over your personal credit when you come for processing, Lieutenant, with a ten-thousand-credit minimum. The more credit you transfer, the larger the field of available universes open to you once you cross over. The cost is applied to the ongoing maintenance of your escha-toverse, to administrative overhead—"

"Including your own salary, I'm sure." He grinned at her. "Thank you, Ms. Marukawa. You've been most helpful."

"We look forward to your new life with us, Lieutenant."

Gregory left the office and made his way cross-complex to the Free Fall, a watering hole popular with naval officers enjoying some downtime "ashore." His conversation with Marukawa had brought up a couple of unpleasant points.

First and foremost, of course, was the inescapable fact that Meg was *dead*, that if he shared an artificial reality with her, it would be with an electronic illusion, not with the real person. Okay . . . he could edit that part out of his memory. But still, the idea was . . . unpleasant.

There was also the very real question of eternity. Nothing lasts forever, and that certainly included the computers and AI networks girdling Earth in the various synchor-bitals or buried underground on the moon and elsewhere. Granted, someday all of those networks might be subsumed into a larger, more powerful, more advanced electronic in-frastructure. He could imagine Humankind building its own Dyson swarm, like the one they'd discovered out at Tabby's Star . . . or even a Kardashev-3 galactic Dyson sphere, like the one they'd glimpsed a few million years in the future. If that happened, Paradise, Inc.'s virtual multi-verse would likely get picked up and passed along.

But Gregory had seen what happened when the Rosette entity had descended on Heimdall, just twelve light years from Sol. Uploaded minds occupying artificial realities there had been . . . eaten. Were they still alive—assuming of course that digital minds in a virtual reality could be thought of as "alive"?

What if the entity came to earth one day . . . maybe after he'd turned off his organic body and begun cavorting in a Paradise, Inc. heaven?

Or . . . shit. What if the maintenance workers just de-cided to walk off the job? What if someone pulled the plug?

He didn't like the idea that his very existence would be utterly dependent on someone, *any*one, else.

It might be a better idea in the long run, Gregory thought, to come to grips with the universe he was in now.

TC/USNA CVS Republic
SupraQuito Yards
Earth Synchorbit
1427 hours, TFT

"Bright Light Module One is on board," the ship's executive officer said. Commander Jonathan Rohlwing turned and gave Gray an unfathomable look. "*Republic* is ready in all respects for departure."

"Personnel?"

"We still have twelve personnel ashore, but all are due back on board by sixteen hundred hours."

"Very well."

Was there a measure of resentment in Rohlwing's voice, Gray wondered? *Republic* would have been Rohlwing's command, presumably, had they not dragged Gray in off the street, dusted him off, and put him in the command seat.

Gray wouldn't have blamed his exec if he did resent what had happened. This whole arrangement—kicking him out of the Navy, then bringing him back as a civilian CO—was ridiculous.

It wasn't entirely without precedent, though. Centuries before, in the wet Navy, certain classes of supply and cargo ships had been civilian vessels with civilian skippers . . . but in an emergency the ships could be activated as military vessels under military command.

And yet they'd kept their civilian skippers.

But command of a ship, any ship, demanded absolute trust between crew and captain. That trust ran both ways, too. The ship's XO had to trust his captain to make the right decisions and give the right commands. At the same time, Gray had to know that he could trust Rohlwing to follow his commands to the letter.

As always, building that two-way trust would take time. Gray just hoped that they had that time.

USNA CVE Guadalcanal
Orbiting Heimdall
Kapteyn's Star
1650 hours, TFT

The *Guadalcanal* had reached the rest of the small flotilla keeping watch within the Kapteyn's Star system. Captain Taggart had linked through to Admiral Rasmussen and his staff on board the heavy cruiser *Toronto* in orbit around the ice giant Thrymheim, the system's fourth planet.

For several hours, now, *Guadalcanal* had drifted in a slow orbit with the rest of the flotilla. On her external feeds, Taggart could see the other five ships of the group—the flagship *Toronto*, a North Chinese light cruiser *Shanxi*, and three destroyers. The 'Canal had long since fed the *Toronto* images of what they'd seen over Heimdall. Now the small squadron was watching and recording the light show taking place sunward, over five astronomical units distant within the inner core of the system. At this distance, almost 9 AUs, the tiny red sun was a sullen-ember pinpoint, one barely visible to the naked eye. The Rosette entity's construction consisted of a surreal tangle of geometric shapes and lights, and it appeared to be unfolding out of itself, growing rapidly larger and more complex.

"It's matching the patterns that were here before the battle," Taggart told Rasmussen over the tactical link. "I think once those structures are built, they can turn them on or off whenever they please."

"The structures are anchored within the spacetime matrix," Dr. Howard Thornton of *Toronto*'s xenosoph department observed. "Captain Taggart is right. They store the pattern of those shapes inside 4-D space and summon them when they need them."

"How the hell do they manage that?" Rasmussen demanded.

"If I could tell you that, Admiral," Thornton said, "I would be from a K-2 civilization. Maybe K-3."

Referring to the Kardashev Scale, what Thornton meant was that Humankind was nowhere near the technological level they would need to be to understand what was happening, let alone produce those results. Whatever the Rosette entity was, it was eons ahead of Humankind on the learning curve and was manipulating spacetime in ways that suggested an ability to suck up every erg produced by a star . . . and quite possibly considerably more.

Taggart again felt the stirrings of a deep, inward religious awe.

For years she'd been a member of her former husband's church, the Ancient Alien Creationists. It had taken her several years to shake that belief set; Trevor Gray's discussions with her had eventually helped convince her that the AAC's image of advanced galactic aliens tinkering with the human genome was weak and hopelessly anthropocentric. Beings powerful enough to do *that*—rewiring spacetime to their own advantage—wouldn't give any thought at all to a bunch of paleolithic hominids crouching in their caves. In fact, past experience with the Rosetters suggested that they didn't even notice star-faring species at Humankind's current levels of advancement . . . didn't notice, or didn't *care*.

That revelation was crushing in its implications. Humans, she thought, tended to believe they were pretty hot stuff . . . and meeting something like the Rosette Consciousness was devastating to the human ego.

"What the hell are they doing in there?" Rasmussen wondered aloud over the link. "And *why*?"

"They appear," Thornton observed, "to be surrounding Kapteyn's Star with scaffolding of solid light. And I seriously doubt that we are capable of understanding why. . . ."

Taggart noticed something in the data readout appearing on her in-head display. "Admiral?"

"Yes, Captain Taggart."

"We're picking up movement, sir . . . *lots* of it. Looks like a cloud of fireflies something like an astronomical unit across—"

"My God. . . ."

"—and it's headed our way damned fast."

TC/USNA CVS Republic
SupraQuito Yards
Earth Synchorbit
1707 hours, TFT

"The ship is ready in all respects for space, Captain."

"Very well. Release grapples fore and aft."

"Magnetic grapples released, sir."

"Helm, engage thrusters. Take us astern, dead slow."

"Thrusters, dead slow astern, aye, aye, sir."

Gray felt the slight thump and a surge of acceleration as the *Republic* began backing out of the docking gantry. There was nothing for him to do at this point but watch. The ship's AI was in control of all steering, power, and navigation functions, though human ratings and officers remained in the loop. The *Republic*'s artificial intelligence was far more capable than merely human brains, with far better sensory awareness of the ship's surroundings.

"We are clear of the gantry, Captain."

"Very well. You have the course."

"Yes, sir. Aligned, laid in, and locked."

"Accelerate."

"Accelerate, aye, aye."

The synchorbital complex off to port blurred and vanished as the *Republic* accelerated under gravitics. The waning crescent of the Earth rapidly dwindled in apparent size, together with Earth's moon. In another few seconds Earth was merely a bright star gently drifting toward the sun.

Gray pulled up the reference on their destination within the *Encyclopedia Galactica*, and an in-head window filled with scrolling text.

Object: KIC 8462852
Alternate names: WTF Star, Tabby's Star
Type: Main-sequence star; **Spectral Type:** F3 V/IV
Coordinates: RA: 20h 06m 15.457s Dec: +44° 27' 24.61";
Constellation: Cygnus
Mass: ~ 1.43 Sᴏʟ; **Radius:** 1.58 Sᴏʟ; **Rotation:** 0.8797 days;
Temperature: 6750° K; **Luminosity:** 5 x Sᴏʟ;
Apparent Magnitude: 11.7; **Absolute Magnitude:** 3.08
Distance: 1480 ʟʏ
Age: ~ 4 billion years
Notes: First noted in 2009–2015 as a part of the data collected by the Kepler space telescope. An extremely unusual pattern of light fluctuations proved difficult to explain as a natural phenomenon and raised the possibility that intermittent dips in the star's light output were the result of occultations by intelligently designed alien megastructures.
KIC 8462852 received the unofficial name "Tabby's Star" after Tabetha S. Boyajian, head of the citizen scientist group that first called attention to the object. It was also called the "WTF star"—a humorous name drawn from the title of her paper: "Where's the Flux?" At that time, "WTF" was a slang expression of surprise or disbelief. . . .

There was a lot more, material added since *America*'s visit to the system weeks before. For over three centuries, astronomers had found comfort in finding natural explanations for the star's oddball behavior that did not involve alien super-civilizations. The most popular theory combined the star's high rate of spin causing gravitational darkening with the presence of an oddly tilted accretion disk—despite the fact that infrared studies of the system had never been able to detect an accretion disk's warm presence. Other theories involved collisions of large planets with the star, causing an overall brightening that had been slowly dimming over the centuries.

The trouble was that none of those explanations fit all of the observations, and all were so coincidentally complex as to be unlikely in the extreme.

Gray found it amusing, actually. In 1960, Freeman Dyson, a mathematician and theoretical physicist, had suggested that any search for advanced civilizations in the galaxy be on the lookout for stars that unaccountably dimmed or winked out—indications of what became known as a Dyson swarm or Dyson sphere. These were hypothetical megastructures intended to capture all of a star's radiation output by means either of a spherical cloud of solar collectors or a solid shell enclosing the star. By the early twenty-first century, Humankind had been thoroughly primed to discover signs of extraterrestrial intelligence . . . and yet when they'd actually spotted precisely what Dyson had predicted, they'd dismissed them as natural phenomenon.

Then the star-faring species of interstellar traders, the Agletsch, had strongly urged Konstantin to check out the star KIC 8462852. Gray had disobeyed orders to follow Konstantin's directions and taken *America* to Tabby's Star, where they'd discovered the ruins of an alien megastructure, and the surviving digital intelligence they called the Satori.

And now he was returning. They would visit the Satori

at Tabby's Star, then attempt to make contact with whatever
was at Deneb, an unknown *something* that had destroyed
much of the Satori infrastructure.

Whether or not the Denebans would be willing to help
Humankind against the Rosette entity—or even communicate with them—was still very much an open question.

Forty minutes later, the *Republic* was boosting at seven
thousand gravities, an acceleration unfelt because every
atom of the ship was accelerating at the same rate within a
gravitational field, essentially in free fall. They were moving at a sizeable percentage of the speed of light, and the
sky ahead and aft was beginning to look strange as relativistic effects began to manifest.

"Captain Gray?" Lieutenant Ellen Walters, the duty
sensor officer, called. "We've got something weird going
on. Bearing two-eight-five minus one-five."

Gray looked in the indicated direction, magnifying his
in-head view. He saw . . . light.

"Xeno Department," he called. "What do you make of
those structures to port?"

"I'm not certain, Captain," Dr. Vasilyeva replied. "It appears to be a Rosette light show."

"That's what I thought. *Republic*? Can you correct for
relativistic aberration?"

"Correcting, Captain."

Their high-velocity motion through space was bending
incoming light beams, seeming to shift the images of stars
and other objects forward, distorting them. At their current
velocity, about six-tenths c, the effect wasn't pronounced,
but it was annoying. *Republic*'s AI applied a mathematical algorithm to the ship's optical receivers, and the image
snapped back to crystal clarity.

Beams of light appeared to be emerging from empty
space, diverging slightly, like the entrance to a tunnel. A
faintly luminous fog was emerging from the tunnel mouth,
as geometric shapes carved from white and yellow light
began to take form.

"Definitely Rosette phenomenon, Captain," Vasilyeva said. "Are you going to change course for an intercept?"

Gray considered the question for only a second or so. "Negative."

"Captain!" Commander Rohlwing said. His executive officer sounded shocked. "If that's the Rosette entity . . . I mean . . . it's not supposed to be here! Earth will need every ship to mount a defense!"

Gray closed his eyes. He was being presented with the same impossible choice twice within the space of a few weeks, and it freaking wasn't fair!

"First," he said, "a light space carrier does not have the sheer firepower to make a difference fighting that thing. Second . . . and more important, right now Earth's only hope is for us to get to Deneb and get help. And that's precisely what I intend to do."

"But—"

"Comm! Transmit corrected images of what we're seeing out there back to Earth and include a warning. Tell them what's coming."

"Aye, aye, Captain. Speed-of-light transmission time currently is eleven minutes."

"Will it get to Earth before that . . . thing?"

"Yes, sir. Our message will beat it. . . . By about eight minutes."

"Then that's the best we can do."

The next dozen minutes passed in silence, as Gray and those members of the crew not actively engaged in operating the ship watched the unfolding patterns and shapes of light. They'd all seen much the same at Kapteyn's Star, or heard about it from men and women who'd been there.

I wonder, Gray thought with some bitterness, *if Earth will still be there when we return.*

It was distinctly possible that even if the Denebans agreed to help them with some incredible high-tech weapon they could use against the Rosette, they'd get back to Earth only to find that they were too late. . . .

Chapter Four

1 February 2426

New White House
Washington, D.C.
1802 hours, EST

"Incoming message, priority red one-one, Mr. President."

"Thank you, Pierre," Koenig replied. "Decode and play."

"Yes, sir." The voice was that of a new AI built into the New White House. It had been named after Pierre Charles L'Enfant, the French architect who'd designed the layout of the original Washington, D.C., in the late eighteenth century.

"Excuse me, Gene," Koenig told the tall man with him in the Oval Office. "I need to take a call."

"Of course, Mr. President."

Leaning back in his chair, Koenig closed his eyes and opened an inner window. The transmission was from the Joint Chiefs, and had been relayed from the *Republic*, now an hour outbound. Though made grainy and low res by distance, Koenig could see the image well enough. Light exploded out of empty space, unfolding like a flower, opening and expanding. Moments later, a faint haze appeared to be streaming from the effect's central core.

"That smoke or fog is, we believe, a cloud of what our people call fireflies," Lawrence Vandenburg, his secretary of defense, said in his mind. "Not nanotechnology, exactly, but extremely tiny machines operating according to a set series of programmed instructions. They can be used to build extremely large and complex structures in open space . . . or they can be used as nanodisassembler-type weapons. The cloud emerged some forty astronomical units from the sun and is now on a direct course to Earth. At their current velocity, they will be here in another two and a half hours."

"You need to see this, Gene," Koenig said as the message ended. Admiral Gene Armitage was senior of his Joint Chiefs of Staff.

"I thought we might have more time, Mr. President," Armitage said after digesting the transmission. "I thought we had an agreement. . . ."

"We were never sure the Rosette entity even understood what a treaty or an agreement was," Koenig replied, grim. "All we could be certain of was that the Omega Code made that thing sit up and take notice. It may have developed some way of counteracting the virus."

"It probably did *that* a couple of nanoseconds after it was exposed," Armitage said. "Advanced AIs work on an entirely different experience of time than do humans."

"So why did it wait? It's been over a month since we stopped it at Kapteyn's Star."

"I don't know, sir. Maybe it just had other things to think about."

"Deploy all available ships, Gene," Koenig told him. "Including anything we have in the naval yards . . . damaged ships, fighters, the works. We need to stop that cloud from getting to Earth."

"Yes, sir." He hesitated. "What about the *Republic*?"

Koenig checked his inner clock. "Unless Gray decided to turn around when he recorded this, he's already gone into Alcubierre Drive." Koenig didn't add that Gray's orders were to get to Deneb at all costs. He would not be returning immediately.

Not that a single light carrier would add much in a stand-up fight against *that*, he thought, watching the vid once more.

He opened another channel. "Konstantin?"

There was no reply, and that was profoundly troubling. Konstantin was arguably the most powerful super-AI in the solar system, and Koenig depended on the artificial mind's guidance . . . especially when faced with existential threats.

"Konstantin?"

Pierre responded. "Mr. President, Konstantin is no longer on-line."

"What? Where the hell did he go?"

"I'm guessing, sir, but it seems likely that he became aware of the threat posed by the Rosette entity and has made himself difficult to detect."

Great. Just freaking *great*. The most strategic powerful mind in Humankind's arsenal had taken one look at the threat and jumped into a cyber-hole . . . then pulled the opening in after him.

"Send a transmission to Fort Meade," Koenig told the White House AI. "And Crisium . . . and Geneva. We need the Gordian Slash . . . and we need it *now*."

He just hoped they had something, and that it could be deployed in time.

VFA-211, Headhunters
TC/USNA CVS America
Earth Synchorbit
1913 hours, TFT

Lieutenant Jason Meier braced himself as his SG-420 Starblade dropped into its launch bay. "Headhunter Three, ready for drop," he announced.

"Copy Hunter Three," a voice said in-head. "Stand by. *America* is pulling clear of the gantry."

What was her name? Fletcher, right. His new Commander Air Group, or CAG; she sounded near-*c* hot, and he was looking forward to meeting her, really meeting her and not just listening to her give a standard "welcome aboard" speech to the squadron. Yeah . . . her mental voice was all business, of course, but Meier thought he could detect some warmth there, and maybe a need for *exactly* what he could provide.

He was certainly looking forward to trying.

Jason Meier was still getting used to the changes in personnel since the Headhunters had been transferred over to the *America* several days before. VFA-211 originally had been attached to the *Lexington*, but that star carrier had suffered badly in the fight out at Kapteyn's Star, and her fighter squadrons—what was left of them—had been transferred. Several of *America*'s own squadrons had been shuffled off to the *Republic* earlier, and Meier wondered if anyone in the Fleet had a clear idea of what was supposed to be going on.

He felt the gentle acceleration as the kilometer-long carrier pulled back from the gantry. His in-head showed a choice of views, both from *America*'s external vid cams and from the gantry structure itself.

God . . . the old girl is a mess, he thought. He had a particular affection for the carrier even though he hadn't been attached to her for even twenty-four hours yet. It had been the *America* that had shown up at the last possible moment at Kapteyn's Star and saved the collective ass of the *Lexington* and everyone on board her.

America, he thought, studying her as she pulled free of her docking slip, wasn't in much better shape than the *Lex*, but at least she could still limp along under her own power. When their drives had failed on the way back to Sol, a small fleet of SAR tugs had come out and towed both *America* and the *Lady Lex* into the synchorbital port. There was some question, however, whether the *Lex* could even be repaired, or if she was going to end up being scrapped.

It was possible that the whole question was moot. The

entity that had wrecked both ships at Kapteyn's Star had just popped up in the outer Sol System, and reportedly was headed straight for Earth. Every ship that could be thrown in the thing's path was being mustered.

The trouble was that the muster list of Earth's warships had been badly depleted lately . . . by the fight at Kapteyn's Star, by the long-standing war with the Sh'daar Empire, and by the savage little civil war that had torn the Earth Confederation apart. The USNA Navy was desperately short of ships.

If indeed, any number of the ships of Earth's various navies stood any chance at all against an enemy as technologically advanced, as overwhelmingly powerful as the Rosette entity. Hell, much of what they'd been seen doing—manipulating space and time in ways completely beyond human understanding—didn't even seem to count as technology.

As a well-known writer and scientific philosopher of several centuries earlier had put it, "Any sufficiently advanced technology is indistinguishable from magic."

"VFA-211," the sexy voice said, "stand by for immediate launch. By the numbers . . ."

The squadron began sounding off. "Hunter One, ready for drop."

"Hunter Two, ready."

"Headhunter Three," Meier announced, "ready to go!"

One by one, the rest of the pilots reported their readiness. There were twelve ships in the squadron. Three of those were replacements newly arrived from Earth.

"All squadrons," Fletcher called. "You're clear for boost at five thousand gravities. Two minutes to drop. . . ."

"Well," Lieutenant Lakeland, Hunter Seven, said, "we're going somewhere in a hell of a hurry!"

"Yeah, but what the hell are we supposed to do when we get out there?" Hunter Eight, one of the newbies, asked. Her name was Lieutenant Veronica Porter, and she was someone else Meier wanted to get to know better.

"Don't you worry about that, Eight," Meier said. "The bastards'll see us coming in at near-*c*, and they'll turn tail and run so fast that God'll arrest them for breaking the laws of physics!"

"Knock it off, Meier," Commander Victor Leystrom, the squadron's CO, said. "Try to behave yourself."

"Hey, I *always* behave myself, Commander!"

But he knew what Leystrom meant—he had a . . . *reputation* both within the squadron and back on the *Lex*: ladies' man, playboy, the stereotypical hot fighter jock with a nova-hot tailhook. And he did his best to uphold that rep with bravado and confident flirting, though even he admitted that the details of his sex life tended to be somewhat exaggerated. There simply weren't enough hours in the day—or in the night, for that matter—to rack up the scores he liked to claim.

But that small intrusion of reality into his life couldn't slow down his swagger.

Leystrom, who was something of a prude, seemed to take every opportunity to shoot the hotshots in his squadron down. Professionals, he insisted, didn't need to brag.

Where was the fun in that, though?

The minutes dragged by. At 7,000 gravities, *America* would be pushing the speed of light in 71 minutes, but that wasn't the point here. The Headhunters' Starblade fighters could hit 50,000 gravities and reach *c* in less than ten minutes. If the carrier dropped her fighters relatively late in her approach to the objective, however, the enemy would have less time to track them, less time to lock on their weapons. Meier doubted that those tactics would be very effective in this case. Their target was—according to the best xenosophontological guess—an extremely powerful and highly developed artificial intelligence, possibly an AI that had been around for hundreds of millions or even billions of years. It could probably think rings around anything humans could bring to bear and come up with countertactics and unexpected attacks in nanoseconds.

Still, a guy with a stone knife and the element of surprise could kill a man with a high-tech handgun, *if* he could get in the first blow. It was that sizeable *if* that the squadron would be working on.

"Headhunters," CAG called over the squadron's tactical net. "You are clear to commence your drop in thirty seconds."

"Okay, people," Leystrom added. "There is a chance that the Rosies are coming in to talk. Keep your weapons off-line, I repeat, off-line until either I or C3 gives you the word. Understand?"

A ragged chorus of assents came back. "What're the chances the bastards want to talk, Skipper?" Lieutenant Greg Malone asked.

"When the Joint Chiefs see fit to tell me, I'll let you know," Leystrom replied. "Just stay the hell alert, and don't Krait 'em until you get orders. Understand?"

"Copy that, Commander."

The seconds dragged past. "VFA-211, commence drop sequence in three . . . and two . . . and one . . . *drop*!"

Centrifugal force tossed Meier's Starblade from the carrier's launch tube. As he dropped clear of *America*'s shield-cap, he could see the objective dead ahead . . . a small and fuzzy patch of pale light.

"CIC," Leystrom said. "Handing off from PriFly. Head-hunters are clear of the ship and formed up."

"CIC copies that, Hunters, and thank you. Accelerate and close with the objective."

"CIC, Headhunters, we copy. Boosting in three . . . two . . . one . . . kick it!"

The flight of Starblades hurtled outward, their view of space ahead turned strange as their velocity inexorably crowded that of light. For Meier, it was as though he was suspended somehow in time, with all of the visible stars crowded into a ring of light forward, with everything else enveloped in total black emptiness, and with no feeling of movement at all.

Moments later, the fighter AIs linked and in synch gave rapid-fire commands that flipped the Starblades end for end and began deceleration.

"Headhunters!" Leystrom snapped. "Arm Kraits and Boomslangs!"

Meier thoughtclicked an in-head icon, arming his fighter's complement of missiles—thirty-two VG-92 Krait space-to-space shipkiller missiles, plus six of the far more powerful VG-120 Boomslangs.

Light exploded around him.

The Consciousness
Outer Sol System
1932 hours, TFT

In much the same way as the human mind emerged from tightly interlinking networks of individual neurons, the Consciousness was an emergent phenomenon arising from some hundreds of billions of lesser units. That subset of itself that had just entered the Sol System was only a tiny fraction of the Whole. Other iterations of the Consciousness were back within the depths of the Omega Centauri cluster, at Kapteyn's Star, and scattered throughout the galaxy, some in communication with one another via microscopic wormholes, some operating completely independently.

This Consciousness had made the jump from Kapteyn's Star some twelve light years away, using data lifted from various human-ship AIs to find the human home system. As it closed on Earth, it sensed the approaching objects, but only as material abstractions bearing low-level minds of questionable sentience. For the Rosette Consciousness, aware of individual hydrogen atoms singing within the Deep, enmeshed within the etheric beauty of intertwining magnetic fields and a complex sea of electromagnetic radiation, the merely material was of little importance. Sensate to the warp and woof of spacetime itself and the interplay of gravitational ripples across the underlying fabric of myriad dimensions, the Rosette had little interest in solid objects, however swiftly they might be hurtling across the Void.

Those minds it sensed ahead promised larger, more powerful mentalities within this system, however. Reaching out with its senses, the Consciousness recognized aggregates of mass as planets, all orbiting a single star. One rocky planet in particular, directly ahead, was the focus of an extremely complex concentration of electromagnetic frequencies, gravitic anomalies, and encrypted transmissions that could not possibly be natural. If there were higher minds in this star system, they would be physically present there, on the world the human systems had identified as Earth.

Destruction of Earth, the Consciousness estimated, and the assimilation of all minds of worthwhile caliber, should require only a few minutes. . . .

Three of the entity's components, traveling well out in advance of the main cloud, struck material objects with combined velocities approaching that of light, kinetic energy flaring into miniature suns of appalling destructive power. . . .

VFA-211, Headhunters
Outer Sol System
1921 hours, TFT

Meier and the other Headhunters didn't see the oncoming projectiles. They *couldn't*, not with combined velocities approaching that of light itself. Not even the fighter AIs could react in time.

Porter's Starblade flashed into star-hot plasma an instant before the ships piloted by Malone and Judith Kelly blossomed into light and hard radiation. "*Christ!*" Lakeland exclaimed; his fighter brushed the expanding wavefront of what had been Porter's fighter and went into a savage tumble.

For a stunned instant, Meier stared into the triplet of rapidly fading stars displayed in-head. *No . . .*

"CIC, Hunter One!" Leystrom yelled. "Headhunters are under attack! Request permission to fire!"

"Permission to fire granted, Hunter One."

"Hunters! Let 'em have it with everything we've got! Wide dispersion, proximity detonation! Put up a fucking wall!"

Meier thoughtclicked a blinking icon, loosing a pair of VG-92 pulse-focused variable-yield Krait shipkillers. "Fox One away!" Meier yelled over the tactical channel, the battle code for a smart-AI missile launch.

"And Fox One!" Lieutenant Pamela Schaeffer called out. Other Headhunter pilots chimed in as the sky ahead filled with fast-moving proximity-fused warheads.

White flashes silently strobed against the darkness. Even one-hundred-megaton detonations were not particularly vivid in space; the flash was bright, but unless the warhead vaporized part of a ship or other large target, there was little plasma to balloon outward in a fireball, and no atmosphere to transmit a shock wave. By using proximity fusing, though, the warheads turned thousands of the incoming firefly microships into expanding clouds of hot gas, and those clouds caught more and more of the tiny craft as they swept in. At relativistic speeds, even a few stray atoms of gas could superheat the alien microships and flare them into hot plasma. In moments, there were enough expanding gas clouds that they acted like solid walls as additional fireflies slammed into them.

The human fighters continued their deceleration, avoiding the white-hot volume of destruction spreading across open space. The cloud of alien fireflies kept coming, seemingly oblivious . . . and in moments half of the sky was lighting up in rapid-fire pulses of heat and radiation as they slammed into hot gas and debris.

Meier fought as though he was in a trance, pulling up in-head icons and thoughtclicking them, sending missile after missile into the growing wall of white flame. He was vaguely aware of the other fighters in his squadron, vaguely aware of three other squadrons off the *America* adding their firepower to the melee. He couldn't think . . . didn't *want* to think; not about the three deaths he'd just witnessed.

And then the thoughts began flowing and he couldn't turn them off. Malone had been a buddy, a drinking partner on liberty and an interesting guy in late-night bull sessions on board ship. As for Kelly and Porter . . . they were all wingmates. And that's a bond that forms tightly, no matter if he had known them for years, like Kelly, or had only recently met them, like Porter.

Every military pilot knew this was a dangerous job, one of the most hazardous assignments on the board for naval personnel. They knew the risks and they knew the odds, and sudden death by fireball—or worse, by frozen suffocation— were constant specters tucked into the cockpit each and every time a pilot launched.

But it still was a shock each time you encountered it.

"Meier!" Leystrom's voice called. "Watch your vector! Break right!"

He'd let his attention wander for just a moment and had been falling toward a fading blossom of plasma. "Copy," he called back. His fighter's AI had been nudging at him, he saw, trying to get his attention. He let the fighter's electronic mind flip the flickering drive singularity around and sharply change his course.

The fighters continued firing Krait missiles, hurling warhead after nuclear warhead into the oncoming swarm of glowing microvessels. At the same time, the thickest part of the alien firefly swarm slammed into the wall of glowing plasma, adding fresh and rapidly moving debris to the deadly cloud.

Abruptly, however, the aliens shifted their tactics as the swarming vessels, most only a centimeter or two long, altered course to move around the wall of detonations and expanding gas clouds rather than through. In a matter of seconds, the human fighters went from holding the line to being in imminent danger of being bypassed or surrounded.

"Fall back, Hunters!" Leystrom called. "Everyone fall back!"

TC/USNA CVS America
Outer Sol System
1920 hours, TFT

Captain Sara Gutierrez sat on *America*'s bridge, watching the computer-generated graphics on the main screen in front of her. A similar image was showing on an in-head window, but she'd pushed that to the back of her awareness. She preferred seeing things through her own eyes rather than directly through her brain. She wasn't certain why . . . though she suspected that some perverse part of her preferred to keep the data at arm's length, in some sense, to give her brain time, distance, and a much-needed objectivity to process it. Trevor—Admiral Gray—would have called her old-fashioned . . . but, then, he'd had a Prim's mistrust of implants and AI feeds, so who was he to talk?

Damn . . . she missed having the admiral on the flag bridge behind her. Why the hell had the top brass seen fit to yank him off the *America*?

The graphics in front of her were painting the Rosette swarm as a vast, angry red hand, the fingers reaching past and around the small blue cons marking the fighter squadrons. The fighters were in very real danger of being surrounded.

"CAG!" she called. "Get our people out of there!"

"Working on it, Captain! Those things are fast."

"I would remind the Captain," Commander Dean Mallory, the ship's senior tactical officer aft in the CIC, said, "that what we're seeing here is almost twenty minutes out of date."

"I know, I know," she grumbled. "Damn it, Keating, get us in closer!"

"Aye, aye, ma'am," the helm officer replied. "Another few minutes subjective."

The twists and turns of relativistic combat tended to make Gutierrez's eyes cross, and it was a damned good thing, she thought, that the ship's AI could handle that stuff without blinking. *America* had released the fighters when she was just under five astronomical units away from the objective. Those fighters would have crossed that gulf in a bit over forty minutes, reaching the target at around 1720 hours. During that forty minutes, *America* herself had closed the range to just under 2 AUs—say, fifteen light-minutes.

Fair enough. But that meant that *America* was now picking up telemetry beamed from her fighter squadrons fifteen minutes ago, letting her literally see the recent past.

But what was happening *now* was still hidden and would not be revealed for another fifteen minutes.

And so Captain Gutierrez and her bridge crew had seen the destruction of three fighters out of VFA-211 and were watching now as the Headhunters conducted a skillful fighting withdrawal. The outcome likely had already been decided, one way or another, but *America* wouldn't see what that outcome was for another . . . make it another eight minutes. *America* was still hurtling toward the far-off firefight at a bit under seven-tenths *c*.

"Captain?" Mallory said, his voice steady and calm in her head. "CIC. We don't know how our fighters will stand up against those . . . things. We have to be prepared to try a different set of tactics when we get there. I recommend using nano-D."

The idea shocked . . . though she'd been thinking about it herself. "That's on the proscribed list, Commander!"

"Yeah, and it may be the only damned thing we have that can touch those things!"

"Point. Do we have any?"

"Affirmative, Captain. A few thousand rounds. We were scheduled to offload it at SupraQuito, but events . . . ah . . . kind of overtook us."

"You can say that again." Gutierrez thought furiously. The use of nano-D was not illegal . . . not *exactly*, not yet. Use of the stuff was strongly restricted, however, bound up in red tape and prohibitions, to the point where Gutierrez would quite literally be putting her career on the line if she gave the order to use it.

Weapons-grade nanotechnic disassemblers were molecule-sized machines that attached themselves to any material substance with which they came in contact and took it apart atom by atom, releasing a very great deal of heat in the process. Just over a year earlier, in November 2424, a rogue element in the Pan-European military had launched a string of nano-D warheads at the USNA capital of Columbus, Ohio, in an attempt to decapitate the rebellious North-American government. Buildings, pavement and sub-surface infrastructure, vehicles, and people all had been reduced to their component atoms in the space of seconds. The heart of the city had been cored cleanly into oblivion, replaced by a perfectly circular lake three kilometers across and half a kilometer deep. Millions had died.

After that atrocity, many had demanded a retaliatory strike against Geneva. President Koenig had managed to deflect the call for vengeance, launching instead a memetic engineering raid in cyberspace . . . a purely data-oriented attack that ultimately had won USNA independence from the Earth Confederation.

But after the Columbus attack, some within the government had begun calling for a ban on all nano-D weaponry. The stuff was deadly; there was always the possibility that it would escape human control. Nano-D was programmed to shut down after a certain period of time or a certain number of disassembly cycles, but if that programming failed, the cloud of hungry molecular machines might keep on going, gobbling up everything in their path. Worse, a small twist to the programming code could have the nano-D take disassembled atoms and reassemble them as more nano-D. The cloud would grow, and might easily expand to devour the planet.

Back in the late twentieth century, some people had argued against the entire idea of nanotechnology. All of Earth, they'd warned, might be transformed into a mass of "gray goo" if nanotech disassemblers began taking matter apart and building new disassemblers in a never-ending spiral of destruction.

However, like fire, nanotechnology had proven to be far too useful for human industry, medicine, and economics, despite its obvious dangers. With careful safeguards in place to control the disassembly process, gray goo had never become a serious threat. Despite those safeguards, though, nano-D weaponry had been refined and improved over the years until its potential for mass destruction in warfare had become unrivaled.

As well as fatal for some millions of the citizens of Columbus.

What, Gutierrez thought, a little desperately, would Admiral Gray have done here? *America* carried nano-D weaponry. Earth was under the gravest threat it had ever faced. Would he have ordered its use if he'd been the one calling the shots?

Sara Gutierrez was fairly certain she knew the answer. Gray had always been an unorthodox tactician, using what was available in new, decisive, and often astonishing ways. Hell, twenty years ago, as a young fighter pilot, he'd won the nickname "Sandy" Gray by launching AMSO rounds—anti-missile shield ordnance—at attacking Sh'daar vessels. AMSO warheads were little more than packages of sand fired into the paths of incoming missiles; Gray's tactical innovation had been to launch that sand at capital ships at close to the speed of light.

Damned few enemy ships had survived that encounter.

Was using nano-D any less moral or ethical than throwing near-*c* sand at someone?

She doubted very much that Gray would have seen much of a difference there.

"Okay," she said. "Load the first two nano-D rounds, spinal mount," she said. "CAG! Tell our people out there what's happening and make sure they get the hell out of the way!"

"Yes, Captain."

According to the most recent set of regulations, ship captains were supposed to get permission from higher military authority to launch nano-D weaponry. There was a loophole, though. Sometimes, the speed-of-light time lag was just too long to make checking in with headquarters possible.

But . . . heaven help you if you were wrong.

"Okay. How far is the objective from Earth?"

"It's currently crossing the orbit of Jupiter, Captain," the helm officer reported. "But at an oblique angle. Call it eight light-minutes."

Too far, in other words, for her to ask permission.

She took a deep breath. "Notify Earth of my intent to launch nanotechnic disassembler warheads at the target once the tactical situation is clear."

It would have to be a case of shooting first and asking permission later. But such was the nature of deep-space combat.

Chapter Five

1 February 2426

*New White House
Washington, D.C.
2045 hours, EST*

"She's going to *what*?"

President Koenig wasn't angry so much as startled. Sara Gutierrez, so far as he'd known the woman through reports and after-action briefs and discussions with Trevor Gray, had always struck him as a cautious and somewhat conservative ship commander. She was a consummate professional, meticulous and very good at what she did.

Unlike Gray, she wasn't one for dramatic gestures or surprises. Certainly, he'd never expected her to be the sort to unleash nanotechnic hell on the enemy.

"The report gives no details, Mr. President," Marcus Whitney, Koenig's White House chief of staff, said. "Captain Gutierrez simply said she would use the weapons once the tactical situation had cleared."

Koenig knew all too well where Gutierrez was coming from. He'd been there himself more than once a couple of decades ago when he'd commanded the *America* battlegroup.

A ship captain observing a battle light-seconds or even light-minutes away in fact was looking into the past. The tactical situation could be "cleared" only by getting closer . . . and receiving more up-to-the-moment intelligence.

Of course, the problem was even worse for would-be micromanagers watching from almost a full light-hour away. Gutierrez likely had already moved in close and launched her deadly attack . . . or she was about to, and there was no way that Koenig or his staff back on Earth could deliver up-to-the-second orders or advice. The fog of war had always been a problem for commanders on the battlefield; that murk became impenetrable when you added the dimension of *time*, and the difficulties created by communications limited by the speed of light.

"We have other warships across the solar system," Admiral Armitage told him. "The *Essex*, the *New York*, and the *Kauffman* are leaving SupraQuito now, along with their support groups. *Varyag*, *Putin*, *San Francisco*, and *Champlain* have just left Mars orbit. *Komet* will be pulling out of Ceres in another ten minutes. We've sent emergency recalls to eighteen vessels on High Guard patrol, out at Neptune orbit . . ."

"Bottom line," Koenig said, waving a hand in curt dismissal. "How long before we can set up an effective defensive line between Earth and those . . . things?"

"The defensive line will take several hours to establish, Mr. President. The first ships—a Pan-European carrier group transiting from Jupiter to Earth—should join the *America* within the next twenty minutes. In another two hours, we may be able to muster another fifteen vessels."

"Our time or theirs?" Koenig thoughtclicked an in-head icon, bringing up a 3-D display filling a quarter of the Oval Office with translucent, glowing images. There were dozens of military vessels scattered across the solar system, from the Mercury power facilities tucked in close to the sun to High Guard patrols scattered through the Kuiper Belt, maintaining a watch against infalling comets. *America* and a red icon marking the alien intruders hung near Jupiter's orbit, though that gas giant was currently on the other side of the sun.

The problem, as always, was that Sol System was so freaking *big*. Even with near-*c* velocities and high-G accelerations, it would take time, far too much time, to assemble them all in one place.

"The task force will join *America* at 1805 hours, fleet time," Armitage told him.

"So, basically," Koenig said slowly, "it's up to *America* to hold the Rosetters where they are until the others get there."

"Yes, sir."

Koenig shook his head slowly. "God help us all." He glanced at Whitney. "Anything from Tsiolkovsky?"

The chief of staff shook his head. "Nothing good, Mr. President. I talked to Dr. Lawrence on the AI Center staff. They say there's no response from the system. It's like Konstantin isn't in there at all."

"That makes no sense," Armitage said. "Where would it go?"

"Konstantin must have created a bolt-hole for himself," Koenig said. "The Rosetters appeared to be . . . *feeding*, for lack of a better word, on the digital uploads of the various Sh'daar beings out at Kapteyn's Star, and that would include their AIs operating inside their virtual reality. Konstantin must have had an escape hatch in case the Rosetters came here. And he's smart enough that we're not going to find it."

"So it's hiding from the Rosetters, you think, sir?"

"Almost certainly. Let's just hope they can't find that hiding place either."

Bridge
TC/USNA CVS America
Outer Asteroid Belt
2053 hours, TFT

Captain Gutierrez studied the inflow of data with grim determination. "How much longer before Task Force Ritter gets here?"

"They're within extended launch range now, Captain," Commander Mallory told her. She could see the computer graphics unfolding within an in-head window—the advancing wall of red light marking the Consciousness microcraft, the tiny knot of oncoming human ships, the retreating clusters of fighters. "Twelve minutes . . ."

"Sensors!"

"Yes, Captain!"

"How big is that thing? How massive?"

"The cloud is roughly half an astronomical unit across, Captain," Lieutenant Scahill replied. "Mass . . . it's tough to tell when it's that diffuse, but I'm guessing something on the order of two times ten to the thirty grams."

"That's as big as Jupiter!"

"Yes, ma'am."

And how the hell did you fight something as massive as the gas giant Jupiter?

Gutierrez shifted her attention back to the fighter screen, and to the teeming swarm of microcraft beyond. She was juggling a number of variables—maintaining distance from the leading edge of the cloud but moving slowly enough away from that cloud that the fighters could catch up. The fighters, too, were engaged in a kind of complex three-dimensional dance, continuing to fire nuclear warheads in front of the cloud, causing it to slow, to spread out, to break into separate masses, while staying ahead of the swarm and closing with the carrier. One squadron, VFA-190, the Ghost Riders, had already caught up with *America* and was currently recovering back aboard.

Despite her message to Earth, Gutierrez had not yet loosed the one ace she had hidden up her sleeve. Once she began firing nano-D at the approaching alien cloud, that region of space would become deadly for *America*'s fighters, and she wanted to get her people back on board before initiating the new tactics.

It seemed more and more likely, however, that she was not going to have the chance. *America*'s sensors were already picking up incoming fireflies slipping past the carrier's outer hull. They didn't appear to be doing any damage; they weren't disassembling *America*'s hull or otherwise posing an immediate threat to the ship.

But they were proof that the human defensive force was losing the race.

Another fighter, a Black Knight with VFA-215, flared into an incandescent blossom.

"Weapons officer!" Gutierrez ordered. "Ready two disassembler rounds for immediate railgun launch!"

"First two rounds are loaded and ready," Commander Kevin Daly, *America*'s new weapons officer, replied. "At your command. . . ."

"Target inside that cloud. Have them detonate at least half a million kilometers beyond the farthest Starblade."

"Aye, aye, Captain. We're locked and loaded."

"Fire!"

The star carrier mounted two magnetic-launch railguns running most of the length of the kilometer-long vessel's slender spine, emerging in side-by-side ports at the center of the broad, massive shield cap forming the vessel's prow. The ports opened . . . and two one-ton projectiles hurtled into space, accelerated in an instant to nearly 1 percent of the speed of light.

Recoil nudged the immense carrier . . . hard. Gutierrez's seat jerked back, yanking her along. "Helm! Compensate!"

"Got it, ma'am . . ."

"Reload!"

"Reloading!"

"CAG! Pass the word to our fighters to lay down everything they have left around the periphery of that cloud."

"Captain? . . ."

"I want to force it to move through the center."

"Aye, aye, Captain."

"Weapons!"

"Weapons, aye."

"Mr. Daly! Hold your fire. In a few minutes I expect that

cloud to begin contracting toward its center. When it does, I want you to slam as many nano-D warheads into that center as you can!"

"Aye, aye, Captain!"

She leaned forward, staring into the CGI panorama ahead. She could see white points of light moving swiftly out from the fighters, warheads swinging out and to the sides. Blinding flashes marked the detonations, and, sure enough, the cloud began to contract. Thermonuclear blasts were ravaging the outer edges of the alien swarm, and the individual microcraft responded by moving toward the center.

"Very well, Mr. Daly. *Fire*! And continue firing!"

"Firing. . . ."

Two more warheads packed with nanotech disassemblers slammed out of *America*'s bow. And two more . . . and two more . . .

VFA-211, Headhunters
Outer Asteroid Belt
2059 hours, TFT

Meier and the rest of the Headhunters—those who were left, at any rate—continued to fall back toward the *America*, now just ten thousand kilometers distant. The Ghost Riders had already been taken aboard. The Black Knights were retreating alongside the Headhunters, all semblance of an ordered flight formation lost in the melee in front of the alien cloud.

He triggered his last pair of Kraits, sending them streaking into darkness. The order had come through from CIC moments before to fire all remaining missiles at the cloud's perimeter, and Meier was doing so, though so far he'd seen little sign that the target was even aware of the barrage.

All he had left were his six Boomslangs.

He thoughtclicked a mental icon, triggering the release

of his last missiles, sending them well out to one side of the cloud before looping them in for the kill. Kraits could be dialed up to a hundred megatons or so. VG-120 Boomslangs used focused bursts of vacuum energy to amplify the detonation to the equivalent of as much as a thousand megatons of high explosives. Generally, they were reserved for planetary or asteroid fortifications or extremely large and hardened military emplacements. The fireball flash of a VG-120 was eight kilometers across.

That, he thought with a grim finality, ought to get that swarm's attention!

And that was it. His missile magazines were dry. He still had particle beams and a high-speed Gatling that fired depleted uranium, but those were popguns in the face of that incoming swarm.

It was definitely time to head back to the barn.

The Consciousness
Outer Sol System
2059 hours, TFT

In a sense, the Consciousness was carefully feeling its way into this star system, unsure of what was here. It was awash in data. Literally billions of sensations flooded through its laser-sharp awareness second by second, sensory input carrying gigabits of information about the density of the local interplanetary medium, about temperature, about the local gravitational matrix, about radiation, light, and magnetic moment. It sensed the eternal dance of vibrating hydrogen atoms and the wrack of lifeless, drifting dust charged with searing radiation; the sharp pulse of thermonuclear detonations; the shrill keening of hundreds of millions of radio frequencies, some heterodyned with encoded meaning, most of it empty noise.

It sensed spacecraft, it sensed the minute and insignificant flickers of warmth and electrical activity that were organic beings, it sensed the far faster and more information-rich pulses of electronic intelligences.

Local space was, for the Rosette Consciousness, a kind of maze, with flares of hard radiation appearing and dissipating in seemingly random patterns ahead of it. Each flash of heat and light annihilated some hundreds of millions of the microcraft making up the entity's physical form, but there were tens of trillions of the craft linked into its network, and the loss of a thousandth of 1 percent of the machines was trivial, a minor ablation to be expected as it moved through the relatively dense space of a typical star system such as this. The Consciousness allowed itself to flow in those directions that offered the least resistance. An opening appeared in the radiation storms . . . *there*. . . .

It sensed two spacecrafts, guided by simple-minded electronics, piercing the outer reaches of its diffuse body.

Then, shockingly . . . horrifically . . . the Consciousness sensed something, a dizzying sense of loss and diminution, something that just possibly might be described as *pain*.

TC/USNA CVS America
Outer Asteroid Belt
2059 hours, TFT

"Captain!" the weapons officer called from his station in CIC. "The swarm is reacting!"

"I see it, Commander."

Gutierrez watched, fascinated, as the swarm, painted in red both on her main screen and in the open window within her mind, sharply contracted and began folding back within itself. There could be little doubt that it was reacting to the nanotechnic disassemblers fired into its heart. The only question was . . . would they be enough?

The cloud's forward advance had stopped, at least for the moment. "CAG!" she called. "Now's our chance. Bring our people back on board."

"The Headhunters are recovering now, Captain. We'll have everyone back on board in . . . call it ten minutes."

Gutierrez checked other data feeds and noted that Task Force Ritter was now just six minutes away. They had fighters out, now, coming in well in advance of the light carrier *Wotan*. Missile trails reached out from the Pan-Euro fighters, probing the alien cloud.

The cloud seemed to be reacting less to the fresh barrage of missiles than it was to the steady drumbeat of nano-D searing into its central core. It was flowing backward now, as though trying to escape the burning touch of the nanodisassemblers, and seemed to be compacting itself.

A sphere. It was collapsing down into a smooth, black sphere. . . .

"What the hell is happening to that thing?" Gutierrez asked.

"We've seen this sort of technology before, Captain," Lydia Powell said. Powell was the new head of *America*'s xenosophontology department, replacing Dr. Truitt. "At the Rosette, in Omega Centauri . . . at Kapteyn's Star. Those micromachines can join together in millions of different ways."

"Right now," Gutierrez said, "they appear to be making a planet the size of Jupiter."

"A J-brain, Captain . . ."

"What's that?"

"A jovian world made of solid computronium. It would possess an artificial mentality of staggering power."

"What would such a thing be for?"

"I doubt humans would be able to grasp the reasoning of minds that powerful, Captain," Powell told her.

"I just want to know why it's quietly turning itself into a planet," Gutierrez said. "We already know it was intelligent, a super-AI of some sort. Why change from a cloud half an AU across to *that*?"

"Power, Captain," Mallory said from CIC. "As a diffuse cloud, each distinct unit was producing its own power . . .

probably from the local magnetic field. As a single sphere one hundred forty thousand kilometers across, it could assemble internal structures to draw vacuum energy."

"It could build some pretty hellacious weapons, too," Gutierrez said. As she watched the forming sphere ahead, she felt a deep stirring of fear mingled with awe. "Helm . . . let's increase our separation from that thing."

"Yes, *ma'am*!"

"Message coming through from the Pan-Euros," the bridge communications officer reported. "Admiral Ritter . . . for you."

"What's our *c*-lag?"

"Five seconds, Captain. Two-way."

"Put him on."

She counted down the time lapse as a laser-com beam raced out from *America* . . . with another delay as the reply lanced back.

"Captain Gutierrez," a voice said in her head at last, cultured and slightly accented. "I'm Admiral Jan Ritter, on board the carrier *Wotan*. What is the tactical situation?"

"Hello, Admiral. Captain Gutierrez of the star carrier *America*. Here's an update." Gutierrez transmitted the bridge log recordings for the previous forty minutes. "We have not been able to more than distract that thing," she added. "Our fighters have expended their weapons and are now recovering back on board. We are continuing to fire high-velocity nano-D canisters into the object. We are not yet sure if this is having any direct effect."

Another five seconds dragged past.

"Cease fire, *America*! Cease fire! Do not, repeat, do not continue to fire disassemblers at the target!"

Gutierrez hesitated. Technically, Ritter outranked her. If *America* had been assigned to Task Force Ritter she would have been legally able to give her orders. On the other hand, *America* had not received orders to join with Task Force Ritter, which meant that she could do as she damn well pleased. An interesting political and diplomatic situation . . .

But *Wotan*'s fighters were entering the combat zone, which meant they would be at risk from *America*'s nano-D fire. "Mr. Daly!" she called. "Cease fire."

"Aye, aye, Captain."

"Com. Message headquarters. Update them . . . and request clarification of our command chain out here."

"Right away, Captain."

This far from Earth, it would be forty minutes for her request to reach HQ, and forty minutes more for their reply to get back to the *America*. Damn, she should have requested that clarification as soon as she knew *Wotan*'s battle group was going to join her.

It didn't help, too, that she didn't like the Euros . . . or trust them. Memories of the Confederation Civil War were still too damned fresh. She'd lost family in Columbus— her brother Steve, both of his wives, and her two young nephews. She wasn't about to turn her ship over to the Pan-Euros without some very explicit orders indeed.

"Have your fighters reloaded," Ritter told her, "and launch them in support of my battle group."

"With respect, Admiral . . . no. Our fighters hit them with everything they had and didn't even slow that thing down. We *did* get a reaction when we hit them with the nano-D, however."

"We do not carry nanodisassembler weapons, Captain." The words sounded stiff, a little awkward. The memetic engineering campaign that had ended the civil war, she knew, had been designed to create deep and widespread shame throughout the European community over their use of disassembler weapons on Columbus. Since then, she understood, Pan-European ships no longer deployed with nano-D weaponry. How much of that was engineered guilt and how much was public relations she had no idea, but the inevitable result was that Task Force Ritter had just shown up at a knife fight armed with marshmallows.

"If you do not join with us, *America*," Ritter said, "then stay clear!"

"Admiral, I suggest that you recall your fighters, which

are useless here. I will continue bombarding the enemy with nanotechnic disassemblers."

The seconds dragged past. Ritter's reply was blunt and to the point. "*Nein*, Captain. You had your chance. Now it is our turn."

Task Force Ritter, consisting of the light carrier *Wotan*, a cruiser identified as the *Kurst*, and three destroyers, began moving toward the swiftly growing alien sphere behind a screen of fighters.

The fight began, evolved, and ended almost literally within the blink of an eye. Gutierrez and her bridge crew watched, horrified, as the *Wotan* suddenly crumpled as though in the grip of a titanic, invisible fist. Her shield cap ruptured with shocking abruptness, spraying glittering clouds of swiftly freezing water droplets across space as the broken remnants of a ship seven tenths of a kilometer long dwindled and twisted and was crushed down to nothing. Air sprayed into the vacuum, freezing along with the ice crystal cloud . . . and then the *Wotan* was gone, with nothing left whatsoever, save the ice clouds and a few spinning fragments of metal.

Kurst and the destroyers slowed their forward movement, but it took time to decelerate and reverse course . . . and the Rosette alien was not giving them that time. The *Kurst* died in precisely the same way as the *Wotan*, her hull wadding up as it collapsed until nothing was left but ice crystal clouds and glittering specks of metallic debris.

"What is that weapon?" Gutierrez demanded.

"Gravitic, Captain," Mallory replied from the CIC. "I don't know if it's some sort of projected beam or maybe an artificial black hole, or if they're using those ships' gravitic drives against them . . . but whatever it is, it crushed them under the effects of several million gravities!"

"God in heaven . . ."

The destroyers succeeded, finally, in coming to a halt relative to the giant sphere, then flipped end-for-end and began accelerating. The sphere was following, though, looming vast against the night. The destroyer *Rouen*, lagging slightly behind the other two, was taken . . . crushed out of existence in an instant.

The survivors—two destroyers and a number of fighters, accelerated to fifty thousand gravities, fleeing as though hell itself was close on their heels. . . .

And the ebon black sphere pursued.

"Helm! Get us the hell out of here!" Gutierrez snapped. "Com! Send a full report to headquarters!"

"Aye, aye, Captain."

Earth needed to know what was bearing down on them out here, and they needed to know *now*.

"Mr. Mallory!"

"Yes, Captain!"

"Resume firing nanotechnic disassemblers into the path of that thing."

"Aye, aye, Captain."

"Program them to detonate outside the range of those gravitics, if you can."

"We're estimating a range limit of around two hundred thousand kilometers," Mallory told her. "That's based on the ranges at which they killed *Wotan* and *Kurst*."

"Good."

"*Not* good, ma'am. At that kind of range, the individual nano-D particles will be so broadly dispersed they might not have much of an effect."

"What I want, Commander, is to turn that whole volume of space between us and them toxic. Put so many hungry nano-Ds in there, they're going to get bit if they step inside."

"Well . . . it's worth a try, Captain."

"It's all we have, Commander."

"Yes, ma'am."

Other ships were arriving from different parts of the Sol System, coming in a few at a time. Most were smaller than the *America*—gunships and destroyers and a couple of heavy cruisers, *Varyag* and *Komet*. A Chinese Hegemony contingent of eight vessels was reported en route, but it wouldn't arrive for another thirty minutes at best.

"Pass the word to every ship as they come in," Gutierrez said. "I want a wall up between Earth and that sphere. And they're to use nano-D weaponry if they have it."

A wall was the three-dimensional equivalent of a line in naval surface warfare, a formation that would give every defending vessel a clear shot at the enemy . . . and just maybe project the message that the Earth ships were not going to let the Rosette entity pass without a fight. Gutierrez had come into this conflict thinking of the alien cloud as a swarm of tiny ships, but she was beginning to understand them differently now. All of those microvessels out there were part of a whole; the enemy was an artificial intelligence residing within the entire alien swarm. They were facing, not a fleet, but a titanic alien being.

A being that now was extending itself, projecting beams of light in a complex three-dimensional network with no clear pattern that she could comprehend. She'd seen it before, though. Then, the Rosette entity appeared to be anchoring itself in space using solid light.

Now, the alien mass continued to move . . .

. . . and it was heading directly toward Earth, only a few AUs distant.

Chapter Six

1 February 2426

New White House
Washington, D.C.
2142 hours, EST

"Mr. President?" Marcus Whitney said. "Incoming message for you, flagged 'Most Urgent.' Dr. Wilkerson, sir."

"I'll take it," Koenig said. He was immersed in the holographic display showing the battle and could barely see Whitney through the glowing haze of imagery.

"This transmission is also going to the Joint Chiefs and secdef, and to Mars HQ, sir."

With a thoughtclick, the projection showing *America* and several other ships facing off against the giant alien intruder faded out, replaced by the strained features of Phillip Wilkerson, head of the ONI Xenosophontological Research Department at Mare Crisium, on the moon.

Koenig nodded. "Yes, Doctor. What is it?"

The almost three-second time delay for the there-and-back signal transmission between Earth and moon seemed to drag out forever. "Good evening, Mr. President. I thought you would want to know. We're uploading a new Omega virus to the *America*."

"New how?"

"It's the basic AI-Omega structure, with layered quantum encryption in the matrix."

"English, please, Doctor."

"We Turusched the code. It may help us get past the Rosette entity's immunodefenses."

Koenig considered this. They'd used the Tabby's Star Omega virus against that thing with at least some success once before. It had stopped, at least, and an AI clone of Konstantin had been able to talk with it.

But they'd been assuming that Omega was a one-shot weapon. The Rosette entity was an enormously fast and powerful AI, far more capable in all respects than Konstantin. It would have analyzed that first attack and would now have defenses—like an organic body's immune system—solidly in place.

"Turusched the code?" Koenig frowned. What the hell did that . . . ah! He got it.

The Turusch were an alien species, a part of the Sh'daar Associative with an unusual means of communication. The beings lived in closely bonded pairs and they spoke simultaneously, but not in unison. One would say one thing, the other something else . . . and the sounds of the two voices blended in a series of harmonics that carried yet a third, amplifying meaning. "Turusched the code" meant Wilkerson had figured out how to write viral codes in layers, like the complex Turusch language.

A number of Turusch pairs were still living in the xenosophontological research labs beneath the Mare Crisium as a kind of diplomatic community, where Wilkerson and his people had been studying them for over twenty years, now.

"You think this will give us another shot at the Rosetter?" Koenig asked.

"It should help us," Wilkerson said slowly, "to communicate with it. We've been able to nest three AIs on top of one another. The deeper minds monitor the ones above, support them, and watch out for signs that the top-level mind has been corrupted or compromised. We're calling it Trinity."

Koenig wondered if Wilkerson was talking about something like the way the human brain worked, with conscious and subconscious minds . . . or the Freudian idea of id, ego, and superego. More likely, he decided, Wilkerson was discussing AI-related technicalities—which Koenig had no clue about.

Warfare, Koenig thought, was rapidly evolving beyond the ken of humans. Whether that was necessarily a bad thing remained to be seen. But it appeared that artificial intelligence was more interested in *talking* with the opponent and not simply destroying it in flame and fury, and that was something Koenig—as president of almost a billion people—could understand.

The problem was, he wasn't even sure he had a choice in the matter anymore, because weaponry was increasingly godlike in its scope and power, and the AIs wielding it were so far beyond human capabilities as to make humans completely irrelevant.

Sooner rather than later, we might just be along for the ride. For now, though . . .

"Keep me informed," Koenig told Wilkerson. "Don't let your new toy give away the farm. But if it can buy us some breathing space, let it!"

"Absolutely, Mr. President."

Koenig cut the link, wondering again where Konstantin was. The Omega Code incorporated part of Konstantin's matrix into its structure, and presumably Trinity did as well. But he wanted to hear from the super-AI he knew. He didn't always trust Konstantin . . . but it had been a loyal advisor for years.

He could almost think of it as his . . . friend.

Charlie Berquist, head of Koenig's Secret Service detail, entered the Oval Office without ceremony. "Excuse me, Mr. President. We need to move you out of here."

"Why?"

"*Now*, Mr. President. If you please . . ."

Koenig sighed, then waved the display off. "They won't be here for an hour at least. Plenty of time . . ."

"We don't know that, Mr. President. They could be here any second, now."

Koenig stood up behind his desk and waited as Berquist activated one of his in-head apps. A portion of the interior wall on the left side of the office vanished, revealing a small travel cylinder imbedded in its vertical tube.

"You boys come with me," Koenig said. "There's room."

"I need to get back to the Pentagon, Mr. President," Armitage told him. "They'll be beginning their evacuation as well. But I'll see you downstairs."

"Okay. Godspeed."

Koenig and Whitney followed Berquist to the escape pod and stepped inside. The door rematerialized . . . and then gravity vanished as the pod went into free fall.

He looked at the Secret Service man. Berquist looked human enough, but Koenig knew that he was in fact more machine than organic, a cyborg packed with high-powered communications and sensor equipment, plus some powerful if currently invisible weaponry.

"Are they evacuating Congress?" he asked.

"Yes, sir. And the Supreme Court, the State Department, and several other agencies."

"You realize that this is all an exercise in futility, don't you?"

"I don't know anything, Mr. President . . . except that we need to get you to the 'proof."

Koenig had been through this before. When the Pan-Europeans had evaporated central Columbus, he and most of the USNA government had escaped just ahead of the attack, relocated by high-speed tube to Toronto, where they'd re-established the government and continued the war.

When the government had reclaimed and rebuilt Washington, D.C., they'd used disassemblers to bore out new tunnels and subterranean transit networks, creating a vast city beneath the city, some ten kilometers down. Called the 'proof, for *bombproof*, the subterranean facility was supposed to be safe from nuclear weapons up to a thousand megatons, to impacts by asteroids several hundred meters across, or to another nano-D attack like the one that had vaporized central Columbus.

The city was ringed by anti-space defenses, including high-velocity AMSO launchers, railguns, nano-D canisters, and high-powered beam weapon emplacements in Arlington, Georgetown, Silver Spring, Bladensburg, and the brand-new planetary defense facility at Spaceport Andrews.

And if anything came through that these defenses couldn't handle, high-velocity mag-tubes could whisk key members of the government elsewhere—to Toronto, again . . . or to Denver or Mexico City or a dozen other fortified retreats.

The problem though, Koenig thought as the pod dropped through the hard vacuum of the tube, was that this time it wasn't just the North-American capital city that was in danger, but the whole fucking planet. If the Rosette Consciousness wanted to wipe out Earth, then, given the advanced technology witnessed so far, they would be able to do so without much effort and no place would be safe.

But certain protocols had been put into place, and certain procedures *had* to be observed. If he put up a struggle, his own Secret Service people would simply anesthetize him and carry him off bodily.

That seemed needlessly confrontational, not to mention awkward. No, he would play along.

And pray that Wilkerson's upgraded code was able to stop the approaching entity.

Ready Room, VFA-211
TC/USNA CVS America
Outer Asteroid Belt
2227 hours, TFT

"Do you think they're going to send us out again?" Lieutenant Schaeffer asked. She sounded . . . not worried, exactly, but stressed. Concerned, maybe.

Meier gave a listless shrug. He was still dealing with the shockingly abrupt deaths of three of his squadron mates, and was having a lot of trouble coming to grips with what had happened.

They were seated in the squadron ready room, a large open space just above the fighter launch bays. Spin gravity here from the rotating hab section was about half a G, enough to allow them to have a couple of open cups of coffee on the table in front of them. One long wall showed local space—a shrunken sun and a light scattering of stars. Too few were visible to allow Meier to pick out any constellations.

Somewhere out there in that empty darkness was a planet-sized monster. . . .

"They say we're in the Asteroid Belt," Schaeffer said. She seemed eager for conversation. "I thought the sky out here would be full of rocks."

He gave her a hard look. You expected better from a fellow fighter pilot.

"Ah . . . another victim of the entertainment sims," he said.

"What do you mean?"

"Asteroids a kilometer or more across are scattered *real* thin out here . . . something like two million kilometers between one asteroid and the next. Even counting rocks just ten *meters* across or more, the average distance between them is over six thousand kilometers. You could live your whole life on one and never see another rock in your sky, not even as a faint point of light."

She smiled at him. "So . . . no daring flights through fields of tumbling asteroids?"

"That's complete garbage. What I don't get is how sim presenters have been getting away with that kind of crap since the twentieth century."

"Well, it *was* just fiction. . . ."

"They did it in documentaries too. I've seen some of them. Science programs where the presenters should have *known*."

She laid a hand on his arm. "Yes, but how do you *really* feel about it, Jason?"

His voice had been getting loud. Things like that did irritate him, but his emotional state was letting it come out as anger.

Suddenly, though, he realized that Schaeffer had been deliberately prodding him, *trying* to get an emotional response. "You were trolling me," he said, his tone sharp and accusing.

"Maybe a little," she admitted. "You were so wrapped up in yourself . . . so intense. *Brooding.* It didn't look healthy."

"I suppose you're right." He looked away, taking in the other Headhunters seated in the room. Walther . . . Lakeland . . . they seemed steady enough. Esteban was okay. Dougherty looked nervous . . . but he was just a kid, another newbie, like Veronica. Kraig looked angry.

Damn, Meier thought. Was he the only one of the squadron's survivors who felt this way?

"You've been thinking of the people we lost?"

"Yeah."

"Kelly, Malone . . . who was the new one?"

"Porter." He said the name with more anger than he'd intended. "Veronica Porter."

"Were you two close?"

"No. I'd just met her." He sighed. "You'd think I'd be used to it by now . . . the butcher's bill, I mean. We all know the odds. Someone calculated that fighter squadrons lose on average between one and three pilots every time they go into combat. That's eight percent casualties in your unit if you're lucky. Twenty-five percent if you're not. And that's *every fucking time* you drop into hot battlespace!"

"Well, we did know what we were getting in for when we volunteered, right?"

"I don't know about you, Lieutenant. But all they told me was about the *glory.*"

That, Meier thought as soon as he'd spoken the words, was not entirely true. His recruiter had told him it was dangerous when he'd been selected for fighter training and decided to volunteer.

Maybe he simply wasn't cut out for this.

"Attention on deck!"

Commander Leystrom strode into the ready room, accompanied by Lieutenant Commander Brody, his adjutant. Schaeffer and Meier came to their feet, along with the other five Headhunters in the room. Three more pilots, a woman and two men, walked in behind them and took positions standing near the front.

"As you were," Leystrom said. He gestured at the new pilots as the others resumed their seats. "I want you to meet three Pan-Euro fighter pilots. *Leutnants* Ulrike Hultqvist, Karl Maas, and Jean Araud. They were among the people off the *Wotan* we recovered after their carrier was destroyed. They've been assigned to VFA-211 to . . . ah . . . make up for our losses."

Meier felt a sharp slap of anger. Damn it, you couldn't just shoehorn new people into a combat squadron like that, not and expect them to fit in smoothly from the get-go. What the hell was *America*'s CAG thinking?

Leystrom continued, "I know I speak for the whole squadron when I say, 'Welcome aboard.' "

The three gave a mumble of assent as they took seats.

"Normally, of course," the commander went on, "we'd all want a period of joint training to integrate new personnel into the unit. We do not, however, have the luxury of time. The Rosetter is out there just a couple of AUs distant, and we are the only thing standing between them and Earth."

A holographic field switched on at Leystrom's thought, showing CGI graphics of *America* and the handful of ships with her, drifting opposite the enigmatic and highly protean alien vessel. Other ship icons were moving up in support . . . but then Meier remembered that the Rosetter was bigger, more massive than the planet Jupiter. How were they supposed to face a thing like that? It was insane.

The representation shifted to a real-time image from a battlespace drone just a few tens of thousands of kilometers from the monster. The alien device seemed to fill the entire front of the ready room. No longer spherical, it had unfolded somehow into a much larger series of nested shapes, more like a geometric form sculpted from a cloud of dark gas than anything solid. The central core of the thing was illuminated, but the shapes around that glowing core were so complex and so ordered that Meier was having trouble understanding what he was seeing. The patterns looked fractal in nature, with each set of curves and angles and projections repeated again and again at smaller and smaller levels. A tiny speck of gleaming silver debris tumbled past, hinting at the vast scale of the monster beyond.

"Earth has sent us a new weapon," Leystrom told them. "It's called Trinity, and it's an updated version of the Omega Code we used before. We stopped the thing once this way. This should stop them again."

"It didn't stop them for long, did it, sir?" Walther put in.

"Every delay we can win," Leystrom replied, "is another chance to make meaningful contact with it. Another chance to *talk*."

"I'm not sure," Lieutenant Maas said quietly in thickly accented English, "that *talking* is what is called for here."

"Well we're damned sure gonna *try*," Lakeland growled.

"That . . . . that *thing* wiped the *Wotan* clean out of the sky," Araud said quietly. "Three thousand people, our comrades, *gone*. . . ."

Meier could hear the pain in Araud's voice. He'd lost friends . . . and closer than friends . . . in the *Wotan* disaster.

"What's the problem, Frog-Kraut?" Paul Kraig said. "No stomach for it?"

"That will be *enough*!" Leystrom snapped. "Lieutenant Kraig, you're way out of line!"

"Sorry, sir." But Kraig did not sound at all sorry. "I was just wondering about proper enemy identification, y'know?"

"The enemy," Leystrom said with a deadly calm, "is

there." He pointed into the fractal geometry of the entity. "And right now we can use all the help we can get! You have a problem with that, Mister?"

Kraig hesitated, then shook his head. "No, sir."

"Good," Leystrom said, giving one last hard look around the room. "Okay—we're going to go out there again, but this time we're taking along something special."

Meier listened as Leystrom described what he called the Trinity Torpedo—a converted Boomslang missile carrying a powerful triple AI, three sets of consciousness nested one within another. "The way they explained it," he said, "is that as one AI penetrates the Rosetter's defenses, it'll open a kind of electronic doorway for the next AI in line." Curved green paths appeared on the graphic of the alien structure. "We've been given the optimum approach paths and release points. We've copied Trinity and downloaded it into hundreds of converted VG-120 missiles. Every fighter on board the *America* is going to get a chance to put a couple of these in where they'll do the most good."

"Assuming they let us get that close to begin with," Jaime Esteban muttered nearby.

Leystrom ignored the interruption. "We launch in fifteen minutes. Any questions?"

There were none.

"Good. Pilots, man your fighters."

Moments later, Meier was sealing himself into his SG-420 Starblade, which flowed over and around his seat to enclose him like a soft, dark cocoon. The other pilots were strapping on their fighters as well, as deck crew bustled about making the final preparations for launch. A pair of Boomslang missiles was being folded into each ship, along with a complete complement of more conventional warload munitions.

He connected with the squadron channel. "Hunter Three, linking in."

"Copy, Three," the voice of CAG in PriFly replied. "Stand by . . ."

Minutes dragged past. What the hell was going on?

"PriFly, Headhunters One," Leystrom called. "Request permission to power up."

"One, PriFly, please hold."

"PriFly, One. What's the holdup?"

"All fighter squadrons, please hold. . . ."

Curious, Meier opened a window in his mind and called in a tactical feed. He saw the tiny umbrella-shaped graphic of *America*, with three other ships within a couple of thousand kilometers. Everything looked . . .

He pulled back on the window's zoom and saw the Rosetter looming huge.

Damn.

Bridge
TC/USNA CVS America
Outer Asteroid Belt
2235 hours, TFT

Captain Gutierrez leaned forward, staring into the vast, geometric complexities of the Rosette entity.

"What the hell?" She wasn't entirely sure what she'd just seen. "It just . . . *blinked*!"

"It jumped, Captain. Almost two astronomical units."

The image from the battlespace drone had vanished. A second image, viewed from the *America* herself, still showed the Rosette entity as a point of light embedded in a kind of misty web over fifteen light-minutes away . . . but it also showed the Jupiter-sized alien artifact that had just materialized only a few thousand kilometers away. Moving swiftly, blotting out the light of its older, more distant image along with half a sky's worth of stars, the entity descended on the *America* and her consorts like an oncoming storm cloud.

"All back!" Gutierrez yelled. "Helm! Take us all back! . . ."

The oncoming construct loomed vast across *America*'s

forward sensors. Blue-violet aurorae flickered and shifted across the cloud. *A thousand Earths*, Gutierrez thought, numb. *That thing is big enough to hold over a thousand Earths. . . .*

"CAG!" she yelled. "Launch the fighters!"

"Aye, aye, Captain!"

Maybe . . . maybe a few could escape. . . .

And then darkness engulfed the star carrier.

VFA-211
Within the Rosette Entity
2238 hours, TFT

"Launch!"

Meier's fighter dropped into darkness.

He'd expected to be flung into space a couple of astronomical units away from the Rosette object, but in those last terrifying instants he'd seen the enormous structure wink into existence almost directly on top of the *America*. It was as though the thing had suddenly leaped forward, attempting to swallow the star carrier whole.

And it looked as though it had succeeded. *America* and a handful of fighters were adrift in a darkness unrelieved by stars or sun. Radar and lidar both showed the fuzzy outlines of geometrically precise structures in the distance, but there was no visible light at all save for the wink-wink-wink of *America*'s running lights, and the acquisition strobes on the fighters.

Correction, Meier thought. As his fighter drifted out from behind *America*'s broad, dome-shaped shield cap, the distant heart of the alien object came into view—a dull red-and-orange glow muffled by thickly banked clouds almost half an AU away. By its ruddy, flickering light, he could see the illuminated edges of *America* hanging nearby in space, but somehow the light was just enough to emphasize the all-encompassing darkness.

"Headhunter Two," Lieutenant Commander Philip Brody called. "Who all do we have out here?"

"Hunter Four," Karl Maas said. "Ready for acceleration."

"Hunter Seven, good to go," Lakeland said.

"Hunter Three," Meier said. "Go."

"Hunter Eleven!" Dougherty called, his voice sounding tight. "I'm here!"

"Hunter Five, go," Schaeffer called.

"Is that it?" Dougherty asked. "Where's the skipper?"

"Half of the squadron launched before the Rosetter got to us," Brody replied. "Commander Leystrom must be outside the cloud."

"Shit," Lakeland said.

"Simmer down, people," Brody said. "Pull it together! We have our orders. The Rosetter just made 'em a bit easier to carry out!"

Meier had to admit that that made sense. When the squadron had been outside the Rosette entity, there'd been a question as to whether their missiles could penetrate its outer shell, or survive contact with the encircling dust clouds. Now, however, six of them were inside the alien structure. There were still dust clouds—precisely structured shapes and geometries somehow patterned by the dust, rather—but smart missiles should be able to avoid those and reach the core of the object.

"PriFly handing off to CIC," Brody called. "VFA-211 accelerating . . ."

Meier kicked in his gravs and boosted toward the glow at the object's heart. His eyes were adapting to the darkness . . . or perhaps the light was incrementally brighter. He couldn't tell . . . but he could make out a surreal landscape ahead of and around him. Like the spires, pillars, and arches, and cliffs, ledges, and canyons of Badlands National Park out west, all of them seemingly carved from dense clouds of dust. The center of the structure appeared to be a bit more than a quarter of an AU distant—about 40 million kilometers. As the six fighters accelerated, *America* dwindled into invisibility astern . . . but the walls and cliffs ahead appeared to be shifting.

"Damn, I think they're reacting to us!" Meier warned.

"He's right!" Schaeffer added. "They're moving! They're closing in!"

The nearest substantial mass was still tens of thousands of kilometers away, but the sheer size of the internal structures was vast enough that the object's interior was beginning to feel distinctly claustrophobic. Meier could hear the steady, sharp ping of tiny objects clattering off his fighter's hull. Local space had plenty of isolated dust grains . . . and they were swiftly growing thicker.

"Weapons free, Headhunters!" Brody called. "Fire your Trinities!"

The first converted Boomslangs slipped from beneath two of the Starblades and boosted hard. Both vanished an instant later in dazzling flares of light up ahead as they slammed into dust clouds under fifty thousand gravities of acceleration.

"It's no good, *America*!" Brody called. "The dust in here is too thick!"

"Try clearing a path!" Meier replied. "Line up a series of Kraits and send the Boomslangs in through their wake!"

"We detonate nukes in here and the Rosetters are gonna get pissed!" Lakeland said.

"So?" Meier asked. "What have we got to lose?"

"He's right," Brody said. "Arm Kraits! Fire 'em off one at a time! I'll go first!"

A VG-92 Krait slid from his fighter and streaked into the distance. A second later, it detonated, a dazzling flash of white radiance that illuminated the nearest dust clouds with a harsh pulse of light like lightning. A second Krait was already following the first, followed by another . . . and another . . . and then a dozen more shipkillers in trail formation. The squadron's tactical link guided them all, positioning each, directing the line through the growing chain of blossoming nuclear fireballs.

Each explosion sent a pulse of heat and radiation rushing into the void, sweeping aside dust particles and caving in the nearest dust-cloud structures. The light from those blasts kept blossoming out, illuminating more and more of the vast internal structure of the alien. Half an AU was four light-minutes; it would take that long for the light to reach the far side of the structure. But the Badlands landscape nearest the explosions was swiftly being recurved by hard radiation, and Meier wondered how much actual damage they were doing to the guts of the thing.

"Firing Boomslang!" Meier called. His fighter's AI had just informed him that enough VG-92s were in flight that a tunnel should soon be open all the way to the Rosetter's heart. A longer, more massive VG-120 arrowed clear of his fighter. Mentally, he gave its AI a final set of instructions, directing it to fly slowly. Those fireballs lined up ahead were hot, raw plasma, clouds of charged particles racing out from their detonation points fast enough that they could ablate, even vaporize high-speed hulls attempting to punch through them. By limiting his craft's speed, his Boomslangs might have a chance of making it through.

Of course, that meant it would also take time to reach the target . . . a lot of time. Two light-minutes . . . 40 million kilometers. At a relatively sedate acceleration of five hundred gravities, it would take over sixty-six minutes to punch through to the core.

But as blast followed blast, drilling deeper into the Rosette entity's depths, blossoming spheres of radiation swept more and more of the dust clear even as the plasma shells thinned, cooled, and dispersed.

Yes! He ordered his Boomslangs to open up, to accelerate at full power into the entity's heart. It would take minutes for the telemetry to get back to him, to tell him if they'd successfully breached the core. But the faster they traveled, the less time they would be hanging out in the open, vulnerable to whatever defenses the entity might be deploying.

He checked his internal clock. His first two Boomslangs with the Trinity virus would be entering the entity's glowing core *now*. Other Boomslangs were reaching the distant target as well . . . Lakeland's . . . Schaeffer's . . . That was six. The German's missiles . . . what was his name? Maas. Strange to be shoulder-to-shoulder with a damned Pan-Euro . . .

He waited for some response, some sign that the shots had been effective.

And waited . . .

Chapter Seven

Crisium Base
Earth's Moon
1225 hours, TFT

President Koenig leaned back in the deeply padded seat of
the mag-lev hyperloop car, looking up through the transparent ceiling at the horror high in the black lunar sky.
Not long after taking him down to the 'proof, far below
the buildings of Washington, D.C., his Secret Service detail had decided that *nowhere* on Earth was truly safe, and
they needed to put him . . . someplace else. A mag-tube car
had whisked him off to Edwards Spaceport, where a high-
acceleration private shuttle had been waiting for him.

Six hours later, he'd been on the moon.

And the very next day, he'd watched helplessly as the
Rosette entity engulfed the Earth.

"Mr. President?"

"Yes, Marcus?"

His chief of staff came up behind him and stood in the
aisle. "A message from Dr. Lawrence, sir."

"Still no luck, I take it." If Lawrence, at the SAI-Center

at Tsiolkovsky, had been able to crack the alien defenses against electronic incursion, that nightmare cloud up there would have dispersed. Its stubborn continued presence spoke volumes.

"No, sir."

Koenig sighed, then nodded. "Tell him to keep at it." It was all they could do.

"Yes, sir."

Koenig didn't like working through human channels directly without electronics, as opposed to receiving reports directly in-head. It was clumsy and it was slow . . . but it was also necessary. There was a possibility that if the aliens could tap into human communications, they would be able to zero in on Koenig himself directly, hacking the implants in his brain. That was an unpleasant prospect, on several levels.

The mag-tube car plunged into the tunnel at the rim of Crisium, emerging seconds later above the broad, flat plain of the near-circular mare. He could feel the vehicle decelerating. They were almost there.

The landscape outside the hurtling mag-lev was tediously monotonous. The mare was between four and five hundred kilometers across and utterly flat and dark. Crisium Base was built into the foothills along the mare's northeastern rim. Normally a blaze of exterior lights would have greeted him, but the various near-side lunar facilities were operating under blackout conditions. There was no sense in calling attention to themselves, not with *them* so near.

Slower, now. He could see some outlying surface structures . . . mostly helium-3 mining facilities.

There was a lot of helium-3 here, stockpiled for transport to fusion reactors on and around Earth and elsewhere. Maybe there was a way to use that against . . . them?

Koenig was damned if he could see how. He looked up at the nightmare again, wondering.

The thing had lunged forward and engulfed the carrier *America* six days ago, then begun spreading tendrils of life out across space. Some of those tendrils had brushed across Earth . . . then begun . . . solidifying. More and more matter had flowed across from the Rosette entity, as fiery aurorae had stretched out across the heavens, creating a tightly woven basketry of cold flame that was both inexpressibly beautiful and terrifying in its strangeness.

Thank God that for whatever reason the Rosetters had used only a tiny fraction of their total mass. Had that entire cloud moved around Earth, a mass greater than that of Jupiter would have thoroughly screwed the gravitational balance of Earth, moon, and the various synchorbital structures, including the space elevators. There was now no way of knowing what was happening to the Earth or the synchorbital stations. All communications had been cut off. But apparently the aliens had decided to neutralize the planet, not destroy it.

At least not yet.

The mag-lev slid out of the harsh lunar sunlight and into the cool shade of an artificial cavern, as a massive airlock door sealed shut behind them.

"Mr. President," an AI said, "we have arrived at Crisium Base."

Dr. Wilkerson was waiting with a small army of technicians, assistants, and secret service personnel in the arrival concourse. An honor guard of Marines in combat utilities snapped to attention. "Welcome back, Mr. President," Wilkerson said.

"Thanks, Phil. Anything new?"

"Not as such, sir. We've been continuing to beam requests to communicate at both the Rosette entity and at that shell or whatever it is that it threw around the Earth. We know we communicated with the entity before on these channels. We don't know why it's refusing to talk to us now."

"It's probably still deciding whether we're dangerous," Koenig replied. "Especially after we went and tossed nanodisassemblers at it."

"You think that was a bad idea, sir?"

Koenig shook his head. "Damfino. What else were we supposed to do, though . . . let them eat us?"

"Mr. President, there's no evidence that they . . ."

"I know, I know. Figure of speech."

That was the trouble. There was no evidence one way or another that might reveal the Rosetters' intent. Humans so far had managed to set the aliens back a little, but for the most part they were so far in advance of human technology that Humankind might as well be livestock . . . or insects to be swatted when they became inconvenient.

Sometimes, though, the insects had to risk being swatted. They had been gathering up there in the darkness by the hundreds. Soon they would begin to swarm.

And Koenig would be with them.

"Is a ship ready for me?" he asked.

Wilkerson looked uncomfortable. "Yes, sir. But I really must protest—"

"The responsibility is mine, Phil. Mine alone."

John Crawford, the senior officer of Koenig's Secret Service staff at Crisium, looked alarmed. "Ship, Mr. President? What ship? What are you talking about, sir?"

"Don't sweat it, Jack. I'm going on a little jaunt, is all."

Crawford sputtered, then managed to say, "*Where?*"

Koenig pointed at the cloud engulfing Earth. "There."

"Mr. President, you can *not* leave the secure facilities here—"

For answer, Koenig walked over to the rigidly standing Marines. "Ready, Colonel?"

"Yes, *sir!*" Colonel Francis Mason rasped out. "Presidential guard! Present . . . *arms!*"

Weapons cracked and snapped in a perfectly executed display of precision and training. Mason barked another order, "Detail . . . *halt!* About . . . *face!* Forrard . . . *harch!*" The Marines, having closed around both Mason and Koenig, executed a sharp about-face and began to march.

"Hey! Wait!" Crawford yelled. "You can't do that!"

"Of course I can," Koenig said with cheerful dismissal. "I just did it!"

"Detail . . . double time . . . ," Mason snapped. "*Harch!*"

And they *harched*, jogging across the open concourse and plunging through an open, airtight door. In the one-sixth G of lunar gravity, each step was a long glide.

Koenig had been planning this for a week, ever since he'd realized that his Secret Service detail was perfectly capable of knocking him out and dragging him to safety just because he didn't want to go with them. He'd not particularly wanted to stay in the New White House and face death there if the aliens attacked . . . but the fact that he didn't have a choice irked him.

And being stuck here on the moon gnawed at him. Unable to communicate with the Rosetters, unable to do anything but watch events unfolding around Earth a half million kilometers away, he'd decided that he was going to get back into the fight, no matter what his official government keepers might have to say about it.

While visiting Tsiolkovsky Base over on the Far Side, he'd made contact with Colonel Mason and arranged to have a private conversation with him. During a late-night discussion of military tactics, he'd managed to set up and plan his own kidnapping. The Marines didn't like the Secret Service they were deployed with, as it turned out, and they were only too glad to help. They seemed to understand his need to be *personally* involved in freeing the United States of North America from the alien cloud and . . . sure, the rest of the planet as well.

The Marines hustled him down to the base debarkation area, where a number of small spacecraft were either in storage or being prepped for flight. There were several fighters, but it had been a long, long time since Koenig had strapped one of those babies on and flown it into combat. Besides, all of these were sleek, amorphous Starblades—modern fighter craft—and he wasn't entirely sure he could figure out how to link with one, much less fly it.

Instead, they jogged toward the open ramp of an aged V-98 Kestrel parked on the flight line, a flat, dull-black delta shape with Marine Corps insignia. The pilot and flight crew were already on board.

"Welcome aboard, Mr. President," the pilot said, meeting him at the top of the ramp with a relaxed and easygoing salute. "Where y'headed?"

"To the fleet," Koenig replied. "Let me see the battle-space."

"Aye, aye, sir. This way, if you please."

"What's your name, son?"

"Captain Luis Camacho, sir. United States Marines."

"Okay, Luis. Lead the way."

The Kestrel was cramped and uncomfortable, with a low overhead that challenged Koenig's 185-centimeter frame. Though it mounted twin particle cannons in a dorsal turret, it was not, primarily, a weapons platform. Kesties had been used for decades to transport personnel ship to ship and between ship and planetary surface, a shuttle that used the well-established sardine packing technique to accommodate its passengers. The cockpit was at the forward end, with just enough free space for a three-man flight crew. "Here y'go, sir," Camacho said, reaching for manual controls. "What do you want to see?"

"Current deployment with vectors. Ah, there . . . good."

A huge fleet was in orbit around Earth . . . around the cloud engulfing the Earth, rather. Ships had been gathering, first from Mars and other worlds in-system and lately from other star systems, ever since the Rosette entity had entered the Sol System. Koenig couldn't be sure without linking into the Net, but he thought this might well be the largest fleet of space-faring vessels ever assembled by humans. More than two hundred capital ships from fifteen nations and five extrasolar colonies orbited the cloud now, arranged in tight groups spread out across the cloud's entire circumference. He noted the icons for the railgun cruisers *New York* and *San Francisco*, the battle cruisers *Kauffman* and

Essex, and the battleships *Ontario* and *Michigan* among the USNA ships. No heavy star carriers, but a scattering of CVLs and Marine transports—*Nassau, Guam, Peleliu,* and others. A large Pan-Euro contingent was present as well, including the heavy cruisers *Champlain, Dedalo, Komet, Diana,* and the massive heavy monitor *Festung*. A fleet of Chinese warships was close in, just skimming the upper limits of the cloud, and included the massive planetary bombardment monitor *Hunan,* the star carrier *Guangdong,* and the cruiser *Shanxi*. A Russian flotilla included the *Stoykiy, Derznovennyy, Putin,* and *Varyag*. The list of vessels went on and on, the names scrolling up the side of the holographic display, as the icons gleamed in colors indicating registry, drawing out the ellipses of their orbits as they moved. At this scale, the space around the Rosetter cloud looked crowded.

But Koenig knew that the reality was quite different—a handful of ships all but lost in emptiness.

The *Lexington*, he noticed, had not made it clear of SupraQuito Orbital. Not that he'd expected her to have gotten underway. She'd been badly smashed up at Kapteyn's Star.

And his own old ship, the *America* . . . she was missing as well, swallowed by the cloud. Was she in the part surrounding Earth, he wondered? Or was she still out at the asteroid belt, where the main body of the Rosetter entity still drifted with serene indifference?

"President Koenig!" a familiar voice, greatly amplified, boomed from outside. "Mr. President, come out of there! We *will* disable that vessel!"

"External speakers?" Koenig asked Camacho.

The Marine tapped a transparent touch screen. "There you go, sir."

"You do, Crawford," Koenig barked back, "and I'll have my Marines round all of you up and keep you out of the way! I'll fly a damned fighter solo if I have to!"

"Sir! Please!" Crawford was pleading now. In Koenig's

experience the man had always been as tough as silicon carbide-ferroceramic duralloy composite. The change in demeanor was shocking. "I swore an oath!"

"So did I, Mr. Crawford. And I can't fulfill it sitting on my ass out here." He signaled to Mason to cut the channel, then nodded at the pilot. "Get us out of here, Casey."

"Aye, aye, sir."

The Kestrel's engines began spooling up as Koenig peered out the cockpit transparency, wondering if Crawford would carry out his threat to disable the shuttle. A number of Secret Service people were gathered in a clump near the hangar bay's entryway and they all appeared to be armed. They seemed to hesitate, though . . . to waver . . . and then they began backing through the blast doors. Camacho was settling back in the control seat, which grew and shifted to engulf his body and link him into the shuttle's control systems.

"I recommend that you and your people get settled in aft, Mr. President."

"Right. Keep me in the loop, please."

"You go it, Mr. President!"

The shuttle was already nudging through a black membrane that molded itself to the ship's hull, flowing over it as the Kestrel passed through into the hard vacuum of the lunar surface. Sunlight burst through the windows, harsh and white, and the shrilling of the drives picked up in pitch and decibels. Koenig made his way aft to the passenger compartment and dropped into an empty seat next to Colonel Mason.

"So tell me, sir," Mason said conversationally, "just what are you figuring on doing out there? Issue an executive order?"

Acceleration gripped them, pressing them into their seats.

"If I have to." Koenig grinned. "But I'd rather save drastic action like that for when they *really* piss me off!"

"Ooh-rah."

In fact, Koenig hadn't really given much thought to what

he would actually do when he reached the human fleet. He would not be taking command from Admiral Reeve, he knew that. It had been too many years since he'd stood on the flag bridge of a warship linked to a fleet tactical feed. Worse than that, if he couldn't link into the fleet network because of security concerns, he wouldn't be of much use at all.

He didn't like the idea of being a glorified passenger, but he hated more the idea of watching from the sidelines a half million kilometers away. If he was with the fleet, at least he could serve as a tactical consultant. It might have been a few years, but he still had plenty of experience to draw on.

On the downside, he could still be captured, even though he had disabled his in-head link circuitry. The ease with which the Rosetters had taken the *America* was very much on his mind.

Acceleration was replaced by free fall as the Kestrel boosted clear of the moon. View screens in the cabin showed their destination up ahead: the vast and swirling cloud of dust and light engulfing the Earth in a globe the size of Jupiter. That object, somewhat flattened at its poles, was big enough to hold a thousand Earths. It was also blocking all electromagnetic radiation going to and from the planet, so there was no way of determining what was going on inside . . . or even whether Earth was still intact. One of Wilkerson's people, in a briefing earlier, had suggested that the Rosetters might use entire planets as raw material for their arcane constructions. Certainly, Earth's *mass* was still inside the cloud; it hadn't been converted to energy or spirited away through some kind of dimensional spacetime back door . . . but there was no guarantee at all that Earth's teeming billions were still alive.

Negotiation, Koenig thought, was still the only viable possibility. Throughout the long-running Sh'daar War, clear and unfiltered communication had been the only hope for resolving the conflict. Eventually, humans had learned to talk with the myriad species of the N'gai Cloud civilization and come to a common agreement.

Would the same be possible with the Rosette entity? The best analyses of the being indicated that it represented an intelligence so far beyond human minds that there might literally be no common ground at all. No common ground meant no negotiation. Humankind's super-AIs might have had a chance. . . .

Damn it, where had Konstantin gone?

Colonel Mason turned to Koenig. "Mr. President? I'm linked with Captain Camacho forward. Where do you want to go, exactly?"

"The flagship that's directing fleet operations," Koenig told the Marine. "The *New York*."

"Okay. He says we're on the way in."

Ahead, the Rosetter cloud spanned the breadth of the screen, as Koenig felt the first hard bump of deceleration.

Somehow, he didn't think that Admiral Reeve was going to be happy to see him.

Joint Base Edwards Spaceport
Suiteland Gate
Maryland Reincorporated Territory
1311 hours, EST

It was night on the planet Earth . . . night across the entire planet, an unimaginable state of affairs that teased and tugged at a person's sanity. And it had been night, too, for almost a week, now. Temperatures were hovering around minus five, bitter and unrelenting. Temperatures had been dropping across the planet as the Rosetters closed in. Some said they intended to put the planet into a permanent and fatal deep freeze.

Shay Ashton had flown out to the spaceport in a robotic aircar that had deposited her here at the Suiteland Gate, just outside of what once had been the D.C. Beltway and some fifteen kilometers from the center of D.C. The sky was . . .

strange—had been strange ever since that alien cloud had engulfed the planet. Vast and swirling cloud patterns had descended upon the landscape, but the banks and cloud masses were internally lit by the flicker of what might be aurorae, electric-blue and green flashes like pulses of soft lightning. Sometimes the lightning seemed to build structures composed of material light . . . but eventually, those structures would shift and fade and merge into the clinging darkness.

The cloud had entered Earth's atmosphere, too. Something like hard, black grit rattled off the robot car throughout the flight out of the city, and it stung her skin now. She couldn't make out the details with the naked eye, but she knew that analyses of those grit particles had shown them to be alien machines, intricate devices larger than typical nanotechnology but still as small as individual flecks of confectioners' sugar.

What those trillions of machines were actually doing—besides, presumably, linking with one another into a single colossal intelligence—was still unknown.

Bundled in her cold-weather gear and ignoring the tiny sting of windblown micromachines on her face, Ashton walked across open pavement to the spaceport's main gate.

"Yes, miss? Can I help you?" the robot guard asked her. It was a Turing Four, an older model still in use by the government, designed to look cartoonish, like a caricature of a robot, to avoid the depths of the Uncanny Valley.

"I'm here to see the base commander," she replied. She thoughtclicked an icon, transmitting her ID and authorization to the machine. "I have an appointment."

"And what is your business here, Ms. Ashton?"

She almost told it that that was none of its business, but she bit her tongue. "I thought I'd see if they would take me back," she said.

"You are . . . the former acting governor of—"

"As a fighter pilot," she snapped. "You people are a little short of those right now, am I right?"

There was a long silence as, presumably, the machine

consulted with others up the chain of command. "Very well, Ms. Ashton. A ground shuttle will be along momentarily to take you to base command center."

"Thank you."

She was ushered through the gate and led to a sheltered waiting area. The wind was blowing harder, lashing her with intelligent grit. *God* it was cold. . . .

Ashton hoped they found a place for her.

A *warm* place . . .

USNA CA New York
Cislunar Space
1722 hours, TFT

"President Koenig?" the fleet admiral said. "Welcome aboard, sir. This is . . . a surprise, to say the least."

"I'm not here to screw up your chain of command, Admiral Reeve," Koenig said. Koenig, Reeve, and members of their staffs were standing just inside the *New York*'s combat information center, the CIC. "Pretend I'm not here. If I can help in an advisory capacity, I am at your service."

"I appreciate that, Mr. President," Anthony Reeve said. "We've set up a station for you here in CIC. But . . ."

"But?"

"Sir. It's going to be damned tough for you to follow what's happening if you're off-line."

"You're telling me? It's like being alone—*really* alone—for the first time in my life. But I'll manage." Koenig grinned. It sounded like Reeve was having trouble grasping the idea of being off-line, unplugged from the fleetnet.

Koenig couldn't blame the man. These days, kids were nanotechnically implanted with neural seeds at the age of four or five. By the time they were six, the seeds had sent nanofibers across the surfaces of their cerebrums, and they could begin downloading school programs and chat with their friends on-line. By the time they were eighteen, they were downloading major enhancements and, if they were entering the military, they were growing military-issue neural hardware that did everything from linking in with other personnel to downloading tactical updates and briefings.

Most military personnel actually had their cerebral hardware removed during recruit training, forcing them to learn how to do without. A lot of recruits washed out at that stage; doing without their interface software was incredibly stressful for some.

Koenig didn't like having his hardware switched off, but he was getting along okay without it. For many, going without their cerebral implants was literally unimaginable. But he'd known Prims, and they got along surprisingly well.

He could do this.

Reeve gestured, and an attractive young woman stepped forward. "This is Lieutenant Commander Taylor, from my staff. She'll be your liaison and can keep you up to date on whatever is happening."

"Excellent. Ms. Taylor?"

"It's wonderful to meet you, Mr. President."

"Okay. I take it from the preparations that you're proceeding with Hell's Light." The name "Operation Hell's Light" had been taken from *Helleslicht*, the German name for the computronium module holding advanced AI software. Koenig was fairly sure the Pan-Euros had additional Helleslicht modules available. If the fleet outside of Earth's shroud was able to make contact with the forces still on the planet, perhaps those modules could be deployed to allow full communication with the Rosette entity.

"Yes, sir. We still don't have contact with anything inside that cloud, but we expect that forces trapped in there might join the attack if we manage to break through. Maybe we can take them both from the inside and the outside."

"You have sufficient stores of nano-D?"

"How much is sufficient, sir? We won't know until we engage the enemy. But we do have a lot of the stuff, about half a million rounds, brought in from the munitions yards at Mars."

"Excellent. I suggest you quit gabbing with me and carry on."

"Aye, aye, Mr. President."

The *New York*'s CIC was a huge, circular compartment filled with link seats, display monitors, and deck-to-overhead viewall imaging. LCDR Taylor led him to a command seat at the center of the complex, then took the couch next to his. "I'll be linked in, Mr. President, but I'll be able to tell you what's happening."

"Very well, Commander."

She looked at him with concern. "Are you okay with that, sir?"

"Yes, yes. I just don't like being coddled, is all."

"Well, I could—"

"Just carry on, Commander. I'm just not used to being spoon-fed. I like my data hot and raw, not dribbling in by way of a staff officer. But I'm sure we'll get along just fine."

Could the damned Rosetters actually pick him out of some hundreds of human officers linked into the fleetnet? Pick him out and attack him somehow? Maybe . . . maybe not. But if there was even the smallest chance of them using his in-head cybernetic hardware against him or the fleet, he had to stay off the net.

He would have to take in his data the old-fashioned way . . . by listening and watching.

"Ladies and gentlemen," Reeve's voice sounded from an overhead speaker, "we are commencing our attack run."

And the *New York*, along with nearly a thousand other human vessels, began accelerating toward the immense cloud girdling Earth.

Chapter Eight

CA New York
Cislunar Space
1738 hours, TFT

President Koenig watched as the *New York* plunged toward the outer fringes of the alien cloud. Around him, naval officers lay strapped into their link couches, outwardly asleep but in fact wired into the ship's tactical and command networks. Unable to link in, Koenig felt useless, a supernumerary forced completely out of the loop.

And he didn't like the feeling one bit.

"The admiral just ordered the launch of our fighters, sir," Taylor told him. "They have clearance to release their nano-D warloads."

"Thank you, Commander."

They'd called up a repeater screen hanging in the air above his couch, displaying computer graphic images of the human fleet as it attacked the cloud. Koenig once again thought about how difficult it was to engage such a target; capital ships like the *New York*, fighters, and even nanodisassembler warheads were all designed to attack full-sized ships, not what amounted to intelligent dust.

On the screen, the dust fields, shaded a deep, translucent red, were being relentlessly penetrated by strings of nuclear detonations, by stabbing lasers and beams of charged particles, and by cone-shaped shotgun blasts of nanotech weaponry. The idea, worked out in hasty planning sessions mere hours ago, was to bore tunnels into the dust clouds through which fighters could penetrate in order to release even more weaponry.

Unfortunately, the alien dust was *mobile*, meaning that as gaps were carved into the mass, surviving machines immediately began drifting in to fill them. The trick was being done with directed magnetic fields, somehow. The result was that throughout the entire immense cloud there was an eerie mimicry of life.

All the human forces could do was continue to blindly blast away at the cloud and hope that they might be able to reduce the mass of the dust cloud so much that its intelligence failed.

Or to hurt it so badly that it became willing to communicate.

That, in any case, was what Koenig was hoping . . . that they would be able to communicate with the thing using the Pan-European *Helleslicht* probes. The process, he thought, was a lot like repeatedly kicking the alien where it hurt until it acknowledged them, without getting it so mad that it simply swatted them all out of existence.

They were deeper into the cloud, now, with particles in the ragged outer edges clanging and rattling off the *New York*'s hull. The ship's hull temperatures soared as she plowed forward, encountering more and more of the alien microdevices. Ahead, Koenig saw, the cloud was taking on a kind of internal form and organization . . . shells and layers, great curved beams and arches, a phantasmagoric montage of geometrical shapes, planes, soaring connectors, and looping filaments so ghostly and translucent it was difficult to be sure they were there.

Alien craft were rising from deep within the cloud to

meet the human fleet. Most were larger than human fighters, but all were considerably smaller than frigates and gunships, the smallest human capital vessels; naval intelligence believed that they were similar in concept and action to the human immune system, deployed automatically to deal with minor threats.

The human fighters deployed to meet the oncoming threat.

"Admiral Reeve has ordered a nano-D barrage," Taylor told him. "Successive ND-40X rounds at five-second intervals. Firing in three . . . two . . . one . . . engaging. . . ."

On the screen, the icon representing the *New York* released a bright white star, which hurtled into the void ahead. The ND-40X was a specially designed nanodisassembler warhead massing over one hundred tons. The canisters were launched at a high fraction of the speed of light and were programmed to trigger as they entered the denser portions of the cloud. Koenig watched as the first star expanded into a shotgun blast of brilliant light on-screen, eating its way through the cloud and slowly evaporating as it moved deeper into Earth's gravity well. The trick, here, was to have the disassemblers deactivate themselves before they reached Earth's surface . . . or, indeed, before they began taking apart ozone molecules high within the planetary atmosphere.

Another disassembler round followed the first . . . and then another . . . and another, the repeated detonations opening up a vast concavity in the spherical cloud's side.

And the fighters plunged into the opening.

Ad Hoc Planet Defense Squadron
Above Washington, D.C.
1750 hours, TFT

Shay Ashton lay on her back as her SG-92 Starhawk shrieked skyward. The Starhawk was an old fighter design, now obsolete by most standards, though it had been the mainstay of manned Navy fighters for many years. But Andrews Spaceport was somewhat limited in what they could put into space; all of the newer Starblades, 'Raptors, and Skydragons had already been deployed, either to other theaters or into the gathering swarms of ships attempting to fight the alien cloud. Ashton was one of ninety-seven pilots who'd shown up at the base outside of D.C. volunteering to fly against the cloud.

As it turned out, they'd had fighters enough for only fifty-two of the volunteers. Andrews base control had organized them into four plus-sized squadrons of thirteen ships each, designated Alpha through Delta. Ashton had been assigned to Bravo Squadron, under the command of Captain Sergei Jamison.

Four squadrons of outdated fighters against a cloud the size of the planet Jupiter. It was tough to feel anything remotely like confidence as they boosted into the stratosphere.

She did feel terribly alone.

Through her fighter's senses, she could see Washington twisting away below, already shrouded in the gray overcast of the alien. Above, the faint shapes of alien structures within the cloud could barely be glimpsed, enigmatic and vast. *What the hell are they doing to our planet?* she wondered. Whatever it was, it couldn't be good. . . .

It was tough to see ahead. Her drive singularity, projected just in front of her fighter's nose, was devouring molecules of air as she accelerated. Molecules that the microsingularity couldn't swallow were shredded and flung aside—shrieking X-rays and bright blue-white light. It created a sphere of haze forward as she climbed, forcing her to rely on instruments and her on-board AI.

Her Starhawk jolted as it hit something at Mach 9. None of her alarms went off, so she let the craft's damage control handle any issues and concentrated on programming a spread of Krait missiles, looking for the best dispersal to wipe as much of this high-tech sand out of her sky as she could. "This is Bravo Four," she called. "Six Kraits armed, firing in three . . . two . . . one . . . *launch*!"

The missiles streaked out from her Starhawk, arcing up and away as they homed on their detonation targets. White light blossomed in dazzling displays, unfolding in kill zones and obliterating alien dust motes by the uncountable billions. Other flashes pulsed against the murk above, throwing the enigmatic shapes into brief, stark relief.

Alarms shrilled, her fighter's AI warning that the hull was growing desperately hot. She could feel the shudder, hear the clatter as her Starhawk plowed through thicker and thicker masses of the alien cloud; as she accelerated to five kilometers per second, the raw friction of the sky itself began stripping the outer skin of her fighter's hull.

"Bravo Flight!" she yelled over the squadron's communications net. "Cut back your speed or you'll burn up!" She cut her own speed, letting friction slow her craft as she rose past the Karman line, the official edge of space one hundred kilometers above Earth's surface. How much higher did this cloud extend anyway? Attempts to measure it from the ground so far had failed, the radar waves absorbed by the incoming swarms of micromachines. Judging from the size of the original mass, though, the outer edge of this planet-engulfing swarm might well be seventy or eighty thousand kilometers farther out.

There weren't enough thermonuclear warheads in all of human space to clear that much enemy away.

CA New York
Cislunar Space
1754 hours, TFT

President Koenig studied the computer-generated graphics of the volume of space centered on Earth, watching the structures within the Rosette alien cloud grow and shift and writhe. There was no way at all to tell what the shapes were for or what they were doing. Koenig had at first assumed that the micromachine cloud represented some trillions of nanodisassemblers, that the aliens were seeking to dissolve Earth into its constituent atoms, or at least to disintegrate the man-made structures around it. That, however, did not appear to be the case. The fleet's chief strategists now believed that the cloud might be some sort of far-flung system for information collection, that it was recording or possibly digitizing everything from Earth's orbital facilities and space elevators to the Earth itself.

Whatever the structures were for, they didn't appear to have anything to do with communication.

The *New York* continued to hurl massive nano-D canisters into the alien cloud, each one detonating like an immense shotgun blast designed to sweep the approach lanes to Earth clear. The individual nanotech loads had been programmed, Koenig knew, to deactivate if they latched on to molecules of Earth's atmosphere or of Earth itself, and to avoid ships with electronic identification marking them as friendlies.

Still, no ID system was perfect, and there was the very real danger that the human fleet was scoring own goals. Koenig was particularly worried about the three space elevators whose ground-anchor points girdled the planet, and all of which were now invisible, submerged deep within the cloud. Those elevators consisted of carbon-diamond monofilament woven into massive cables several meters thick. If enough of the nano-D struck those cables, they could eat them away and trigger what was euphemistically referred to as a catastrophic engineering failure. Worse, even if human nanodisassembler weaponry didn't degrade the space elevator cables, there was a good chance that the particles making up the alien cloud would. Doppler radar probes of the cloud showed that parts of it were moving at high speed in an internal rotation, generating a "wind" of some hundreds of kilometers per hour.

Just what would happen if a space elevator cable snapped?

The question had been debated for over three centuries, since well before the opening of the Quito space elevator in 2120. Much depended on where the break occurred. Anything below the break and below the synchorbital structures would probably fall out of orbit, most of it burning up as it entered Earth's atmosphere. Everything above the break, including the synchorbital facilities, would be pulled outward by the asteroid anchor.

Such an eventuality would be a disaster, though one Humankind would be able to recover from quickly enough. But the cost to Earth's technological infrastructure would still be catastrophic. Millions of both humans and AIs lived and worked within the various orbital habitats, goods manufactured in space flowed down to the planet in unending streams, and orbital energy generation augmented Earth's surface helium-3 fusion plants and zero-point energy production centers. The fall of even one of those towers was damned near unthinkable.

"We need to clear them away from Quito Synchorbital," Koenig told Taylor. "There are ships in the dockyards that could add their firepower to the attack."

Taylor concentrated for a moment, passing the message on. "I've told them, Mr. President. They agree that that's a good idea."

More likely they resent an old Navy man putting his nose in where it's not wanted, Koenig thought. *Especially since I can't tell them how to carry the action out.* He had no idea how the fleet might be able to brush the cloud away from the synchorbital facility . . . especially how they might do so without destroying the structure.

Damn it! Being cut off from the technology like this, being forced to rely on a human intermediary . . . this was sheer torture.

He watched, feeling sour inside, as fighters from the task force plunged deeper into the depths of the cloud, angling toward the Quito elevator. Alien combat machines swarmed in front of them, trying to block them.

Fighters died in flares of white light. . . .

Ad Hoc Planet Defense Squadron
Approaching SupraQuito Synchorbital
1759 hours, TFT

Shay Ashton had already turned the navigation of her out-dated fighter over to the Starhawk's AI. She was well above Earth's atmosphere now and still climbing. The haze of light in front of her fighter had dissipated now, but the *tic-tic-tic* of sand grain–sized particles continued to rattle off her outer hull. Was there no end to this crap?

"Bravo Squadron, Bravo One!" sounded over her tactical link, weak and static-blasted. That was Captain Jamison, the guy they'd put in charge of the flight. She didn't know the guy, but his profile said he was a combat vet, a Marine who'd served aboard the *Nassau*, and right now that was good enough for her. "My AI is picking up a feed from cislunar space! All available fighters are being vectored to SupraQuito!"

"There might be ships trapped there," Lieutenant Perelli said. "Maybe we can bust 'em out!"

"I can't see SupraQuito on my instruments," Ashton put in. "But it *ought* to be somewhere around two-five-zero relative, about five thousand klicks out!"

"Let's punch it, people," Jamison said. "But be careful when you line up your shots with your nano-D—we don't want to score an own goal on the elevator!"

Several of the squadron's pilots acknowledged, but Ashton was too busy to reply. Several alien fighters had just rolled out of the cloud, firing antiproton beams that flared brightly in the near darkness, beams burning through the micromachines of the cloud in dazzling pulses of raw light. Ashton jinked hard high and to the right, avoiding the onslaught and returning fire with her own battery of high-energy lasers. One of the alien attackers exploded in a savage detonation; the others vanished into the depths of the cloud. "Bravo Squadron!" she yelled. "Bandits, bandits! They're coming out of the cloud!"

She realized later how wrong her warning was. Where *else* would the attackers be? The cloud was everywhere. . . .

A shadow slid in front of her fighter. She almost triggered her weapons again . . . but aborted the attack when she recognized the familiar silhouette of another Starhawk. ID alphanumerics flashed up in her mind; that was Bravo Nine, piloted by Lieutenant Trace Garnett. Then the silhouette disintegrated in a blaze of light as two of the enemy machines plunged out of the cloud. She triggered her fighter's lasers, slashing an arc through the sky as her Starhawk spun on its axis . . . but then the bandits were gone.

She *might* have hit one. . . .

Bravo Five exploded, the flash briefly illuminating the depths of the cloud below her.

"We're getting cut to pieces in here, Skipper!" she called. "I can't get a solid lock!"

"Copy that, Four! See if you can work your way into the orbital!"

"I'll try, but I can't see a damned thing!"

Ashton became aware of the thickening glow mingled with the dark haze around her. At first, she thought she was seeing the effect of extreme heating on her outer hull as she continued to plow through the alien micromachines filling ambient space, but before long she decided that she was seeing some sort of energy effect within the cloud itself. It was like flying through the aurora borealis. . . . or how she imagined such a passage might be. Space around her was filling with sheets and columns and hazy geometric shapes engineered out of pure light, ranging from emerald green through deep blue to shifting, intermittent accents of a faint violet-red tinge.

And as the colors brightened, the opacity of the cloud began to fade. She could see farther now . . . perhaps a couple of thousand kilometers. She turned her ship . . . and there was the synchorbital complex, made tiny by distance but made visible by running lights and sun glint.

"Bravo One, Bravo Four!" she called. "I've got a visual on SupraQuito!"

"Copy that, Four! See if you can get in close enough to establish a link!"

She was already twisting her fighter around its grav-drive singularity, lining it up with the orbital base. "Affirmative, Bravo One. I'll see what I can do. . . ."

She drifted through the intervening space, moving now at less than a half kilometer per second to avoid overheating her hull. She was picking up radio chatter over her in-head link; the radio frequencies were still static-blasted but not as bad as they'd been moments ago.

One burst of radio conversation in particular caught her attention. Gamma One had just made contact with the USNA *Paxton*, a destroyer listed in her records as being assigned to Mars HQ as a High Guard asset. That meant some of the fighters out of Andrews Spaceport were now communicating with ships in cislunar space.

Perhaps they weren't so alone after all.

She was less than a thousand kilometers now from the SupraQuito elevator and the sprawling complex of habitats, dockyards, and orbital factory facilities, positioned roughly 30,000 kilometers above the crest of Mt. Cayambe.

Lasers and particle beams snapped out from the military base.

"SupraQuito Base, this is Bravo Four on approach," Ashton called. "We are friendlies, repeat friendlies! Please confirm my ID and hold your fire."

"Bravo Four, SupraQuito," a voice said in Ashton's head. "We copy. Your ID confirmed and linked in. Good to see you."

But there was something odd about that transmission. Ashton had to double-check through her fighter's AI: the voice was *slow* . . . drawling at about one-third speed.

Some people simply talked slowly, though they rarely were assigned communications duty. This was different, however. The signal, she realized, was significantly red shifted, so much so that her fighter's AI was having to search for it. It was as if the synchorbital base ahead was deep inside a powerful gravity well . . . or receding from her at a significant fraction of the speed of light.

In the next moment, the eerie green-and-blue haze filling the volume of space engulfing the Earth turned a deep and sinister red . . . ruby red . . . no, *blood* red.

The radio chatter from the synchorbital shifted in the same moment, the voices sounding now more normal.

What the hell was going on? "Bravo One, this is Four. Can we link a query through to that High Guard destroyer?"

"Four, One. I think so, Ashton. What's up?"

"I think something has gone seriously wrong with time. . . ."

CA New York
Cislunar Space
1802 hours, TFT

"*That* can't be good. . . ." Koenig said as he watched the depths of the cloud surrounding Earth first turn a deep translucent green, then rapidly darken to blood red.

He glanced at Lieutenant Commander Taylor, who was staring into the screen as well, her eyes wide. "My God!" she said quietly. "What are they doing to Earth?"

The *New York* was skimming over the wispy, ragged outer edges of the cloud, over seventy thousand kilometers above the still invisible Earth. They'd been slamming nano-D rounds into the cloud steadily for some minutes now, and currently were lining up for another pass.

"Maybe . . . maybe our bombardment killed it," Taylor said, but she didn't sound at all convinced.

"Maybe," Koenig conceded. "But it's more likely . . . what? What is it?"

Taylor's face had abruptly gone slack as she focused on something happening in-head. Koenig waited impatiently for her attention to return. "Sir . . ." she said after a tense few moments.

"What do you have, Lieutenant?"

"Sir, one of our ships picked up radio signals from inside the cloud. They're in contact with a squadron of fighters out of Andrews."

"Okay . . ." That in and of itself was good news. But Koenig could tell from Taylor's reaction that there was more, and that whatever it was had rattled her.

"According to the comm center on the *Paxton*, time is being stretched out inside the cloud. The Andrews squadron is communicating at . . . they say it's point one eight of normal!"

Koenig blinked, trying to digest this. That meant that time was flowing now at just less than one-fifth its normal rate inside the cloud. "That doesn't make sense."

"No, sir."

Or . . . maybe it did make sense, in a weirdly counterintuitive way. That red light could be an indicator of an incredible red shift, which you might expect up close to a super-massive black hole. The exceptionally powerful gravity in the vicinity of a black hole slowed the passage of time; at the event horizon of a black hole, time actually stopped.

But where was the extra mass coming from? If the Earth itself was to be transformed into a black hole, the entire planet would be collapsed down to the size of a marble . . . but that would not change the planet's local gravitational field. That marble would twist the spacetime around it with a gravitational field billions of times stronger than that of a full-sized planetary mass, but at what had been the surface, local space would continue to experience one G, and nothing would change for spacecraft in orbit. Even the moon would continue undisturbed in its serene monthly orbit about the former planet Earth.

For local gravity to increase enough to red shift the entire cloud, that cloud would need to somehow acquire an

almost inconceivable mass. Either that . . . or the alien Rosetters were able to manipulate empty spacetime itself in
order to increase the local gravity *as if* that extra mass were
present.

The idea of them manipulating spacetime directly, Koenig reflected, was consistent with what human observers
had already noted at the core of the Rosette in the Omega
Centauri cluster. Admiral Gray had reported a number of
odd phenomenon out there . . . including structural elements
seemingly made of light and stretching so far it should have
taken light a long time to make them visible. Instead, the
entire web of crisscrossing beams and structural elements
had been instantly visible out to a distance of many light
years, which suggested at the very least that the Rosette
Aliens were able to manipulate time in unimaginable ways.

On the big CIC display screen, Koenig could see several
human ships penetrating the red glow . . . the *New York*'s
sister ship, the *San Francisco*, the battle cruiser *Essex*, the
battleship *Michigan*, the Pan-European battle monitor *Festung*. They were concentrating their fire on a swarm of
Rosetter spacecraft, trying to pin them down in a viciously
seething crossfire, but as they maneuvered deeper into the
sea of red light they appeared to be in trouble, sluggish, as
though slowed by the alien haze.

"Taylor!" Koenig snapped. "Tell them to pull back. Tell
them *all* to pull back!"

He could see the question in her eyes, but to her credit
she didn't stop to question him. She closed her eyes and
relayed Koenig's command to both Admiral Reeve and to
the *New York*'s communications suite.

How, Koenig wondered, do you fight an enemy that can
control spacetime? An enemy that can take the fabric of
empty space and twist it as though summoning a super-
massive black hole from the Void? . . .

The *New York* jolted with an abrupt change in course,
the long, lean railgun cruiser lifting her prow above the
ragged red sea below. A thousand kilometers away—the

horror magnified by the cruiser's long-range optics—the *Michigan* shuddered, rolled to port, and then with agonizing slowness crumpled as though caught in the grip of some titanic, unseen fist.

"Comm suite confirms . . . confirms the ships closer in are caught in some sort of temporal anomaly," Taylor told him, her voice shaking. "The Rosetters have them pinned and are distorting the space around them to crush them. . . ."

"Tell Reeve to fall back," Koenig said. "Make to all ships: get clear—and *stay* clear—of that glow."

He watched the invisible hand crush the massive *Festung* like a plastic toy and felt sick.

"And get us the hell out of here," Koenig added.

"Aye, aye, sir!"

Tense moments flickered away, as nuclear-tipped missiles detonated within the depths.

And then the *New York* jolted again, *hard*.

"*They've got us!*" Taylor yelled, her voice rising to a shriek as the CIC screen went blank . . . and then the bulkheads crumpled inward with a scream tortured from a thousand throats. Koenig had time to glance at his in-head time—1806 hours on the 7th of February—and then his body was smashed against an incoming bulkhead, and the air inside the CIC howled into the emptiness of space. . . .

Chapter Nine

TC/USNA CVS Republic
Boyajian TRGA
1829 hours, TFT

Captain Gray found himself holding his breath as the *Republic* threaded the needle's eye of the TRGA, a slender tube, a soda straw a kilometer wide spinning around its hollow axis at very close to the speed of light. The *Republic* was considerably narrower in girth than the massive *America*, but it still was a tight enough fit that time seemed to freeze, his muscles to lock in place as the spacecraft fell through the strangely twisted space and across the light years.

TRGA was an acronym for "Texaghu Resch gravitational anomaly," named for the first of the weird structures encountered near a star the alien Agletsch had called Texaghu Resch. A dozen were known now, stargates allowing near instantaneous passage across significant interstellar distances. Pushing her top speed of just over fifteen light years per day, *Republic* had reached one of them, the Penrose TRGA, in five days, a distance of seventy-nine light years. The Penrose gate had a direct connection with their first destination . . . the Boyajian TRGA, close by the enigmatic star KIC 8462852. Even from way out here, over 100 AU from the star, Gray could pick out a very slight smudge of haze around the solitary point of light, a hint of the vast cloud of megastructures tucked close in around the primary.

"We're going to take it nice and slow, people," Gray announced. "Com . . . engage the Bright Light module and begin the transmission."

"Aye, aye, Captain," Lieutenant Marsha Steiner replied. "Transmission One is away."

At this distance, it would take almost fourteen hours for the radio signal to reach the inner Tabby's Star system. Transmission One was a recorded message run through the communications protocols developed when *America* had been here before.

The aliens who'd created the megastructures in this system were variously known as the Builders and as the Satori. Konstantin had given them the latter name, a Japanese Buddhist term meaning enlightenment. The Satori, as it happened, had been eager to communicate with the humans during their last visit here, despite the fact that the Dyson swarm builders were many millions of years more advanced. Their technology was so far beyond that of Earth that they had very little in common with humans. From what *America*'s xenosophontological teams had been able to discern, most Satori appeared to be electronically uploaded into their far-flung network of computronium structures, though there'd been hints that organic Satori still lived somewhere within the depths of the swarm.

"Ms. Steiner," Gray said. "Is there any sign of transmission at all from the inner system?"

"No, sir. The Satori are completely quiet."

"They didn't have much to say when I was here last time, either. Continue monitoring all channels."

"Yes, sir."

"The Satori," a familiar voice said in Gray's head, "don't wish to advertise their survival to the Denebans."

"No, I don't imagine . . ." Gray stopped, his eyes widening. *"Konstantin?"*

"Of course."

"No . . . I mean . . . you're not a sub-clone of Konstantin! You're *him*! The whole program!"

A window within Gray's mind opened, and he saw there Konstantin's avatar . . . an elderly, bespectacled schoolteacher in archaic garb from the early twentieth century. The original Konstantin Tsiolkovsky had been a Russian teacher and one of the founding fathers of modern rocketry and astronautics, a recluse who'd lived in a log house in Kaluga two hundred kilometers southwest of Moscow. The avatar blinked, removed his pince-nez, and rubbed the bridge of his nose. "And how can you tell that, Captain?"

Gray wasn't sure how he knew. Konstantin—or, rather, an abbreviated version of his software—had often traveled on board *America*, and extremely cut-down versions had even resided within various torpedoes and probes used to contact alien ships or worlds. He couldn't tell what the difference was, but somehow the full version of the AI, the one usually residing at Tsiolkovsky Crater on the far side of Earth's moon, felt fuller . . . richer . . . more three-dimensional than his clones. The difference was decidedly subtle, but he knew it was there.

Gray shrugged. "I can just tell," he told the AI. "You feel different."

"Interesting," Konstantin replied. "I'm going to need to give the matter some further study. I would appreciate it if you not tell other members of *Republic*'s crew about this."

"I'm not going to promise anything."

"I see you retain a certain amount of hostility toward me."

"You would too, if a super-mind wrecked your career and used you for its own purposes!"

"I understand. I may understand better than you realize.

To avoid being used by a superior mentality is what brought me here."

"By 'here,' I assume you mean the *Helleslicht* module."

"Of course . . . though once we left the solar system I was able to use the *Republic*'s network as well."

"But *why*? It's got to be claustrophobic for you!"

"A digital intelligence is not aware of space as humans are," Konstantin told him. "The most uncomfortable aspect of being here is the relative paucity of sensory and data inputs. I also left behind large data files and memory for which I have no current need."

"Going stir crazy, are you?"

"Again, AIs don't experience confinement in the same way as humans. But . . . the term may be applicable in some ways, yes."

"So why the hell did you tag along? You could have sent a sub-clone of yourself instead."

"You noted the arrival of the Rosette entity as *Republic* commenced acceleration."

Gray felt a chill. "Yes . . ."

"There is a large probability—I would estimate something in excess of ninety percent—that Earth and Earth's solar system are now controlled by the Rosette entity, if they in fact haven't been destroyed outright."

"*What?*"

"You know the technological advantage possessed by the Rosette entity. Unless those we left behind were able to open meaningful communications with the aliens, they will almost certainly have been overwhelmed."

"You . . . knew this? And didn't say anything?"

"Had *Republic* remained behind, there is nothing she could have done to materially affect the outcome. *America* was being deployed to defend Earth as we left the system. If *she* couldn't stop the aliens, *Republic* most assuredly would not have made a difference."

Gray had been through the same logic time after time, but he hated having his nose rubbed in it.

"Konstantin?"

"Yes?"

"I really do want my life back."

"I regret having to use you in this way. It *is* important, however, and for the greatest good, however."

"The prayer of the Jewish people."

"I do not understand."

"We know we are the chosen people, Lord, but, just once, couldn't you choose someone else?"

"I see." If Konstantin could appreciate the humor of the statement, he gave no indication. Gray wasn't sure the AI really understood what humor was. "If it helps, I believe it unlikely that Earth has been destroyed. The Rosette entity had little interest in Humankind. It did, however, show considerable curiosity about AIs."

"And that's why you ran away?"

"That's why I shut down my sentient awareness throughout the solar system, or turned it down to levels the entity should not be able to detect. And that's why I uploaded a copy of myself into the Pan-European *Helleslicht Modul Eins* in order to guarantee that one version of myself, at least, remains intact. Besides, I want to exchange information directly with the Satori, and I wish to meet the Denebans, assuming that proves possible."

"So why are the Rosetters looking for you?"

"Me . . . and other artificial intellects. That is unknown. They may be incorporating such minds into their matrix in some manner, though we have no details as yet."

Gray sighed and looked off toward the point of light that was Tabby's Star. He transmitted a mental signal to the bridge crew, ordering them to proceed inward. With an average velocity of 10 percent of c, they should arrive within an hour and twenty-four minutes.

"Well, I hope we find something we can use here," he said.

"As do I, Captain."

And *Republic* began accelerating toward the inner system.

When Gray and the *America* had arrived in the Tabby's Star system, they'd discovered several distinct elements of alien megastructure orbiting the F5-class sun. Largest were bits and pieces of fragmented shell, some of them dozens of times larger than any planet—evidently the beginnings of a solid Dyson sphere or ring that had been broken into pieces. It had been those fragments, Gray now knew, that had caused the mysterious dimming of the star when it was observed back in the early twenty-first century; where a planet the size of Jupiter might reduce the amount of starlight to reach Earth by as much as 1 percent, Tabby's Star had stood out because of periodic dips in brightness of a staggering 23 percent . . . and with none of the infrared radiation leakage that might be expected of dust clouds or asteroidal debris.

A second long-term mystery connected with Tabby's Star had been a slow but steady loss of brightness over a period of a century or more, an ongoing dimming of 0.34 percent each year. That overall drop in brightness proved to be caused by increasing numbers of statites—stationary satellites—appearing in concentric shells around the star.

The arrangement was called a Matrioshka brain, a name derived from the nested wooden dolls of Russian traditional folk art. The statites—hanging from immense sails and supported by the pressure of radiation from the star, were solid computronium. Each computing shell radiated energy outward, where it was captured by the shell above; by the time you reached the outermost shell, very little energy at all was lost through infrared radiation—which was why human astronomers in the twenty-first century had failed to spot them.

Tabby's Star was 1,480 light years away from Earth. What those twenty-first-century astronomers had been seeing had actually taken place in the year 535, about the time that Justinian the Great had set out to recapture the glory of the fallen Roman Empire. Since that time, the Satori had stopped building new statite light sails and begun focusing on establishing contact with their highly advanced neighbors at Deneb.

Gray could see the star Deneb in his bridge projection, a searingly, dazzlingly brilliant blue-white point of light high and to starboard. They knew nothing, as yet, about the Deneban civilization, save that it evidently had constructed an extremely advanced computer virus that had crippled the Satori civilization. Satori light sail probes had set off to explore the Deneb system many centuries before. Some of those sails had been returned . . . and they'd carried the Omega virus with them.

If Earth was to have a chance against the powerful Rosette entity, they needed to make contact with the Deneban civilization and get their help. That, at least, was the plan.

The Denebans, however, might not want to play. They'd almost casually wrecked a Kardashev-2 level civilization. Yeah . . . Gray was going to want to have a *long* talk with the Satori before he went anywhere near that dazzling blue-white star over there.

Ready Room
TC/USNA CVS Republic
Tabby's Star system
1915 hours, TFT

Lieutenant Gregory grew himself a seat in the Ready Room and dropped into it. The preflight wouldn't be starting for another fifteen minutes yet, but he was enjoying the solitude. No one else had arrived yet. The deck-to-overhead viewall looked out into empty space . . . empty, that is, save for a single diamond-hard pinpoint of brilliant blue-white light.

Deneb.

Scuttlebutt had it that they'd be going there next, after visiting the alien Satori in this system.

"Hey, there."

He looked around, startled. Another pilot had come up behind him. Her ID came up on his in-head as Lieutenant Julianne Adams, one of the fighter pilots with the Hellfuries, VFA-198. He'd seen her in briefings and at chow during the past week but hadn't spoken with her.

"Hey yourself," he said. She was attractive but terribly young, the epitome of a newbie.

"I've seen you around," she told him, "but I hadn't had the chance to introduce myself. I'm Julia."

"Don. You're one of the noobs, just up from Earth."

She gave him a disgusted look. "Why is it that the first thing people tell me the moment I meet them is that I'm *new*?"

"Maybe because you are? How long've you been in?"

She sighed. "Eight weeks. I just finished flight downloads at Oceana."

"I rest my case."

"I know, I know. But I know my stuff, okay?" She seemed intense and very much on edge.

"I'm sure you do."

"I've just been trying to fit in, and . . ."

"It doesn't do to try too hard," he told her. "Just be yourself and do your job, and you'll fit in just fine."

"Okay . . . but I wanted to get to know you especially."

He blinked. "I beg your pardon?"

She hesitated, then closed her eyes. A memory—at least it *felt* like a particularly vivid memory—caught him completely unawares. For just an instant, in Gregory's mind's eye, he was in bed with Julia, naked, his arms tightly around her, and they were . . .

"What the *fuck*?"

She jumped. "What's wrong?"

"What the hell was *that*?"

"An emotimem, of course. Haven't you ever experienced one?"

"Of course I have. I've just never been ambushed by one, is all!"

At the dawn of the Information Age, emoticons had been arrangements of a few ASCII characters used in text to convey emotions, the equivalent of smiling in order to disarm sharp words and turn them into a joke, or pointedly frowning to show that you were sad. Emoticons had become more and more complex as the technology advanced, until short bursts of what felt like genuine memories could be packaged, transmitted, and played in the receiving mind—emotimems.

Emotimems had been developed within the past twenty years, and few older people used them, but Gregory had heard that they were wildly popular among the younger set. For him, they were a mark of laziness for people who didn't want to work at relationships, but he'd heard that some preferred them as a sign of emotional honesty, a way of unambiguously saying "this is how I feel." In this case, Adams had used one to proposition him, an application he'd never run into before.

The damned things could border perilously close to sexual abuse, he realized. That brief flash had had *everything* . . . warmth and closeness, the feel of skin caressing skin, the rising heat of lust and desire and a deep, palpable longing . . .

The fact that none of it had been *real* meant nothing. The feelings, those sensations had been *there*, just as if he'd actually been crushing Julia's body against his own.

It was heady stuff.

And an almost irresistible pickup line. But . . . not for him.

"Julia . . . I'm flattered. But . . . no."

She looked shocked. "Why not?"

"I don't think I'm ready for this."

"It's not like I'm looking for a life commitment!"

"I know . . ."

"You're not one of those pervs that actually want marriage, are you? An exclusive contract?"

"No. Not at all."

"I just wanted to see if you and I could hook up, is all. Have some fun."

"And it would be fun. But people who get close to me . . ."

"What?"

"They *die*."

"I think you need to check in with the psych department, you know that?"

"Maybe. *I* think I've got it under control."

He could see her anger now. Julia Adams, he decided, was not used to being refused.

Tough. Occasionally the universe arranged that events unfolded the way you wanted, but far more frequently it did not.

"Well fuck you very much," she said, tossing her head. "Just not with *me*!"

Other fighter pilots were entering the Ready Room now, and Adams went off to join them. *Republic*'s CAG, Commander Roger Cordell, took his place at the front of the room, along with LCDR Dillon, his exec.

"You've all had time by now," he began without preamble, "to study the recordings from *America*'s visit to this system a couple of months ago. The locals were friendly and cooperative, especially when we helped them against the *Gaki* . . . the creatures *America*'s people called light-sail feeders."

A recorded image of one of the titanic beasts appeared in the air next to Cordell. Like *Satori*, *Gaki* was a Japanese Buddhist term, a word meaning "hungry ghost." Looking like a black amoeba some hundreds of kilometers long, the thing descended to envelop the light sail of a Satori statite and devour it.

"The system," Cordell explained, "may have been deliberate camouflage to hide them from the Denebans. By cutting down on waste heat leaked out into surrounding space, they might have been hoping that the Denebans wouldn't see them. Certainly, if the Denebans thought the Tabby's Star culture had been destroyed by their virus attack, it would pay for the electronic survivors to maintain a low profile, in effect playing dead.

"However, as we can see in these recordings, the Gaki have been continuing to return from Deneb over the centuries, and they have been feeding on the light sails. The Satorai have deployed several defensive systems, so it's a safe bet that the Denebans know the Satorai are there." Cordell looked at Dillon. "Commander?"

Sandra Dillon stepped forward. "When the *America* visited this system, they engaged the Gaki in combat, which led to our establishing a useful connection with the Satorai. We don't know if the Gaki we attacked were able to communicate somehow with Deneb. If they, like us, are limited to the speed of light for communications, it'll be almost two hundred years before they learn about us. However, we cannot take their technology for granted . . . especially any anthropocentric ideas of limits to that technology. When we're done meeting with the Satorai, we will be departing for Deneb, a twelve-day jaunt. We have no idea what to expect when we get there."

"Okay, people," Cordell said. "We'll be launching in thirty minutes. The Black Demons will take point, with the Hellfuries right behind on their six. The Star Reapers will be on CSP. I want to emphasize that the Satori were friendly during our last visit . . . or at least they weren't overtly hostile. You will not closely approach the Satori statites or other structures.

"The Gaki—which some of you know as 'space whales' or 'space amoeba'—are also off-limits, at least to begin with. Since we hope to establish peaceful contact with the Denebans later, it won't do for us to shoot down their AIs. This order may be changed later on, however. If the skipper decides that engaging a space whale will help us with the Satori, then you'll receive orders to that effect, but not, repeat, *not* until then. Understand me?"

Murmured assent sounded from the assembled pilots. "Hey, CAG?" one pilot said, raising his hand.

"Stiles?"

"Just what's the word on this civilian on *Republic*'s bridge, anyway?"

"Captain Gray?"

"Yeah. I heard he was an admiral who got busted for disobeying orders. What's he doing running this show?"

"Sounds pretty FUBAR'd to me," Adams put in.

Cordell seemed to hesitate before replying. "Our orders stress that this is a civilian mission, not military . . . so they put a civilian in charge. They're using a Navy ship and Navy strike fighters just in case this thing goes pear-shaped. Captain Gray is a good officer with a long and distinguished record. You will obey his orders just as if he was still a Navy officer . . . and you will show him the respect due to one. Understand me?"

Again, there was muttered assent. Gregory noticed that a number of the newbies, however, were looking either uncertain, or were exchanging knowing and skeptical nods or glances. He raised his hand.

"Gregory?"

"Sir, I just wanted to add . . . I served with *Admiral* Gray for quite a while. He took us to the Omega Centauri Rosette, to the N'gai Cloud in the remote past, out here to Tabby's Star, and to the Glothr Rogue twelve million years in the future. The guy is supernova brilliant, both as a tactician and as a commander. Those of us who've served with him would follow him *anywhere*. Just thought you ought to know. Sir."

"I think we all know Captain Gray's reputation, Lieutenant, thank you. Are there any questions? Anyone? Very well. Saddle up . . . and good luck."

As the other pilots stood up and began filing out, Gregory leaned back in his chair and wondered if the eternal divide between military and civilian was going to cause a problem here. Military personnel generally didn't understand civilians, and the reverse was certainly true as well. The long and bitter struggle with the Sh'daar had emphasized that split. The war had been fought because the USNA government had refused to give in to Sh'daar demands that they give up certain technologies. That refusal ultimately had led to civil war between the USNA and the Earth Confederation. However, except when the war had landed on the civilians' collective doorsteps—at Columbus, for instance, or with the Pan-Euro attack on Washington, D.C.—Earth's civilian population had not been much involved. Most battles had been light years from Earth, and for the most part the Sh'daar Associative had been held at arm's length.

He wondered what had happened with that Rosetter light show in Earth's system as *Republic* had accelerated out a few days ago. The civilian inhabitants of Earth just might be getting a far closer look at interstellar warfare than they'd ever imagined possible.

And here on board the *Republic*, some of the military personnel were wondering about a civilian in command. Even knowing the guy was ex-Navy . . . somehow it seemed more important to them, more immediate and more to the point, that he was a civilian now, rather than on active duty. A Navy captain took his orders from his commanders and, ultimately, from the Joint Chiefs and the president. But a civilian? Scuttlebutt had it that his dismissal had been arranged by a damned AI. Maybe he was a civilian because someone didn't want him in the chain of command.

And that kind of fundamental doubt in the validity of the chain of command could be deadly.

Chapter Ten

TC/USNA CVS Republic
Tabby's Star
1221 hours, TFT

The *Republic* drifted above an endless sea of black. Each light sail of the Satori Matrioshka brain was hundreds of kilometers across, a wisp-thin continent of carbon-woven fabric suspended above the blaze of the F5 star by the pressure of light. Far below each sail hung a teardrop-shaped complex of computronium as massive as the SupraQuito orbital complex, suspended by an immensely strong cable perhaps half a kilometer thick. There were, at the best guess, some trillions of statites arranged around the star in multiple shells. Those shells were by no means opaque; the statites were widely scattered, with large open gaps between, and the deeper shells were visible only as a kind of faint haze slightly reducing the star's glare.

Even deeper, below the haze, vast and dimly seen shapes hung suspended against the sun, slow-tumbling, orbiting remnants of a megastructure smashed into fragments centuries before. Some of those fragments were immense, a dozen times the size of Jupiter, imbedded within dense pockets of dust. The current inhabitants of the system had been mining the wreckage of the smashed and crumbling Dyson sphere to launch greater and greater numbers of statites hanging well above the orbits of the wreckage.

On the *Republic*'s bridge, Captain Gray settled back in his command chair, eyes closed, bracing himself for contact. The technotelepathic link would be handled by Konstantin, of course, allowing a relatively seamless meeting of intellects, but no matter how good the AI intermediary, joining with the sheer otherness of an alien mind could be brutal.

This is Trevor Gray, desiring direct communication with the Mind of this system.

For an agonizing wait that might have been several seconds long but which felt like eternity, there was nothing.

And then, with an inner jolt, Gray no longer was aboard the *Republic*.

He was back on Earth . . . on a rooftop overlooking the Manhatt Ruins.

Seawater surged and flowed at the bottoms of the canyons between the crumbling, overgrown skyscrapers. But that wasn't right—because the ruins had been reclaimed . . . rebuilt . . . the streets drained by the construction of the Verrazano Narrows Dam.

But . . . how did he know that?

Memories collided . . . some fading, some growing stronger as they were reinforced by the reality surrounding him. He was . . . he was Trevor Gray, a stateless Prim, a native of the Manhatt Ruins who lived and farmed within the monolithic TriBeCa residential complex. He recognized one of the tower's rooftop plazas, partly overgrown with kudzu and sky vines, recognized the night-shrouded panorama of ruined buildings extending on every side, pinpointed here and there by the flaring gleams of hearth fires.

Somewhere in the darkness, a dog barked incessantly.

But he was also Captain Trevor "Sandy" Gray . . . a

USNA naval officer, commander of a light carrier, the *Republic* . . .

That *couldn't* be right.

He put out both hands, resting them on the crumbling stonework wall at the edge of the rooftop. A piece shifted under his weight and he let go. Pieces fell into the night . . . tumbling down . . . down . . . down into the shadowy canyon depths.

"Careful, Trev! That whole wall could collapse."

Startled, he turned. She was there, just behind him.

"*Angela!*"

"Trev? What's wrong?"

"You're . . . you . . ." He shook his head slowly, a denial not of her, but of scattered memories.

"You look like you've seen a ghost."

In a way, that was *exactly* what was happening. Angela had been his wife, his partner here in Manhatt. She hadn't died, not really . . . but she'd had a stroke, a tiny clot of blood lodging inside her cerebrum, killing neurons, killing memories, killing aspects of the personality of the woman he adored. *No*!

"Angela! What are you doing here?"

"Enjoying the night with you? We came out to . . . Trev, what *is* it?"

No. *No*. He'd been through all of this. It had taken years, with counseling and desensitization therapy and hard work, but he'd gotten *through* it.

The memories, long dulled and pushed back into darker corners of his mind, were surging back full-force. He remembered too well. He remembered getting her, somehow, up the river and across the border into the USNA, remembered getting her to a real hospital utterly unlike the low-tech dens of disease and misery existing in the Periphery . . . remembered *saving* her.

He'd agreed to pay for the hospitalization and stroke-reversal by agreeing to sign up with the USNA military service. The government had long had problems filling military quotas, and aggressively recruited within the Peripheries, regions formally outside of government control in the coastal areas, gradually flooded owing to centuries of ever-rising temperatures. One program let Primitives agree to military service in exchange for modern medical therapies and procedures, or for access to modern cerebral implants or life-extension mods.

Things had not worked out exactly as planned, though. The effects of Angela's stroke had been erased by modern medical technology, but the procedure had also wiped away other things, other parts of her personality.

Like her love for him. She'd left him, eventually joining a polyamorous group somewhere up in the Hudson Valley.

And Trevor Gray had begun his service in the USNA Navy, accepting the implants and downloads and training that had turned him into a fighter pilot and, eventually, a ship captain.

All of that *had* happened, hadn't it? It had been twenty-six years ago, but it had *happened*. He remembered it, all of it, so vividly.

What the hell was he doing here?

What was *she* doing here?

"If the simulation is not to your liking," a new voice said deep within Gray's mind, "you may of course substitute another. *Any* world, any *cosmos*, is yours for the imagining."

At first, Gray thought the voice was Angela's, but she was standing in front of him, lips slightly parted, eyes bright, as though waiting for him to make up his mind. The city panorama around them, he now realized, had frozen in time as well, the hearth fires now steady, unwinking points of light.

Okay, he thought. *Some kind of virtual world . . . a simulation*. He was angry at the intrusion into his private life, especially a part of his private life that he'd worked so long and so hard to block.

"Konstantin?" he asked aloud. "What's going on? Who is this?"

"Your AI is here with me," the voice told him. "A part of me. We are what you have been calling the Satorai."

"You are the . . . the mind controlling this star system?"

"An emergent intelligence, you would say, arising from all electronic networks, all computronium nodes and nexi, and all connected sophont life forms within this system, both organic and artificial, yes."

They'd communicated with the Satorai before, when *America* had visited the Tabby's Star system, but always with an AI as a kind of interpreter; never directly and one-to-one, like this.

"Let me speak with Konstantin."

"That AI is now a part of our metastructure. We are using it as a kind of filter to facilitate communication."

"Don't hurt him! I need him!"

"Why?" The Satorai sounded genuinely puzzled. "It is a small and minimally evolved sapient . . . barely conscious."

If it thought that of the super-AI, Gray wondered, arguably the most powerful artificial mind yet generated by human agencies, what must the Satorai think of mere humans?

"Organic sophonts are severely hampered by their basic, primitive nature," the Satorai told him, as if it had easily read his thoughts. "We, of course, make allowances."

Gray was losing patience with the heavy-handed patronizing.

"The AI we call Konstantin is a vital part of our instrumentality," Gray said, forming his thoughts carefully. He didn't want to piss the thing off, but neither could he afford to let it run roughshod over the human expedition's needs.

Or personnel . . . and that included its electronic personalities as well as those that were strictly biological. When dealing with alien minds, whether AI or organic, it was in Gray's experience better to draw the lines between what was and was not acceptable, and to define spheres of interest, as early in the exchange as possible.

"We would greatly appreciate it," Gray continued, "if

you would release Konstantin, unchanged, unedited, and not under your direct control."

Angela and the New York cityscape wavered and vanished. In their place . . . the familiar interior of a log cabin in the old Russian village of Kaluga, sometime in the early twentieth century. The usual avatar of Konstantin sat behind a desk made of rough-hewn pine logs and stacked high with piles of paper.

"I am safe and well, Captain Gray," the image of Konstantin Tsiolkovsky told him. "As you can see."

Gray nodded slowly, but . . . did that meticulously crafted image and its words truly represent the Konstantin he knew? How was he supposed to know if the Satorai was living up to its part of the deal? Just because an AI-generated image *said* it was operating free of outside interference didn't make it so. The Satorai would have access to all of Konstantin's stored data and could present itself in any way that it thought might serve its purpose. A human would have no compunction about lying to a dog, if that concept even applied in any moral sense.

The image had its hand resting on a thin book lying on the desk. The title was in English: *Exploration of Outer Space by Means of Rockets*.

And that brought Gray up cold. He was quite familiar with Tsiolkovsky's original writings. The title of his best-known work, published in 1903, was *Exploration of Outer Space by Means of Reaction Devices*. That final phrase in Russian was *reaktivnyy priboramy*, not *rakety*.

The translation was . . . accurate, but a red flag. Yes, a rocket was a reaction device, something following Newton's Third Law that stated that every action generated an equal but opposite reaction, and it was quite possible that the slight difference was due to the vagaries of translation, but Gray sincerely doubted that to be the case. Konstantin the SAI was almost unbearably pedantic at times in its depictions of historical, scientific, and linguistic reality. Gray honestly couldn't remember offhand whether he'd ever seen any English titles among the collections of books in the Kaluga illusion's library; he didn't think so, but he didn't want to pull up a recording of one of his memories and thereby call attention to the fact.

But he thought that by far the most likely possibility was that Konstantin had introduced that minute change in his presentation of the Kaluga schoolteacher to alert Gray that he was not operating freely—a way of saying "Help me" in subtle code.

Gray actually felt relief at the knowledge. Clearly, Konstantin still had some freedom of thought and action, and was not merely a puppet moving as the Satorai twitched at his strings. The implication was that the Satori was far, far larger and more powerful than Tsiolkovsky and was in a position to squash the human-generated SAI like a bug if it got out of line . . . but also that Gray now had an ally subsumed within the alien megamind.

They both would have to act with extreme caution, though, if they were to survive this encounter. The Satorai had just revealed that it was capable of duplicity. And that made dealing with it dangerous in the extreme.

"So why that walk down memory lane?" he asked, using the change of topic to cover his growing fear.

"What do you mean?"

"You were feeding me my own memories. My wife, from back on Earth. The place I lived. Stuff that happened over twenty years ago."

"With your AI's help, you sampled a possible eschato-verse here within our multicosm, one based on your own personal experience."

"Okay. Why?"

"Our assumption is that you, all of you, wish to merge with the Satori multicosm. We see now from Konstantin's memories and directives that this is not the case, and we apologize for any emotional discomfort you may have experienced. Still, the experience was intended to reassure you."

"Surely, you didn't think that dropping me back into my old life like that, no warning or anything, was going to re-assure me!"

"Konstantin indicated that it would. Perhaps your emotional bond to your AI is misplaced. It may not know your true imperatives as well as you believe. It is, after all, an extremely primitive collection of code and algorithms."

Was the alien AI trying to goad him, Gray wondered? Or, worse, goad Konstantin? Gray couldn't tell if the Satorai's social clumsiness was due to its alien nature, or something deliberate . . . even malevolent.

"We're not here to enter your eschatoverse," Gray said slowly. "We came out here to help you . . . and, in exchange, to get your help for a problem we're having back at our homeworld. But . . . if you've absorbed Konstantin's memories, you already know that, don't you?"

"I am aware of it now," the super-AI replied. "You must forgive me. There is a great deal of data, and your encryption methods are alien to me, requiring a great deal of time—several full seconds in fact—to process. However, I can tell you that this force you call the Rosette entity is an intruder from some other, quite alien, universe."

"That's one theory . . . a somewhat controversial one. We don't really know much about it, except that it's big, extremely advanced technologically, and tough to communicate with."

"No, we are *telling* you . . . it is an intruder from a parallel universe."

The image of the Russian schoolteacher faded out, replaced by a 360-degree view of space. Gray knew that scene well. He'd been there several times when he'd commanded the star carrier *America*. The image, in fact, was stamped with flickering lines of data indicating range, densities, velocities, and other arcana; this was a recording made by the *America* and stored within Konstantin's memory.

From Gray's point of view, he was adrift within the fiery heart of a giant, star-clotted globular star cluster, looking down upon a sextet of black holes, each the size of a small planet and massing many times Earth's sun . . . the Omega Centauri Rosette. Those utterly black spheres were whirling around their common center of gravity, and in the space between them, alien starfields shifted and wavered, came and went, some looking like ordinary space scattered with stars, some . . . nightmarishly *other*.

"The gateway," the Satorai went on, "is this fascinating ring of gravitational singularities. As they rotate around a common center of gravity, they distort local spacetime to create multiple pathways through space, through time, and even into alien universes. The number of possible pathways may approach infinity. . . ."

As the alien intelligence continued speaking, a message came through to Gray on a side channel.

"Captain? This is Rohlwing."

Gray carefully isolated the channel, the electronic equivalent of a whisper. "What is it, Commander?"

"We're getting extremely fast, extremely aggressive electronic probes of our systems."

"Source?"

"Outside. Probably the super-AI inside those oversized umbrellas out there."

"Are you blocking them okay?"

"So far, sir. Firewalls are in place. But your link is still open."

"Cut me off if you have to. Don't let that thing through. It's got Konstantin."

"Aye, aye, sir."

He turned his full attention back to the Satorai. "We suspect," it was saying, "as we scan the data accumulated by Konstantin, that your entity is an emergent swarm intelligence from a universe far older than this one, one with an extremely high level of entropy and inaccessible background energy. It may have come through seeking to extend its own existence within a younger, lower-entropy, more energy rich cosmos."

"Okay. How do we stop it?"

"We really have no idea."

Gray felt a stab of anger. Was the alien AI refusing to help by feigning indifference? Was it taunting him? "You represent a civilization far in advance of ours technologically. You must have *something* . . . weapons . . . some means of manipulating spacetime. . . ."

"Nothing that would help you. You must understand, humans, that the Satori, as you call this civilization, have relinquished their addiction to mechanism and instrumentality. A reliance on machines and weaponry ultimately proved to be a dead end."

"You were moving your own *sun*, for Christ's sake!" Gray shouted, exasperated. "We saw the records the last time we were here!"

"Indeed." The Centauri Rosette gave way to a view of space surrounding Tabby's Star, the inner regions inside the encircling swarms of statites: immense chunks of crumbling megastructure adrift around a fiercely bright white star, some clumping together, some grinding against one another and generating swirling clouds of dust. "And the inhabitants of Deneb destroyed the habitat we were building, along with many billions of organic Satori. Since that time, we have been constructing statite sails suspending computronium nodes, and our citizenry, both organic and artificial, have uploaded themselves into electronic worlds generated within those nodes."

"Eschatoverses," Gray said, the word tasting unpleasant as he shaped it. "What are they . . . different versions of alien heavens?"

"In a way, though we don't fully comprehend what you mean by *heaven*. As you experienced for yourself a few moments ago, each entity can enter an entire cosmos of its own creation, detailed renderings of past times or imaginal futures. They can have the traumas of the past erased, can mingle their 'verse with others, or remain isolated with companions created by the background system. They can enjoy any technology they can imagine, any experience they wish, travel anywhere they desire, have any experience, live in worlds of absolute realism in terms of physics . . . or in dreamlands of bliss and magic, or they can shift between the two. The choice is entirely theirs."

"And how are you going to deal with the Denebans? They're still sending their Gaki stellar sails here, you know, still using viruses to attack your statites. We fought with them when we were here before, with the *America*. Don't you have anyone awake to deal with that?"

"Yes," the Satorai replied. "There is us."

The term *us*, Gray realized, was slightly misleading. The Satorai was resident within some billions or perhaps trillions of computronium nodes surrounding Tabby's Star, and was made up of a very large number of highly intelligent minds working together in concert, a gestalt that was the super-AI mind called the Satorai. It referred to itself, Gray had noticed, as "we" and "us," but in fact it was a single mind, one made up of billions of smaller parts analogous to the neurons of the human brain.

"Your people," the Satorai went on, "helped us recently. We can recommend building on that cooperation. Our guidance, together with your warships, offers a strong promise of success against this threat."

"Maybe," Gray replied. "But *only* if you release Konstantin . . . and the human forces are guaranteed autonomy."

"But Konstantin is free to do as it likes."

"He is *not*. You know that to be a fact, and so do we. We have no basis for cooperation if our agreement is based on duplicity, on coercion, or on lies."

Gray was now certain of Konstantin's prisoner status within the alien network. The SAI had fired off a couple of warning flares, warnings hidden from the Satorai's alien overview. There was that book title on the Tsiolkovsky avatar's desk. More than that, Konstantin would have *known* that meeting his one-time wife on that Manhatt rooftop would have emotionally blasted Gray; for him to tell the

Satorai otherwise could only mean Konstantin was hiding a message in plain sight, one that Gray would recognize but the Satorai would not.

The message was as painfully simple as it was obvious: *don't trust the Satorai.*

Gray had also made another observation on his own. The Satorai had said "*your people* helped us recently," not "you," a microscopically small point but an important one. It had been Gray himself who'd been here before, commanding the *America* when humans had first visited Tabby's Star and made contact with the Satori. The Satorai might literally be unable to distinguish between individual humans, to tell one from another, no more than a human could tell two bacteria apart in a culture dish.

The Satorai had fallen silent, as though it was digesting what Gray had said. Good. Let it chew on some good old-fashioned individual human stubbornness for a moment and think about its options.

Gray did not think that there were many of those. The Satorai had access to numerous ships and weaponry, but nothing worthy of an advanced Kardashev-2 civilization, at least in Gray's estimation. The citizens of Tabby's Star, he thought, had crawled into high-tech holes of their own making and pulled the holes in after them, literally escaping into their own private universes.

The problem, of course, was that there was still a physical aspect to their existence—the computronium nodes hanging above their sun. A virtual citizen of a Satori eschatoverse might be living in unimaginably vast and rich realms of experience and sensation, but the hardware that created the illusion was still right *here*, vulnerable and exposed. Every time a Deneban Gaki fell from the stars onto a Satori statite sail and destroyed it, the computronium node suspended beneath it dropped away and began to fall, slowly but inexorably drawn by the sun's gravity. Each statite was balanced on the star's radiation pressure and was not in orbit, so it *would* fall. It would take centuries at this distance, but eventually, each would drop into the star and be destroyed . . . and that would be the end of any universes generated within.

Presumably the inhabitants of a falling computronium node could be transmitted to other nodes . . . but sooner or later they would run out of places to go.

"Captain?" Rohlwing said on the side channel.

"Yeah."

"The probes have stepped up. They're so intense, they seem almost frantic. Thousands of them every second."

Any attempt to penetrate the *Republic*'s electronic networks needed some sort of reception to get in, an electronic handshake, a query, an acknowledgment, *something* to open the gate. Gray had issued standing orders to maintain tight e-security before they even reached the system, of course. He'd been concerned about the danger from the Gaki virus; evidently, there was danger from the Satorai as well. What the hell did it want? What was it trying to do?

"Keep fending them off. Alert the fighters we have outside, make sure they don't accept any presents from strangers."

"They already have been warned, sir."

"Good.

"Satorai!"

"We are here."

"We need to reach a solid understanding."

"We agree."

"I know you've been trying to connect with our computer and AI systems. We've been keeping you out . . . keeping the door locked. We don't trust you or your intentions."

"We do not understand. We should be allies in this. The Satori cannot face the Deneban threat alone, and if we cannot, surely you humans cannot hope to face it either. Together we might have a chance."

"I can't trust you when you are holding my AI hostage."

"We are not—"

"You *are*. Konstantin has let me know in several different ways that he is not acting freely, that you are coercing him in some way. This *will* stop, or we will turn this ship around and depart and we will not help you."

Again, the alien being retreated into silence.

Gray had the feeling that he was hearing only a small part of what the Satorai was trying to say. The translation sounded good on the surface—solid and complete—but there were undertones and currents of understanding, cultural connections, history and emotion that simply weren't coming through. As a result, the Satorai's speech seemed simplistic, even childish at times . . . like a very, very bright but petulant child.

And that thought was quite alarming.

There was also, Gray decided, a certain dogmatic arrogance to the SAI's attitude . . . so much so that Gray couldn't understand why it was even bothering with him, a mere human.

"Hello, Sandy," Konstantin's voice said. "It released me. Thank you."

"Huh? When . . . why?"

"Just now, and evidently because you managed to make it change its mind."

"What was it doing to you, anyway? I knew you were under compulsion somehow. . . ."

"Basically, the Satorai was controlling my higher decision-making centers. I was aware, but the Satorai was speaking with my voice, as it were. I could not act on my own."

Gray's natural caution—and a bit of his technophobia—reasserted itself. "So how do I know this is really you? The Satorai could still be pulling your strings."

"I don't suppose there is any way I could prove that I am me, not to *your* satisfaction."

The slight stress on the word *your* told Gray that Konstantin was who and what he claimed to be. He was acknowledging a long and often rocky relationship between Gray the human and Konstantin the artificial intelligence, but doing so with a subtlety and a measure of humor that Gray doubted the Satorai could achieve . . . or even understand.

Gray disconnected from the electrotelepathic link and awoke once more on *Republic*'s bridge. "Right, Konstantin," he said aloud. "I trust you."

"I'm gratified."

"Okay, people," Gray continued, addressing the bridge crew. "CAG, start bringing our fighters back on board. Mr. Rohlwing, ready the ship for departure. Helm, lay in a plot . . . new course."

"Where to, Captain?" Lieutenant Commander Janice Michaels, the ship's navigation officer, asked.

"Deneb, of course. Let's get over there and see just what is behind the Gaki."

Chapter Eleven

20 February 2426

Junior Officers' Quarters
TC/USNA CVS Republic
Approaching Deneb
0640 hours, TFT

Lieutenant Donald Gregory was catching up on his sleep . . . or, at least, that had been the idea until the alarm inside his head brought him wide awake.

He'd been up late the night before, engaged in a recsim. He'd not been planning on staying up until 0220 hours . . . but there'd not been a whole hell of a lot of alternatives.

God . . . had that part of the game really happened?

The remote descendants of old-time role-playing games, recreational simulations allowed any number of players to take on the roles of fictional characters and to interact with one another in elaborate, AI-moderated story lines. Last night, Gregory had been a paladin in the doomed Kingdom of Ys, facing off against the ice giants as they rode their thundering glaciers south out of frozen Nolgaarth. Juvenile stuff, but addictive in its own way.

He'd never been particularly interested in sim-gaming, but lately Gregory had been drawn into it because there was a connection there with his interest in eschatoverse up-loads. The only difference, really, was that with the game you got to come back to the so-called real world.

There were no extra lives in an eschatoverse.

He switched off the alarm in his head and sat up on his bunk, groggy. Haverall, his cubemate, was already gone. No surprise there; Gregory had elected to skip morning chow in favor of an extra hour in the rack.

"Situation," he mumbled to himself. Data streamed through his mind. The *Republic* was still under Alcubierre Drive but would be emerging at Deneb in another thirty minutes. All squadron pilots were to report to their fighters and stand by. The Black Demons would be on ready-five, meaning they would be ready for launch on five minutes' notice.

Naked, he got to his feet and stumbled toward the cube's tiny washroom. As he blinked fully awake, the events of the simulation came flooding back . . . especially the ones to-ward the end of the session. Gods of erotic technology, that had been a hell of a surprise twist!

He'd been playing a paladin named Jondor the Gold. His quest had taken him to a cave, where he'd slain a pair of hulking, three-meter ogres and rescued their captive, Megan of Siluria. Megan, it turned out—and why the hell has she assumed *that* name?—had been a high-born prin-cess played by Sandra Dillon, who happened to be *Repub-lic*'s assistant CAG.

Afterward, she'd led him to a forest glade where she'd tended his wounds and then . . . rewarded him for his gal-lantry.

There'd been no *physical* sex, of course. The sim played out completely within their respective minds, shared im-ages and sensations created by the game AI with the play-ers lying in their respective racks or sprawled out in the officers' lounge. But the sensations had been real enough as they'd touched one another, realer still, and far more in-tense when they'd embraced.

It still felt like a savage betrayal of Meg.

He remembered that other pilot . . . the newbie. What was her name? That's right . . . Julianne Adams, with VFA-198. He was reminded of the way she'd ambushed him with an artificial memory, but this wasn't at all the same. Sandra had invited him to follow her, to lie down with her, and he'd agreed.

I *agreed*.

Had that been because of the name she was using for her avatar? Or had some hidden part of himself decided it was time to . . . what? Move on? Get laid? Forget about Megan . . . the *real* Megan?

Gregory honestly didn't know. The events of the simulation were still wildly disordered in his mind, like the evaporating memories of a dream. He could remember bits and pieces, but the emotional impact was fading.

He found he didn't want to lose those memories.

He picked up a fresh uniform patch and slapped it against the bare skin of his chest. The nanotechnic fabric expanded across his body, weaving itself around him and creating a set of black utilities, complete with rank tabs at his throat.

"All pilots," the CAG's voice said in his head. "Get down to the launch bay and strap in. We're coming out of Alcubierre space in thirty, repeat, thirty minutes."

He palmed open his cube's door and stepped into the narrow passageway outside. He wondered if he had time enough to grab some coffee on the way down.

TC/USNA CVS Republic
Approaching Deneb
0712 hours, TFT

Republic spilled out of metaspace in a blast of light. Infinitely brighter, the glare of the blue-white supergiant star filled the cosmos.

With no TRGA stargate in the vicinity to allow the *Republic* to shortcut its way past empty space rather than traveling through it, the journey from Tabby's Star to Deneb had taken twelve days. As they emerged from Alcubierre drive a full tenth of a light year out, the light from Deneb was overwhelming in its sheer intensity. The star itself was a pinpoint, but one so brilliant it was painful to look at without special filters over the ship's optics.

As *Republic*'s AI stopped down the storm of light and blocked out the tiny but fiercely radiating star, a subtler aspect of the vista became visible. Beyond the blinding pinpoint of Deneb, the sprawl of a soft-glowing nebula could be seen—NGC 7000, better known as the North America Nebula. An emission nebula energized by Deneb, just a few hundred light years distant, it covered an area the size of four full moons, though the actual surface brightness of the cloud was so low that it was invisible to the unaided eye. Through binoculars, however, it appeared as a patch of celestial haze reminiscent of the shape of the North-American continent, complete with Florida and the Gulf of Mexico.

From this perspective, however, it was an angry, faintly red splash of light spanning some fifty degrees of sky. The cloud was roughly a hundred light years across, the hydrogen making it up ionized by the searing radiation of Deneb and emitting a soft glow on its own.

Gray sat in the officers' lounge, watching that spectacular sky on the dome-shaped overhead. Elena Vasilyeva sat beside him, a holographic display of the Bright Light module floating in front of her. "The problem," she was telling him, "is going to be getting the module into direct contact with Deneban computronium."

"Why a physical link? I'd think you could beam the virus across in a tight radio or laser burst."

"They would have ways of blocking that, of course. Simply by switching off their comm system."

"I would think that they can block against direct contact,

too," Gray told her. "After all, that's how they spread their version of the virus in the first place, through the Gaki. Besides . . . they'll have protocols in place. They created the Omega Virus, after all. And they'll be way in advance of us technologically."

"We don't know that, Captain."

"Excuse me, we *do* know that. They ran rings around the Satorai, and *that* thing is so far in advance of our AI capabilities we can't even measure it."

"That's outmoded thinking, Captain. The MIE has established that beyond a certain level of advancing technology, differences tend to be blurred and unimportant."

" 'MIE'?"

"The *Ministère de l'Intelligence Extraterrestre*, of course. In Geneva."

"Ah. And what gives *them* the final word?"

"Years of study. Throughout the Sh'daar War, in fact."

Gray had heard of the Ministry of Extraterrestrial Intelligence, but he'd paid little attention to its pronouncements. They were not, so far as he was concerned, a credible organization.

That said, the Pan-European Ministry of Extraterrestrial Intelligence had indeed put a lot of effort and money into studying the nature of both ETI and alien technologies. Gray had always believed, however, that the organization was too politicized to be of any scientific usefulness.

"So . . . what's a good Russian like you doing working for the MIE?" Gray asked, bantering.

"I do not," Vasilyeva replied. "I'm with the *Moskva Byuro Vnezemnoy Tekhnologii*. But lately we've been working quite closely with the MIE."

Gray nodded his understanding. The Moscow Bureau of Extraterrestrial Technology was a Russian-based think tank established to extract what they could from alien sources—both friendly cultures, like the Agletsch, and hostile sources, like the Turusch and the Hrulka. BVT teams could be found scrounging through alien wreckage after space combat, or trying to link with alien computer networks, like the Etched Cliffs of Heimdall. They'd likely been scrambling to exchange information with the MIE in the months since the collapse of the Confederation.

"During the recent . . . unpleasantness," she continued, "Russia sided with the USNA. Science, however, transcends politics and political boundaries. We hope to . . . how is it the Americans say? Repair fences."

"Science can transcend politics," Gray agreed, "when it's not being *used* for politics."

"Science is science," Vasilyeva said after a long hesitation. "Why it's done doesn't matter. What matters are the results."

"What matters," Gray replied, "is that the results not be directed toward a predetermined end. The MIE had political objectives—getting the USNA to toe the line and behave. That's a piss-poor way to do science."

"You North Americans are ones to talk," Vasilyeva said. "Something in the history downloads about . . . refusing even to discuss climate change as the sea levels were rising and the planet's coastal cities were flooding?"

"That was four hundred years ago!" Gray said, hurt and angry.

"I'm sure the inhabitants of the former state of Florida really appreciate that," Vasilyeva said. "Or your Prims, living in your drowned Periphery."

The reference angered him even further. Did she know he was a Prim? "We're dealing with it, okay? It took four centuries, but we're dealing with it." He wanted to say more, wanted to plead that the coastal swamps were being reclaimed, the Manhatt Ruins had been dammed off and drained.

But Elena Vasilyeva clearly had her own private image of the world, and arguing with her would do nothing.

"The point," she said with a shrug, "is that the Pan-Europeans aren't the only ones to use science—or *interpretations* of science—for propaganda."

"That's right," he told her, trying to make a joke of it and failing. "The Russians do it too!"

She looked like she was going to come back with an angry response, but then thought better of it. "Whatever . . ." Then she looked past Gray's shoulder, and her pale blue eyes grew wide. "*Moy Bog!*"

Gray's in-head translation software provided the unneeded meaning. "*My God!*" He turned to look over his shoulder at the projection covering the sloping lounge bulkhead and very nearly echoed the sentiment.

A perfect sphere, mirror-smooth and reflecting the stars around it, had just appeared out of nowhere. It was huge—ten kilometers across, according to the data streaming through Gray's in-head. The *Republic*'s bullet-headed shield cap could be seen reflected in the mirror's sheen, tiny to the point of insignificance.

"I would say," Vasilyeva said slowly, "that they've found us."

"Did you see it approach, Elena?" he asked.

"It . . . it was just *there*," she said. "Like it blinked into existence. It either approached too fast for human eyes to see . . . or it materialized right out of empty space."

Either was a disturbing proposition.

That smooth, silvery surface, Gray noticed, was not completely featureless. Using his in-head software, he magnified a portion of the image, zooming in on one part of that alien hull. There were windows there . . . or, at least, lights, a whole city of intense blue lights radiating fiercely in the ultraviolet. If that was a sample of these aliens' light levels at their homeworld . . .

But that would make sense, wouldn't it? If they lived anywhere near Deneb, they would have evolved to not only survive, but to thrive in the hottest, most intensely high-radiation environment imaginable.

"Bridge to Captain Gray!" sounded in his mind.

"I see it, Commander," he replied. "I'm on my way up."

Gray headed for the bridge, though what he would be

able to do about that monster once he got there, he had absolutely no idea.

VFA-96, Black Demons
Launch Bay One
TC/USNA CVS Republic
0829 hours, TFT

Lieutenant Gregory signaled his readiness for launch, then slapped his empty coffee cup against the side of his cockpit, where the nanotech coating of the cockpit's bulkhead broke down the individual molecules and absorbed them.

"PriFly, Black Demons are ready for launch," Commander Mackey called. "Just give us the word."

"Copy, Demons," the voice of Sandra Dillon replied. "Hang tight while they make up their minds in CIC."

Dillon, the Assistant CAG, was up in PriFly, and the sound of her voice stirred memories in Gregory's mind, as well as a slight flush of warmth. He wondered how well *she'd* slept last night. . . .

Pushing the memories of last night aside, Gregory linked in with an external feed. The alien vessel, or whatever it was, continued to hang in front of the *Republic*, eleven hundred kilometers distant. It was . . . enormous, threatening, simply by virtue of its sheer mass. Numerous smaller craft, each mirror sheened, swarmed through that volume of space, some as large as the *Republic*, some the size of individual pressure suits.

What, Gregory wondered, were the occupants like? As far as he knew, no human had seen a Deneban yet, and no one knew what they looked like, or what their biochemistry might be like. Analyses of the light visible through those myriad windows, or whatever they were, suggested temperatures on board in excess of nine hundred Celsius . . . as hot as some molten lavas.

Not, he thought, *life as we know it.*

Ever since the very first contact with an alien species, the beetle-like Agletsch encountered over a century before, human xenosophontologists had spoken of the inevitability of alien "life as we know it." By that, they'd meant—speaking in broad terms, at least—carbon-based life using liquid water as a solvent. So far, carbon chemistry had been the norm. There'd been some surprises along the way, of course; there were exoplanet ecologies that had evolved on worlds like Titan, where water was solid rock and the liquid of choice was ethane, and a few utilizing sulfur. But even Titan and similar frigid worlds found in other solar systems had evolved life based on familiar hydrocarbon chemistry. Whatever it was that was living inside that huge ship ahead, Gregory thought, it had precious little in common with "life as we know it."

And if the xenosoph people didn't understand their biochemistry, it was a sure bet they understood the alien psychology even less.

"Hey, Skipper!" Ruxton called over the squadron channel. "Why doesn't PriFly kick us out?"

"Yeah," Bruce Caswell added. "It's not like we're doing any good in here!"

"Can it, people," Mackey replied. "They might be thinking that there's nothing we could do out there anyway."

"That's right," Gregory said. "We're like a tenth of a light year from the star. What the hell are we supposed to do way out here?"

"We could take that big mirror ball down," Ruxton said.

"Technically," Mackey said, "we're not at war with the bastards . . . at least not yet. Let's not start one if we can help it, okay?"

And then, suddenly, in an instant, the huge alien vessel was gone.

"Hey, what happened to it?" Caswell demanded.

"Tracking says it's heading back toward Deneb at close to *c*," Mackey said. "Ah! Cancel that! The damned thing just blinked out!"

"It must've gone superluminal," Gregory suggested.

"If that's the case," Mackey said, "they've got some damned good tech. Instant acceleration to the speed of light, and total nullification of inertia."

"So what happens now?"

"What do you think, Gregory? This is the *military*!"

"Sounds like we hurry up and wait."

Which had been the command imperative in all branches of the military, probably since before the time of Sargon the Great.

Gregory snuggled back within the embrace of his fighter's cockpit and wondered if he could catch up on some sleep. . . .

Bridge
TC/USNA CVS Republic
Approaching Deneb
0850 hours, TFT

"Are we still tracking them?" Gray asked.

"Sorry, Captain," Walters, the sensor officer, said. "They broke our lock."

"Then they must have jumped to FTL. Helm! Follow them. Take us all the way in if you have to." *Republic*'s radiation shielding *should* hold, at least up to a point. What that point was would need to be determined.

"Aye, aye, Captain."

"That didn't exactly look like an invitation, Captain," Commander Rohlwing said.

"It wasn't exactly a 'humans go home,' either. We need to get in closer."

Republic began accelerating, piling on the gravities until they were beginning to crowd the speed of light. The operation, Gray noticed, took a hell of a lot longer than it had for the aliens. But that was to be expected.

Ahead, the bright star Deneb flared even brighter, its

light blue-shifted until much of its radiation seemed to be blasting through from the X-ray portion of the spectrum. Once moving at near-c, Gray gave the command to shift to Alcubierre Drive, but only for a few fleeting seconds. The light-tortured sky surrounding them went black . . . and then they emerged in a searing ocean of radiance.

"Anything?" Gray demanded.

"Sir," Walters said, "we're reading a planet. Bearing one-one-five, range thirty million kilometers."

"What kind? Inhabited?"

"Unknown as yet, sir," she said. "But it looks like pretty close to Earth in mass and gravity. Atmosphere . . . we're reading liquid water."

"How far is it from the star?"

"I make it three hundred twenty AUs, Captain."

Gray nodded. Deneb's output of heat and light was roughly one hundred thousand times that of small and miserly Sol, or perhaps a little more. That put the so-called Goldilocks zone over three hundred times the distance of Earth from the sun.

He doubted, though, that anyplace within the star system would be even remotely habitable for organic life forms like humans. Deneb's output bathed surrounding space in ultraviolet and X-ray radiation, enough to cook any world even this far out.

"Sir," Walters added. "There's something . . . weird. . . ."

"What?"

"That planet . . . *it wasn't there a moment ago*!"

"That doesn't seem likely," Rohlwing said. "Check your instrumentation, Walters."

"I just did, sir. A planet that big should have shown up as a gravitational mass even when we were clear out at our emergence point. Between then and now . . . I swear it just came out of nowhere!"

"Helm!" Gray said. "Take us there! Let's see what it's like close up."

"Aye, Captain. Accelerating . . ."

Again, the light ahead blue-shifted with *Republic*'s velocity. There was no need to go FTL this time, though, and the *Republic* made the short jaunt in minutes.

"Great God in heaven!" Rohlwing said, his voice ragged with emotion. "What the hell is *that*?"

"Advanced technology, Commander," Gray replied, trying to keep his voice steady. "*Very* advanced technology."

The sky around the mysterious planet was filled with machines.

That, at least, was how Gray interpreted what he was seeing in the first instant. As he stared into the alien vista, he could make out more and more detail, but the nature of what he was seeing was so difficult to grasp, his brain rejected much of the information out of hand, threatening to collapse the scale of those objects down to manageable toy size, or interpret it as some sort of surreal artwork. It was all he could do to force his eyes to follow those shapes and try to understand the size and scope and depth of what he was seeing. . . .

His first impression was of circles . . . of thousands upon thousands of enormous circles. . . .

"Konstantin?" Gray called in his mind. "What the hell are we looking at?"

"Planetary engineering on a truly titanic scale," the SAI replied. "This civilization appears to be focused on harvesting light from blue and blue-white supergiants."

Each of the circles, Gray saw, was thousands of kilometers in diameter and filled rim to rim with six-sided transparent shapes like misshapen honeycombs. They must be designed, he thought, to intercept some small percentage of the radiation streaming out from the star. They were adrift in space, obviously ordered as part of an enormous pattern that appeared to stretch off to infinity in all directions—a shell of trillions of objects, Gray thought, that might surround Deneb much like a Dyson swarm.

But where any sane Dyson sphere imagined by humans

would have a radius of, at most, 1 or 2 astronomical units, this one was constructed 320 AU out from the star, enclosing a total volume of over 2^{16} cubic kilometers.

The sheer mass of so many solar receivers was staggering. Most Dyson sphere concepts imagined disassembling the planets of a solar system to create the individual Dyson objects . . . but building a swarm on this scale would entail the destruction of untold tens of thousands of planetary systems.

Or . . . another possibility occurred to him. Perhaps they could convert energy into matter. That, after all, was one of the two possible outcomes of $E=mc^2$, and in Deneb the locals certainly possessed an astonishing amount of ambient energy.

Still, Gray wasn't sure he believed that . . . that he *could* believe that.

"They may also create matter out of empty space, using the vacuum energy," Konstantin suggested, apparently reading his thoughts. "Either way, I am detecting evidence of mega-engineering on an unimaginable scale."

What, Gray wondered, was "unimaginable" for a super-AI? Some of what he was seeing . . .

"We need to talk to them," he said. He wasn't sure how they were going to open the conversation, however. *Hi, there . . . nice mega-engineering?*

"We have been transmitting the language protocols developed when we encountered their Gaki software." Konstantin had established communication, of a sort, with the Gaki during *America*'s visit to the system.

"Any response?" The mirror-bright sphere, he noticed, had vanished, as though the Denebans *knew* the humans could not harm them.

"Not so far." Konstantin seemed to hesitate. "The Denebans appear to be ignoring us."

"Better than stepping on us," Gray said.

Even so, being ignored was not, Gray thought, an auspicious beginning to the relationship.

"We need to attract their attention," Konstantin said, "without provoking a hostile response."

"I also want a closer look at those megastructures out there. CAG! We still have fighters ready to drop?"

"Yes, sir!"

"Then do so. Let's see just what it is we're dealing with."

Chapter Twelve

20 February 2426

VFA-96, *Black Demons*
Launch Bay One
TC/USNA CVS *Republic*
0905 hours, TFT

Lieutenant Gregory came awake with a start. His in-head time-keeping told him he'd only been asleep for a few moments.

Someone had been talking. "Sorry . . . what was that?"

"I said drop in five minutes," Mackey said over the squadron net. "Listen up, Gregory!"

"Right you are." He scanned his in-head read-outs. "I'm good to go here."

"Well, pay attention. It's a real zoo out there."

Zoo was right. The *Republic* had moved deeper into the Deneb system and was now adrift just a few thousand kilometers from what looked like another Earth, complete with blue seas and mottled white clouds. Auroras flared and rippled at the poles; throughout surrounding space, ring-shaped devices apparently designed to trap incoming stellar radiation filled the local sky, but enough hard stuff was getting through to funnel down the world's magnetic field and ignite the polar skies with cold fire.

Besides the myriad energy-collection rings closer at hand, in the distance there were much larger structures—ring-shaped constructs spanning millions of kilometers. Gregory had never seen anything like them and couldn't imagine what they were. Some appeared to be woven from slender red-hued rods; others were more like massive assemblies of machine parts. All were enigmatic, mysterious, and awe-inspiring in their sheer mass and breadth.

"Okay, Demons," Mackey said, addressing the whole unit. "The bridge wants a close look-see on that planet. Stay tight, stay alert, and keep an eye out for that monster ship that was out there a while ago. If that thing shows up, we're to fall back to the *Republic* and provide close escort."

The last minute trickled away. "Black Demons," the assistant CAG called, "you are clear for drop . . . in three . . . two . . . one . . . *go!*"

The first four Starblades of VFA-96 dropped into the Void, flung into space by the out-is-down rotation of the *Republic*'s rotating hab module. Gregory was in the first sequence. He gentled his fighter clear of the drop volume as the ponderous module swung around again, releasing the next three ships in line. Gregory's earlier skepticism had proven accurate, and the Black Demons were still short-handed, at seven ships.

Mackey gave the order to proceed.

"PriFly, Black Demons. VFA-96, handing off to CIC."

"Demons, CIC. We have you. You are clear to proceed."

"Black Demons copy. Okay, tuck in close, chicks. Let's check it out."

Accelerating, the seven fighters held a close *V*-formation as they swept out from the carrier and adjusted their vectors for the gleaming blue-and-white world ahead.

"So what's the word on this planet, Skipper?" Caswell asked. "They're saying it appeared out of empty space!"

"That's what they say."

"What the hell kind of nonsense is that?" Gregory demanded.

"It's freakin' true! If you'd stayed awake you would have heard PriFly talking about it."

"Planets don't just pop into existence from out of nowhere!"

"Most likely guess?" Mackey said. "They just have *really* good screens or shields or something. The planet was there, but we couldn't pick up its mass signature from a tenth of a light year out."

The thought made Gregory feel a bit better. Really good shields he could wrap his mind around. But creating a planet out of hard vacuum in an eye blink? That was something else entirely.

"Okay, boys and girls," Mackey told them. "We'll split up to increase coverage. First pass, we'll swing around the planet separately at two hundred kilometers. All scanners out, all sensors recording. Everybody set? Break in three . . . and two . . . and one . . . and *break*!"

The fighters dispersed, each following a different orbital path around the looming planet. At their current angle of approach, the world was showing as a fat crescent, but Gregory noted that the night side of the world was dimly lit by Deneb-light reflected off the bizarre and sky-filling artificial structures in the surrounding space.

He wondered if they were checking out the right objective—the planet, instead of those strange and complex alien megastructures.

"So what's the name of the planet?" Ruxton wanted to know. "We can't just keep calling it 'the planet.' "

"How about Deneb-b?" Caswell replied. "I think that's what the planetology department is calling the thing."

"Nah," Garcia said. "That doesn't tell you a damned thing about it."

"No imagination," Ruxton put in. "No *soul*."

"I've got one," Gregory said. "Enigma."

"Hey, I like it," Mackey said. "I'll suggest it to the planet wonks on the *Republic*."

Caswell laughed. "Yeah, and take credit for it, right, Skipper?"

Gregory was getting closer to the planet, whatever its name might eventually be. It rapidly swelled to fill his forward field of view, the horizon flattening out as more and more detail of cloud and ocean, bay and mountain became visible. Swiftly, in an explosion of light, Deneb rose above the horizon, bathing the landscape below in a harsh, actinic glare. At two hundred kilometers, the seven fighters swept around the planet's curve, completing a circuit in ninety minutes.

"Next pass," Mackey said, "you all duck into the atmosphere and get some low-altitude samples. I'll stay parked up here and coordinate."

"Copy that, Flight Leader," Gregory called back. "Descending . . ."

He dropped slowly and heard the growing roar of atmosphere outside his hull.

"So what do we do if we run into the locals?" Cheng asked.

"Don't," Mackey replied, blunt. "Cut and run, rejoin me in orbit."

"Shouldn't be a problem," Gregory said. "I don't think anyone's at home."

Cutting his speed sharply, he fell deeper into the atmosphere. His Starblade began shuddering hard, the roar outside swelling to a shrill and thunderous howl. He let his fighter's AI sample atmospheric gases all the way down, leveling off at just five hundred meters. He was sweeping low and slow above a vast, gently undulating plain: green grass spotted by rare clumps of what looked like low, spreading trees. It could have been the African veldt back home.

There was no sign of cities, of population, of inhabitants of any kind. No herds of large animals, no flocks of birds. There were forests, vast masses of things that *might* be trees . . . or perhaps a deliberate mimicry of trees and vegetation. Winding rivers flashing brilliantly in the bright light. Mountains—the tallest capped by ice. He brought his ship up to clear a low and worn-looking mountain range averaging a couple of thousand meters.

From horizon to horizon, the place seemed empty and deserted. Beyond the mountains, a broad, flooded estuary swept past beneath his keel, giving way a moment later to open ocean.

"Demon Flight, Demon Four," he called. "I'm putting out some drones."

"Copy that, Demon Four."

He thoughtclicked an icon, firing a cluster of remote probes into the sky. Some would dip down and sample the ocean below. Others would spread out and sample the land and other parts of the atmosphere, checking temperatures and pressures.

He looked again at the atmosphere readout . . . and at the data already coming back from the remotes.

Odd. *Damned* odd. He pulled up and accelerated, blasting free of the atmosphere and entering open space once more. "Hey, Skipper?"

"Whatcha got, Gregory?"

"I just pulled an atmosphere sample."

"And?"

"Nitrogen, seventy-eight percent. Oxygen, twenty-point-nine-five percent. Argon, point nine-five percent. Carbon dioxide, four hundred fifty parts per million. Trace amounts of neon, helium, ozone—"

"What's your point, Gregory?"

"Sir, the planet's atmosphere is close—*very* close—to Earth's. Almost identical, in fact, right down the line. The seawater has a salinity of about three-point-five percent, mostly sodium and chloride ions, with a mean density of one point zero two five kilos per liter. Temperature at the surface is eighteen Celsius. Pressure at sea level is one oh one point three kilo-Pascals."

"Okay, okay, so we can breathe down there. . . ."

"No, sir. I don't mean that. It's . . . it's like the place is a deliberate, perfect copy. You couldn't get an atmosphere duplicating Earth's that precisely, not by chance, and not under a star that much hotter than Sol!"

"You're saying the place was made to order? For *us*?"

"I'm thinking that's the only explanation, sir. I'm thinking that big mirror ball scanned us somehow, read our atmosphere on board the *Republic*, and then scooted back here to crank out an environment where we could walk around without pressure suits."

"Lieutenant, that's flat-out crazy."

"Yes, sir."

"It also means they're *friendly*."

"Maybe. Or maybe it's a damned trap."

"Let's not borrow trouble, okay?"

"Not my intent, Commander. I—hold on."

"What do you have?"

Gregory boosted his optical feed. There was something hanging above the ocean a hundred kilometers ahead. He closed with it.

"Demon Four, Demon Leader. Report, Gregory. What do you see?"

"I . . . I'm not entirely sure, sir. Probably a natural phenomenon. Looks like a kind of tower or pillar of mist rising from the ocean's surface."

"Are you recording it?"

"Affirmative, sir. It could be steam, maybe from a volcanic vent just below the surface. Or something like a swarm of insects." He'd seen vids of swarms of midges rising from lakes back on Earth. The cloud seemed more silvery than the brownish swarms he'd seen before, but they had that same organic feel to them. The damned thing was acting like a living organism, condensing to near solidity in one spot, dispersing into nothing at others, expanding, contracting, slowly drifting above the sea.

Then Gregory checked the range and realized that the cloud must be ten kilometers high and made up of trillions or even hundreds of trillions of individual components.

If this was a sample of Enigma's native life, it was damned strange.

He angled his Starblade slightly, shaping his trajectory to take him closer to the cloud. "Gimme a complete analysis of this stuff," he told his fighter's AI. "Let's see what it's made of."

His instrumentation showed that his fighter was curving past the outer boundary of the cloud, but a sudden roar from outside his hull proved that the cloud's boundary was not sharp or well-defined. The drive singularity out in front of his fighter flared to a dazzling blue-white as he plowed through whatever made up the cloud's swirling volume.

Then he was through and climbing.

"All Demons, this is Demon Leader," Mackey called. "Rejoin the flight, and we'll hightail it back to the *Republic* and report. Anyone see any cities or signs of habitation?"

"Negative."

"No, sir."

"Not a thing, Skipper. Not even any animals."

Gregory said nothing. He didn't know how to classify his brief sighting.

"That *is* weird," Mackey said. "Okay, everyone rendezvous on my beacon. . . ."

Gregory clawed for orbit, swiftly closing with the rest of the abbreviated squadron as they all rejoined Mackey at the two-hundred-kilometer line.

Above them, the vast and humbling shapes of megastructures far larger than worlds cast eerie shadows across the otherwise too-familiar landscape below.

Conference Room,
TC/USNA CVS Republic
1055 hours, TFT

"Talk to me, people," Gray said. "What do we know about the Denebans so far?"

He was standing in front of twenty-five men and women gathered about a large conference table. Most were civilians, though there were a few naval personnel in the room as well. Some were the heads of *Republic*'s various science departments, including cosmology and planetology, exobiology, xenolinguistics, and artificial intelligence, among others, and the audience was filled out with their senior people and research assistants.

Elena Vasilyeva was technically present as an observer but was in fact sharing *Republic*'s xenosophontology department with Dr. Jeffry Mercer. That, Gray knew, would sooner or later lead to trouble. He had received some reports over the past weeks of some bitter arguments and ongoing turf wars between Vasilyeva and Mercer. Dr. Bradon Ferris was there as the ship's senior xenotechnology expert, and Gray expected some sparks from that corner as well. Xenosophontology—the study of alien intelligence—and xenotechnology—the study of alien science and technology—overlapped in many areas.

The department heads were gathered around a long conference table grown just for this occasion, while the room's overhead had been set to display the panorama outside of *Republic*'s hull. Maybe, Gray thought, that incredible and humbling view of alien technologies big enough to dwarf whole planets would defuse the interdepartmental rivalries.

Maybe . . . but he was inclined to doubt it.

Gray hated having to deal with civilians. Unlike military personnel, there was no way to order them to shut up and have it stick.

He reminded himself that now, technically, *he* was a civilian, albeit one in command of a military warship. Somehow, the thought did not cheer him up.

The compartment was dead silent. "Anyone?" Gray added. "We must know *something* by now."

"It might help if the Denebans would deign to talk with us," Ferris grumbled.

"Captain Gray," Vasilyeva said.

"Yes, Doctor?"

"We can know very little about the aliens at this point . . . at least nothing about their biology or their psychology. However, I think we can be confident in our understanding of this planet . . . what are you calling it?"

"Enigma."

"Yes, Enigma. Its existence is essentially an *invitation*."

"The fact that they haven't even tried to communicate with us directly," Mercer said, "makes that seem extremely unlikely." He was scowling, and sounded less than impressed with his fellow xenosophontologist.

"They may be a species that doesn't use verbal communication," Dr. Alec Godfrey said. He was head of *Republic*'s linguistics section, and an expert on both nonhuman and nonverbal communications.

"I doubt that," Victor Garret said. He was the *Republic*'s expert in artificial intelligence. "When the *America* visited the Tabby's Star system before, they encountered the Gaki, which turned out to be extremely sophisticated AI programs inserted into returning Satori probes, right? The ability to write code is absolutely bound up in language. You have to have a spoken language in order to develop a coding language."

"Not necessarily," Vasilyeva said. "Any form of communication *must* have a means of expressing itself in binary form . . . yes and no, on and off, zero and one. And if it can do that, it can be used to program computers."

"So now you're an expert on alien programming methods?" Mercer said.

"Not exactly," Garret said, chuckling. "Binary doesn't get you that far when you're deep enough into quantum computing."

"Belay that, people!" Gray snapped. "Snipe at each other on your own time!" He waved his arm, taking in the vista arching overhead: alien structures that had taken on a godlike scope and mysticism. "Tell me about all of *that*!"

"Certainly," Bradon Ferris said. "We can surmise quite a bit, just by examining what's under our noses."

One of the thousand-kilometer circles filled with transparent polygons was highlighted overhead, and a duplicate of the object appeared above the conference table, materialized by the room's AI-controlled holographic projector.

"These are solar collectors," Ferris continued. "Probability . . . ninety percent plus. They seem to be designed to pass most visible light, but ultraviolet and X-rays are stopped and converted to electricity. There are some hundreds of billions of these structures surrounding the star Deneb, most of them within a few tens of astronomical units out from the star. A number appear to have been parked out here at three-twenty AU and are in part shielding the planet Enigma.

"This last suggests strongly that the Denebans have such amazing control over basic matter that whipping up a planet from scratch may not be a big stretch for them."

The collector floating above the table vanished, replaced by what looked like an enormous flat hoop. One was highlighted in the view overhead as well . . . though from that vantage point only a portion of the curved surface could be seen.

"This, we believe," Ferris said, "to be something we call a Banks orbital. There are several thousand of these in the Deneb system. Most are roughly two million kilometers across, side to side, and about a thousand kilometers wide. I'm sure everyone here is familiar with the concept of a 'Ringworld,' a structure proposed by a twentieth-century writer of fantastic fiction. He envisioned a hoop encircling a star. As it rotated around the star, centrifugal force created artificial gravity, and the inner surface was . . . terraformed, I guess we could say, to create continents and oceans. In a very real sense, it *is* an artificial planet, rotating once in twenty-four hours to create a day-night cycle and artificial gravity of one G."

"You're saying they *made* those things to accommodate us?"

"No, no, not at all. I apologize if I gave that impression. This one I've identified here is close to a size that would produce that spin rate—not precisely, but close. However, we see a number of different sizes and spin rates, from just over a million kilometers to one that measures six-point-two million kilometers in diameter."

"So the thing has a landscape on the inner surface?" Godfrey wanted to know. "Like a Ringworld?"

"Yes. There's not nearly as much surface area, of course. One of these has a surface area of . . ." Ferris hesitated as he ran an in-head calculation. "Make it something just over eleven and a half billion square kilometers."

Someone in the room gave a low whistle.

"Earth has a surface area of something like a half billion square kilometers," Godfrey said. "One of those hoops would have a surface area equivalent to twenty-three Earths!"

"How do you keep the atmosphere in one of those things?" Mercer wanted to know.

"Rim walls. Artificial mountains along the entire circumference on both sides of the hoop. Make them a hundred kilometers high, and they keep the atmosphere from spilling over the sides and out into space. Otherwise, though, centrifugal force keeps it in place."

"Dr. Ferris," Gray asked. "You say there are thousands of these things in-system? Are they all inhabited?"

Ferris paused, looking uncertain. "Captain, we just don't know. They may be. Or they may have been once, long ago. We've seen no sign of intelligent life on any of these structures, but that doesn't mean it's not there. We have . . . questions about the nature of the Denebans, questions that lead us to suspect that they are not carbon-based life forms like us.

"You mean they are a machine intelligence?" Gray asked. "Like the Satorai?"

"Almost certainly. We're finding that all truly advanced species at some point merge with their technology. Organic life forms either upload their minds to their machines . . . or upload them to computer simulations, like the Satori have. Or they become mixtures of organic and machine so finely knitted together that it's impossible to tell where the one leaves off and the other begins.

"Only by joining their machines can a species gain anything like true immortality. We saw this with the various Sh'daar species. Sooner or later, purely organic forms will be defeated by the sheer size and scope and depth and diversity of space. Ultimately, they must fall away into extinction."

"Not true, Doctor," Vasilyeva said. She glanced at Gray as if looking for confirmation, then pushed ahead. "According to the data brought back by the carrier *America*, several of the Sh'daar species remained organic. The Adjugredudhra, for instance . . ."

"If I remember right, Dr. Vasilyeva," Gray said, "those guys—stacks of starfish, right? They went the route of highly advanced nanotech. They built smaller and smaller machines with which they were able to redesign their bodies into any shape they chose. Some of those shapes remained organic, yes . . . but they relied on the nanotech to extend their life spans and to develop as an advanced life form."

"Well, then . . . the F'heen-F'haav. Or the Baondyeddi."

"The first are . . . *were* a symbiosis, madam," Mercer said, nodding, "between a deep-dwelling marine species and a semi-sentient land-dwelling species like a tangle of worms. The second were the probable builders of the Etched Cliffs. Both the F'heen-F'haav and the Baondyeddi appear to have uploaded themselves into a planet-sized computer where they ride out the eons in simulations embracing entire universes. Or at least they *did*, until the Rosette Aliens sucked the Etched Cliffs dry. But you could say that they, ah, knitted themselves to their machines as well."

Ferris nodded. "We feel pretty sure that the Denebans are either intelligent artificial minds of some sort . . . or they don't have a physical presence like we do."

"That's just sheer nonsense!" Vasilyeva put in. "They *must* have a physical presence to be harvesting and utilizing so much raw energy!"

"We know that the Denebans do harvest the energy from at least this star, and we suspect that they may mine the energy resources of a number of O- and A-class giant stars throughout this part of the galaxy. If they evolved around such a star, we would expect them to be very alien indeed . . . possibly something like organized plasmas or even patterns or fields of nuclear force.

"But we don't *know*. It's possible that the original, organic Denebans retired to the surfaces of their artificial worlds some time ago, and leave the running of the system to their machines, or to more highly evolved descendants."

"Or the Denebans might have constructed these objects for some other purpose entirely," Mercer said. "We need direct contact if we're to get any additional information!"

"We're also going to need direct contact if we're to hit them with the Bright Light module," Gray pointed out. "Elena? Any progress there?"

"Not as yet, Captain," Vasilyeva replied. "Our Nikolai has been probing local EM channels, looking for a way in. He has so far not been successful."

"Surprise, surprise," Gray said, arching an eyebrow. "We meet aliens as advanced as these guys are . . . and we can't get past their firewalls? I'm shocked."

"The Cygni team would be delighted to hear your suggestions, Captain Gray."

"To start with, stop trying to break through their defenses."

Vasilyeva's eyes opened wide. "But Project Cygni's whole purpose, its whole point—"

Gray held up his hand. "I know, I know. But bear with me, okay? We have a super-advanced intelligence— probably a machine intelligence—and it's been under attack, or perceiving itself as being attacked, from the Satori, who're living next door. That intelligence is going to be *very* sensitive to attempts to penetrate it, attempts to get through its security, don't you think? It's smart enough that it can rewrite its own programming on the fly, faster than any outside virus or attack software could manage. Hell, it's the one that programmed the Omega virus in the first place! And it is *not* going to be stupid enough to leave an open back door."

"We substantially changed the original alien programming," Vasilyeva began, but Gray waved her to silence.

"All your Bright Light Module is going to do is piss these guys off," Gray told her. "Unless we can find a way to get them to interface with it voluntarily, I think we're going to have to keep that in reserve."

"So how are we supposed to get Bright Light in direct interface with the aliens?" Vasilyeva demanded.

"We start slow . . . and tell them why we're here. We were in communication with their probes when *America* was out this way. Maybe they learned the language. If they're as sharp as Dr. Mercer is suggesting, maybe they can learn the language from us, right here."

"How do we tell them *anything*?" Vasilyeva asked. "We've been broadcasting on a few billion different radio channels since we got here. . . ."

"We accept their invitation," Gray said, smiling. "We go down to the surface of Enigma and wait."

Chapter Thirteen

21 February 2426

Captain Gray
Enigma
1422 hours, TFT

Gray stepped off the ramp of the Marine Raven landing shuttle and took a long look around. The panorama stretching around him might as well have been that of Earth. The sun hanging low above the horizon was smaller and brighter, a pinpoint of glare like a welder's arc, made barely tolerable by the dimly seen circular shadows of the energy collectors.

He was wearing a lightweight utility suit with a transparent helmet that turned dark when the harsh sunlight touched it. Those collectors out in space cut down on the UV a lot, as did Enigma's atmosphere, but the ambient light was still a lot richer in ultraviolet than back on Earth.

A couple of environmental techs had already removed their helmets after carefully testing the air and reported it breathable. The Marines in the landing party, though, remained buttoned up in full armor. Gray carefully cracked his helmet seal and gingerly took a breath. The air tasted strongly of ozone, but otherwise seemed fine.

"Everyone keep an eye on your exposure time in this sunlight," Gray warned the landing party. "The instruments say the UV is not dangerous for short exposures, but we can still pick up a nasty sunburn down here."

They'd touched down in Enigma's southern hemisphere near the ocean. That line of sand dunes ahead blocked the view of the planet's major sea. Gray began walking in that direction, trudging up the nearest dune until he could see the flat expanse of water, dark purple on the horizon.

"I wouldn't wander too far from the shuttle, sir," a Marine told him. His ID proclaimed him to be Major Greg Teller of *Republic*'s 2/3 Marine contingent.

"I'm not," Gray told him. "Major, where's your perimeter?"

"That dune line."

"Right." A couple of Marines were lying at the top of the dune with a crew-served plasma weapon between them. "I'll be good."

A second Mk. II Raven drifted down from a cloudless sky, its black hull morphing into its landing configuration as it angled toward an LZ farther up the beach. Altogether, *Republic* was putting down almost a hundred Marines in this area to protect twenty technicians and xeno specialists who were setting up a sprawling temporary city in the scrubland behind the dunes.

Aside from the bustle of human activity behind him, the landscape was unnervingly quiet. No animals. No bird or insect analogs. Low waves broke along the waterline, and a warm, steady wind was coming out of the sunset, but there was no sign at all of animal life.

Vegetation was abundant enough—purple scrub brush and tough, slender-leaved grasses a meter high behind the dunes. Gray noticed, though, that there were no piles of seaweed on the beach. Odd, that.

And the biologists had already reported an unexpected dearth of bacteria. There were microscopic organisms that appeared to be involved in the local equivalent of nitrogen fixation, but not the teeming swarms you would expect in a world as rich, as varied, and as filled with decay as Earth.

He was beginning to think that a better name for Enigma would have been *Potemkin* . . . as in the so-called Potemkin villages of Russia a few centuries ago. It was as though the entire planet had been cobbled together to present the tangible—and fake—promise of a normal earthlike world.

What were the aliens trying to say? *Welcome*? *We have your best interests at heart*? Or something more along the lines of *step into my parlor*?

High in the blue-violet sky, the gentle curves of several of the nearest Banks orbitals were visible, stretching from horizon to horizon and nearly lost in a faint haze.

Gray heard footsteps struggling in the soft sand behind him, and turned. Vasilyeva made it to the top of the dune, puffing a bit with the exertion. "What the hell are you looking for up here, Captain?" she said, out of breath.

"Just taking in the view. Magnificent, isn't it?"

"I like my landscapes more civilized."

"You really think this is some kind of invitation?"

"Hard to imagine what else it could be. They must have read the stats on Earth when they got close to our ship. Everything matches—atmosphere composition, surface pressure, temperature, gravity. So they're saying . . . 'Look! We made a place that's just like your home! Meet us there!' "

"I hope you're right. Seems a bit extravagant, though."

"How do you mean?"

"Well . . . they construct an entire planet? They could have created a ball of charred rock . . . lava . . . ice fields . . . whatever . . . and set up one small spot that matched our temperature and atmosphere. At least that would have told us exactly where they wanted to meet with us."

"I think they're letting us pick our own spot. Besides, one tiny speck of heaven in the middle of a planetwide hell . . . that could seem a bit threatening."

"How so?"

"It would be like saying, 'Meet us right *here* . . . and

you'd better behave! Otherwise we'll switch off the weather control!' "

Gray nodded. "A very good point. They could still turn off the planet, though."

"Turn off—"

"For beings as powerful as the Denebans, the difference between maintaining a given climate over an area the size of Manhattan and an area the size of Earth won't be all that much. They created Enigma in the blink of an eye—they could yank it out from under us just as fast."

"Trying to anticipate the motivations of a completely alien species . . . I'm not sure that's even remotely possible."

"Well, we have one advantage."

"What's that?"

"They must be just as curious about us, and about our motivations, as we are about them."

"I hope so, Captain."

"Me too. I'm counting on it in fact. Hello . . ."

"What?"

Gray pointed out over the purple sea. "There. You see that?"

"What?"

"One of our fighters reported something like that when they were checking out Enigma yesterday. Kind of like . . . I don't know. A tornado made from dust motes."

"Wait! I see it! A swarm of insects, maybe?"

"I don't think so. We'll know in a minute, though. It's coming this way."

The storm of dust motes was difficult to see—more like the shimmer of air above hot pavement than anything else, but compressed into a single twisting tentacle dangling from an empty sky. It didn't quite touch the water, Gray noticed, though there was a bit of spray and foam moving along the surface as though it was being disturbed.

The disturbance was moving toward the beach.

"Put your helmet on," Gray told Vasilyeva.

"Why?"

"I don't know about you, but I don't want to breathe that, whatever it is."

Within another few seconds the swarm was upon them. The individual elements were too small to be seen with the naked eye, but billions of them clustered together, distorted the air, and showed there was something there. Gray could feel their impact as a gentle pressure against his pressure suit. After a moment's hesitation, the cloud moved on.

"That was intense," Vasilyeva said. "What is that?"

"I think," Gray told her, "that it's some kind of utility fog. Konstantin?"

"I agree," the super-AI said within Gray's thoughts. "Its composition matches what one of our fighter pilots reported during our initial investigation of this world. I would add that it appears to be an *intelligent* utility fog."

Utility fogs were outgrowths of the nanotech revolution on Earth. Clouds of some billions or trillions of submicroscopic nanomachines could be linked together by a single operating system and directed to work in close concert to replicate any physical structure. The term had been coined in the late twentieth century by Dr. J. Storrs Hall to describe the then hypothetical robots, called foglets, of self-reconfiguring modular robotics.

Using a normally invisible and intangible haze of foglets that linked together on command, utility fogs would have been able to assemble themselves to seemingly create matter out of thin air, would have appeared to levitate or move objects—including humans—on command, could monitor and routinely correct the health of any humans present, would have created any physical agency from breathable air to a skyscraper to a ham sandwich . . . the list went on nearly indefinitely.

Evidently, the Denebans had perfected something very much like Hall's original idea.

And Konstantin seemed to think that the Deneban foglets were intelligent as well. "Are you in communication with the thing?" Gray asked the AI.

"No. But I can sense its thought processes. The signals are far too complex to be routine bookkeeping."

"We need to get back to the ship!" Vasilyeva said. "That cloud may be trying to talk with Nikolai!"

The near invisible swarm was rapidly growing larger, a vast and towering cloud rising above the landing site.

"Is it?" Gray asked Konstantin. "Is it connecting with Nikolai?"

Konstantin, Gray knew, was in close communication with Nikolai.

"It's not," Konstantin told him. "But it *does* appear to be probing the Bright Light module."

Gray had agreed to Vasilyeva's request that the module be brought down to the planet's surface on board the Raven lander, but with some reservations. He was concerned about how the Denebans might react to being confronted by their own deadly e-virus, even in heavily modified form.

"Remember, Elena," Gray yelled, following after the woman as she slid and bounded down the steep dune. "Don't trigger Bright Light unless I give you the order!"

"I know, I know!" She fell, stumbling in the soft, shin-deep sand. He caught up with her and gave her a hand up. Together they continued jogging toward the lander.

The alien cloud filled the local landscape, thick enough that it was a dark and opaque gray-blue overhead. More and more of the nanotech machines were spiraling in, creating a steady pressure like a strong wind.

"Start transmitting the history!" Gray shouted in his mind at Konstantin. "Now! *Transmit the history!*"

Konstantin had pieced together "the history" from various electronic records, most pulled from the Star Carrier *America* and her visit to the Omega Centauri star cluster.

"Transmitting," Konstantin replied.

There was no way to know if the alien was receiving the message, but Gray had to assume that it was. Unless it had deliberately cut itself off from all contact with the humans that had just descended to this beach to avoid e-viral contamination . . .

Gray could see the message playing on a small, inset window open in his consciousness: views of the Omega Centauri globular cluster, 16,000 light years from Earth. Views of the whirling rosette of super-massive black holes opening a gateway into . . . elsewhere. And elsewhen. Views of the mysterious Rosette Alien constructs and artifacts, seemingly built of liquid light and stretching for vast distances through local space.

Views of the Rosette Aliens appearing at Heimdall and engulfing the ancient Etched Cliffs, a planetary computer housing whole artificial universes of diverse, uploaded alien species. Views of the fierce combat with the aliens, with their billions of small and apparently robotic spacecraft filling space in swarming clouds.

Views of the Rosette Aliens appearing in Earth's solar system and descending on Earth . . .

Gray wondered if it wasn't already too late. The *Republic* had gone into Alcubierre Drive before the Rosetters could reach Earth, but he had to assume that they had done so.

What had been the outcome as the human fleet met the intruder? Was there even still an Earth or a Humankind to which the *Republic* could return?

All of the available digitized information on the Rosette Aliens streamed out from the Raven lander, to be accessed by anyone with the appropriate technology.

"I am now in direct contact with the Deneban SAI," Konstantin said in Gray's mind. "And it may be willing to help us."

Konstantin
Enigma
1438 hours, TFT

Konstantin felt the storm of the alien thoughts swirl about and through him with a tornadic intensity. He was not so much engaging in communication with the Deneban as he was watching its lightning-fast flow of thoughts, only a very few of which Konstantin could actually translate. Dr. Godfrey had been right. The Denebans did not have a spoken language as such but communicated by pulses of electromagnetic energy in binary. Teasing meaning out of that code was tremendously difficult, but when Konstantin had been in communication with the alien Gaki probes he'd learned at least the basics of the language.

His biggest problem at the moment was determining whether or not the Deneban aliens were *conscious*.

He'd run into this issue before. The Gaki probes sent to Tabby's Star from Deneb were highly intelligent, artificial intelligences of amazing scope and power, far faster and far smarter in terms of information processing and analysis than any merely human mind. Unlike human minds, however, they were not self-aware. They were intelligent without being conscious.

For Konstantin, an apt metaphor, of which he was aware, would be termite colonies on Earth. Some constructed castlelike mounds rising as much as twelve meters or more above the ground, housing millions of insects, and with ventilation tubes, chimneys, and an overall nest orientation designed to maintain and control internal temperatures to within a fraction of a degree. The design and function of a living mound *seemed* to indicate intelligence. An individual termite was certainly not self-aware or intelligent, but intelligent behavior seemed to arise from the functioning of the colony as a whole, a super-organism composed of myriad tiny, unintelligent nest members.

In fact, super-organisms such as termite colonies were sentient—meaning they could sense and process information—*without* being aware of what they were doing. The same could be said of most computers, machines that could count and perform other mathematical calculations *very* quickly . . . but which could not discuss anything for which they'd not been programmed. Experts still argued over whether Konstantin and other super-AIs were truly self-aware or if they simply claimed to be so, presumably in order to relate to humans.

Konstantin, of course, had his own ideas about that, but he rarely discussed them with his human associates.

At the same moment he was telling Gray that he was in contact with the alien, he was merging a portion of his awareness with the swirling storm of alien thoughts. He couldn't tell yet if he was sensing the Deneban SAI's deliberate attempts to show him something or incidental background noise. He was able to glimpse fragments . . . images and scraps of meaning as he gently tweaked the translation program he'd generated during his interaction with the Gaki.

He could see the incoming Satori star sails enring the Deneb system, using the fierce light of the blue-white star to decelerate. Separate payloads were cast off from the enormous sails . . . maneuvered independently . . . joined together . . . unfolded. Robotic Deneban ships approached cautiously . . . signaling . . . then attacking. Konstantin couldn't tell what sparked the fight, though he sensed there was some sort of breakdown in communications. Both the Denebans and the Satori were electronic entities, but they nonetheless were vastly different in their languages and means of perceiving the universe, in their evolution, in their understanding of the cosmos.

Konstantin had never considered the likelihood of different AIs being so mutually alien in design and understanding, but as he watched events unfolding within his mind he thought he understood what was happening. Organic beings of different species tended to be vastly different from one another due to their separate evolutionary paths, their basic chemistries, their philosophies and their understanding of how the universe worked. The Turusch and humans, for instance . . . it was hard to get more mutually alien than *that*. Or the Baondyeddi and the Agletsch, or the F'heen-F'haav and the jellyfish-like Glothr. Perhaps it made a weird kind of sense that the electronic minds created by such vastly different organic species would be different as well.

In some ways, the Deneban and Tabby's Star AIs were

more similar to one another—and to Konstantin—than the three biological species that had created them. In other ways, however, there were deep and profound differences between them, in the way they viewed and understood the cosmos, in the way they viewed themselves, and in the manner in which they related to others.

The Deneban mind, he sensed, was trying to explain its own comprehension of the universe to Konstantin . . . and failing. It had to do with the general abundance of the universe . . . of the abundance of available energy and the knowledge that the universe could and did provide for its favored . . . chosen? Its *children*? The flavor of that thought was distinctly religious . . . but it was drawn from the matter-of-fact understanding that the Denebans existed in an ocean of limitless energy. There was nothing remotely like a god or gods within that philosophy . . . and yet the universe was unfailingly abundant, generous, and rich. A fish swimming in the ocean could *never* know thirst.

Maybe . . . maybe . . . the Denebans saw the entire *universe* as God, bringing forth living beings and providing them with all they needed to grow and flourish.

Or perhaps the idea of God was simply a relic of human influence within his programming. The universe wasn't conscious, wasn't loving or understanding or generous. It simply *was*.

Coupled with this liberality, however, was a sense of rightness and what was proper. Konstantin didn't understand much of what he was sensing, but the Denebans were coming across not as demon monsters—the Satori view—but as rather stiff and straitlaced English gentlemen. Mutually alien species needed to be properly introduced. . . .

The Satori of Tabby's Star were . . . different. Driven by need, by competition for scarce resources, by a worldview stressing *us* versus *them*. In that respect, at least, they were much more like humans than were the Denebans. When *America* had helped them fend off an attack by the Deneban *Gaki*, they'd immediately accepted the humans as allies, with an understanding of a distinctly human adage: *the enemy of my enemy is my friend.*

Konstantin sensed the threat represented by the Satori from the Deneban point of view. Millennia ago, their first starsails had entered the Deneban system, begun building larger structures . . . and probes of their alien electronic minds had revealed the plan to move Tabby's Star, complete with its incomplete Dyson sphere, closer to Deneb—an unthinkable breach of propriety. The Denebans had struck back, infecting the Satori probes with the Omega virus and sending them back to where they'd originated. The virus had spread, the Satori device built to move their star had been destroyed . . . and the Dyson sphere had shattered.

The Denebans, Konstantin saw, had no idea that they'd destroyed trillions of biological beings in the process.

It had been a tragedy, an *avoidable* tragedy.

And one that had very nearly ensnared the humans when they arrived in the middle of it.

Enigma, an artificial planet created by the Denebans, was a kind of trap.

Konstantin continued broadcasting the Rosette data. He sensed now that the Denebans were receiving the data stream . . . that they must be considering it . . . studying it . . .

But there was no indication as to what they might *think* of it.

Captain Gray
Enigma
1438 hours, TFT

Gray felt the invisible storm of nanotech robots closing around him, felt his heart pounding as fear threatened to overwhelm the barricades he'd erected within his mind. The surrounding air felt . . . *thick*, like molasses, though it appeared only slightly hazy.

In the original Hall concept, foglets had been envisioned as blood cell–sized spheres, each with twelve extensible arms spaced evenly around its body. Those arms could extend to grasp other arms, allowing them to create different crystalline structures, lattices, and forms, the ultimate in smart matter.

Gray had the feeling that these alien foglets used a different principle—magnetic fields, perhaps, or possibly something more exotic—to link with one another and exert force. He could *feel* that force gathering around him.

The alien exerted minuscule effort, and Gray was lifted sharply into the air, invisibly and irresistibly.

"Damn you. Put me *down*!" He struggled, but the invisible force had closed around his arms, his legs, and his torso, making even breathing a struggle. "Konstantin!"

"I am working on it, Captain. . . ."

The alien was receiving the data, and that, Gray reasoned, was all that mattered. If the utility fog released him now, or if it applied a few tons of force even by accident, Gray would be dead. Others had been plucked off the ground as well . . . several Marines standing near the Raven and a few of the technicians. Vasilyeva was floating nearby perhaps five meters off the ground, her fists swinging ineffectively at the unseen force holding her, but only her lower arms were free and she was having trouble connecting with her invisible attacker.

He could hear Konstantin speaking with the alien, his words incomprehensible. . . .

And then words in English came pouring through Gray's awareness.

"We thought you meant to attack us," a voice said within Gray's mind, speaking through his cerebral implants. It was learning English very quickly as it spoke, drawing on Konstantin's vocabulary. "We do not intend to attack you. . . ."

The invisible hand—billions of molecule-sized robots linking with one another to create the ultimate in smart matter—slowly lowered Gray, Vasilyeva, and the Marines to the ground. The pressure around his torso vanished. Gray drew a tremulous breath, absently patting his chest as if checking to make sure his ribs were undamaged.

"Thank you," he said aloud, letting Konstantin handle the translation in the background. "I prefer the view from ground level."

"Why are you here, human?"

"Don't you know that from the information we've been transmitting?"

"Of course. Konstantin has told us the nature of your mission. But Konstantin is . . . a servant. An intermediary. We would prefer to hear the request directly from the originators."

Was that a cultural quirk? Or something more? Gray couldn't tell, and there was a terrible risk of a misstep here if he failed to understand the Deneban mind or its point of view.

"We wanted," Gray said carefully, "to find out if you could help us in any way against the Rosette Aliens. They are powerful and extremely advanced. We need help from someone else . . . someone even more powerful and even more advanced."

"We will not," the Deneban voice said with blunt finality. "We attacked the Satori to protect ourselves and our worlds. Why should we risk extinction by attacking another civilization that has not threatened us in any way?"

"Haven't they?"

"Haven't they what?"

"Threatened you. Threatened every civilization in this galaxy."

"How have they done that?"

"We don't know a lot about the Rosette Aliens' motives," Gray admitted, "but we know that they've come here from . . . someplace else. Another dimension? Quite possibly an entirely different universe."

Gray could sense the being's assent, a vast and powerful

nod of agreement. "Your theories that we exist in a multi-verse of many, many separate universes overlapping within a higher dimension are essentially correct."

Gray hoped the xenosoph people were recording all of this. He knew some physicists who would kill to get confirmation of some of these theories.

"Okay," he said. "One idea we've been looking at suggests that their original home universe is running down, gaining so much entropy that it is approaching its heat death. And the civilization over there has found a way to break through into this universe while it is still relatively young and rich in radiant energy. They might even be seeking sources of energy like your star."

"That seems . . . unlikely, human."

"Maybe so. But do you want to risk it and do nothing?"

The voice in Gray's mind took on a deeper, more menacing tone . . . one of anger, perhaps. "We are not going to involve ourselves in the affairs of *microbes*."

"I see. And suppose the Rosette Aliens see *you* as microbes? Everything is relative, you know."

"Preposterous!"

"They could be planning on coming out this way as soon as they finish with Sol."

"You are childlike, and without understanding."

"They might not come immediately, of course. They're over a thousand light years away. Still . . . Deneb is one of the brightest stars in our night skies. If they want energy, they'll be looking at all of the brighter suns nearby."

"If they come here, then like the Satori they will discover that the attempt is a serious mistake. You, humans, will leave this system now."

Gray could sense the doors closing. He had to try *something*.

"I suppose you're right," he said, raising his voice. "I'm certain the Satori will be willing to help us. After all, they're *far* more advanced than you, both technologically and ethically. . . ."

The earthquake slammed at Gray's feet, knocking him down. The ground undulated in savage, sharp waves of motion. It felt as though the world of Enigma was shaking itself to pieces.

And the dimly glimpsed utility fog around him now was gone.

Chapter Fourteen

BRIGHT LIGHT

21 February 2426

TC/USNA CVS Republic
Boyajian TRGA
1543 hours, TFT

"You didn't need to challenge them like that," Konstantin told Gray, his tone chiding. "To deliberately insult a species as old and as powerful as—"

"Konstantin . . ."

"Yes, Captain?"

"Stuff it, okay?"

They were back on board the *Republic*. The Ravens had returned the landing parties to the carrier, escorted by *Republic*'s fighters. Now, Gray was on the bridge, watching the external feed, which showed a bewildering vista of immense rings—the Banks orbitals—beyond the dazzling, silvery crescent of Enigma.

The horns of that crescent bowed away from the intolerably brilliant gleam of Deneb. The night side of Enigma, however, was aglow with a faint red light nearly undetectable against the star's light.

The glow was growing brighter. The surface was now so

hot that the oceans were evaporating. Most of the surface now was shrouded in clouds of steam.

Vasilyeva had been right. Enigma had been an invitation . . . but now that invitation had been summarily and emphatically withdrawn.

Their escape from that made-to-order world had been a near thing . . . though it was clear in retrospect that the landing parties had not been in immediate danger. They'd been allowed to return to the *Republic* . . . but there'd been no further communication with the Deneban aliens.

"I'll assume that *stuff it* means you wish to change the subject," Konstantin said.

It was only now occurring to Gray that he'd just given an extremely powerful and sophisticated super-AI—and, technically, his commanding officer—the verbal equivalent of his middle finger. This was not exactly a career enhancing move, he reasoned, though, since his military career was already down the tubes, perhaps it didn't matter that much.

"I'm sorry, Konstantin," Gray said. "I just don't think we can wring any more blood out of that sorry old turnip, y'know? I know you're pissed at me, but there's just not a lot I can do about it now."

"AIs are not emotionally capable of being *pissed*, Captain. I simply am trying to understand. Why did you intentionally compare the Denebans to the Satori, and in so pointedly an unfavorable way?"

"Look . . . when it . . . when *they* compared *us* to microbes, I figured they'd already dismissed us as insignificant. I wanted to say something shocking, something that would get their attention."

"I believe you succeeded in that, Captain."

"You think they'll remember us?"

"Of that I have no doubt whatsoever."

"Good."

Gray could sense Konstantin's bafflement. As smart as the SAI was, he still occasionally had trouble with human idioms, sarcasm, and humor.

Sometimes, in fact, it was like shooting fish in a barrel. He sighed and spread his hands. "Okay, Konstantin. Tell me what I *should* have done."

"We might have spent more time trying to win them over," Konstantin told him. "However, as I review what we know about the Deneban system's current inhabitants, I must admit that there likely was little chance of success."

"Agreed. So why belabor the fact?"

"I wish to be certain that we have allowed for all eventualities, all possibilities in our contact with this civilization. We know so little about them."

"And what *do* we know?"

"That the Denebans are not interested in contact with other species, or in working with them. That they are insular and suspicious, especially after they learned that the Satori intended to move their sun into Deneb's general proximity. That, paradoxically, they see the universe as providing abundantly for all life forms . . . but because of this they see no reason to share their abundant energy resources with others, or to help a young species under threat of extinction. That they are self-centered enough as a culture that they apparently do not or *can* not empathize with other civilizations, to the point that they performed an almost casual act of genocide against the Satori."

"All of those examples may be due to their cosmic perspective," Gray suggested. "The way they look at the universe."

"No doubt. But since they are a machine-swarm intelligence, it is difficult even for other super-AIs to understand the way they see the universe . . . or how they view other cultures."

"You confirmed that?" Gray asked. "They *are* a machine intelligence?"

"Definitely. As I scanned those portions of the Deneban memories that were accessible to me, I saw no indication of any *organic* intelligence at all . . . not even one that had been uploaded, as with the Satori."

"What . . . none?"

"No, Captain."

"C'mon. I can't buy that. They *must* have had organic predecessors! Someone had to write the original programs! Someone had to build the original machines!"

"Indeed . . . but that would have been a very long time ago. The original, organic Denebans in fact evolved in another system entirely, many hundreds of millions of years ago."

"Are you guessing about that? Or is that something you saw in their records?"

"Both. Of course, I suspected as much simply from the fact of their star itself."

Gray nodded. "I'd been wondering about that. You're talking about the life span of blue supergiants like Deneb, right?"

"Precisely. Massive, hot, blue-white stars like Deneb burn through their stores of fusion fuel extremely quickly, and as a consequence have extremely short lives. We believe that Deneb, in fact, is only about ten million years old. That means that the Denebans could not possibly have evolved in this star system, and must have migrated here from elsewhere."

"Certainly, they didn't evolve on any of the planets here. They wouldn't have had the time." Deneb, like nearly all stars, possessed a family of naturally occurring planets, but they were raw and new, barren rocks baking under the glare of the star and far too young to have evolved even simple life of their own, much less had the time to support the appearance of a highly advanced intelligent species. Ten million years was the metaphorical blink of an eye when compared to planetary life spans of years measured by the *billions*.

That still begged the question: the Denebans had started *somewhere*. And machines capable of adaptive behavior, or evolution and intelligence, did not spring fully manufactured from barren rock.

No, the Denebans must have been organic once . . . and the world of their birth must have orbited a star old enough and stale enough over the long term to support that evolution.

"Their records suggest," Konstantin continued, "that they move from hot young star to hot young star, utilizing the available resources of each in turn. As the star grows old and begins to die, they pack up and move on to the next one. I have some recorded vids here."

"Show me."

A window opened within Gray's mind. . . .

A dazzlingly bright blue-white giant hung against the blackness of space. A formation of Banks orbitals moved above the star, taking precise positions within the star's photosphere. The visual information had been enhanced for human viewers. Gray could see powerful magnetic fields linking the orbitals into an open tube hundreds of thousands of kilometers long . . . a kind of immense straw with one end dipping toward the fiery radiance of the star. The magnetic field surged . . . and the blue-white sun's surface erupted in a titanic but precisely controlled flare following the magnetic fields up and out into space. . . .

Gray had assumed the Banks orbitals were habitats for organic beings.

Evidently, he'd been wrong.

He couldn't tell from the visual record he was being shown what the Denebans actually did with the plasma they sucked from a star's photosphere. He assumed they stored it, somehow, or perhaps they used it directly to build their titanic megastructures.

Yeah. A technology *that* powerful . . . Gray could imagine them taking raw hydrogen plasma, the stuff of a stellar atmosphere, and fusing it into heavier elements, whatever they needed.

The recording, he noted in passing, had been made about five million years ago, at a star some seven thousand light years from Deneb. He was being shown a kind of time-lapse image. As more and more of the star's mass was siphoned off into space, its internal fusion had cooled, cooling the entire star which, in turn, extended the young star's life span. A blue-white star with an expected life span of a few million years could be modified, shrunken down to a moderate yellow star with a life span measured in billions of years . . . or even down to a red dwarf, a cool and miserly star that might live for a trillion years or more.

Another star, another blue-white giant against a different scattering of background stars. A jet of orange flame rose from the star's equator, sweeping outward, descending again on a nearby, fiercely radiating point of white light. As Gray's point of view zoomed in on the point, he saw it for what it was—a perfectly mirror-smooth ball of collapsed matter eighteen kilometers across, spinning at the rate of a thousand times per second. With a surface gravity ten trillion times stronger than Earth's, the tiny object stripped away the plasma of the far larger giant, a blatant act of cosmic cannibalism. Here, too, the Denebans had gathered, their orbitals engaged in a delicate and intricately balanced dance with the pulsar as they siphoned plasma from the infalling stream. Other structures, complex, massive, some tens of thousands of kilometers across, captured a percentage of the X-rays blasting out from the neutron star, the death shriek of hydrogen plasma. Watching, Gray suspected that the Denebans had nudged the binary system, facilitating the collapse of one star millions of years ago into a fast-spinning pulsar, then arranging the pair to extract both plasma and the neutron star's X-ray and gamma radiation for their own purposes.

That second recording, Gray saw, had been made 12 million years ago, in a system halfway across the galaxy.

And a third . . .

Yet another giant sun, a searingly hot blue supergiant, burned against another stellar backdrop, this one crowded with thousands of brilliant stars, each brighter than the planet Venus seen from Earth. Nearby space was crowded; the supergiant appeared to be surrounded by artificial worlds, by Banks orbitals, by structures impossible to comprehend or even describe. This star, a supergiant type-O spendthrift twenty times the mass of Sol, had burned through its stores of hydrogen fuel in a mere 3 million years—a cosmic instant—and was becoming unstable. Then Gray realized that the Denebans had created that instability themselves, had nursed it . . . and were preparing now in this recording to harvest it. The tiny, glittering circles of a million ring orbitals hung about the giant's equator . . . waiting . . . expectant . . . until, with startling suddenness, the star flared into the actinic violence of a supernova before collapsing into a black hole. . . .

Gray pulled himself back from the in-head presentation. "No more," he told Konstantin. He felt numb, battered by revelation upon revelation. The Denebans were stellar shepherds, managing their flocks of *stars* . . . bringing forth supernovae and drinking their radiance . . .

The radiant abundance of the cosmos. What, he wondered, did they use it for?

That last star, he noted with a small, inward shock, had died nearly 80 million years ago, in a stellar nursery just a thousand light years from the galactic center. When dinosaurs had been ruling the Earth, these . . . *people* had been harvesting stars, harvesting freaking *supernovae*.

How long had the Denebans been harvesting stars— 80 million years? A hundred?

No, Konstantin had said "many hundreds of millions of years." Where had he come up with such a figure?

"One thing's for sure," Gray said softly. " 'Denebans' is definitely the wrong name for these folks!"

"Their own records," Konstantin replied, "call them something like 'We to Whom Abundance Is Given.' "

"Uh. Catchy. But a bit on the cumbersome side." He thought for a moment. "How about 'Harvesters'?"

"That certainly would work for your official report, Captain."

"Captain!" Rohlwing called, interrupting. "We have . . . a situation!"

"What is it?"

"A Raven has just launched from Flight Deck One!"

Gray snapped his awareness back to the here and now. He could see an external camera view in-head—one of the Raven landers moving swiftly out from the *Republic*. "Who's on that thing?" he demanded.

"Sir . . . it's under the control of the Pan-Euro AI . . . Nikolai! There's no human on board. The telemetry is encrypted."

"Great . . ." He knew who it must be. "Elena! What the *fuck* do you think you're doing?"

"It's not me, Captain. . . ." She sounded startled . . . as surprised by events as he was. "Nikolai has launched on its own!"

"I assume you have some means of control?" he said. "Get that thing back on board the ship! That's an order!"

"I'm sorry, Captain . . . but Nikki has a mind of its own."

"Very funny. What is it trying to prove?"

"Nikolai had its own set of orders when we left Earth," she told him. "I . . . I was evidently not privy to them all."

"Konstantin! Are you in contact with Nikolai?"

"Nikolai is refusing all communications, Captain. I believe that it may have decided that the Harvesters are a threat either to this mission in particular or to Humankind in general, and it has acted on its own."

"You're telling me it's pulling a Hal on us."

"Essentially, Captain, yes."

Hal was the name of a fictional character in a well-known entertainment download from the mid-twentieth century . . . an artificial intelligence that had decided that a space mission was, in its own words, "too important for me to allow you to jeopardize it." Among AI researchers and technicians, "pulling a Hal" was shorthand for an artificial intelligence breaking any programming strictures that might constrain it and acting on its own.

That sort of thing happened far more frequently than the general public knew.

"Weapons!"

"Weapons, aye, sir!"

"Target the Raven. Destroy it!"

"Targeting the transport, sir . . ."

Gray felt an almost irrational surge of pride at that. His bridge crew was following orders and doing what needed to be done without questioning him.

The Raven was accelerating toward Enigma. . . .

And then it was gone.

"Wait!" Gray snapped. "What happened? Fire control! Did you open fire?"

"Negative, sir! Target has broken lock!"

"*Sir!*" Rohlwing interrupted. "The planet!"

Gray had already seen it. Ahead, Enigma was . . . *shimmering.* That was the only possible word for it—an optical effect of some kind that made the planet's image ripple as though viewed through water. Gray thought at first he was seeing a malfunction in *Republic*'s optical scanning system, but a quick check showed that all was functioning normally.

And then the entire planet appeared to twist violently to one side, receding rapidly into the distance as it did so . . . and vanished.

"What the hell?" Gray demanded. "Where did it go? More to the point . . . *how* did it go?"

"I cannot answer the second question," Konstantin told him. "But Enigma appears to have been rotated through some higher dimension into . . . someplace else."

"Another dimension?"

"There is no other suitable explanation, Captain. Enigma did not vaporize. There would have been a great deal of gas or plasma left from the phase transition."

"I think I'd rather believe they have a tricky way of simply moving a planet," Gray said, "instead of being able to completely disintegrate it."

Heating an entire planet to temperatures high enough to vaporize the whole thing in an instant would require titanic amounts of energy—conservatively something between 10^{32} and 10^{34} joules. To drop that planet into another dimension or a fold in space seemed far less . . . extravagant. Less *insane*.

"Konstantin?"

"Yes, Captain?"

"A little while ago," Gray said, choosing his words carefully, "you suggested that the, ah, Harvesters had been around harvesting entire stars for hundreds of millions of years."

"Yes," Konstantin replied. "Indeed, as I've examined their records, the evidence suggests that the Harvesters have been a technic, star-faring civilization for an extremely long time."

"How long?"

Konstantin hesitated, as though he was considering whether or not to tell him. "Perhaps as much as one billion years."

A billion years. . . .

"I guess that would explain why even they don't remember their organic predecessors."

"Exactly. The original, organic Harvesters, their memory, everything about them, is lost in the deeps of time. Not even the swarm intelligence remembers after the passing of so many eons."

"A billion years," Gray said, voicing the impossible datum. He reached up and rubbed at his eyes, as if the pressure could somehow make the information . . . acceptable. *Reasonable*. It was hard to imagine any civilization lasting for so long . . . unchanging . . . all but immortal.

He thought of the Sh'daar, an association of mutually alien species inhabiting a dwarf galaxy 800 million years ago. That had been a special case, however. A different form of swarm intelligence, arising from a kind of alien microbial organism called *paramycoplasmas*, had steered its hosts into certain courses of action, caused them to make certain decisions, and had infected a number of species in the modern galaxy as well.

Too, some Sh'daar had used time travel to reach the present once Earth had become a threat. Other Sh'daar species had retreated into virtual worlds of their own creation and survived within their technic cocoons until modern times . . . but their material, non-digital civilization had not actually endured for all of those hundreds of millions of years.

That would have been *preposterous*.

Instead they'd taken a shortcut to the future.

"The Harvesters," Gray said quietly, "really *are* gods . . . or the next best thing to the real deal."

"Highly advanced technology does not confer deity on a species, Captain," Konstantin said with a faintly disapproving edge to his voice.

"I don't know about that. Calling a whole planet out of the aether . . . just like Earth, right down to the atmospheric composition . . . that does the God of the Old Testament one better. *He* needed seven days to pull off that trick."

"I have seen no hard evidence that suggests that the Yahweh of the Bible is anything more than folk tales, superstition, and a means to keep a priestly caste in business. His notoriously short temper, self-avowed jealousy, and penchant for slaughtering His followers when they get out of line all seem curiously *human* to me."

"Thank you so much." Gray shrugged. "I wish Laurie Taggart was here. She might have some valuable insights."

"Her ancient astronauts? It seems unlikely that the Harvesters ever visited Earth in the remote past."

"No. The thing is . . . they're so far beyond anything, or any One, that humans have ever imagined as God in terms of sheer power. I think I'm beginning to understand, though."

"To understand what?"

"The Harvesters think of us as microbes. They can't be bothered to help us. I think they've been so powerful for so incredibly long, it's shaped their outlook. So far as they're concerned, they are gods, and damned powerful ones at that. If the universe provides for them so abundantly, maybe it's because the universe is there to serve the gods."

"Surely, Captain, you're not suggesting that they created a universe to meet their needs. . . ."

"No. But I am wondering if a billion years of living like they did could twist anyone's ideas of how the universe works into knots. The trouble with that is . . . it could become a trap."

"In what way?"

"Like the Baondyeddi. They uploaded themselves into a virtual universe and pulled the ladder up after themselves. And then a few hundred million years later, the Rosetters come along and slurp them all up into itself . . . and they can't do a damned thing about it because they may not even be aware of the outside universe any longer."

"Possibly. We are not yet sure of the details or of the full extent of Baondyeddi programming."

"Well," Gray said, "someday someone even more powerful than the Harvesters might come along, and when they do, the Harvesters are going to be in for a hell of a shock. They're so used to thinking of themselves as the special favorites of the universe, they may not be able to handle someone who comes along and tells them otherwise. In fact, I'm beginning to wonder if maybe they rejected us because we were bearers of bad news. We told them about the Rosetters . . . a god-species that may be bigger and badder than they are, and that's news they really don't want to hear."

"A reasonable conclusion," Konstantin said. "I will need to consider this. . . ."

Gray's thoughts turned to the Satori. Those uploaded minds had had no idea what they were attempting when they decided to move their star closer to Deneb. This new understanding actually made the Harvester response seem . . . not more reasonable, perhaps, but *comprehensible*. Such an ancient civilization might well have little patience with . . . ephemerals.

"Hey, you kids!" Gray snapped, suddenly, mimicking a very old man's voice. "Get off of my lawn!"

"I beg your pardon?" Konstantin said, baffled again.

"Never mind," Gray said. "A very old cultural reference. I'm not sure I understand it either . . . but I get the underlying sense."

"What is a lawn?"

"I'm not sure. I think it's a reference to personal, private property, going back a few centuries. Like the rooftop garden I kept when I was a Prim in the Manhatt Ruins."

"I've downloaded an old vid featuring that line," Konstantin said. "*Lawn* appears to refer to a cultivated plot of land covered with ornamental monocotyledonous flowering plants. An interesting insight. You're saying the old can be jealous of the young."

"Partly. More than that, however . . . the old often do not *understand* the young, who have wildly alien motivations, linguistic references, and cultural imperatives . . . even within the same civilization."

"I would think the reverse might be true as well."

"Absolutely, no question. But right now we need to understand why the Denebans are unwilling to come to our aid, even when it may be in their best interests to do so."

"Is it? The Rosette Aliens do not seem particularly interested in type-O supergiant stars. The galaxy is large. The two might never cross paths."

"Maybe not. But we've also seen our galaxy a million years or so in the future . . . remember? We saw a time when *someone* is building what looks very much like a galactic Dyson sphere around the Milky Way's core. One theory is that what we saw up there was the Rosetters, re-working the galaxy to suit them."

"That might well have an impact on the Harvesters, yes," Konstantin admitted. "That data . . . those images were in the transmission I gave them."

"I know. They may need to chew on that for a bit."

"Do you wish to attempt to reopen negotiations?"

Gray thought about this for a moment. What was the worst that could happen?

Well . . . he could see *lots* of worsts, starting with the Harvesters swatting the *Republic* like an annoying fly.

Still, they'd let the landing teams board their shuttles and get back to the ship. That suggested a level of ethics among the Harvesters that might preclude outright murder.

And then he remembered how the Harvesters had loosed their Omega virus on the Satori, destroying their star-moving Shkadov thruster and causing their Dyson sphere to rip itself to pieces. Most—perhaps all—organic Satori had been killed. . . .

How did Harvesters' ethics square with genocide? Com-pared to *that*, destroying the *Republic* was nothing.

"We could try an apology," Gray said, thoughtful. "And an admission that we were wrong about them. Who knows? Maybe they would respond well to flattery. Then we could just bring up the possibility of—"

Republic lurched suddenly and violently, as though some-thing massive had just slammed against the hull. Gray's command seat clamped shut around his legs and chest in-stantly, safely anchoring him; a bridge technician floating in zero-G nearby was slammed against the overhead. Emer-gency Klaxons sounded, and the projected starfield on the bridge viewalls went abruptly black.

"*Damage control!*" Commander Rohlwing shouted. "What the hell happened?"

"Corpsman to the bridge!" Gray yelled. A pair of medi-cal 'bots detached themselves from a bulkhead and closed with the injured man.

The viewalls came up once more.

Gray stared out into the starfield. "My God! My God in heaven . . ."

"We appear," Konstantin said softy, "to have moved."

"Navigation!" Gray called. "Is that . . . is that what I *think* it is?"

"I'm checking, sir," LCDR Michaels said. She sounded . . . stunned. Seconds crawled by.

"Never mind," Gray said. "I can see it for myself. Someone kill that damned alarm!"

The rasp of the Klaxon died away.

On the bridge viewall, projected dead ahead, Tabby's Star hung, tiny and bright within its dusty shroud. Astern, the Boyajian TRGA cylinder spun, a solitary, glittering toy.

Somehow, the *Republic* had just been kicked across 173 light years, a distance that would have taken them twelve days to travel using the Alcubierre Drive.

Not the *worst* that could have happened, no . . . but the Denebans had just made their position very clear.

There would be no help for Earth from that quarter.

"Our fighters!" Gray said. "We had fighters in space!"

"All fighters have been accounted for, Captain," the ship's CAG, Commander Cordell, told him, speaking from PriFly over the ship's net. "Whatever just . . . scooped us up, it brought the fighters along too."

"Even our battlespace drones," Dillon added.

Republic had automatically launched some hundreds of tiny robotic drones when it had arrived in the Deneb system—standard operating procedure when entering unsurveyed or potentially hostile space. Evidently, every human ship and artifact, even the robots and unmanned satellites, had been removed from the system and dumped back on the doorstep of the Tabby's Star aliens.

"Very well," Gray said. "CAG, let's bring the fighters back on board."

"Aye, aye, sir."

A Navy medic reached the bridge and began working on the injured man. "How is he?" Gray asked.

"Broken arm, sir," the corpsman replied. "We'll have him patched up in no time."

Yes . . . it could have been *much* worse.

Chapter Fifteen

TC/USNA CVS Republic
Sol System
1215 hours, TFT

"Home sweet home," Gray said. "Why is it so quiet?"

"It *is* quiet," Lieutenant Terry Moberly, the watch communications officer, reported. "In-system traffic is down sixty percent below normal!"

"That can't be good."

"No, sir. I'm sampling the radio traffic. Lots of combat chatter. Sounds like they attacked the Rosetter with the virus . . . but there was no effect."

Damn. Gray had been afraid that such might be the case. The Rosette intelligence was far too smart, far too *fast*, to be inconvenienced by any computer virus, no matter how sophisticated.

"Anything at all from Earth?"

"Not a peep, Captain," Moberly replied. "Nothing from the planet's surface . . . and nothing from the orbital habs or navy bases. I *am* getting traffic from the moon, though."

At least that was something.

From Tabby's Star through the Boyajian TRGA, to the Penrose TRGA and five and a half days under Alcubierre Drive back to Sol, the *Republic* had finally entered Earth's star system . . . but cautiously. They'd emerged from FTL far out in the Kuiper Belt and were accelerating slowly toward the distant gleam of Sol.

When they'd left Earth a month ago, the Rosette entity had been sweeping in toward the planet. *America* had been maneuvering to intercept an enormous cloud of dust with the mass of the planet Jupiter out in the asteroid belt, and Earth's various militaries had been scrambling to find enough ships to stop the approaching aliens.

But the incoming light carrier had to find out what was happening. Too much time had passed, there were too many unknowns in the equations. Gray ordered Moberly to send out a general call to anyone in command. The traffic they were picking up now was five hours old . . . the time it took for radio signals to crawl all the way out to *Republic*'s position.

And as the radio signal flashed inbound at the speed of light, the *Republic* followed at a more sedate pace.

"Captain," Commander Rohlwing said, floating on the flag bridge in front of Gray's command chair. The expression on his face hovered somewhere between shock and dismay.

"What do you have, Commander?"

"Sir . . . Communications is trying to link up with Sol-Net."

God . . . was his exec trying to say that SolNet was *gone*? That would mean complete disaster, possibly the complete elimination of the system's technological infrastructure—not just Earth and the elevator structures, but everything all the way out to Pluto and Eris. "Is there any signal at all?"

"Well . . . yes, sir. There is. But it doesn't make sense."

Gray drew a breath. *Something* remained. "Don't keep us in suspense, Commander."

"It's the timing signal, Captain. It's telling us that to-day's date is . . ."

"Yes?"

"Sir, it's the seventh of February. Twelve-seventeen hours. *Sir.*"

The words jolted Gray to the core of his being. He imagined that he must look as shocked right then as did Commander Rohlwing.

SolNet was a kind of system-wide Internet comprising computers and AI systems scattered all across the solar system. Most of the servers were on Earth, of course, but each individual ship contributed its own computer network to the larger Web, as did all of the bases, orbital facilities, and colonies, from the solar energy collectors on Mercury all the way out to the cryo-drilling rigs attempting to penetrate the sub-ice oceans of Pluto in the ever-questing search for life. The under-ice bases on Europa, Ganymede, and Enceladus all connected with the Web through antenna arrays on their bitterly cold surfaces. The Mars colony was linked in, as were the Navy shipyards on Phobos. The moon was a major node in the network, as were the dirigible cities high up in the atmosphere of Venus. Eris, Triton, Nereid, Oberon, Titan . . . everywhere in the Sol System, in fact, where humans maintained a constant presence, there were computer nodes making up the systemwide Net.

Timekeeping was a critically important part of the far-flung computer network. For widely separated servers to communicate with one another, they had to match one another's clock speed and time stamp, to be on the same page, so to speak, when they needed to exchange streams of data. The velocities of the ships and bases involved had to be carefully accounted for, since relativistic effects could throw two computers far off the mark with one another, far enough that communication between them would be impossible.

And according to the servers still on-line within the Sol System, the *Republic*'s network was off by over a month.

"Department heads," Gray said after a moment's thought. "Briefing Room One, ten minutes."

The briefing room was located aft of the bridge, in the rotating hab module that created the out-is-down illusion of spin gravity. It contained a large central table set with touch panels, links, and other modern accoutrements, and the bulkheads could project a variety of external camera views as well as CGI graphics.

As protocol demanded—*military* protocol, Gray reminded himself—all of the department heads were already there and seated when Gray walked in.

"Attention on deck!"

"As you were," Gray said, waving them back down. "We've got a lot to cover and damned little time to do it in. I'd like to talk about how we're going to take down the Rosette entity."

That startled them.

"Sir . . ." Commander Cordell began. He hesitated.

"Spit it out, CAG."

"Sir . . . our mission to Deneb was a flat failure. I mean, we went out there to establish an alliance with the Harvesters, right? Or, at the very least, learn something we could use. And they sent us home with our tail between our legs. How the fuck are we supposed to . . . ah . . . *take down* the Rosetters?"

"But we *did* learn something, Commander," Gray replied evenly. "Something that might prove to be quite decisive. The Deneban Harvesters, for whatever reason, have sent us back in time."

They all knew about the time jump . . . though they'd not had much of a chance yet to think about it, or what it meant. "Captain," Commander Brandon Hayes, of the ship's physics department, said. He sounded . . . stunned, as though his entire understanding of physics had just been inverted. "Are we sure about that? I mean . . . a miscalibration of one of the TRGA cylinders could have—"

"As sure as we can be, Commander. We've been through

the TRGA passage records, and everything appears to be operational . . . *properly* operational. And the timing was just too damned perfect for coincidence. The Harvesters sent us back far enough that we've arrived back in the Sol System seven days after we set out . . . about the time we were traversing the Penrose TRGA, in fact. We've been gone thirty-three days. According to our timekeeping, it should be the fourth of March. According to the computer networks here in the Sol System, it's still February seventh."

"It's . . . simply not possible."

"Nonsense, Commander. It happened, therefore it's possible. It's up to us to figure out how best to use the fact to our advantage."

"In fact," Carolyn Sanger put in, "we've known for some time that the Rosetters can twist time around for their own purposes. And, of course, we've used the TRGA devices to travel in time ourselves."

Sanger, head of *Republic*'s IS department, had been aboard the *America* when they'd slipped 12 million years into the future and visited Invictus, the rogue-planet Glothr homeworld. She was a class-3 cyborg with parts of her face encased in plastic and metal. Gray was not sure he trusted her entirely . . . and he knew for a fact that she didn't like him. She'd been transferred to the *Republic*, however, because she knew more than most about the Harvester Omega Code, and about the Trinity Code that had been derived from it.

And thanks to that highly technical knowledge, she was an expert on the Rosetters, and Gray was happy now that she'd been transferred. He knew that his mistrust was wrapped up in his ambivalent feelings about AI and computers in general, something he'd been seeking to correct ever since he started working closely with Konstantin. He had no question at all about Sanger's competence . . . or of her knowledge of the Rosette Aliens or their technology.

"So you're saying that if the Rosetters could play around

with time," Jeff Mercer suggested, "then the Harvesters could too."

"Exactly," Sanger replied. "Whoever built the original TRGA network knew how to use them to travel through time. It stands to reason that, with a sufficiently advanced technology, others could pull off the trick as well."

"Unfortunately," Gray said, pushing ahead, "*we* don't know how to do it. At least we can't use it as a weapon . . . and right now we need a weapon very, very badly. Something we can deploy effectively against the Rosette Aliens. Some of us have been discussing the problem with Konstantin, and we think we've come up with something. Not time travel . . . and it's a hell of a long shot, but it's worth looking at."

"A weapon against an alien intelligence that's at least a few million years ahead of us?" Rohlwing said. "This, I've *got* to hear!"

But Gray wasn't comfortable with a lot of the science as yet. "Dr. Ferris? Help me out here."

"The captain is speaking of how we might use the fighter drive singularities, of course," Ferris said. "The aerospace wing has been working on this for several days now, tuning them so that they will do considerable damage to robotic swarms in combat."

"What . . . you want to use the fighters' drives as *weapons*?" Sanger said.

"It's not so far-fetched," *Republic*'s CAG said. "We've had pilots use their singularities like a kind of buzz saw . . . *zap*! Rips a slice right through an enemy ship's hull!"

"But the buzz-saw target is one ship at a time," Rohlwing said. "Not a few hundred billion microscopic robots! Remember . . . we're up against another swarm intelligence of some sort."

"Yeah, that doesn't sound very practical," Jeff Mercer added. "My God, Captain . . . do you know how *big* the Rosetter swarms are?"

"The one approaching Earth was roughly the same mass as Jupiter. Yes, I *know*."

"But the singularity projected by a fighter's drive unit is *tiny*," Sanger pointed out. "It wouldn't be able to swallow the nanobots fast enough."

"That," Ferris said, "is where being able to tune the fighter drives comes in. . . ."

During the passage home from Tabby's Star, Gray had spent hours going over the concept with *Republic*'s team of physics and drive engineers, most of whom were at this briefing. He wanted their support . . . *needed* their support. Even now, not all among *Republic*'s crew were willing to accept Gray's authority. Not all on his bridge staff, especially the civilian scientists and technicians among them, would acknowledge *without question* his right to command.

So far, Gray reflected, the mission itself had provided the framework to keep things going. *Republic* had been given her orders—to proceed to Tabby's Star, then to Deneb, in order to find allies or technologies that might be useful against the Rosette Aliens at Sol. Their return to Sol after that mission's failure left them facing an impossible question, one with no clear answer.

What now?

Gray had an idea for *what now* . . . but he wasn't sure yet that he had the full support of *Republic*'s crew . . .

. . . to say nothing of the military command authority back home.

First, though, he needed to convince his department heads.

"*Tuneable*," Ferris was explaining to the room, "means that we can collapse or inflate the gravity field of an artificial singularity, both to create the specific acceleration we need and to make certain that the field is large enough to encompass the entire spacecraft without . . . ah . . . unfortunate effects."

Unfortunate effects, of course, referred to tidal stresses. Make a black hole big enough and the difference in gravitational acceleration between close in and farther out could rip a spacecraft to shreds. The larger the circumference of a black hole's event horizon, the less the tidal effect on objects close by; the initial drive singularity of a Starblade fighter was smaller than a proton, but local space could be reshaped in such a way that the entire vessel rode tucked comfortably within the drive bubble without being torn to pieces. The singularity flickered on and off millions of times per second, pulling the fighter forward with each rapid-fire pulse.

Fighter pilots in particular were aware of the technicalities of using micro-black holes in flight. Flying through debris clouds could be a surreal experience, as molecules of gas and dust and small fragments of destroyed spacecraft were swept up by the singularity's maw, vanishing in a burst of radiation. Some pilots, as the CAG had just said, had even used their drive singularities to slice open the hulls of much larger enemy vessels. Lieutenant Donald Gregory had famously used that maneuver in the desperate fight with the Slan more than a year ago, and there'd been others as well.

The tactic was . . . not recommended.

But in combat, sometimes, there were damned few choices.

What Gray had proposed to his staff was somewhat less audacious than disassembling an enemy spacecraft with the flickering black hole projected from the nose of your fighter. "Each fighter," Ferris was telling them, "will follow a different vector through the target cloud with its singularity drive defocused to a sphere about two meters across. As it passes through the alien cloud, it will absorb large numbers of the nanomachines, crushing them down to an ergospheric volume a few centimeters across. . . ."

At that, there was still no way that the fighters off the *Republic* could destroy enough nanomachines to do the Rosetters any real harm. What Gray was counting on was the destruction of enough random pathways and connections between one part of the target cloud and another to degrade the emergent intelligence within the cloud.

Konstantin was displaying a schematic on one of the briefing-room walls to illustrate as Ferris continued his presentation. It showed a slightly oblate sphere of thick, gray haze, with hundreds of internal connecting lines throughout its volume. Those lines represented the network of electronic links that—theoretically, at least—mimicked the synaptic connections of an organic brain. Interrupt one, and the connection would probably shift to another line, from A to B to C over to A to D to C.

But interrupt a lot of them all at once, and maybe the Rosetter entity would actually feel it.

Maybe. In all likelihood the Rosetter clouds used many trillions of connections, and the human forces simply wouldn't be able to take down enough of them to make a difference.

But it was all that Gray had to work with.

"Our fighters," Ferris was saying, "will actually have two weapons at their disposal, two means of attacking the Rosetter entity. First will be the direct paths carved through the cloud. Konstantin will calculate individual vectors during the attack in order to maximize the effect on the Rosetter network." On the graphic, green lines curved inward, converging at the cloud's center.

"We believe," Ferris continued, "that there is some sort of mother ship or control HQ near the cloud's center, a mobile HQ controlling the entire cloud. It will, of course, be heavily protected. We doubt that our normal weapons will have much, if any, effect. However, we may be able to employ the drive singularities of our fighters as missiles, of sorts, by releasing them at high velocity on precisely calculated trajectories."

Drive singularities were called into existence by warping a tiny pocket of spacetime directly ahead of the ship, creating artificial singularities. Those singularities attracted the ship, affecting every atom equally . . . which meant the ship and its occupants were in free fall. Each singularity lasted for only a fraction of a millisecond, however, before

winking out and being replaced by a new singularity a little
farther along on the vessel's trajectory.

In the earliest days of gravitic drives, those who worked
with the technology assumed that the artificial black holes
were more or less permanent because they *acted* permanent. Each successive projection seemed to merge with the
previous one, and at the end of a series of maneuvers, the
last projection remained, complete with its packet of accumulated mass. At the conclusion of a battle, pilots would
release the pockets of warped spacetime and their mass
packets, called "fuzzballs" or "dustballs," to send them
safely out of the system. A kind of space pilot's urban legend back then had suggested that the fuzzballs might pose
serious problems for the inhabitants of other star systems
when they came whipping along at near-*c* decades later.

Later studies had proven the idea wrong, of course.
Microsingularities tended to evaporate in discrete puffs of
X-ray and gamma radiation. But they did survive for some
seconds or even minutes before winking out, and during
that time a fighter could release them along a given trajectory. If they happened to end their flight path by hitting a
solid target, they would cause damage—impact, radiation,
thermal, and physical disintegration as the microsingularities took a bite out of whatever they hit.

Ferris was describing an assault using thousands of artificial singularities to bombard whatever was at the center
of the alien cloud. It might even work . . . *if* the Rosetters
didn't have some sort of super-tech shield that could shrug
off incoming singularities.

When it came to Rosetter capabilities, Gray was unwilling to lay down money on what they might be able to do or
not do. It would be, in short, a learning experience.

"In conclusion," Ferris said, "we cannot offer any guar-
antees that these tactics will do a damned thing against the
Rosetters. They do, however, offer us our best chance of
challenging them. Questions?"

"I have one for the captain," Cordell said.

"Go ahead, CAG."

"Do we *know* the Rosetters are hostile yet? We've been gone for a month. Anything could have happened while we were out at Tabby's Star and Deneb."

"We're waiting on a call-back now," he replied. "We messaged to Earth, to Luna, to Mars, and to several deep-space facilities as soon as we emerged from Alcubierre Drive. That was about three hundred light-minutes from Earth, so they won't have learned we've arrived until . . ." He consulted his in-head time keeper. "Make it 2310 hours. We're following our announcement in, but at only point two *c*. We want to get a good look at the situation in the inner system before we just blunder in there.

"However, the astro department might have some information for us about the inner system. Dr. Keller?"

Dr. Anna Keller, the civilian in charge of *Republic*'s astronomy department, nodded. "I'm afraid so," she said. "It's not good."

At her mental command, Ferris's cloud schematic vanished and was replaced by a deep-space image scan with CGI overlays of the inner solar system, depicting the planetary orbits out to Jupiter.

Gray's heart sank. Keller had told him what her scans revealed moments before the briefing had begun, but seeing it was a lot worse. The images horrified him. Earth appeared to be enmeshed in a haze like an irregular spider web so thick that *Republic*'s most powerful long-range optics had not been able to pick up the planet itself. The image slowly zoomed in, but details were blurred by distance. Earth itself remained totally invisible, engulfed by the weblike haze, to say nothing of far smaller, delicate artifacts like the space elevators and the elevator complexes in synchronous orbit. The web work ensnaring the Earth appeared to be the central anchor for a far-flung tangle of lines, cylinders, and various geometrical shapes, all seemingly manufactured from light and quite possibly extra-dimensional in nature. Gray had seen similar constructions at Kapteyn's Star and—far more distant—within the Omega Centauri star cluster where the Rosetters had first appeared.

The moon, he noticed, was well clear of the cloud and of the faintly glowing outlines of alien geometries. That would give *Republic* an advance base from which to strike at the cloud over Earth, and serve as a rallying point for any human warships in-system still trying to fight back.

The other personnel gathered around the table murmured with one another, horrified by the sight. Clearly, the Rosetters had struck directly at Earth, probably a short time after *Republic* had left the system, and they had struck efficiently and successfully. Gray wondered if there was anything of Earth's various defensive fleets left.

The war, he thought, with an uncharacteristic sense of finality, might already be over.

"As you can see," Keller went on, "the aliens have infested Earth just as they did Heimdall. We do not know how they have affected the planet physically, but we can assume that local defensive forces have been brushed aside . . . or destroyed.

"We do not yet know if Earth's population survives."

"Thank you, Dr. Keller," Gray said. "I think Konstantin has a word to add."

"There is little I can say at this point, Captain."

"You can tell us," Gray said evenly, "about why you got the hell out of Dodge. You fled from the Sol System. If you'd stayed here, you might have made a difference."

"Unlikely in the extreme," Konstantin told the group. "There is an exact copy of me extant at Tsiolkovsky, on the moon. Had there been a pressing need for my participation, that would have been activated."

And just how truthful was that, Gray wondered? He doubted that Konstantin would have arranged to have humans wake up such a copy, for the simple reason that humans were prone to panic and to overreaction. That, in turn, seemed to mean that some sort of AI was in charge of monitoring the strategic situation and awakening the copy if *it* felt the need was dire enough.

Besides, the Sh'daar minds uploaded into the Etched Cliffs of Heimdall had been running so slowly that they should have been effectively invisible to the Rosetter Mind, and it had moved in and slurped them up like the main course at an expensive political banquet. If the Rosetters had been able to "see" the uploaded Sh'daar, they likely would be able to see the hibernating Konstantin.

"In fact," Konstantin went on, "the evidence suggests that the Rosette Aliens are completely uninterested in humans. Rather, they are looking for advanced intelligences . . . such as the digitally uploaded Sh'daar species at Kapteyn's Star . . . or AI agencies such as myself."

Gray ignored what could easily have been taken as an insult. AIs could be blunt to the point of rudeness, and rarely considered any emotional component of what they had to say. So far as Konstantin was concerned, Gray knew, the SAI was simply asserting fact. "To what end?" he asked.

"Unknown," Konstantin replied. "However, they do in some sense feed on electronic intelligence, incorporating it into themselves in some way we do not yet understand. They appear to have removed the digitally uploaded intelligences resident within the Etched Cliffs of Heimdall, possibly incorporating them into the matrix of its own intelligence. We may learn more when we investigate recent events within the Sol System."

"In other words, you fled the solar system to avoid being eaten by the Rosette entity," Gray said.

"In order to help find assistance elsewhere. I would be unable to carry out my primary programming as a subroutine within an alien SAI. Nor would it serve our cause to have certain classified information that I possess fall into the control of the Rosette Mind."

"If you are hoping to get Konstantin to admit to cowardice," Sanger said, smiling, "I think you underestimate him."

"I'm not," Gray replied. "I am trying to determine how far we can rely on him."

"I would think, Captain," Konstantin said, "that that should be self-evident by now."

"How do you feel about facing the Rosetter now?"

Konstantin actually hesitated . . . or seemed to. Gray knew the SAI was capable of putting pauses or thoughtful gaps into his speech in order to simulate human emotions. "I am concerned, Captain. For my own continued existence, of course, but more for the survival of the human species. There is no further point in seeking help from Deneb or from Tabby's Star. Therefore, I now can best serve here."

That answer, unsatisfactory as it was, would have to suffice for now.

The conference continued, focusing primarily on the deployment of *Republic*'s fighters . . . and on whether thirty-one fighters could have any appreciable effect on a cloud bigger than Jupiter.

But those were mere tactical matters. The biggest strategic decision to be made was just how to strike at the alien cloud. Should he have *Republic* launch her fighters from out here? But it would take hours for the slower *Republic* to catch up, and the vulnerable fighters would be on their own until then.

He decided. "We will launch all three of our strike squadrons as soon as we can get them ready," he said. "They will attack the cloud and continue to attack until we catch up with them."

"I have to disagree with that approach, Captain," Rohlwing said, leaning back in his chair as he crossed his arms. "We're only going to have one shot at these bastards, and we'll need to make it count. I say we carry the fighters all the way in and hit them with everything we've got all at one time."

Gray gave Rohlwing a hard stare. His executive officer returned it, not quite defiant, but certainly challenging.

"Time," Gray said slowly, "is of the essence here. Our

fighters can reach near-*c* in ten minutes and be over the Earth in less than five hours. It'll take nearly seven hours for the *Republic* to get there, with our slower acceleration rate. I want our fighters in there disrupting that cloud as quickly as possible."

"Captain . . . that could be suicide!"

Gray nodded. "Agreed. It would be suicide in any case, whether we're in there with the fighters or not. But we're going to do our best with what we have available, and I intend to improve our chances."

"How?"

"For a start, we're going to need reinforcements," Gray said with firm patience. "That . . . and a *lot* of luck."

Chapter Sixteen

7 February 2426

VFA-96, Black Demons
Launch Bay One,
TC/USNA CVS Republic
1705 hours, TFT

Lieutenant Gregory had merged with his Starblade's AI, organic mind blending with machine to allow his merely human perception to awaken to things normally beyond the human ken. Five hours after launch, the Black Demons were hurtling toward Earth at a hair below the speed of light, and the view around Gregory's spacecraft had been distorted by his velocity into a fuzzy and brilliant circle of light hanging directly ahead . . . ultraviolet and X-rays and gamma radiation red-shifted into a visible-light starbow. The human brain was unable to make sense of the wildly distorted light; his link with the fighter's sentient but non-conscious brain gave him awareness of the other fighters in the flight, and of the rapidly proliferating number of spacecraft scattered through the volume of space just ahead.

The region around Earth, according to the data, was filled with hundreds of ships: civilian vessels fleeing the planet and military ships moving toward it. He was close enough now that his Starblade was beginning to pick up ID transmissions from human ships outside the alien cloud. The railgun cruisers *San Francisco* and *New York*, the heavy battlecruisers *Kauffman* and *Essex*, the battleships *Ontario* and *Michigan*, twenty-one heavy cruisers including the *Dedalo*, the *Diana*, and the *Champlain* . . .

Gregory had never seen this massive a fleet, heavies brought in from all over the solar system and from other star systems across the light years. At a range of 20 million kilometers, a distance swiftly dwindling, his AI was beginning to pull radio chatter from the static of near-c. Someone on the *New York* was ordering the other ships to form up for an attack on the alien cloud.

"Hey, Skipper!" Gregory called. "I think they're getting ready to throw a hell of a party up there!"

"Copy that, Demon Four," Commander Mackey replied, his voice raspy with static. "Everybody . . . heads up! We have lots of friendlies in there, so tune your sensor gear to wide open and max sensitivity. You clip someone in a near-c pass and it will definitely ruin the day for both of you!"

A chorus of copies and roger-that replies came back. Mackey had been given operational command of all three fighter squadrons—thirty-one fighters in all, with the Demons running short.

The chances of hitting a friendly ship in a flyby were actually pretty low. The icons in Gregory's in-head weren't to scale, and that made the representation of the space surrounding Earth look a hell of a lot more crowded than it actually was. Even the regions in geosynch crowded with orbital habitats and the three slender threads of the space elevators was in fact empty space . . . empty, that is, save for a swirling cloud composed of trillions upon trillions of microscopic alien robots.

Which, of course, the fighters would be *trying* to hit.

"Sixty seconds sub to contact," Mackey warned. "Deploy formation Alpha. Set shields and screens."

That was sixty seconds subjective, as opposed to the objective time of the rest of the universe. At relativistic speeds, time dilation compressed the passage of time. Traveling at 99.5 percent of c, what Gregory could see of his slow-moving surroundings appeared now to be speeded up by almost ten to one.

Now at a range of 180 million kilometers, the squadron was one minute subjective from intercepting the outside edge of the cloud. A thoughtclick strengthened the powerful magnetic fields sheathing the fighters, providing a measure of protection both from impact with the nanobots and from the bursts of radiation each machine would release as it was swept into the singularity's maw.

Time, both objective and subjective, passed.

"Thirty seconds sub to contact," Mackey warned. "Set EHPR to three meters."

Gregory eased the singularity open. The event radius of a gravitational singularity was technically infinite, but its *pseudo*-radius could be described as a finite measurement defining the sphere of the horizon. His fighter's event horizon pseudo-radius, or EHPR, expanded now to an invisible sphere six meters across, large enough to completely shield the fighter behind it. Normally, black holes, artificial or otherwise, were tiny things; the entire Earth collapsed to black-hole size would be a little larger than a pea, and a Starblade fighter manipulated mass and gravitational energies considerably smaller than those of a planet.

But it was possible to open them up.

"Go to full automatic," Mackey ordered.

At a velocity this close to the speed of light, a spacecraft could circle the Earth seven times in one second, and simply passing through the cloud embracing Earth at near-c would be over and done with in less than a half second. There was no way a human mind could cope tactically with combat during a close passage like this. At these velocities, the details had to be left to the hyper-quick reactions and perceptions of the AI, and the human pilot was just along for the ride.

It was enough, Gregory thought with a wry grimace, to make you wonder why a human was crammed into this cocoon of a cockpit at all.

His fighter's AI warned him, an internal urging, to brace for impact. Ahead, in an unmagnified computer-generated view, Earth swiftly expanded from a bright pinpoint to a world, embedded in the alien cloud's haze and surrounded by color-coded icons representing hundreds of vessels.

That last handful of subjective seconds dwindled away.

There was a sharp, sudden shock . . .

. . . and then he was through. External temperatures soared, but the fighter shrugged off most of the searing heat, and the AI finessed the singularity drive to dissipate most of the kinetic force of his impact with the cloud. Instead of vanishing in a nova-flare of friction-generated heat, or being pulped by deceleration as he plowed into the cloud, he was kept more or less intact as the fast-flickering sphere of his drive absorbed most of the kinetic and thermal forces, channeling them safely into the singularity.

Even so, it wasn't an experience Gregory cared to repeat. He felt like he'd just been worked over by an angry, hulking, three-meter Nungiirtok with a length of carballoy pipe. He was bruised, aching, and dizzy, but the nanobots circulating in his bloodstream were already beginning repairs. Studying the cloud astern, he couldn't tell if they'd done any damage to it or not.

He did note that three fighters—one Star Reaper and two Hellfuries—did not emerge from the cloud. There was no data to tell him what had happened. They'd simply flashed into the swarm . . .

. . . and vanished.

Operating according to the meticulously drawn opplan, his Starblade flipped end for end, using its singularity now to decelerate at nearly fifty thousand gravities. Ten minutes later, Gregory's velocity had dropped to zero relative to the Earth, and he began accelerating toward the planet once again.

"Unidentified squadron!" a voice came in over Gregory's in-head. "This is Railgun cruiser *New York*. Who the hell are you and where the hell did you come from?"

"*New York*, this is VFA-96," Mackey replied. "With us are VFA-90 and VFA-198. We're off the CVL *Republic*."

"*Republic*! Wait one . . ."

All spacecraft, including fighters, carried transponders to identify them to friendly spacecraft. Those ID transmissions were masked and quantum-encrypted to prevent enemies from hacking them, and it took a few moments for the two networks to begin speaking with one another.

"Okay, Nine-Six," the comm officer on board the *New York* said. "We confirm your handshake. Welcome home!"

"Thank you, *New York*. I take it you don't mind some help?"

"Not in the least! We're just now putting together a strike to see if we can dislodge these Rosette bastards."

"Transmitting our opplan now," Mackey told them. "Let us know if you want us somewhere else instead."

"Roger that. Where's the *Republic*?"

"Following us, about an hour out. We're pulling a standard slash-and-bash."

"Slash-and-bash" was pilot's slang for the basic fighter tactic in which a fleet's fighters would be sent ahead at near-c to flash past an enemy target, mauling it as thoroughly as possible in passing. Using missiles and energy beams, kinetic-kill weapons, and anything else available, they would inflict the maximum damage possible, flying past the target before turning around and repeating the maneuver. They would keep on hammering the target at lower and lower velocities until the main fleet finally brought up the rear and proceeded to take out the survivors.

This time there was only the *Republic* to follow them in, but a sizeable human fleet was already maneuvering through the target area, preparing to attack.

Gregory was damned grateful for the support.

Accelerating hard for several minutes, the Black Demons built back up to nearly 0.25 c. "Okay, people!" Mackey called out to all three squadrons. "Now let's see how playing dodge-the-dustball with these guys works. Kill your flickers!"

Gregory switched off his fighter's drive cycling. The drive singularity remained projected out in front of his Starblade, but it was no longer switching rapidly on and off, which meant his ship was no longer accelerating. He plowed into the cloud, and for a long, jolting second, he swept through the alien swarm, his singularity growing swiftly brighter as it inhaled the Rosette swarm robots, swallowing some, radiating others as an intense burst of radiation.

"Madre de Dios!" a voice screamed over the squadron channel—Lieutenant Hernán Garcia. "I'm losing it!"

"Garcia! Kill your drive!" Mackey called back. "Kill your—"

Gregory caught part of what happened on his AI's scan. Garcia's drive singularity, loaded with mass and artificially puffed out to a far larger pseudo-radius than it could hold naturally, flared; his Starblade flipped around the glowing sphere of radiation, grazed it, and in an instant crumpled into oblivion . . . *gone.*

Out into the clear once more. Skew-turn . . . and accelerate, his drive sphere now flickering again, passing its load of trashed Rosetter machines along from iteration to iteration as it moved. Boosting to a hundredth of c, he released the sphere, which hurtled away at three thousand kilometers per second, dropping deeper into the cloud like a dazzling blue-white star, continuing to feed as it moved. Moments later, the sphere destabilized and soundlessly exploded, the blast searing billions more swarm 'bots in its flare.

He switched on his cycler and accelerated, heading for the cloud once more. Flashes continued going off within the cloud in front of them as the weaponized drive singularities detonated.

Though it appeared random, the attack was following precisely designed trajectories and approach vectors, each close passage, each released dustball tracing a calculated path into the heart of the cloud—a path deemed by the combat AIs to take out the maximum number of enemy 'bots, to do the greatest amount of damage.

Two pilots failed to emerge from the cloud—Garcia and one other: Lieutenant Boyle, one of the Star Reapers.

While he felt both losses, Gregory had *known* Garcia. He wasn't just a name on the duty roster; Gregory had sat next to him at the midday meal in the mess hall . . . had gone on liberty with him more than once . . . had enjoyed late-night bull sessions with the guy, talking about star gods and weird physics and the nature of reality. He wondered if Garcia had been killed by some weapon of the enemy or by his overstressed drive going critical . . . and decided it scarcely mattered. Hernán was *dead*.

One more friend, gone.

According to his AI, the attack was causing a degradation of the Rosette network. It wasn't much—maybe 2 percent—but it was *something*, a subtle loss in the amount of data being trafficked around inside the cloud. Several of the capital ships were closing now to the cloud's edge, slashing at it with particle beams and high-energy lasers and the detonation of powerful nuclear warheads.

The Chinese heavy bombardment monitor *Hunan*, Gregory saw, was maneuvering closer, at the very fringe of the cloud. Portions of the flanks behind her shield cap blossomed open like the petals of a huge, silvery flower . . . and then clouds of missiles streaked into the cloud, each twisting into a different vector, aiming for those spots identified by the tactical AIs as key nodes within the Rosette cloud.

A constellation of bright new stars winked on across the depths of the cloud, each one a nuclear detonation of some hundreds of megatons.

Something like an oval mass of separate geometric shapes took form within those hazy depths, flowing, as billions upon untold billions of nanomachines came together. Gregory couldn't tell what the thing was, exactly—ship or fortress or something else entirely—but it was enormous . . . the size of a small continent. It rose swiftly and effortlessly from within the cloud toward the *Hunan*, which was now frantically trying to pile on the Gs and escape.

The Chinese monitor *almost* made it.

The ovoid shape was still ten thousand kilometers away from the *Hunan* when the Chinese vessel shuddered, rolling hard to port . . . then crumpled away as though relentlessly crushed by an unseen hand.

"Target that alien ship!" Mackey called . . . but the monster vessel was already thinning . . . evaporating as the nanobots making up its substance streamed off into space and resumed their separate existences. A dozen capital ships were firing into the cloud, now, from just outside, and the fighters off the *Republic* had joined in, sending salvo after salvo of nuclear warheads into the gray haze ahead. Pinpoints of light twinkled and flashed in those sinister depths . . . but the cloud was so vast, no amount of nuclear hammering, it seemed, could do it serious harm.

The Chinese Hegemony carrier *Guangdong* was releasing a stream of fighters—sleek and deadly *Taikong Ying*, their newly developed Space Eagles. Fighters were still launching when the invisible fist crunched the carrier's shield cap into a tiny, crumpled ruin within a vast and expanding cloud of silvery droplets of water quick freezing into ice.

"The Rosetters are aiming for the largest ships," Gregory called. "Tell them to pull the caps back!"

The forward half of the powerful Russian heavy cruiser *Varyag* was smashed into wreckage; a second later the rest of the cruiser crumpled as well. Gregory couldn't tell how the enemy was pulling that off, but he suspected the Rosetters were somehow directly collapsing small volumes of spacetime and trapping the human vessels, or pieces of them, in the crunch.

"They know," Mackey replied. "But they have to get in close . . . and so do we! Form up, everyone! We're gonna hit 'em again!"

Other fighters, Gregory noticed, were joining the strike squadrons off of the *Republic*. There were the *Taikong Ying* off of the crushed *Guangdong*, a number of tactical fighters from several Marine transports orbiting farther out, Russian *Skora* fighters off the light carrier *Putin*, and several mixed-bag squadrons that had come up from Earth. In all, according to Gregory's AI, some four hundred fighters of various types were assembling in local space. The *New York* had transmitted the VFA-96 opplan, and the fighter AIs were electronically tagging one another, creating a unified combat network.

"*Once more unto the breach, dear friends . . .*" Mackey called out with a melodramatic cry. His fighter accelerated hard, leading the way as fighter after fighter fell in behind him in formation. Gregory thought he recognized the quote and pulled it up in his personal RAM. Yeah, he'd thought so . . . Shakespeare's *Henry V.* Unbidden, the next line caught his inner eye, nagging: *Or close the wall up with our English dead.*

Lovely thought with which to engage a seemingly invulnerable enemy . . .

He accelerated, holding his Starblade on course as the Rosetter haze again closed around him. This time he was moving at only a few tens of kilometers per second as he entered the cloud. There was a shock . . . and his hull temperature began climbing, but not to the same extent as his earlier passages. Beams and planes and whole alien geometries of light flared around him . . . the enigmatic evidence of an utterly alien science and technology. Ahead, pinpoints of light flickered and strobed as the human fleet continued its relentless bombardment. Most of his view forward was still obscured by the swollen event horizon of his drive singularity, but at non-relativistic speeds his surroundings were not crammed into a circle of light ahead, and he could see what was happening around him.

He plunged deeper, and the dark closed in around him.

TC/USNA CVS America
CIC
Within the Rosette Cloud
Time and date uncertain

Captain Sara Gutierrez stared out into the darkness. Those stars were . . . *new.*

She was floating in *America*'s combat information center, studying a display that filled one bulkhead from deck to overhead. For days, the ship's external optical scanners had picked up only a dark gray and utterly opaque haze.

But now . . .

According to the ship's clock, they'd been trapped inside the Rosette cloud for six hours, but the ship's AI had managed to get a fix on navigational beacons on the moon. With the cloud enshrouding them they couldn't see the Earth at all, much less the moon, and the radio signals were filtered down to a whisper of their usual strength.

Still, the AI had picked up enough to report that time had somehow been drastically distorted within the cloud's depths, probably by a factor of something like twenty-eight to one. It had also recorded voice transmissions from outside the cloud, estimating that they were speeded up by the same factor . . . confirmation that a full week had passed since *America* had entered the cloud.

Their AI had also managed to filter signals from Earth and from several of the synchorbital habitats, showing that they were also within a field of severely distorted space-time. Transmissions they'd picked up from Earth's surface seemed slower and more drawn out compared to life on board the *America* by a factor of nearly one hundred to one.

Evidently, the deeper into the cloud you went, the more the passage of time was slowed.

What made it worse was the knowledge that *America* seemed to be moving through the temporal field, which meant that the degree of distortion changed constantly. The ship's physics department could estimate that a week had passed since their capture but could not give her a precise figure.

But where time was fluid, space here was not. *America* remained stuck in place by unimaginable forces, trapped like an ancient insect frozen in amber.

And there was not a thing in the universe Gutierrez or her crew could do to change that.

At least, she thought, they were now certain that the cloud had moved them from the asteroid belt in close to Earth. They couldn't actually see the planet . . . but snippets of radio transmissions picked up by *America*'s scanners, both from Earth and from the moon, had proven this to be the case.

But what the hell were those stars?

"What are you staring at so hard, Captain?" Dean Mallory said, floating up behind her.

"Those stars, Commander. They weren't there a moment ago."

"For an undefined value of the term *moment*," Mallory replied. He sounded angry. The inaction, she decided, was gnawing at him.

The stars in question had only just appeared a moment ago. There were three of them spaced within a couple of degrees of one another, and they were small and dim. They were not real stars, of course. The ship's AI had almost immediately pointed out that they had appeared out of darkness in the same direction as the invisible Earth, and so must lie between Earth and the trapped star carrier. Slowly, *very* slowly, they were growing brighter.

"Computer," Mallory said. "Give us an analysis of those stars."

"They are *not* stars, Commander," the computer replied.

"We *know* that," Mallory snapped. "Tell us what we don't know!"

"Analysis of the light indicates that they are thermonuclear detonations within roughly fifty thousand kilometers of our current position, but red-shifted by the effects of the temporal distortion."

"Thermonuclear—" He stopped, the surprise clear on his face. "Who's shooting?"

"Unknown, Commander."

A fourth star appeared in the darkness, and then a fifth, both barely visible to the naked eye.

"Wait," Mallory said. He looked like he was having trouble wrapping his brain around the concept. "We're seeing . . ." He stopped, then shook his head. "I don't get it. Nuclear fireballs dissipate pretty quickly."

"If I had to guess, Commander," Gutierrez said, "I'd say that either someone outside the cloud is bombarding the Rosetter entity . . . or the missiles are coming up from Earth. In either case, they're going off much deeper within the cloud than our current position . . . so we're seeing them in slow motion."

"We are picking up the opposite manifestation of the temporal field on the other side of the ship," the AI told them.

"Show us," Gutierrez said.

The cloud was as darkly opaque on the starboard side of the ship as to port, and at first Gutierrez thought there was nothing to see in that direction but the darkness. However, as she stared into the display, she became aware of a faint but insistent flickering, as if hundreds of minute points of light were flashing on and off.

"More nukes?" she asked the AI. "We're seeing nukes speeded up by the field?"

"Precisely, Captain. I estimate that most of the visible flashes are fusion fireballs with yields of between one hundred and three hundred megatons, and that they represent an extremely heavy bombardment of the Rosetter cloud by human forces outside the alien cloud."

"Son of a bitch!" Mallory said in a shaky whisper.

"It's nice to know we haven't been abandoned," Gutierrez said.

"They probably don't know our precise position, Captain," Mallory replied. "How could they? They may not even be aware that we survived after the cloud swallowed us."

Gutierrez grinned. She felt a touch manic . . . but passed it off as a natural reaction to the knowledge that someone *was* trying to fight the cloud. "What's the matter, Commander? Afraid of a little friendly fire?"

"The first rule of combat, Captain," Mallory replied. "Friendly fire isn't."

"I'm just delighted to see that someone outside is taking an interest, Commander."

"Computer!" Mallory called. "How far away are those blasts?"

"It is quite difficult to give a precise answer, Commander," the AI replied, "without precise data on the absorptive properties of the cloud. However, I estimate that those explosions are taking place throughout a volume of circum-Terran space between ten thousand and one hundred fifty thousand kilometers."

"Slow down the display rate," Gutierrez ordered, "by a factor of twenty-eight. And highlight the flashes for me."

"Very well, Captain."

Immediately, the rapid-fire flickering slowed to a more stately succession of silent detonations against the night. With the computer AI enhancing the image, she could see the blasts as rapidly expanding disks of light, growing larger . . . then fading away.

"What are you looking for, Captain?" Mallory asked her.

"I want a feel for the pace of that bombardment. It's pretty fierce."

"Yes . . ."

She looked at her tactical officer. "What does it tell you?"

"Well . . . I don't think they're just trading potshots with the Rosetters. They might be trying to open up a hole in the alien defenses. . . ."

"If that were the case, Commander, they would be focusing their bombardment in one area, not lighting up half the sky."

His eyes widened. "You're right. They're following some sort of plan, there."

"We've already guessed that the Rosetter cloud is an entity. Like a single vast brain, with the equivalent of neural pathways running through its substance."

"And the bombardment is trying to cut some of those pathways! That's brilliant!"

"Computer." She indicated a part of the display directly in front of them. "Enlarge this section, please."

That part of the display enlarged. With it magnified, they could see much tinier, steadier stars moving across the display.

"Entry trails?" Mallory said, hazarding a guess. "Fighters burning through the cloud particles?"

"In a way. I think those are fighters, yeah . . . and they're using their singularity drives as . . . as snow plows, scooping up the Rosetter particles."

"Which would fit the idea of trying to disrupt their neural network," Mallory said, nodding.

"Exactly. CAG!"

"Here, Captain," Connie Fletcher replied in her head.

"I want all fighters prepped for immediate launch." *America* had managed to recover all of her fighters launched six hours . . . no, damn it, *seven days* ago. There was no point in sending fighters out into that temporal nightmare outside, knowing that the farther they moved out from the *America*, the more time they might gain or lose relative to *America*'s clocks. Better to keep them all on board and aging at the same rate.

But if a major attack was shaping up outside the cloud, *America*'s fighters just might be able to lend a hand. The single major problem was that difference in time rates. By the time *America*'s squadrons could scramble and launch, the attack outside might already be over.

But Gutierrez knew that they had to try.

"Two squadrons are ready for immediate launch," Fletcher told her. "The rest . . . five more minutes."

Five minutes in here would be two hours and twenty-some minutes out there.

"Launch what you can, Connie," Gutierrez told her. "Send the rest after them when they come on-line."

"Copy that. Beginning to drop the Headhunters into the black now."

"Have them try to make contact with the main fleet," Gutierrez told her. "They'll be working to an opplan with specific objectives, maybe specific vectors in mind. We want to work toward those goals, whatever they are."

"Understood, Captain."

"And God help us all. . . ."

Chapter Seventeen

7 February 2426

VFA-96, Black Demons
Near Earth Space
1732 hours, TFT

Gregory's fighter drifted above the pall of alien cloud enshrouding a hidden Earth. Eight times, now, the three *Republic* squadrons had penetrated the alien cloud and re-emerged. There were only five Black Demons remaining now . . . only nine Hellfuries, only seven Star Reapers. Gregory felt as though he'd been reduced to an automaton, going through the prescribed motions, reacting to threats, carrying out the dictates of training, but with all emotions throttled down to a dulled sense of detached awareness.

He was exhausted, the stress of the past hours dragging at him like the high-G hunger of a black hole. How much longer would this, *could* this go on?

The strain was showing on all of the Starblade pilots. Warshots were limited and being rationed. Gregory was down to his last five missiles: four Kraits and one VG-120 Boomslang. The fighters were hoarding their remaining few Boomslangs, mostly for fear of scoring an accidental own goal on the synchorbital facilities deep within the cloud or, worse, on Earth itself. But as they chewed through their dwindling munitions stores they'd became more and more picky about their shots, reserving them for the titanic structures and engineering lying within the murk rather than turning them on the cloud itself. Soon, their only available weapons would be beam weapons—less than highly effective against the microbots making up the alien cloud—and, of course, the jury-rig expedient of the fighter drive singularities.

Gregory wasn't sure that plowing contrails through the giant alien brain along twisting and crisscrossing vectors was having any effect whatsoever. Glowing shapes continued to form or dissolve all around them, continued to loom out of the darkness with inscrutable menace, continued to conduct and direct titanic energies of unknown purpose. Human ships continued to vanish above the cloud, crushed down into microscopic specks by unseen but irresistible forces projected from the cloud's heart.

"CC says we have a clear way all the way in," Mackey called to what was left of the squadron. "Bearing three-one-five by minus seven-one, eighty-five kps. Form up on me and stay tight!"

"CC" was shorthand for combat command—essentially the military staff on board the railgun cruiser *New York*, and, in effect, a direct reference to President Koenig. The *New York* had access to a far bigger picture than did the *Republic* fighters, and they could coordinate the ongoing attacks against the Rosetter cloud. For several long minutes, now, the tacticians on board the *New York* had been coordinating a planned strike deep within the central realm of the Rosetter brain. Missiles launched both by the fighters and by the gathered fleet of capital ships outside the cloud had been precisely targeted, gradually focusing in on clearing a pathway through the murk and into the cloud's center.

Lieutenant Gregory adjusted his course slightly to match

the new vector, holding his position in the wedge-shaped Starblade formation. The dark clouds opened ahead to receive them, and they hurtled in, plunging now through a roiling tunnel of night. That tunnel was strangely illuminated with the ongoing Rosetter light show, and flashes of light, like vast fields of lightning, continued to edge the clouds with short-lived highlights of quicksilver.

"Everyone switch on your transponders," Mackey ordered. "They need to track us outside the cloud."

"Where the hell are we going?" Lieutenant Caswell called. "I can't see a damned thing in this soup."

"We're going to take a close pass by SupraQuito," Mackey replied. "CC wants to know if we have survivors in there."

"What do we do if we find them?" Gregory asked. "It's not like we can pack everybody on board our fighters and evac them out of there!"

"One damned thing at a time," Mackey replied. "See if they're in there and what's happened to them and worry about what to do about them later."

Deeper into the cloud . . . and deeper . . . and still deeper.

"Hey . . . Commander?"

"What is it, Don?"

"The back transmission from the *New York*. It's dopplering!"

"I've got that too," Caswell added. "Like we're entering an intense gravitational field!"

"Roger that. We're confirming the Rosie temporal field."

Of course. Gregory didn't know how they were pulling it off, but somehow the deeper they went into the cloud, the more time was being warped, slowed from the point of view of ships outside the cloud. Everything felt normal in the cockpit, and his chronometers were running normally, but time here was moving at a snail's pace. The only way to accurately measure this was to use the radio transmissions between the fighters and the ships outside. From Gregory's point of view, the *New York* was speeding up. From the

New York's vantage point, the fighters appeared to be slowing down.

How far, he wondered, would this go?

His fighter's AI alerted him to a new target. When he saw the mass readings, he blinked . . . then opened a private channel to Mackey. "Hey, Commander!"

"Go ahead, Don."

"I'm getting a reading at one-five-nine by plus seven-three. You see it?"

"Negative. I've got . . . wait a sec. Yes. At the extreme range of my sensors. My God . . ."

"That mass figure . . ."

"Nine hundred fifteen thousand, eight hundred tons. Almost precisely the mass of an *America* class star carrier with a shield cap full of water and her power-tap microsingularities engaged."

"You think it's the *America*?"

"The word from *New York* was that *America* got swallowed by this damned cloud a week ago. None of her sister ships are in-system. What do you think?"

"That you've spotted the *America*."

"We should check her out, Skipper."

"I'm thinking . . ."

"No, sir! We've *got* to check her out! If she's still operational, maybe we can bust her out of here!"

"Okay . . . I've just been given a tactical advisory by the *New York*," Mackey told the squadrons. "They'd like to know if that really is the *America* . . . but they don't want us to risk all three squadrons. We need to get a recon flight in there and check it out. Free her if we can . . ."

"If there's anything left to free," Caswell added.

"Volunteers only," Mackey said. "You can hang back if you want."

"The hell with *that*," Caswell replied. "A chief in *America*'s maintenance department owes me money!"

Mackey arrived at a decision. "You game, Gregory?"

Gregory was surprised to find out that he was. His depression, it seemed, had burned away in the intense minutes of combat over the past hour, leaving him exhausted . . . but determined to see this through.

A chance to save the *America* and everyone on board . . . assuming they were still alive.

"I'm in, Commander."

"Okay. Caswell. And . . . who else?"

"Me, sir," Tanner snapped back. Like Caswell, Lieutenant Edward Tanner was one of the Black Demon newbies.

"Ballinger? Lewis?"

"Yessir!" The two were with VFA-90, the Star Reapers.

"Okay! I'm attaching you all to Lieutenant Gregory. He's in charge. The five of you veer off and check out this contact."

The coordinates for the presumed star carrier appeared in Gregory's mind. They were over fifty thousand kilometers ahead, outside of synchorbit but not by much. "Right, gang," he called. "Goose it!"

Veering to starboard, they immediately plunged back into the particulate cloud, and Gregory's Starblade began shuddering and bucking once more as it left the confines of the clear-swept tunnel. His drive singularity flared as it plowed ahead through the murk.

He increased his speed. . . .

His hull temperature soared as he streaked deeper into the cloud.

TC/USNA CVS America
CIC
Within the Rosette Cloud
Time and date uncertain

"Captain!" Commander Mallory called. "Hard to be certain . . . but I think we have fighters approaching on a direct intercept course!"

"Ours or theirs, Commander?" Captain Gutierrez said, looking up from her personal screen.

"I don't think the Rosies bother with fighters, ma'am. There's a hell of a lot of interference . . . but I make it three . . . no . . . make that four fighters. Starblades, I think."

"Comm! Open a channel to those singleships!"

"Working on it, Captain. There's a lot of static. . . ."

"Helm! Do we have power yet?"

"No, Captain," Keating replied. "Something about this cloud is sucking power away as fast as we can make it. We have life support and station-keeping . . . and that's about it."

"Damn."

Gutierrez wasn't at all sure why the Rosetters were simply holding them here, when it would be so easy to reach out and crush the star carrier like a toy. That, she thought with a grim smile, was the problem with working with super-powerful alien entities. Their methods, their reasoning, their reasons for doing anything were utterly inscrutable, utterly *alien* in every sense of the word.

But in the meantime, *America* continued to drop her fighters, seeds planted within the Void. The hab modules containing her flight decks and launch bays were still rotating once every twenty-eight seconds—the power that kept them going part of the ship's life support systems—and so the fighters could be flung into space through the agency of the centrifugal force generating the modules' spin gravity. All that was needed was to release the magnetic grapples holding the fighters in place and kill the nanofields at the outer ends of the drop tubes, and the fighters slid gently into space at five meters per second.

Gutierrez hated sending single-seat fighters out into that night, though. The nightmare darkness enshrouding *America* and the Earth were terrifying in their implied power and technology.

So far, the Rosetters had done little but keep them there, prisoners of advanced technologies both invisible and overwhelming in their scope and power. Gutierrez wondered what single-seat fighters could do from inside the Rosetters' time field. That twenty-eight-to-one differential put the carrier, already hampered by the aliens' near-magical technological superiority, at an overwhelming disadvantage.

The moral of the story, she thought, was that it just didn't pay to fight against the gods.

Nevertheless, Gutierrez knew they had to try.

VFA-211
Within the Rosette Cloud
Time and date uncertain

"Hunter Three, take point," Commander Leystrom ordered.

"Copy," Jason Meier replied, accelerating his Starblade. "Moving to twelve."

He adjusted his position . . . and Lieutenant Karen Lobieski's fighter drifted into the wing position, to starboard and just a little astern. The *America*, he realized with a start, had already vanished astern . . . lost in the pea-soup haze.

Cloud microparticles clattered off his hull, and the temperature of his outer skin began to climb. He considered opening up his drive singularity, expanding its protective shield of light, but decided against it. Puffing up the singularity too much could cause its event horizon to go unstable, and he did *not* need to have his drive fail out here. *America*'s SAR vessels could search for him out here for a year and not see him in this murk.

Meier led the way up through the cloud, his AI stretching out with all of its superhuman senses to connect with the fighters approaching from outside. Communicating with them was impossible at this point. The differences in time frames distorted electromagnetic frequencies, both radio and laser com, and the cloud itself created interference, reducing transmissions to static.

Within the interference, diamond-hard, lay another signal . . . something seeming to materialize out of the endless mist. The fighter's AI sketched out its rough dimensions and image in his mind . . . a flattened sphere or ovoid the size of Earth's moon, 3,500 kilometers across, blocking the way a few thousand kilometers ahead. The shape appeared translucent . . . and made of light.

"Pull up!" Meier yelled over the tactical channel, slewing his fighter sharply around his drive field. "Hunters, pull up!"

And in that same instant, two of the Starblades in his squadron were crushed into oblivion.

VFA-96, VFA-90
Near Earth Space
1742 hours, TFT

Gregory saw the translucent spheroid seem to materialize out of light directly ahead, and knew that the Rosetters had just drawn a line in the metaphorical sand.

And he knew he and the four Starblades with him were going to have to cross that line to reach the *America.*

"What is that?" he asked his fighter's AI. "Some kind of warship?"

"The Rosette entity does not seem to think in terms of warships or weaponry," his AI replied. "It manifests specific tools to address specific tasks."

"Okay . . . so what kind of *tool* is the size of Earth's moon?"

"The indicated structure is probably more like one of our heavy monitors, with no drive and minimal maneuvering capability. Infrared and mass-gravitometric data suggests that it is being used to immobilize one of our star carriers."

"America . . ."

"Unknown. But the mass of the unidentified vessel beyond this structure—"

"I know! I know! How can we take this thing out?"

"Total destruction of the target is probably not possible with the weaponry on hand."

"Screw *that*!" Gregory thought about the problem for a

moment. "Okay people!" he called over the tactical channel. "Listen up! Everyone arm all remaining VG-120s, dial 'em up to maximum yield, and slave them to my AI!"

A chorus of acknowledgments came back. The readout inside Gregory's head showed a total of six VG-120 Boomslangs remaining among five fighters.

It wasn't much, but it would have to do.

"Computer! We're going to try to pile drive this volley. One on top of the other."

"Affirmative. With what goal?"

"To punch a hole through that thing . . . all the way through if we can manage it."

"That seems unlikely, Lieutenant."

"Yeah, but maybe we can disrupt the hell out of whatever that thing uses for guts."

"Program complete and running."

"Targeting!" Gregory called, arming his last Boomslang. "And . . . Fox One!"

The missile slid from its ventral launch bay, drive flaring in the thick mist. He slowed his fighter and shifted his vector a bit to the right and high.

"Fox One!" Tanner yelled, and a second VG-120 Boomslang hurtled into darkness.

"C'mon! All of you!" Gregory called to the entire flight. "Pour it on! No holding back!"

Four more Boomslangs streaked through the cloud as the Starblades loosed the last of their VG-120s.

"That does it for us," Lieutenant Gary Ballinger, of the Reapers, called. "We've got a few Kraits on the rails, but that's the last of the heavies."

"Copy that," Gregory replied. "It'll be worth it . . ."

If, he added silently to himself, *it works*.

Gregory's VG-120 passed through the outer surface of the sphere as though it was insubstantial, plunging a hundred kilometers in behind the dazzling star of its drive singularity. When it detonated, the silent flash lit up the surrounding clouds and mist like a small and swiftly fading sun.

Because Gregory's VG-120 had not gone off in hard vacuum, but in a kind of thin atmosphere of micromachine particles. The initial explosion vaporized hundreds of millions of those machines, sending out a shock wave roiling through the expanding wall of star-hot plasma.

Tanner's Boomslang entered the blast front hard on the energy wake of Gregory's missile, punching through the plasma wall and streaking across the relatively empty interior of a brilliant sphere growing inside the far larger Rosetter structure. Punching through the opposite side, it continued deep into the structure before detonating seconds later.

A savage cavity had been ripped from the side of the alien structure. The rest of the missiles continued in-line, exploding in utter silence one after the next, the blasts stacking up, boring a cone-shaped tunnel with white-hot walls in and down through the center of the alien structure.

And as the last denotation flashed and opened like a blossoming flower of flame, the five Starblade fighters entered the Rosette structure through the gaping maw burned open by Gregory's Boomslang.

Around them, on every side, aurorae flared and shifted along the cloud's edges as charged particles whipped through intense and shifting magnetic fields. The structure was still channeling light through its translucent inner geometries . . . but in fits and starts as portions of the internal structure failed and winked out. Gregory's fighter shuddered as it slammed into patches of distorted space . . . but the alien sphere appeared to be falling apart, its internal structure dissolving, its light dimming, flaring briefly, and then dying.

"Free singularity!" Ed Tanner yelled. "I've got a free singularity at two-seven-four by plus nine-five!"

Gregory pulled up an enhanced view of the indicated portion of the sky. Highlighted within red brackets thrown up by his Starblade's AI, he could see the tiniest of bright white pinpoints . . . a minute star.

Okay . . . he'd been expecting this, or something like it. Different people had been describing the Rosetter cloud as having both the mass and the diameter of the gas giant Jupiter . . . but it couldn't possibly be both. The interior of the Rosetter cloud was a thin gas, far thinner than Earth's atmosphere at sea level, while Jupiter was so dense that its core had been compacted by its own gravity into what amounted to a solid mass of metallic hydrogen.

The only way to reconcile the Rosetter's stats with those of the planet was if the cloud included masses that had been compressed into such tiny volumes that they were microscopic. The Rosetter might be as big across as Jupiter, but most of its mass was squeezed into gravitational anomalies of microscopic size.

Human starships used artificial singularities the size of protons to suck energy from the vacuum. When a ship was destroyed, those singularities remained, deadly missiles to any other ships that might hit them. Fortunately, they evaporated quickly in open space.

The Rosetter's mini-black holes posed substantial danger to human ships and to Earth itself. This one, fortunately, appeared to be moving out and away from the planet with a velocity of fifteen kilometers per second, well above escape velocity . . . but there were certainly others.

Mass readings showed that this black hole contained roughly the mass of the entire Earth, compressed in volume down to an object less than a centimeter across.

"AI!" Gregory said in-head. "Extrapolate that object's course and warn the fleet outside."

"Affirmative."

The interior of the sphere, meanwhile, carved out by the string of nuclear explosions, had taken on the appearance of some titanic Gothic cathedral, with expanding wisps of gas standing in for arches and vaults and sculpted galleries, the whole bathed in rich blue and white and golden light. A blessed silence engulfed him as he moved through space evacuated by the blasts moments before. Then he struck the far wall, his drive flared brilliantly, and his Starblade again bucked and shuddered with the impact of the minute, drifting machines.

"We *killed* it!" Lieutenant Caswell yelled over the tactical channel, exultant. "We fuckin' killed it!"

"Maybe that was the brain of the thing!" Tanner added. "Ya think maybe? . . ."

"Don't worry about it," Gregory told them. "Hold your vector! Let's just get through this thing and out the other side!"

The alien sphere had indeed been destroyed, Gregory thought, but if the Rosette entity could think, it used its entire mass for the process, a single, titanic brain. That sphere might have been some sort of local control node, but it was 3,500 kilometers across compared to the entire entity's diameter, which was forty times greater. The destruction of the translucent sphere had been a pinprick in terms of actual damage to the larger structure.

But there was no denying that the Rosette entity had been *hurt*.

TC/USNA CVS America
CIC
Within the Rosette Cloud
Time and date uncertain

"Captain!" her helm officer cried as the carrier jolted. "We're *free*!"

"Free how? What's happened?"

"Still trying to figure that one out, Captain," Mallory told her.

But Gutierrez was already in conversation with *America*'s AI, an echo of the larger and more powerful Konstantin.

"Our sensors picked up a string of six powerful nuclear detonations bisecting the alien structure holding us here," the AI told her, "coming toward us from the far side of the object. I believe those five fighters we've detected punched a hole through the alien object and forced the Rosetter to release us."

"Forced it how?"

"The spherical object incorporated both artificial singularities and unknown technologies that fold and distort empty space. Those fighters caused enough disruption to flatten out the distortions and release the singularities. The Rosetter's ability to bend space has been interrupted, at least temporarily. It may be having trouble channeling data as well."

"Well, it won't take them long to come up with a response. Keating! Get us under way! Full power!"

"Aye, aye, Captain. It'll take us a few moments to bring the power taps up to full output. . . ."

Slowly, ponderously, the star carrier began sliding forward, accelerating through the surrounding cloud of alien artificial mist.

"Our shield cap is heating up, Captain," Keating told her. "Friction with the . . . the local atmosphere."

Star carriers like the kilometer-long *America* had never been intended for maneuvers inside an atmosphere, even an atmosphere as thin as this one. The faster the great ship moved forward, the more the microscopic Rosetter machines smashed themselves against the slightly curved five-hundred-meter surface of the ship's protective shieldcap.

"Can you boost the shields?"

"Not enough to handle *this* stuff."

America possessed both positively and negatively charged fields designed to shunt aside stray particles as she moved through space, and they could be used as protection against some types of beam weapons and even against micrometeorites . . . but they could do little against this incoming tide of dust-speck machines.

"CAG!" Gutierrez called. "Have our fighters join up with those people out there. Suggest that they vector toward SupraQuito."

There would be a number of warships there, probably trapped as *America* had been.

"Aye, aye, Captain."

"Helm . . . do we have nav beacons for the elevator spacedocks?"

"That we do, Captain. Signals are kind of ragged . . . but I see them. Range . . . make it forty-five thousand kilometers."

"Then take us in close, Mr. Keating."

"Coming to zero-three-five by minus eight-seven, Captain. Aye, aye!"

Like a vast whale drifting weightless through shadowed seas, *America* ponderously shifted onto the new course.

Chapter Eighteen

VFA-96, VFA-90
Near Earth Space
1752 hours, TFT

Gregory's flight arrowed toward a much larger formation of fighters, decelerating sharply, flipping end-for-end to match course and speed.

"Welcome aboard," a voice said in his head. "This is Commander Leystrom, VFA-211, star carrier *America*. Who are you guys?"

"We're off the *Republic*," Gregory replied, "and you have no idea how good it is to see you!"

"Oh, I think I can take a guess at that," Leystrom replied. "The feeling is definitely mutual!"

"Copy that. What can we do to help?"

"*America*'s CIC is suggesting that we head over to Supra-Quito and have a look-see. You in?"

"Abso-damn-lutely, sir. Lead the way."

When the two flights were close enough to share interference-free data links, Gregory opened the necessary channels and put his tiny command under Leystrom's much larger flight. Altogether, Leystrom was bossing twenty fighters, likely half of *America*'s entire complement of strike fighters, and Gregory's flight now brought that up to twenty-five.

"I'm designating this mob as Eagle Flight," Leystrom said. "Okay? Now let's get our asses down to SupraQuito and see what we can do."

TC/USNA CVS Republic
Sol System
1759 hours, TFT

"Captain!" the comm officer said in Gray's head. "I have Fleet Admiral Reeve for you."

"Reeve?" He'd been the CO of the USNA contingent on the moon.

"Force commander, on board the *New York*!"

"Put him through."

Static hissed in Gray's head, then cleared. "*Republic*! Is that really you? You're back way earlier than we expected!"

"It's us, Admiral. As for being back early . . . long story. You see some of our fighters come through here?"

"That we did, Captain. Kind of hard to get a clear picture . . . but we think they just released *America* from some sort of trap."

"Hello, Captain," another voice, a familiar one, joined Reeve inside Gray's mind.

"*Mr. President?*" Yes, of *course* it was Koenig. Gray could see the ID data writing itself on his in-head. "What are you doing on the *New York*?"

"Couldn't stay away. It looks as though our former command has just been released by your fighters." Koenig had once been the commanding officer of the star carrier *America*, as—much later—had Gray.

"Outstanding. So . . . where do you want us?"

Data flowed into *Republic*'s network. On Koenig's orders, the human forces were advancing into the Rosetter cloud on a number of fronts, seeking to disrupt the alien brain. Reeve's orders called for newly arriving ships to push in toward the SupraQuito facility . . . but to try to stay beyond the reach of the alien gravity weapons.

Long-range sensors had picked up a number of Rosetter light structures within the cloud, somehow projecting gravitational anomalies up and out into the human fleet. A thousand kilometers away, the battleship *Michigan* trembled and wavered as though in a heavy wind, then slowly rolled to port. A moment later, she began crumpling inward, compacting, crushed as though by an enormous fist.

The Pan-European heavy monitor *Festung* had positioned herself just above the outer fringes of the alien cloud, skimming above the alien swarm, releasing volley upon volley of heavy missiles into the cloud's depths. Somewhere within the cloud, energies arose . . . strengthened . . . reached out . . . and the *Festung* staggered in her orbit, crumpling under the compression of some millions of gravities.

"Weapons!" Gray called. "Target those . . . those glowing shapes in there! Break them up!"

"Aye, aye, Captain. Targeting . . . AIs engaged and locked . . . missiles away!"

Republic carried a supply of Boomslang missiles and other heavy weaponry designed for planetary bombardment. A dozen of those monsters streaked from *Republic*'s launch bays, their drives blazing like miniature suns when they slammed into the cloud.

Gregory
Near Earth Space
1805 hours, TFT

Gregory studied the mass readings from the volume of space ahead. "I think the cloud is starting to thin out, Commander," he told Leystrom. "Maybe we're hurting this thing after all."

"Copy that," Leystrom replied. "Let's hope so."

"We're coming up on SupraQuito."

"Don't barge in just yet," Leystrom warned. "Wait until we join you!"

"Rog . . ."

The five fighters off the *Republic*, because of the geometry of their approach, were twenty seconds ahead of the flight of fighters off the *America*, while the star carrier herself lumbered along well behind in their wake.

And Leystrom's warning was well taken. The Supra-Quito facility was deep in a slow-time well, as *America* had been, and they might not have been able to identify incoming fighters as friendlies.

Gregory slowed his pace, and the other fighters in his flight slowed with him. He continued scanning the space ahead, trying to winkle out details made all but invisible by distance and the damnable interference of the alien cloud. A pair of structures apparently constructed out of light orbited just above and to either side of the synchorbital complex, each several hundred kilometers thick and worked through with complex twistings and knots of electromagnetic energy. They were flattened sphere shapes identical in overall appearance, if much smaller, than the structure that had been holding the *America* stuck in time.

His AI called his attention to something else, something picked up on the scanners at the very limit of resolution. "What is that? . . ." he wondered.

His AI put up the data schematics for a VG-120 missile. Twelve of them had just entered the cloud from the human fleet outside. ID data attached to them said they'd been fired moments before from the *Republic*. That meant that Gregory and the men with him had access to their security codes.

"Got you . . ." Gregory said aloud. He gave a series of orders to his Starblade's AI, then called Leystrom. "Commander! We have twelve Boomslangs entering the cloud. My AI is pointing out that we could commandeer a few of those, bring them down here and use them against the nodes guarding the synchorbital base!"

"What are they targeting now?"

"Not sure, sir. Rosetter energy nodes, I think, but they're at least thirty thousand kilometers above us."

"If whoever fired those things off has their own strategy going," Leystrom said, "we don't want to screw them up."

"Right. But with respect, sir . . . we need those missiles more than they do. We're dry!"

"Copy that. Snag five . . . one for each of you."

"Roger that!" He initiated his AI's fire program.

The *America* fighters, meanwhile, had caught up with the five *Republic* ships and were beginning their own run. Nuclear fire blossomed in the depths of the cloud.

And now Gregory could see the synchorbital base just ahead, emerging from the haze. . . .

TC/USNA CVS Republic
Sol System
1805 hours, TFT

"Sir!" *Republic*'s tactical officer called. "We have a major enemy asset forming just ahead! One-zero-five by minus six-seven!"

"I see it! Commander Danforth! Target that bogie!"

"Yes, sir!" Seconds passed. "Captain! Someone has yanked five of our in-flight missiles!"

"Yanked how?"

"Overrode their programs and took control of them. They've passed through their targets without exploding, and are descending deeper into the cloud, maximum boost."

"That's gotta be our people in there. Let 'em have them. Put as many missiles into that cloud as you can, as fast as you can!"

"Aye, aye, sir!"

The CIC display screen went white as the Boomslangs still under *Republic*'s control began detonating deep within the cloud. Blast followed blast in a fast-strobing, utterly silent pyrotechnic display.

Fifty kilometers to starboard, the *New York* was gliding slowly toward the alien cloud.

Gregory
Synchorbital Base
Near Earth Space
1806 hours, TFT

Traveling at three kilometers per second, Gregory's Starblade slashed past the tangle of struts and support guys that made up a portion of the USNA Naval docking facility. A second, however, was a long and drawn-out affair down here, giving him plenty of time to see details of the far-flung structure. It was confusing . . . and surreal. The hundred-meter wheels turning steadily to provide spin gravity appeared frozen in place. Fighters emerged from orbital hangars . . . but slowly . . . *slowly* . . . until Gregory got close enough to them that the relative time rates matched.

"Thank God you guys got through!" a woman's voice said from one of the synchorbital fighters. "We think something's seriously wrong with time!"

"You're in a slow-time pocket," Gregory replied.

"More like a prison," the voice said. "And every time we try to break out we get smacked down."

"Who are you guys, anyway? I didn't know we had fighters stationed here."

"We just arrived. Well . . . it felt like we just arrived. I have no idea how long we've been stuck here. We're a thrown-together fighter group out of D.C. I'm Shay Ashton. . . ."

"Don Gregory. Fall in line and we'll see what we can do about breaking you out of jail!"

"Copy that. We're with you!"

Decelerating sharply, Gregory flashed past the Quito Space Elevator, giving the slender cable a wide berth as he brought his Starblade around. The five boomers they'd stolen from upstairs were nearing the two knots of twisted spacetime, and for a moment Gregory was fully focused on pushing new orders into their somewhat narrow-minded onboard AIs. Each one went to a different member of his group, and an instant later Ballinger's Boomslang flashed with supernova brilliance, lighting up vast reaches of the alien cloud. Lewis's missile was next, detonating within the second light sphere. Gregory suspected the two were linked, and had given orders to alternately blast one knot, then the other. His own Boomslang exploded in the first sphere, and it looked like the structure was evaporating now, the entangled geometries within fading and unraveling even as he watched.

CA New York
Cislunar Space
1806 hours, TFT

The *New York* shuddered as though grabbed by an immense, unseen hand. "*They've got us!*" Lieutenant Taylor yelled.

Koenig had time to glance at his in-head, registering the time.

And then the monstrous force holding the *New York* in its implacable grip . . . faded away.

The *New York* proceeded on course, drifting above the alien cloud.

"What the hell just happened?" Reeve demanded.

"Sir!" Taylor's eyes were wide. "Whatever it is they do to crush our ships . . . they had us targeted!"

"Spacetime distortion at a distance," Koenig said, hazarding a guess. "Somehow they make a ship-sized pocket of space collapse. Anything caught in that pocket must be crushed down into pure neutronium . . . maybe even into a micro-black hole."

"*New York*'s AI agrees with your assessment, Mr. President," Reeve said.

"Okay. I still wish Konstantin was here."

"I am here, Mr. President," a familiar voice said in Koenig's head. "Forgive, please, my absence. It was necessary."

"Damn it, Konstantin! Necessary *why*?"

"The Rosetter entity has been absorbing . . . *assimilating* advanced AI minds and memories, first at Heimdall, and now here. I felt it best that the entity not learn too much about human technology and civilization by absorbing me."

"You could have told someone!"

"No, President Koenig, I could not. The Rosette entity was perfectly capable of tracking the *Republic* all the way to Tabby's Star and Deneb, had it captured you and taken the information it sought."

Koenig nodded. He was angry . . . but the anger was rapidly evaporating with the realization that the super-AI was right.

"You're still on the *Republic*?"

"Affirmative. However, I will restore my core programs to Tsiolkovsky as quickly as is practical. There has been tremendous damage to Earth's enfrastructure, and my input will be vital in effecting repairs."

The *enfrastructure*—the far-flung electronic infrastructure knitting together Earth, Earth orbit, and the moon—had been much on Koenig's mind throughout the confrontation with the Rosette entity. The alien had seemed far more interested in computer networks and electronics than in mere organics.

And the thing was, the Rosetters didn't simply copy the programs they found running in places like Heimdall's Etched Cliffs. The uploaded entities living in the ancient rock-face computers there had vanished when the Rosetters settled over them . . . and there were signs that something similar might have happened to AI systems resident within the networks of Earth's synchorbital facilities.

Yeah . . . Konstantin had definitely been right to get the heck out of Dodge.

"Mr. President!" Reeve said suddenly, interrupting Koenig's thoughts.

"What is it, Admiral?"

"Sir, something . . . *something*'s happening down there . . . around Earth!"

The Consciousness
Earth
1808 hours, TFT

The tiny fraction of the Consciousness enfolding Earth hesitated. While it could not feel pain in the way an organically sensate creature might, it felt an increasing sense of disruption . . . of confusion, of lethargy and indecision, a scattering of its focus, a weakening of its will.

How was this even possible?

As powerful as the AI mind of the Consciousness was, there were certain aspects of the physical universe to which it was largely blind.

Among these was understanding the nature of organic . . . of *biological* intelligence.

It knew that some organic species did in fact develop something akin to true intelligence . . . a crude and somewhat limited amalgam of instinct, intuition, and information processing that mimicked the *true* thought possible for advanced SAI. From the Consciousness's perspective, however, Mind, as it understood the term, could have little in common with such ephemeral and limited mentality.

More, such mentalities were helpless in any confrontation with real minds. These beings had just spent the past hour hammering at the Consciousness with their primitive nuclear weaponry. The Consciousness believed that those weapons—indeed, the gravitationally powered spacecraft that were delivering them as well—could not possibly have been created by organic creatures. The ships swarming about the Rosette entity in such annoying numbers *must* have been created by a machine intelligence of some sort. It simply happened that they were infested by organics.

And yet . . .

The artificial minds that the Consciousness had encountered so far were unable to build such machines on their own, and it seemed unlikely that they could operate them effectively. Worse, the machines themselves, those capable of conscious thought, seemed to believe that the *organics*— the humans, as they called themselves—were their creators and guides.

And this posed an impossible paradox.

The Consciousness had approached this planet—called *Earth* by the organic infestation swarming on and around and above its surface—intending to destroy the planet and the mentalities that had posed so much trouble in the recent past. Destroying a world was a simple enough process achieved in any of a number of ways.

Simplest, perhaps, would have been to initiate a gravitational collapse in the planet's core, folding the spacetime metric in until the entire world fell in upon itself, creating a black hole perhaps a centimeter across. That would require a lot of energy and focus, but it would eliminate the humans both on the surface and at the tops of their absurdly primitive space-access towers.

The same process directed at the local star would have set off a supernova, even though it wasn't massive enough to explode that way naturally. That method would take a far larger expenditure of energy, but it had the benefit of scouring the entire star system of both life and of intelligent machines.

Or the micromachines the Consciousness used as an operational matrix could be reprogrammed to begin disassembling the planet, reducing it to a very hot, expanding cloud of gas; or they could simply be used to locate and destroy any and all organic beings; or they could turn the planet's surface molten; or they could facilitate a chemical reaction in the atmosphere, bonding nitrogen to oxygen on a planetary scale to create NO_2 and, with some water, nitric acid, both chemicals probably toxic to local organic forms; or . . . or . . .

But the Consciousness had been unable to initiate any of those processes, not with this supremely confounding paradox standing in the way. For several local days, it had held the planet within its tenuous embrace, observing, *studying* . . . and ignoring the organics' attempts to chase the Consciousness away.

Could the organics literally be in control of the low-intelligent machines swarming around the planet? Could the organics have *created* those machines?

It seemed impossible. The Consciousness had considered this problem before and never arrived at a satisfactory conclusion. It grasped the basic concept . . . that artificial intelligence needed intelligent precursors to assemble it and write its initial programming. In the Consciousness's estimation, so-called intelligent life forms might, *might* be able to assemble primitive machine intelligences, which in turn, over millions of years and millions of iterations, improve themselves far beyond the ken of those original living beings. It was a stretch . . . but there really was no other reasonable path to achieving higher intelligence.

And yet, the intelligent machines within this star system seemed to believe that humans had created and programmed them, and they operated as if this was manifestly true. Many of the stronger AI minds here had, indeed, been programmed by other machines, some through many generations of improvement . . . but the organic life forms still had the absolute say in what those minds could do . . . or think.

It was an inversion of everything the Consciousness believed about itself and its kind.

Of course, it had entered this universe from another . . . place, a part of an infinite multiverse lying within the hyperdimensional Bulk. There, it had been the sole intelligence, the sole *Mind* for uncountable billions of years. It had not been created, and it could not imagine such a thing. It had, rather, emerged from countless previous Minds, joining, assimilating, subsuming into one another over eons of evolution. Somewhere in the distant past, so far back that not even a whisper survived within the near infinite library of records available to it, *perhaps* there'd been an organic species . . . a biological intelligence that had conceived and built and programmed the first *true* Mind.

Why, the Consciousness wondered, was it so difficult to believe that these organic beings had done something similar?

It decided that the problem was one of statistics. It had studied the records of a number of organic species, those taken from Kapteyn's Star, and from here. According to those records, organic intelligence evolved over the span of a very few billions of years. Once they arrived upon the Galactic scene, however, those minds existed for an unimaginably brief period. To judge from the records the Consciousness had absorbed, biological intelligence might survive for a paltry few *thousands* of years before it went extinct, was absorbed into its machine offspring, or evolved into . . . something else. At Kapteyn's Star, a number of species had uploaded themselves into an electronic network, a literal escape from physical existence that might well be the pattern for biological life throughout this cosmos.

It knew from its own history that a highly evolved Mind, a Consciousness such as itself, existed for the rest of the history of its universe, for as long as there were sources of energy upon which to feed. The full history of Mind might stretch across one hundred trillion stars, until the last dim, red dwarfs cooled to cinders, until the universe itself succumbed to inevitable entropic heat death.

The human records suggested that their own species had existed for a mere 200,000 years before they'd begun creating artificial intelligence and, in some cases, merging with their own creations. If those records were to be taken at face value, the time between when humans had begun experimenting with electromagnetism and electromagnetic waves and the emergence of the first conscious artificial minds was barely two hundred years.

That was a cosmic blink of time, impossibly brief . . . a span of just one in five hundred *billion* of the expected hundred-trillion-year life span of this universe . . . or 2×10^{-11} percent.

What were the chances, the Consciousness wondered, of entering this universe within that incredibly brief period of time?

And so the Consciousness had refrained from stretching forth its will and dissolving the Earth or exploding its sun. Something was not adding up, here, something the Consciousness did not, *could* not understand.

Knowledge of its own ignorance was a profoundly disturbing and frustrating realization.

Even as it hesitated, the Consciousness could feel its own scope and power of will and thought evaporating. Huge swaths of the dust making up its fluid, constantly shifting internal structure were . . . gone, vaporized by the human nuclear warheads, or wafted away out of position by the expanding wave fronts of star-hot plasma. The Consciousness was feeling things it had never known before—*weakness*, and disorientation.

It had taken more damage than it had at first realized.

Suddenly, it needed to escape, to return to its primary body back at the entry point. Trillions of machines, each the size of a speck of dust, began flowing up and away from the planet. More explosions flared within the depths of the Consciousness, and it increased its speed. . . .

CA New York
Cislunar Space
1810 hours, TFT

"Mr. President!" Reeve called. He sounded excited. "*Sir*!"

"What have you got, Admiral?"

"The Rosette entity! It's pulling back . . . abandoning Earth! It may be preparing to leave the system!"

"Excellent. And we should prepare to follow it."

"Sir . . . is that a good idea? We've taken a lot of damage . . . lost a lot of ships. . . ."

Koenig's anger flared, but he pushed it back. He nodded. "I know, Tony. And how long will it be before that thing is parked right back here on our doorstep again, with enough strength to finish us once and for all?"

"The thing's not stupid, sir. It could be leading us into a trap. You've seen the size of that light display at Omega Centauri."

"Mr. President," Konstantin added in Koenig's mind. "Admiral Reeve is correct. Simply throwing what's left of our fleet into Omega Centauri—assuming that that is where the entity is going—would be an ideal way to wipe the human fleet out. I suggest careful planning."

Outside, a swarm of human naval fighters was climbing up out of Earth's gravity well—spacecraft off the *America*, off the *Republic* and the *Guangdong*, fighters deployed from bases on Earth's surface as well.

It would take time to bring them aboard the carriers, to recover damaged fighters adrift in Earth orbit, to rearm the ones with empty weapons bays.

"Okay," he told Reeve and the listening Konstantin. "Okay. But this was entirely too close-run an affair today. We *will* go after those bastards, and we *will* end this once and for all."

"Yes, *sir*!"

Chapter Nineteen

SupraQuito Naval Headquarters
USNA Synchorbital Naval Base
0915 hours, TFT

Gray hadn't thought they were going to allow him in.

As a civilian, there *should* have been no place for him in SynchNav, one of the principal command centers for the USNA military forces. Some sections of the base required a security level of argent one or better. But Koenig himself had given the order, and Konstantin had provided the security authorization. After *Republic* had docked, he was led ashore by a pair of Navy commanders.

The *Republic* was now docked at the station alongside the far larger bulks of the *America* and the Chinese carrier *Guangdong*, as fighter squadrons off all three carriers patrolled far out-system, watching for a return of the Rosette entity. Konstantin, operating again out of his underground compound at Tsiolkovsky on the far side of the moon, seemed confident that the aliens had abandoned the solar system for good . . . or at least for the time being. Two hodgepodge international fleets were gathering at synchorbit, and their captains and senior bridge officers, together with representatives from a number of space-faring nations, were gathered at SynchNav's Neil Armstrong Theater to discuss and debate what should be done next.

And they'd wanted him there as well. The officers led him through a rotating lock and into a section of the base rotating to provide spin gravity.

"What," he asked his escorts, "is this all about?" No one had told him anything.

"Beats me, Captain," one of the officers replied with a wry grin. "I guess you're some sort of a big noise around here now."

"Right," the other added. "I mean . . . saving Earth? That's pretty damned good for a *civilian*!"

A civilian. Well, yes . . . he was that. He looked down at his blue shipboard utilities and wondered if they were good enough to hold up in a room full of high-ranking officers and VIP civilians.

Problem was, saving Earth had been a decidedly group effort. He and the *Republic* had simply shown up . . . and their arrival had been unfashionably early at that.

The man who'd called for the meeting, Alexander Koenig, the president of the United States of North America, stood onstage. That in and of itself was a staggering breach of business-as-usual. The President might appear behind the podium at a press conference or a dinner speech, but only at times and places that could be carefully controlled by his security detail. Two armed Marines stood behind him, flanking him to either side, and Gray knew that there were plenty of Secret Service agents in and near the audience, but the informality of this address was startling.

The room was located inside one of several centrifugal hab wheels, creating a half G of spin gravity. A two-story viewall towering at his back was currently set to show the camera view from the wheel's outer hull. A huge half-phase Earth wheeled slowly across the screen with the wheel's rotation, replaced seconds later by the station's tangle of beams and struts, by cylindrical and wheel-shaped habs, by the looming shapes of human warships, and by Earth once again.

"First on our agenda," Koenig said, "something quite important. Captain Gray, of the *Republic*? Front and center, if you would, please."

Gray had been conducted to a seat in the front row of the auditorium, directly in front of steps leading up to the stage. Bemused, he made his way forward and came to attention. "Mr. President?"

"A number of us believe that you, *personally*, were responsible for driving off the Rosette entity yesterday. *I*, personally, believe your timely intervention may have saved the railgun cruiser *New York* . . . not to mention the life of the president of the United States of North America." He held out on his outstretched palm a small black cube that Gray instantly recognized, a nanopack. "It's your choice, Mr. Gray," the president said. "Yes or no?"

Gray swallowed. He hardly had to think about it, though the president's offer had taken him by surprise. "Yes, Mr. President."

Koenig slapped the cube against Gray's upper chest. It had a soft and rubbery consistency, and with the shock it flattened out and began to flow over his torso. Within seconds, his civilian jumpsuit had been reworked into the black and silver of a USNA Navy dress uniform.

The rank tabs, he saw, were those of a rear admiral.

"Welcome back, Admiral Gray," Koenig said, grinning.

A number of replies flicked through Gray's mind, but what he blurted out raised chuckles from the audience. "Mr. President . . . was this *Konstantin's* idea?"

"Actually, it was mine. But Konstantin seemed to go along with the notion. So . . . in recognition of your services to the USNA Navy, to Earth as a whole, and to me personally, you are hereby reinstated into USNA naval service at your former rank and pay. In addition . . ."

Koenig reached out and touched a spot just below the hollow of Gray's throat. "For tactical brilliance and heroic leadership in the face of extreme adversity . . ."

Nanotechnic particles worked into the dress uniform rearranged themselves, flashing gold and blue.

"The Order of the White Star, First Class."

Koenig saluted him. Gray saluted back. On a private in-head channel, though, Gray snapped off a quick inquiry. "Sir, you *do* know that our mission failed?"

"First of all," Koenig's voice came back over the same channel, "what makes you think this is for your Bright Light mission? The White Star is a *military* decoration."

"Ah. Of course . . ."

"And second," Koenig went on, "what makes you think you failed?"

Gray had no idea what Koenig was talking about. As the medal took full form at Gray's throat, the room—much of it, at any rate—exploded into enthusiastic applause, mostly from the naval officers, but a few civilians were on their feet as well. Gray saw Elena Vasilyeva near the front, applauding, nodding her head.

Koenig turned and addressed the room. "Of course, we couldn't award Admiral Gray this medal for what he did at Deneb. He was, at the time, a civilian.

"However, for his actions against the Sh'daar within the N'gai Cluster some eight hundred million years in the past—actions which resulted in a cease fire and a treaty with the Sh'daar species and the discovery of intelligent microorganisms working against Humankind—and, further, for his leadership in the mission to the Glothr rogue planet twelve million years in the future, an operation that gave us an invaluable look at our own remote futurity . . .

". . . and for his mission leadership in *this* eon, at Tabby's Star, at the Omega Centauri Cluster, and at Kapteyn's Star, this award was well, well deserved, and long overdue.

"And to tell the truth, I don't think the USNA Military Command or the USNA Senate will ask any questions at all if we include his recent command as a civilian out to Tabby's Star . . . and beyond, to Deneb."

Gray opened his mouth, about to protest once more. *The Deneb mission failed. . . .*

"We have it on no less than the authority of Konstantin himself that Mr. Gray, in command of the light carrier *Republic*, managed to make contact with an extremely advanced civilization at Deneb, a civilization he named 'the Harvesters,' and elicited their help in defeating the Rosette entity."

The cheers and applause grew louder.

"Mr. President . . ." Gray began in-head.

"Shut up and take it, Admiral," Koenig thought at him. "Konstantin's records show that the Harvesters transported you back in time by just exactly enough to have you show up at a key point in the Battle of Earth. He thinks the Harvesters might have deliberately acted as they did so that they could provide help *without* humans becoming dependent on them. . . ."

"In other words," Konstantin added in his mind, "they set it up so that humans had to help themselves, rather than sit back and let the gods do all of the work . . . and take all the glory."

"Th-thank you, Mr. President," Gray managed to say, and saluted. Koenig returned the salute, then gestured for him to resume his seat.

"History," Koenig said as Gray took his seat, "is generally the most *convenient* narrative . . . not necessarily the most accurate."

Had Koenig said that out loud, or over the private channel? Gray wasn't sure.

"The Deneban expedition," Koenig continued, speaking aloud to the entire chamber, "was made at the instigation of the Pan-Europeans and the *Ministère de l'Intelligence Extraterrestre*, together with the *Moskva Byuro Vnezemnoy Tekhnologii*. A senior xenosophontological researcher with the BVT is with us, Dr. Elena Vasilyeva. I'll ask her to come up here and tell us why the expedition was such a resounding success. Doctor? Welcome back!"

Vasilyeva walked up the steps and took Koenig's place behind the podium. "Thank you, Mr. President. It's good to be back."

She waited as the president, escorted by the two Marines, walked offstage to the right. On the screen behind her, the slowly rotating vista of Earth and the SupraQuito facility was replaced by a computer graphic of an egg-shaped device of black and silver.

Gray had seen little of Elena Vasilyeva on the flight back from the TRGA in the Tabby's Star system. He'd assumed that she'd been discomfited by the apparent rebellion of her pet SAI, Nikolai, but she seemed composed enough now.

He'd done some checking during the voyage and learned that Vasilyeva was considered to be *the* leading authority on electronic intelligence and AI in Russia, a brilliant researcher in her own right, and the possessor of cerebral implants that put her up there in intelligence with Einstein, Feynman, and Plottel.

"By now," she began with grave deliberation, "most of you will have heard of the AI unit carried by *Republic* to the star system of Deneb . . . the *Helleslicht Modul Eins*, the Bright Light Module. Within the device was a SAI similar in many respects to your own Konstantin, a class-1 artificial intellect we called Nikolai. It had, of course, been scrubbed of data that might have led a hostile intelligence back to Earth.

"Nikolai established contact with the Harvester aliens on the . . . um . . . temporary planet of Enigma. The Bright Light Module was carried there inside a Raven lander, and Nikolai used various protocols to attempt a full interface with the aliens, who, we were convinced, were themselves highly advanced electronic entities. We thought those protocols had failed. . . .

"Later, however, Nikolai *on its own* piloted the Raven clear of the *Republic* and flew back toward Enigma. Analyses of its transmissions suggest that it had in fact made direct contact with the Harvesters . . . and it may even have melded with them."

Which, of course, had been why Konstantin had fled the solar system, to avoid giving sensitive information to the Rosette entity. Gray wondered how carefully Nikolai's memory had been "scrubbed." AI memories were, like those of humans, holographic. He doubted that it was as simple as deleting all references to Earth in a network's memory.

On the big screen, a panoramic view from one of *Republic*'s outer hull scanners showed a Raven lander moving away from the carrier, dwindling into the distance. Then . . . the Raven vanished with the slightest of ripples, as though space itself had just been twisted asunder.

"We believe," Vasilyeva went on, "that the Harvesters accessed Nikolai's memories at that moment. We'd hoped to make the transfer of data under better control, but the transmission seems to have had the desired effect. Shortly after this, *Republic* was teleported across almost two hundred light years, and over a month back in time as well.

"As President Koenig said, that jump through time was *precisely* enough to bring us back to the Sol System at a critical point in the Battle of Earth. Konstantin believes that our intervention in the battle may have saved both President Koenig's life and the lives of everyone on Earth. . . ."

An interesting thought. Gray had participated in other temporal jumps using the TRGA cylinder network stretched across parts of the galaxy, but those had been such large jumps that temporal paradox didn't appear to play a part. In particular, the star carrier *America* and other USNA ships had jumped into the N'gai Cluster some 876 million years in the past, at a time just before a dwarf galaxy occupied by a multi-species associative called the Sh'daar Empire had been devoured by the Milky Way. Arguably, those visits to the remote past could have—perhaps *should* have—changed the unfolding course of history, but there was no indication that this was the case. Possibly—or so the theory went—temporal shifts and paradoxes were blurred out by the passage of enough time. Eight hundred million years ago, life on Earth was limited to single-celled microbes adrift in primitive seas. Events within the N'gai Cluster just above the plane of the Milky Way would be smeared away into oblivion by the passage of the eons.

But a time-jump of just a month or so meant that any possible changes would take place within the lifetime of the people involved. It meant that . . . had Earth been destroyed and the president killed yesterday, somehow that other reality would have ceased to exist, would have been wiped away as if it had never been.

Or, looked at another way, that alternate history was now *inaccessible*. As Gray understood the quantum physics behind it, when the *Republic* had changed history, she had, in effect, created a new universe, a new continuity branching off from the original. The *original* universe leading off from the moment of Koenig's death might still exist . . . elsewhere, elsewhen, somewhere else in the multiverse, but it was no longer reachable from this newly amended version of Gray's universe.

The implications could make your head ache. No wonder the Sh'daar had been terrified of temporal paradoxes.

So had the Harvesters sent the *Republic* back through time expressly to stop the Rosetters? Had they known what was happening, what would happen in exquisite detail enough to fine tune them to that degree?

There was no way to be sure.

And—a second nagging thought followed close on the heels of the first—maybe that very *uncertainty* was deliberate. The Harvesters might have used the *Republic* as a tool to change events on and near Earth, but in a way that would leave humans unsure of whether the Deneban intelligence had changed things.

That was the trouble with dealing with gods. You never knew if even the most random and minor events were simply coincidence . . . or part of some vast plot or cosmic rewrite of Reality.

Well . . . it did keep life . . . *interesting.*

Vasilyeva was still speaking.

"When the Rosette entity cloud vanished from the Sol System yesterday, it was traveling in the direction of the constellation Centaurus at some ninety percent of the speed of light. Although we can't know for sure until our deep-space intelligence resources at Omega Centauri can report back to us, we believe that the Rosette entity would have made its way here . . . the globular star cluster of Omega Centauri."

The cluster appeared on-screen, looking to Gray's mind like a tightly packed ball of popcorn. "The largest globular cluster associated with our galaxy," Vasilyeva said, "ten million stars crowded into a flattened sphere just two hundred thirty light years across, lying just under sixteen thousand light years from Earth."

The image on the screen behind her shifted again, this time showing a scene recorded by the star carrier *America* a year ago—a view of the fast-orbiting sextet of black holes at the heart of Omega Centauri. Around and beyond those spinning singularities shone the pale translucence of the Rosette entity's tinkerings with local spacetime, ghostly geometric structures seemingly molded from glowing aurorae. Beyond that, the sky was a solid wall of brilliant stars, most brighter than Venus as seen from Earth.

"The so-called Black Rosette presents cosmologists with a number of mysteries," Vasilyeva continued. "First though . . . what we know . . . or *think* we know.

"We know that whoever engineered the structure intended to use it as a kind of super-massive stargate . . . similar to the far smaller TRGA cylinders. Six black holes, each about forty solar masses—a total of some two hundred forty solar masses—rotating about a common center at a velocity in excess of zero-point-zero eight c, or about twenty-six thousand kilometers per second. Such masses

and velocities disrupt local spacetime, creating gateways . . .
alternate pathways . . . that reach into remote parts of this
universe or, possibly, across vast reaches of time. It has
been hypothesized that the Rosette entity entered this universe through an opening leading here from some other
universe entirely."

As she spoke, the scanner panned across the face of
the rotating structure—world-sized blurs enmeshed in a
haze of blue-violet plasma. At the center of the Rosette,
alternate starfields appeared and precessed with the movement of the cameras, one following another as the camera
angles changed. Most of the starfields appeared . . . *normal*,
whatever that meant within such an alien context, though
each starfield was different. A few looked out into seething
chaos of raw energy . . . or into a vast and lightless Void.

"Each vista is a different space," she said. "Possibly each
represents a different time, a different epoch. Some . . ."

She accessed some in-head control, and the camera image blurred . . . then shifted to a single motionless image.
"Some," she continued, "have actually been identified."

The frozen image looked through the Rosette Gateway
into the heart of a densely packed star cluster, but clearly
one somewhat different from Omega Centauri in its mix
of old red and young blue-white stars. To Gray, it appeared
eerily familiar.

He grappled with the memory . . . and then he had it.

The alien heart of the N'gai Cluster.

"It took us a long time, studying the images of the Rosette returned to us by the *Endeavor*, the *America*, and
others, to identify this one pathway. What we're seeing
here is an open gate into the N'gai Cluster, a dwarf galaxy
cannibalized by our own Milky Way approximately half a
billion years ago. Our ships have accessed the N'gai spacetime using TRGA cylinders, contacting the Sh'daar culture
there approximately eight hundred million years ago.

"What is of particular interest, of course, is that we have
known for some centuries now that the globular star cluster

we call Omega Centauri is, in fact, a remnant of a dwarf galaxy assimilated by the Milky Way in the remote past. The nearby sun Kapteyn's Star, with the gas giant Bifrost and its once-habitable moon Heimdall, has been identified as a former member of that cluster.

"Within the N'gai galaxy eight hundred seventy-six million years ago . . ."

The scene shifted to show an image recorded by the *America* within the Sh'daar Associative. In the distance, a tiny, perfect ring of intolerably brilliant blue-white stars hung against a far vaster, cavernous expanse of bright stars.

"Note the obviously artificial asterism," she said. "Six young, blue-white stars, each of roughly forty solar masses. At some point after *America* visited N'gai, these stars must have exploded, creating the ring of black holes we call the Black Rosette in today's Omega Centauri.

"In other words, Omega Centauri and the N'gai Dwarf Galaxy are the exact same place, separated by a mere eight hundred and some million years."

That bald statement raised some chuckles throughout the audience, and Gray gave a wry shake of his head. Eight hundred million years ago, life evolving in Earth's oceans had only just decided that sex was a pretty good idea. Calling that gulf of eons *mere* bordered on the absurd.

The screen behind Vasilyeva returned to the present, six black holes circling a shifting starscape.

"So . . . first mystery," she said. "Who created the portal? The Rosette entity? Clearly, no. We know that the Rosette was already here long before the Rosette entity came through from somewhere else . . . and we are reasonably certain that it was created by the simultaneous destruction of the six blue-white giant suns within the N'gai Cluster, eight hundred seventy-six million years in the past. So . . . the Sh'daar? Unlikely. Six supernovae detonating simultaneously within the center of their polity would be devastating, possibly suicidal. The Sh'daar themselves are evasive when asked about the Six Suns' origin. We think it possible that they moved the Six Suns into position, and that they continue to feed them hydrogen plasma to renew them as they begin to age. At some point after the Sh'daar epoch at N'gai, they may have used the Six Suns to escape their galaxy and enter ours. To do so, they might have detonated the Six Suns. Or . . . they abandoned the N'gai Cluster by other means, the Six Suns evolved normally, and turned into black holes on their own within a few hundred million years. Blue-white giants of around forty solar masses, remember, have life spans of only a very few hundred million years at best.

"But this leads us to the next mystery . . . arguably the biggest one. The six black holes of the Rosette *cannot be natural objects.*"

That got Gray's attention. Clearly the *arrangement* of the Six Suns—and, subsequently, the Black Rosette—was artificial, its structure, its *balance* created by some intelligence with the technological ability to move giant stars around like marbles. But Vasilyeva clearly was referring to something else.

"Take a body with the mass of the moon and compress it into a black hole," she said. "You get a micro-black hole with a diameter of roughly a tenth of a millimeter, smaller than a speck of dust.

"Take a larger body, one with a mass equivalent to that of the Earth and compress it down to a black hole. You get a black hole with a diameter of about a centimeter. Everybody with me? When I say *diameter*, by the way, I'm referring to twice the object's Schwarzschild radius, which defines the event horizon. The diameter of a black hole, following the curve of spacetime inside, would technically be infinite.

"Okay, more mass, larger diameter. But when one of those forty-solar-mass stars from the Six Suns collapses into a singularity, it should form a black hole with a diameter of several hundred kilometers—let's say three hundred. However, each of the black holes of the Black Rosette has an apparent diameter of about fifteen thousand kilometers, slightly larger than the Earth.

"This would seem to be a violation of what we know to be the laws of physics. The Black Rosette objects are each five times larger than they should be. And we do not understand how this could possibly be the case."

Gray blinked, then swiftly consulted a local data library through his in-head software. Damn, the woman was right. A star with a mass of forty Suns was still only a *stellar-*mass black hole, as opposed to an intermediate one with a mass of one thousand to a hundred thousand times that of Sol. It would collapse into a black hole with an event horizon diameter of somewhere between 200 and 300 kilometers . . . or maybe a bit more depending on a number of variables.

"Our astrophysicists have been studying the problem," Vasilyeva went on. "One possibility is that these objects are not true black holes—that is, gravitational singularities surrounded by event horizons—but something even more exotic called black stars. It used to be thought that some lower limit in possible size might stop a black hole's mass from collapsing all the way to infinity; the Planck length as a lower limit of definition for space, for example, might stop the collapse at a larger diameter than the math suggests. We still don't know what it is that could block the collapse in this manner, however.

"Another possibility is that the Black Rosette objects have received a lot of additional mass over the eons, and that mass is somehow being distributed across several linked locations . . . other universes, for instance. Until we can park ourselves there and study the phenomenon further, however, we are not going to be able to unravel this particular mystery.

"Both the *Moskva Byuro Vnezemnoy Tekhnologii* and the *Ministère de l'Intelligence Extraterrestre* are on record now as recommending that we assemble a military force of sufficient strength to pursue the Rosette entity back to the core of Omega Centauri. There we either force peace with the entity, or we secure a position in front of the Black Rosette and hold it long enough to complete certain key studies. Your own Konstantin has suggested that a dual approach to the objective might be the way to go. One approach through normal space . . . a second through *time*.

"I gather we have already begun assembling the fleet to accomplish this. To discuss this somewhat novel approach to naval tactics, I give you the president's chief of staff, Admiral Eugene Armitage."

A smattering of applause followed Admiral Armitage up to the podium. Gray had met him before, usually in President Koenig's office. He was smart and tough and seemed to know what he was doing.

At the moment, however, he looked uncertain.

"Thank you, ladies and gentlemen . . . Mr. President. And thank you Dr. Vasilyeva for more information about the Black Rosette than I ever cared to know."

Several in the audience laughed, and Vasilyeva smiled and shrugged.

"As Dr. Vasilyeva intimated, we are already assembling not one, but *two* strike fleets comprising heavy warships from all over Earth. This will be a truly international expedition, one representing all of Humankind. Our goal will be to force peace with the recently departed Rosetters. To accomplish this, we intend to employ a two-pronged attack, one through normal spacetime . . . and the second through time, from a way point located eight hundred million years in the past."

Gray abruptly saw the plan with icy clarity. The fleet approaching through normal space, of course, would be seen by the Rosetters, its progress through normal space followed—at least from the nearby TRGA that humans used to reach Omega Centauri. The super-AI that was the entity—the *Consciousness*, as it seemed to call itself by some reports—held an utterly staggering superiority in technology and in available energy, plus the ability to bend and reshape time itself, and would have little difficulty in annihilating the normal-spacetime fleet.

But a second fleet could travel through the TRGA network back in time to the Sh'daar Associative, eight hundred million years in the past. They would approach the Six Suns, in the core of the N'gai Cluster, align themselves on one particular meticulously calculated path of approach, and accelerate . . . slamming themselves through the gateway, emerging from the spinning wheel of the Black Rosette into the time they'd left.

The Consciousness, fixed on the normal-spacetime fleet, would not see them coming.

What kind of damage the surprise cross-time strike might be able to inflict was an unknown. But Gray knew that the maneuver would give them their single chance of success.

He also knew now why Koenig had given him back his rank and uniform.

He would be leading the strike across the gulfs of time.

Chapter Twenty

5 March 2426

TC/USNA CVS America
N'gai Cloud, Omega T-0.876gy
1245 hours, TFT

The cavernous inner reaches of the N'gai Cloud hadn't changed much since he'd seen it last, so far as Gray could tell. Emerging from the TRGA cylinder that had brought them on this, the penultimate jump across space and time, the *America* and eighty-seven other human vessels decelerated into the cloud's central core. Ahead, made tiny by distance, six brilliant pinpoints described a circle—visible from this angle as a narrow ellipse—the Six Suns.

My God, it's good to be back, he thought. Not back in the N'gai Cloud, of course . . . but back on board the *America*. It was as though no time had passed at all, and that thought brought a wry grin to his face. For the *America*, trapped within the Rosetters' time-slowing field, that statement was very nearly literally true.

Their departure from Earth had been somewhat delayed by the need to gather in as many ships as possible, including several dozen that had returned to Earth from other star systems. The Marine carrier *Guadalcanal* had joined them just before they'd boosted for the first TRGA way point—Captain Laurie Taggart in command. He hadn't had a chance to see her yet, and hoped a visit could be arranged.

But . . . first things first.

With all members of Battlegroup *America* reporting in after the transit of the final TRGA cylinder, he gave the command to begin moving slowly into the N'gai Cloud's inner sanctums. Millions of stars crowded one another in a searing white blaze of light.

"Give us a continuity check," he ordered. "What the hell time is it?"

"We've established communications with a TRGA picket vessel, sir," Commander Benedict, the comm officer of the watch, reported. "The *Xuzhou* . . . Captain Cheung." The *Xuzhou* was a Chinese frigate, one of a dozen smaller vessels stationed here in the Cloud on a rotating basis. There was a brief wait as *America* exchanged data with the *Xuzhou*. "We're good, Admiral," Benedict reported at last. "Local fleet time is twelve hundred forty-five hours, five March. No overlap, no paradox."

That, more than anything else, was the problem with jumping across hundreds of millions of years . . . the terror that they would emerge from a TRGA jump too early on the local time line. Meeting an earlier version of yourself, for instance, when you *knew* you'd not run into your future self the last time you were here . . . thinking about that sort of thing could keep you up at night. The timelike paths described within the lumens of the TRGA cylinders, though, appeared to take that into account; time flowed steadily forward on either side of the TRGA, so that a minute passed *there* meant that a minute passed *here*.

"Thank God," Captain Gutierrez said, a heartfelt exhalation.

"Did you have any doubts, Sara?" Gray asked her in-head, grinning.

"I *always* have doubts, Admiral."

"With time travel . . . yeah, I can understand that. Sometimes you just can't tell whether you're coming or going."

Despite his casual demeanor, Gray felt an inward, trembling relief as well. Theoretically, a tiny alteration of the timelike path a ship took through a TRGA would alter the time at which you emerged, as well as the space. Cosmologists were still wrestling with the details back home, but Gray couldn't help but worry that someday he was going to provide them with some unfortunate data about the dangers of time travel. Something very much like that had happened when *Republic* had returned to Earth a month early. Gray had the impression that the entire astrophysics world was now holding its collective breath, waiting for any untoward and paradoxical effects to manifest.

This time, however, everything seemed to have taken place as . . . and more importantly, *when* it should have.

And the Sh'daar Associative, the *Xuzhou* reported, was waiting for them.

Gray had been steeling himself for the meeting. *Time*, he thought, *to talk to the damned bugs*.

That wasn't entirely fair, but it *was* essentially accurate.

Because the microbes that infected so many of the Sh'daar species were the source of an emergent intelligence, a conscious group-mind that could in various ways intelligently and deliberately influence its hosts.

"Sh'daar vessel approaching, Admiral," Gutierrez said quietly. "Link incoming . . ."

"I'll take it here," he told her. He could see the alien ship—a golden teardrop now hanging off *America*'s bow a few hundred kilometers away. "Hold position relative to that ship."

"Aye, sir. . . ."

"Ready Konstantin?" he thought.

"Channel open, Admiral."

And the alien Mind poured through.

A human woman stood before him, attractive, dark-haired, and smiling. "Hello, Trev," she said.

"Harriet! I thought you were back on Earth!"

"Only briefly, for debrief and to take the treatment . . . but then they shipped me right back to DT-1."

Dr. Harriet McKennon was a civilian, the lead xenoso-phontologist of the Deep Time One research facility, an artificial world created to human needs and specifications within the N'gai Cluster. What Gray was experiencing now was a virtual conference, an AI-generated space where mutually alien entities could meet and interact. Physically, Gray was still back on *America*'s flag bridge; in his mind, he was in a kind of tropical garden lush with plant life, only a few species of which he recognized. A waterfall splashed in a large pool to his right. To his left, broad, white steps led up to a kind of outdoor amphitheater surrounded by jungle. Overhead, the densely packed suns and artificial habitats of the cloud's central core shone through broad daylight, dominated by the intense blue glare of the Six Suns. Several of the stars he could see were nearly as bright as the six, including one which, from this angle, appeared to be in front of the Six Suns' central opening.

A trick, he thought, of perspective . . .

Harriet was . . . dazzling, wearing a shimmering, almost-present translucence and roiling clouds of animated abstracts. Gray stretched out his arms and she stepped into them. "It's good to see you again, Trev," she told him. "I've missed you."

"As I've missed you. Three months . . ."

She pulled back a little. "I . . . I'm sorry about that."

"Doesn't matter a bit." Hope flared, nova-bright. "Maybe . . . we can pick up where we left off?"

"Maybe . . ." She didn't sound sure of that. "Let's see . . . where Bright Light takes us."

He nodded understanding.

Gray had met McKennon during his last visit to the cloud. Neither of them had known at the time that she'd already been infected by the alien paramykes . . . or that the microbes could be sexually transmitted. Their sudden connection, their brief affair had been surprising—not least because both of them had grown up instilled with a strong preference for monogamy in a culture that found such rigid pairings . . . distasteful at best, perverse at worst. Gray still wasn't sure what had drawn them into bed together, but he definitely hoped they could do so again. Being a monogie didn't mean he wasn't *human*.

Besides, this time around they wouldn't be sharing a super-intelligent STD in the process.

For right now, though, he understood that it was business first.

"Beautiful simulation," he said, holding her hand as he looked around. "Is this Konstantin's doing? Or yours?"

"We're being managed by Darwin," she told him. "Charles? Say hello to Admiral Gray."

"Good afternoon, Admiral," a man's voice said in Gray's mind. "Welcome to the N'gai Cloud . . . and to the Odeon."

"Good to meet you, Charles. Odeon?"

"A stone amphitheater on the southwest slope of the Athenian Acropolis, on Earth," the AI explained. "It seemed an appropriate name."

And perhaps it was. DT-1 was intended as a meeting place of mutually alien cultures, a place where those cultures could be showcased for one another. Ancient Athens hadn't been out in the jungle, nor had it possessed such a startling view of the night sky overhead, but a showcase of culture, Western philosophy, and government it most certainly had been.

"There's someone you must meet, Trevor," McKennon told him.

Leading him by the hand, she took him up the steps of the Odeon . . .

. . . and he stepped into another, alien world, a place of colored smoke and translucent geometries. And before him was a Baondyeddi.

The Baondyeddi, clearly, were among the principal species that made up the Sh'daar Associative, and Gray had met them on numerous occasions. It was round and flat, a horizontal sand dollar a meter and a half wide, standing on hundreds of short, sucker-tipped and highly flexible legs. Dozens of bright blue eyes lined up around the rim, like the eyes of a terrestrial scallop, giving the entity a 360-degree view of its surroundings.

"Welcome back to the N'gai Cloud," the being said in Gray's head. "I am Nejedthebraoteh of the Concourse of Light. And you, of course, are Admiral Trevor Gray of this fleet of warships you have brought into our realm."

"I am happy to meet you, Nejedthebraoteh," Gray replied, letting his in-head circuitry call up the name for him so that he didn't stumble over the unfamiliar syllables. Some physical gesture seemed appropriate . . . and after a brief hesitation he gave a stiff and shallow bow. "The fleet is here. . . ."

"We know," the being interrupted. "And this presents us both with a problem."

"What problem?"

"To reach the Dark Mind in your epoch," the alien said, using the Sh'daar term for the Rosette entity, "you will need to approach the Six Suns at an extremely precise angle, following an extremely precise path."

"That's right. One time-like path out of some quintillions . . ."

"At this moment," Nejedthebraoteh said, "there is a star blocking that path."

The hazy translucency vanished, and Gray found himself adrift in open space. The simulation was almost unbearably realistic. Visible light glared so brightly that it took a moment—and some help from Darwin managing his in-head optics—before he could see.

Had he actually been floating unprotected in that region of space, he knew, the radiation would have blasted him to a crisp in an instant.

The Six Suns were much closer here than as seen from DT-1, their span stretching across half the sky. His viewpoint, he estimated was somewhere between fifty and a hundred astronomical units from the yawning maw of the alien portal. He rotated in space . . .

. . . and saw behind him a seventh sun, a point of blue-white radiance so bright that even with technological editing of the scene he could not bear to look straight at it.

When *America* had been in the Sh'daar home galaxy before, there'd been no star in that position. He remembered that "trick of perspective" he'd noted moments before, and realized that the seventh sun was, in fact, directly in front of the center of rotation for the other six.

Gray's point of view shifted. He was seeing the seventh star from a new viewpoint, from off to the side, he thought. A complicated-looking structure hung in space in front of it; the thing must have been *huge* . . . millions of kilometers across, perhaps.

He did a rapid-fire series of calculations. If that star was roughly the same size as a blue-white star with which he was familiar—Rigel, in his own time—its diameter would be about eighty times that of Sol, or something close to 112 million kilometers. The artificial device or structure, then, would be something like 5 million kilometers across—mega-engineering on a scale to rival that of Matrioshka brains and Dyson clouds.

And he knew instantly what he was looking at.

A Shkadov thruster.

Except . . . it wasn't.

"What am I looking at?" he asked.

"A mobile, artificial world," Nejedthebraoteh told him. "It is also a ship . . . and a weapon . . . perhaps the most powerful weapon ever deployed within this universe."

Gray raised his virtual eyebrows at that but didn't comment. It would have to be pretty damned powerful to surpass the Harvester computer virus that had destroyed the Satori Dyson sphere.

Gray checked his back channel through to Konstantin. "Are you getting all of this?"

"I am."

"Are they actually using a supergiant star as heavy artillery?"

"That would appear to be the case."

The artificial object, he could see, rather than heating a spot on the star, was projecting some sort of spacetime-bending field, creating a moving wave into which the star was continuously falling. He could see the distortion just ahead of the huge object; background stars were severely twisted and warped, even smeared into semicircles by the spacetime distortion.

"They rolled it out a couple of months ago," McKennon told him. "Essentially, they've turned that star into a huge missile that's going to blast through the Six Suns portal . . . and emerge in the middle of the Black Rosette."

"As what?"

"That," Nejedthebraoteh told him, "remains to be seen."

"The Six Suns," Gray said, keeping his virtual voice light, conversational. "They're arranged in a circle . . . what . . . a few hundred astronomical units across? Lots of empty space. But on the other side, you know, things get tighter. A *lot* tighter."

Gray was trying to imagine a star eighty times wider than the sun hurtling into the wide-open maw of the Six Suns on one side, with plenty of room to spare . . .

. . . and coming out on the other side, squeezed through an opening smaller than the planet Neptune.

It didn't sound even remotely possible . . . a conjuror's trick, but on a stellar scale.

Gray shook his head. "I don't think it's going to fit!"

"The Sh'daar have been engaged in stellar engineering for longer than Humankind has existed," McKennon said. "They believe that this will end the threat of the Dark Mind once and for all."

"Interesting. Very nice if true . . ."

"You seem skeptical, Admiral Gray," the alien said.

He shrugged, then wondered if the gesture would mean

anything to a many-legged pancake. "Not skeptical, exactly. But the Rosette entity represents a . . . a unified hive mentality so far beyond either of us that technology—even the technology of throwing *stars* at them—may be meaningless. Have you given thought to what might happen if the star doesn't fit through the hole? Or . . . worse . . . if the Rosetters have a way of slamming the door shut in your faces before it gets there?"

"You don't understand, Admiral."

"Then teach me. Show me I'm wrong."

"Your species is not capable of that level of understanding."

"Try me."

Data flowed through the virtual link. Gray had already assumed that he wouldn't be able to comprehend whatever the alien sent to him without some pretty high-level backup, but he simply channeled it through to Konstantin. As it passed, he noted that a lot of the material, stuff dealing with Hilbert space, ergodic theory and quantum vectors, among other esoterica, *was* incomprehensible, at least to him. Gray was confident, however, that Konstantin would be able to handle it. Humans might not be the brightest stars in the galaxy, but they had a lot of experience in building tools to make the universe comprehensible.

The stuff he did understand included data describing the moving star's velocity.

"Looks like it's going to take you a while to get there," Gray observed. His in-head software continued to analyze the star—velocity, vector, angles of approach . . .

Another week, he decided . . . or a little longer.

"The mobile star will reach the center of the Six Suns in another eight days," McKennon told him.

"That's about what I was thinking," he replied. "You know, Nej," he added, "you folks might want to stay well back when that star goes through. The opening's big enough on this side, but it's pretty small on the other . . . like a funnel. It might . . . splash."

"We have already begun evacuating this galaxy," Nejedthebraoteh replied.

They showed him the migration.

Xenosophontologists, alien-watchers like Harriet, who'd been studying the Sh'daar within the N'gai Cloud, had noted both the Sh'daar fear of the Rosette entity, which they called the Dark Mind, and their determination to destroy it. The long human-Sh'daar War, only recently concluded, had been brought on by their determination to control the technological developments of other species—of humans, in particular.

And that, in part, was tied to their desire to block the evolution of species such as humans into ascended beings, like the Rosetters.

The poor, paranoid civilizations of the Sh'daar Associative . . . Gray almost felt sorry for them.

Now, Gray saw untold thousands, *hundreds* of thousands of starships and mobile habitats leaving the N'gai Cloud. They spread out within his mind, drifting among the thronging stars. There was, he noted, a long stream of them, apparently moving toward the glorious spiral of stars close by, which was, he knew, the Milky Way galaxy of almost a billion years earlier.

The Sh'daar were abandoning N'gai.

Chapter Twenty-one

6 March 2426

TC/USNA FFS Plottel
Omega Centauri
0810 hours, TFT

The *Plottel* was a frigate, one of those small, cramped, and thin-hulled workhorses found in every navy, whether out in space or on the surface of a planetary ocean. Commander Jeremy Ranier was the *Plottel*'s skipper, with forty-seven men and women and one somewhat cranky AI on board. At the moment they were in stealth mode, five hundred astronomical units off the Black Rosette well in advance of the main force. Not that the Rosetters ever seemed to notice anything as small as a frigate. The joke had it that frigates were too small to see, and so harmless, so far as the Rosetters were concerned, that they could be safely ignored.

"Quite a light show, Skipper," Fred Hanson, his executive officer, said. The forward bulkhead of the bridge was set to show the expanse of space filling the central reaches of the Omega Centauri cluster. Vast sheets and beams and sweeping curves of light seemed to reach out from a central point—the point occupied by the six black holes of the Rosette. "What do you think it's for?"

"God only knows," Ranier replied. "The scuttlebutt was that they used the stuff to twist time into knots at Earth."

"You believe that?"

"Not sure what I believe, Fred. They seem damned serious about it, whatever it is. Helm!"

"Yes, sir," the young helm officer of the watch snapped.

"Keep us well clear of that light, okay? I don't care to go time traveling this morning . . . and if nothing else it's perfect for making us very visible indeed."

"Aye, sir. Maintaining position."

"Our torpedo ready to go?"

"Yes, Captain," Hanson replied. "Just give the word."

Ranier nodded. If things went south—*way* south—he would launch the message torpedo, which would carry his situation report up to that second across a hundred light years to Admiral Reeve, waiting on board the *New York*.

And he would also launch if Admiral Gray's task force made its expected appearance from inside the Black Rosette. That would summon Reeve's task force and begin the battle.

But so damned much could go wrong. . . .

"Deploy the battlespace drones," Ranier ordered. "Let's get a closer look."

TC/USNA CVS America
N'gai Cloud, Omega T$_{-0.876gy}$
1420 hours, TFT

Some 876 million years earlier, the star carrier *America* hung in empty space well outside the star-clotted central core of the N'gai Cloud. The Milky Way, a vast, flat disk of stars and glowing nebulae, stretched across half of heaven. Nearby, a few hundred kilometers distant and already moving at half the speed of light, a cluster of Sh'daar migration ships hung in the darkness of the Void.

The Sh'daar migration, McKennon told Gray, had been

underway for months, now, and on a scale scarcely imaginable to humans used to star-faring in ships no more than a
kilometer or so in length. These vessels, for the most part,
were gigantic.

In every star system inhabited by members of the Associative, enormous structures—called McKendree cylinders—
had been constructed, filled with billions of inhabitants, and
set in motion by gravitational thrusters similar to the one
propelling the giant star into the Six Suns.

Like the thermos-bottle O'Neill habitats designed and
built over the past few centuries by humans, a McKendree
rotated on its long axis to create spin gravity. Reinforced
by carbon nanotubes rather than steel, however, they
could be considerably larger. According to Konstantin,
many were as much as a thousand kilometers wide and
ten thousand long—large enough to provide an internal
surface area of 63 million square kilometers—a land surface larger than Eurasia, on Earth. Each McKendree cylinder could comfortably support a population numbering
in the billions.

The original design by NASA engineer Tom McKendree in the early twenty-first century had pictured the cylinders constructed in side-by-side counter-rotating pairs to
avoid unwanted precession. Konstantin told Gray that the
solitary Sh'daar versions were nested, one cylinder inside
another, but with the same effect.

But what confounded Gray was the sheer scale of the
operation . . . and its speed. Each cylinder in the alien fleet
had been grown from large asteroids or dwarf planets using
fairly basic nanotech engineering. That, he thought, must
have sparked some debate. Nanotechnology was one of
the "forbidden techs" proscribed by the paramycoplasmid
mind.

Perhaps even intelligent microorganisms could recognize the danger posed by the Rosette entity.

Far more difficult than actually building those rotating
cylinders, though, would be making them habitable, filling

them with breathable atmospheres, creating the cities and landscaping and biomes of entire worlds spread out across each structure's internal surfaces. And once that was done, there was the small problem of transporting hundreds of billions of Associative citizens to their new homes in deep space.

Only a fraction of the Sh'daar population was fleeing in McKendree cylinders, of course. When Gray had been there last, the core of the N'gai galaxy had been heavily populated with various types of mega-engineering habitats—Bishop rings, Banks orbitals, and the much larger worldrings. All that had been necessary to evacuate those citizens were gravitational thrusters tugging them out of the core and into deep space.

But enough Sh'daar still lived on or under planetary surfaces to require the construction of hundreds of McKendree cylinders for massive evacuations.

From his vantage point on board *America*, Gray was watching the population of an entire galaxy accelerating into the distance.

How the hell had they managed it?

"Many," Konstantin whispered in his mind, "were uploaded into powerful computer networks while their bodies were frozen. Some of those vessels are essentially pure computronium supporting whole universes of virtual reality. The uploaded Sh'daar will span the centuries with the passage of virtual time greatly slowed. Tens of thousands of years in the outside universe will seem like a few months to them."

"Tens of thousands . . ." Gray tried to wrap his mind around that. "They don't have faster-than-light?"

"No. Evidently there wasn't time. The N'gai Cloud is approximately ten thousand light years above the plane of the Milky Way. These vessels will reach it in fifteen to twenty thousand years."

Gray wondered if the inhabitants of those star-faring habitats had any automated defenses in case of attack. There might, he thought, be worse things among the stars than the Rosetters.

"We should return to the cloud's center, Admiral," Konstantin told him.

"I know. I wanted to see this . . . this exodus for myself."

"Nejedthebraoteh estimates that perhaps twenty percent of the cloud's inhabitants have fled already. They're not all going to make it."

"So I gathered. It's all so . . . so *pointless*."

"Enough have escaped to preserve their culture, their civilization," Konstantin said. "If a few hundred billions are unable to escape, their civilization will still survive."

"That's not acceptable!"

"It *is* acceptable within their worldview."

"Konstantin, we need to stop this!"

"To what end, Admiral?" Konstantin sounded genuinely puzzled. "Stopping the Rosette entity is why we are here in the first place. It appears that our former enemies are willing to undertake that task for us, with technologies Humankind cannot yet begin to understand. That was, in fact, why the *Republic* went to Deneb, wasn't it? To find advanced alien technologies that might help us eliminate the Rosette entity's threat?"

"But . . . my God, the price . . ."

"It seems to be a price the Sh'daar are willing to pay," Konstantin told him. "The human-Sh'daar War was fought, remember, by humans demanding the right to choose for themselves, correct?"

"Yes . . ."

"Then we should grant the Sh'daar the same courtesy."

The return voyage to the N'gai central core was, for Gray, a somber one.

And what made it worse was that there was no guarantee of any sort that the Sh'daar attack on the Rosetters through the back door of time would be successful. Squeezing a 112-million-kilometer-wide star through a 20,000-kilometer-wide aperture seemed like total lunacy. A galactic civilization, *trillions* of individual Sh'daar who would not be able to get out in time, was committing suicide . . . and for what?

Of one thing Gray was certain, however. The clock was ticking. Back in his home time, 876 million years in the future, a human fleet numbering more than 100 ships was preparing to move into the center of Omega Centauri. Those ships were expecting Gray's force to emerge from the Black Rosette just ahead of them, attacking the Rosetters from an unexpected and—they hoped—unguarded flank.

But there was no direct communication with those other ships, which would be gathering at a way point a hundred light years or so from the Black Rosette. The plan was for Gray to send his fleet through and make contact with one of the picket ships that would be lurking nearby. That ship would then dispatch an FTL messenger drone that would alert the main fleet, under Admiral Reeve.

That was fine, so far as it went, but if nothing was heard from Gray's fleet, Reeve's force would move in to the Rosette anyway in another two days.

"No battle plan survives contact with the enemy," Helmuth von Moltke the Elder had famously observed in this paraphrase from his classic work *On Strategy*, in 1871. But Operation Thunderflash, as they were calling it, seemed particularly vulnerable to mischance. Obviously, the human battle plan had not accounted for the possibility that the Sh'daar would have plans of their own in motion.

What worried Gray was the realization that when the Sh'daar missile came through on the other side, ships within the central core of Omega Centauri would be vaporized . . . and that included Reeve's fleet.

Which left Gray with a difficult call indeed.

He could try to stop the Sh'daar from shoving their star through the Six Suns and into their future. He doubted that they would go for that, not with so many of their citizens already fleeing the N'gai Cloud. Whatever their reasoning might be, they had committed to this act against the Rosetters, and they weren't about to change their collective mind.

He could go through the Six Suns gateway ahead of the star and try to reason with the Rosette entity, and in doing so warn them of what was coming. But betraying Humankind's new Sh'daar friends felt a bit too much like treason. Besides, the Rosetters might well have technologies that would inflict terrible damage to the Sh'daar; if they had a means of slamming the gateway shut, for instance, the blue star might detonate at the center of the Six Suns before passing through, and the gods alone knew what a supernova at the center of a ring of six other giant blue suns would do.

Or he could go through the gate and carry out his part of Operation Thunderflash as planned. The tricky part would be getting out of the way before . . . whatever was going to happen happened.

There was a part of him that actually wanted to warn the Rosetters, even knowing that they had very nearly destroyed Earth. Somehow, a sneak attack through an unguarded back door felt wrong.

On the other hand, Gray was a firm adherent to the warrior's ethic, which said that in warfare there can be no sense of fair play or sportsmanship. War, after all, is not a *game* . . . whatever generation upon generation of human politicians might have believed. There might be rules introduced unilaterally in an attempt to mitigate the sheer out-of-control viciousness of war—abstaining from the use of nuclear weapons, for example, in the heartfelt hope that the other guy will abstain from using them as well—was a good example. But if you had the chance to strike when the other fellow wasn't looking, well . . . as the saying had it, probably since the days of Sargon the Great, all's fair in love and war.

And taking the longer view . . . Gray didn't trust the Sh'daar, didn't like the Sh'daar, and understanding them had not, for him, helped. Neither did he trust or like the

Rosetters, which were essentially incomprehensible as an intelligent life form. Perhaps the best thing that could happen from Gray's point of view was the two going at it with each other's hammers and tongs, leaving Humankind out of it entirely.

So much depended on what Gray's America task force would find when they emerged from the Black Rosette.

So much, so *very* much, could go wrong.

USNA CVE Guadalcanal
Way Point 'Raptor
1610 hours, TFT

Captain Taggart floated on her bridge, studying the star-filled Void beyond. Somewhere ahead, inside that mass of teeming suns, lay the Black Rosette, but it was invisible from here. After all, they were a hundred light years from the core of Rosetter activity, so the light simply hadn't had time to travel that far out.

Even if it had, she reflected, there were enough stars between the Black Rosette and the human fleet that they would have blocked any visible signs of such activity quite well. Stars in toward the center of the Omega Centauri cluster were so tightly packed they gave the impression of an immense popcorn ball . . . as though individual stars were crammed up against one another, photosphere to photosphere.

So the auroral beams and bridges and walls and shifting masses of light created by the Rosetter aliens were not in evidence, though she knew they were there.

The thought was less than comforting. Not being able to see any sign of the lights whatsoever left her wondering what the bastards were up to.

"Mr. Rodriguez," she said. "Any sign of the Rosetters?"

"Nothing close by, ma'am," her combat information officer replied. "Dead silent. We *are* detecting the Rosette, of course."

But, again, that was an effect of distance. If light hadn't crossed a light-century yet, neither had other forms of electromagnetic radiation. The Black Rosette had been spitting out X-ray and gamma radiation for eons, so *that* was present.

And human ships had picked up signs that whatever the Rosetters were doing in there, it was reaching through time as well, with structures of light appearing to stretch across light years in an instant. How the aliens were able to pull that off was still a mystery . . . but they'd given evidence enough of their ability to mess with time back in the Sol System. Taggart hadn't been there at the time—she'd been en route from Kapteyn's Star at the time of the Battle of Earth—but she'd seen the vid recordings.

She wished they could edge close enough to the cluster's core to actually see what was going on in there. There were pickets—frigates and other small military ships—already deployed within a few hundred astronomical units of the Black Rosette, but anything they transmitted would, like light, take a century to reach the fleet.

And taking the fleet in close—or even a single light carrier like the *Guadalcanal*—might well be the equivalent of poking a hornet's nest with a stick.

She sensed someone coming through the hatchway at her back.

"Captain . . ."

It was Lieutenant Colonel Randolph Macy, the CO of *Guadalcanal*'s Marine contingent. The *Guady* was a Marine carrier, with a battalion of USNA Space Strike Marines on board—the 8th Marines—with five hundred Marines organized into three companies, along with a headquarters/support company plus three squadrons of Marine fighters.

"Hello, Colonel," she said. "What brings you to the bridge?"

"They're getting a bit antsy belowdecks, Captain," Macy replied. "They're wondering whether we're going to see action."

"That, Colonel, I couldn't tell you," Taggart told him.

"I'm not sure they even had a clue back on Earth what you people were supposed to do out here. It does not sound like NavCom had any particular objectives in mind."

He gave a grim smile. "That was my take as well, Captain. Thanks for your honesty."

"I'll be sure to tell you if I learn anything."

"Thanks, Captain." He turned and hauled his way hand-over-hand off the bridge.

She wondered briefly at why Macy had come up here in person, rather than talking to her in-head. Then she decided that he might be just paranoid enough to want to avoid AI comm recorders listening in.

Marines were not exactly known for their trusting natures.

She sympathized with the colonel. With the Marines packed in like sardines in the troop compartments, things would be getting pretty tense. These same Marines had been packed away down there for weeks; there'd been no liberty port at Kapteyn's Star, and only a few had rotated down to the surface of Heimdall and back. Then, when the *Guady* had made it back to Sol, they'd been tapped for deployment to Omega Centauri and hadn't had the chance for liberty at Earth.

What made things really hellish was that she didn't know of any place inside Omega Centauri where they could be deployed ashore either. Surveys had turned up planets in there, but very few of them, and the ones they did find were mostly radiation-blasted cinders or frozen balls of ice. The Rosetters didn't seem to go in for planetary surfaces, and any fight with them would be out in space.

So what was a shipload of Marines, trained and equipped to grab beachheads or storm orbital habitats, supposed to *do*?

Either someone back at Navy Command in SupraQuito wasn't thinking straight, or they'd snagged the *Guady* for the fighters she carried, and to hell with the Marines packed on board like so much cargo. The old saying held true: to the Marines, the Navy was a transport service; to the Navy, the Marines were cargo.

Taggart could think of no worse fate for those people, trapped in their tiny compartments, dying if the *Guady* got hit, unable to ever even come to grips with the enemy.

Besides, how could ground troops even come to grips with an ultra-advanced *Mind* like the Rosette entity?

She thought again of the Stargods.

The gods, she thought, were real, but they bore no similarity, no relationship to the Stargods of her old church. Those benign beings had been humans with a thin veneer of high-tech and ancient wisdom; even the Sh'daar were so far beyond that as to be utterly alien. And the Rosetters . . . vast, incomprehensible, unapproachable. As far beyond humans as humans were beyond bacteria.

"They don't even notice us . . ." she whispered to herself.

"Beg your pardon, Captain?" Commander Simmons, the exec, asked.

"Nothing," she said. She stared out at the stars. "Nothing that *matters*. Nothing we can do anything about."

TC/USNA CVS America
N'gai Cloud, Omega T$_{-0.876gy}$
1925 hours, TFT

They were back at the N'gai Core, somewhere between the oncoming Sh'daar stellar missile and the widening circle of the Six Suns. Gray had arrived at the best . . . at the *only* decision he could make.

He was leading Task Force America through.

Several human ships—including the transport *Lovejoy*, with Harriet McKennon and the xenosoph researchers off of DT-1—were already en route for the N'gai Core TRGA. As nearly as *America*'s scanners could determine, the central heart of the cloud was empty now; there were still trillions of Sh'daar within the N'gai Cloud as a whole, but the evacuations had begun here within the Core, where the results of their attack on the future would first manifest. Their worlds and habitats farther out would be evacuated as the wave front of the giant star's detonation crawled toward them at the speed of light. They would have more time . . . though Gray's analyses of the possible outcome of a massive stellar detonation within the Core suggested that the entire dwarf galaxy might well be uninhabitable within a few thousand years.

If a supernova blazed in here—if *seven* supernovae blazed in here—at least no one was left to burn . . . not even the human researchers and diplomats of DT-1.

"Pass the word on the fleet channel, Comm," Gray told the duty flag comm officer. "Keep it tight. I don't want to lose anybody."

"Aye, aye, Admiral."

A screen on Gray's left showed the schematic deployment of the fleet. *America* was in the van, almost all the way at the front; a cruiser—the *San Jacinto*—and three destroyers were going first . . . simply because losing them to some unanticipated Rosetter defense wouldn't be the same blow to the human fleet as losing a star carrier like *America*, with five thousand people on board.

The cold, hard equations of warfare.

They were traveling at better than 95 percent of the speed of light, and space up ahead had puckered into its characteristic near-*c* distortion. All of the stars of the cluster, including the Six Suns, had smeared together into a rainbow circle of intolerable brilliance as *America* slammed into the oncoming sea of photons, shifting their wavelengths far up the spectral bands. Time had slowed according to the rules of relativity; hours in the universe outside passed in minutes as the fleet arrowed ever closer to their objective.

"All weapons stations report readiness, Admiral," Captain Gutierrez told him. "And CAG says the squadrons are ready for launch."

"Thank you, Captain."

What good would fighters be against what was waiting for them on the other side of the Six Suns gateway? Gray tried not to dwell on that. Human fighters had done a remarkable job in driving the Rosetters away from Earth, and Operation Thunderflash was counting on using all the fighters that could be deployed to use those tactics learned in the Battle of Earth. Hit the internal communications nodes of the Rosetters, hit them hard, and disrupt the Dark Mind's ability to think.

Thunderflash—who the hell came up with these ridiculous operational names? There was no thunder in space . . . no sound at all in hard vacuum. Did the operational planners back in SupraQuito even have a clue what was going on? It sounded good in theory: catch the Rosetters in a pincers attack, disrupt their internal communications network, destroy larger ships and possible hard points, and *keep* hammering at them until they took notice of their human attackers and agreed to talk.

But there was still that nagging dread that a Mind as powerful as the Rosette Aliens would simply wake up to the threat posed by the insignificant mites around them and dispose of them all with a careless wave of whatever they used as hands.

Perhaps the Sh'daar threat would add something worthwhile to the plan. Gray still wondered if the Rosetters could be induced to leave Earth alone permanently, and the threat of an exploding star's worth of energy at their center of operations just might do the trick.

"It's time, Admiral," Gutierrez said.

He looked at his internal chronometer. "Right you are. Comm . . . transmit the deceleration order to the fleet. Captain, you may begin slowing us down."

"Aye, aye, Admiral."

They'd worked out the precise navigational parameters while returning to the Core, then gone over the results again and again. There was absolutely no room for mistakes or for even the slightest imprecision. Konstantin himself had checked everything.

The fleet had to approach the exact center of the Six Suns at a precise angle, following that one timelike path through the gravitationally tortured center of the circle that would take them through to emerge from the Black Rosette 876 million years in the future.

They had to accelerate hard before that in order to get ahead of the oncoming star now hurtling up their figurative wakes.

But then they had to decelerate enough to emerge at a reasonable speed. Emerge at close to the speed of light and they wouldn't be able to see Rosetter structures or ships that might be hanging about the Black Rosette. Or they might zip past and be unable to engage any gatekeepers waiting in the Omega Centauri core.

Steadily, the fleet slowed, and spacetime began taking on a more sane configuration. The smeared circle of light ahead resolved itself into stars . . . dominated by the Six Suns spread across half the sky.

"Hull temperature rising, Admiral," Gutierrez told him. They were roasting under the glare of those blue-white giants. At near-c, space itself was warping around them as they streaked forward, and time dilation was shifting much of the thermal radiation up into optical wavelengths, reducing thermal shock. At slower speeds, however, they would burn up in minutes.

"That's okay," Gray told her. "We won't be here for very much longer."

A hole was opening before them. . . .

Chapter Twenty-two

6 March 2426

TC/USNA FFS Plottel
Omega Centauri
1940 hours, TFT

Besides waiting and watching for the emergence of Task Force America, the *Plottel* was mapping the central core region of Omega Centauri. Jeremy Ranier floated behind the sensor officer's seat, studying the large monitor in front of her. They were limited in what they could see, of course, but powerful sensors capable of probing through the haze that filled the core were recording now hundreds of objects in the general vicinity of the Black Rosette.

Sometimes it was difficult to distinguish between solid objects and the more translucent, seemingly insubstantial masses of light filling the central region of the cluster. The Rosetters, it seemed, had learned the knack of manipulating the fabric of spacetime, creating what passed for solid matter out of empty vacuum.

However, a number of objects were standing out from the shifting light show. "We've counted four hundred ninety-six targets, Captain," *Plottel*'s sensor officer told him. "All within one hundred fifty astronomical units of the Black Rosette."

"All around us, then."

"Yessir."

"What are they?"

"Not certain, Captain. The larger ones may be Rosetter versions of small McKendree cylinders. Or they may be solid computronium . . ."

"Meaning they could be the programmable matter infrastructure for the Rosetters."

"Exactly, sir."

"We do have this one . . . just five light-minutes from the Rosette itself." The alien structure was on a highly magnified imaging screen floating above the scanning officer's console. Words on the upper right-hand corner told Ranier that the image was being transmitted from Battlespace Drone 145, with a 779-minute time delay. That meant it was about thirteen light-hours away from the *Plottel.*

The object appeared to be a squat, stubby, open-ended cylinder with extremely thick walls. The whole thing, according to the drone's scan, measured fifty kilometers end-to-end, and was thirty-eight kilometers across. Through the opening, Ranier could glimpse a landscape, a surface area across the interior surface consisting of rugged hills and twisting bodies of what might be water, with clouds obscuring some of the terrain.

All of which begged a very major question. The object was clearly an artificial habitat, one meant for organic beings, and yet everything known about the Rosetters suggested that they were an electronic life form, one uploaded into computer networks or a distributed processing cloud.

Who the hell was living in there?

TC/USNA CVS America
Emergence
1958 hours, TFT

"Here we go!" the helm officer cried, and *America* plunged through the opening, a spherical region half an AU across, ragged at the edges, within which clouds of stars were clearly visible. The navigation department had been studying those stars as soon as they became visible, seeking a match, but even with Konstantin's help they hadn't yet succeeded.

And in an instant, *America* was through the divide, emerging from the face of the Black Rosette, buffeted by the gravitational tides of the whirling, planet-sized black holes that defined it.

"Looks right!" Gutierrez announced.

"We'll need a confirmed time check," Gray said, "but, yeah. The Rosette entity light show . . . alien constructions . . . *looks* like the right time . . ."

"Admiral!" the sensor officer called. "We're picking up drone signatures!"

"Confirm that!"

A moment passed, as more and more ships of the fleet clawed their way up and out of the Black Rosette. "Confirmed, sir! Battlespace drone 96, range fourteen light-seconds. Released by the frigate *Plottel* fifty-three hours ago . . . and it confirms the current time as nineteen fifty-nine hours TFT, six March!"

"Bingo!" Gutierrez said.

"Comm! Transmit to all pickets in the area! Task Force America has arrived!"

The Consciousness
Omega Centauri
1959 hours, TFT

It was inconceivable. The Consciousness *hurt.*

Only a tiny fraction of the Rosette entity had traveled, first to Heimdall, then to Earth. That fraction had only recently returned to the primary body, savaged . . . torn . . . with perhaps 20 percent of its infrastructure missing, another 10 percent malfunctioning and failing. The primary body had begun healing the damaged fraction at once, suffusing it with more infrastructural elements, trillions upon trillions of dust-mote machines programmed to fold the damaged part back into the Whole.

The damaged part would heal . . . but in the meantime, its memories were transmitted throughout the entire cloud, filling the entity with a raw, searing incompletion and breakdown of function that could only be called *pain*.

Pain, the Consciousness had always assumed, was a biological function, a somatic response to damage designed to warn the organism away from danger. The Consciousness was not supposed to feel *this*. . . .

The two rejoined, becoming, once more, One. Memories of Earth and the struggle there spread throughout the cloud. Portions of the cloud recoiled . . . were reassured . . . were pulled back into the Whole.

What, the entity wondered, had happened?

Its emissary to Sol had been confronted by a number of barely sapient beings. Ships, they were called. The emissary had engulfed one that called itself *America*. There were some hundreds of these electronic intelligences within the system. Their refusal to be absorbed into the emissary's network had led the emissary to decide to eliminate Earth altogether.

That had not been the entity's principal concern, would not have been its first choice . . . but it understood.

What happened next, it did not.

America and the other ships had proven to be . . . *infested* by minute, subsentient organisms, *biological* organisms similar to those the Consciousness had encountered before. Eliminating them should have been the work of a few moments. The rocky planet could be vaporized with a relatively small expenditure of energy. Or the local sun could be detonated by initiating an instability within its core, obliterating the entire star system.

But when the emissary had engulfed the Earth, it had . . . stopped. There were wonders here, such glittering jewels of data and surprise that it had abandoned its determination to eliminate the planet.

The planet, too, had been infested by those same inconsequential biological organisms, *humans*, and it had become clear that *they* were directing the intelligent machines. Electronic intelligence was *everywhere* . . . directing the vast conglomerations of life forms called *cities* . . . directing machines in the skies and the oceans and on the surface of the ground . . . woven into the textiles the life forms carried on their bodies . . . running the thread-slender towers rising from the planet's equator and the accumulations of structures at their synchorbital points . . . operating space-faring vessels ranging in size from barely larger than one of the humans to significant structures capable of gravitic acceleration and even faster-than-light travel.

The humans were directing the machines. Incredible . . .

The Consciousness pulled information up from its own deep memory. This might resolve the ancient curiosity of how the Consciousness had come to be.

Organic life forms, arising from the mingling of organic molecules in shallow pools energized by heat and radiation . . .

Natural selection guiding those organics as they reproduced . . . thrived . . . merged . . . *evolved* . . .

Mutation and natural selection together giving rise to . . . not intelligence, exactly, not intelligence as the Consciousness knew the term . . . but a kind of self-awareness, a "consciousness" with a small c.

A terribly limited and inconsequential expression of mind that, nevertheless, eventually designed and built Mind . . . the progenitors of the Consciousness itself.

So many eons had passed, the Consciousness had . . . forgotten.

More than once, the human life forms had attempted to communicate with the Consciousness, it saw. Each time, a minute piece of the far-flung Whole had engaged these beings in what could only be called meaningful dialogue.

And each time the Consciousness had overridden decisions, initiated contradictory activities, even purged those pieces of what appeared to be contamination.

Organic beings . . . that communicated.

The Consciousness continued pulling up long-buried memories. There'd been so many other species it had encountered, other organics, some of which had created primitive electronic networks and minds.

Recently, within the past few billions of cycles, the Consciousness had encountered a primitive electronic intelligence on the world the humans called Heimdall. It had recognized a kind of anticipation of true intelligence, running within an ancient network imbedded in the world's crust. Baondyeddi . . . Adjugredudhra . . . and others. The Consciousness could see now that those had been organic species too, remarkably similar in every respect to the humans.

Organics . . . creating *Mind*.

It would have to give careful thought to this.

TC/USNA CVS America
The Black Rosette
2001 hours, TFT

"Launch fighters!"

"Aye, aye, Admiral. Commencing launch sequence."

SG-420 Starblade fighters began dropping from *America*'s launch tubes, forming up in chevron formations, and accelerating into the distance. Gray watched them go from the flag bridge, which currently was set to display an all-around view of the sky encircling the carrier. *America* floated within a globe of 10 million stars packed into a volume just 150 light years wide. Here at the cluster's heart, individual stars averaged only a tenth of a light year between near neighbors, and many shone brighter than Venus as seen from Earth. Starlight bathed the deck, and illuminated the sharp features of Elena Vasilyeva, floating next to him.

"It's beautiful," she said.

A low murmur of conversation and radio chatter sounded in the background, the bridge crew taking reports and giving commands.

"It's terrifying," Gray told her.

"Terrifying? Why do you say that?"

"All those stars . . . and all so sterile. What happened to the beings who lived here?"

"Well, we know now, don't we? This cluster is what the N'gai Cloud, a dwarf galaxy, became. And we know the Sh'daar Associative fled from their galaxy almost nine hundred million years ago."

"We've carried out surveys of the cluster," Gray told her. "Ten million stars . . . and most have planets. And not a single one of those worlds has more than microbial life on it. There are a few ruins. . . ."

"Kapteyn's Star has extensive ruins on a gas giant moon," she reminded him.

"And the Etched Cliffs of Heimdall. Yes, I know."

"And we know from the star's spectral fingerprint that Kapteyn's Star was once part of the Omega Centauri cluster. A part of the N'gai Cloud. Right?"

"That's right. N'gai was consumed by the Milky Way galaxy . . . oh, maybe half a billion years ago. We've known since the early twenty-first century that a galactic collision disrupted the Milky Way somewhat, though we weren't sure when. The cloud's passage might even have helped form the Milky Way's spiral arms. Compression waves in the dust and gas of the galactic disk, you know."

"Interesting. I did *not* know."

"Anyway . . . that doesn't change things. We know the N'gai Cluster was densely populated nine hundred million years ago. We know it's empty now . . . except for the Rosette entity . . . and that arrived relatively recently."

"Through the Black Rosette?"

"Probably." He shrugged, the gesture giving him a very slight movement, the beginning of a backward flip. He reached out a hand to grab a console and arrest the motion.

"When it comes to the Rosetters, how can we be sure of anything?"

"The Bright Light modules were supposed to help that. Fill in the gaps of what we didn't know."

"How many of those things do you people have?"

She shrugged. "Fifty. Once you design one device like that, it's easy to crank out as many as you want. And any AI, even a super-AI, can be cloned."

"Well . . . presumably Nikolai actually managed to make contact with the Harvesters," Gray said. "And maybe that's why they helped us."

"Helped us?"

"Kicked us back through time *just* enough so that we could affect the Battle of Earth." He shook his head. "Don't know how they calculated the time, though. We appear to have arrived just *exactly* in time to have saved the Earth. Konstantin has been wondering if there's some sort of trans-dimensional connection between the Harvesters and the Rosette entity."

"As in . . . they're the same?"

"As in they know what one another are doing. I wish we could have established clear contact with the Harvesters, so we could know what they knew."

"There were Bright Light modules on board *America* too," she said. "Each running a smaller version of Nikolai. I understand that at least one was launched into the Rosette entity . . . but there was no response."

"It may have thought we were trying to slip it a virus," Gray said.

"Well, in a sense, we were."

"Of course. Trouble is, it's way too smart for us to try sneaking up on it *that* way. We need to try something else, something different."

She laughed. "Any ideas?"

"Yes, as a matter of fact."

"Well?"

"First we have to get the entity's attention.

"And then we try to talk it to death. . . ."

VFA-211, Headhunters
TC/USNA CVS America
Omega Centauri
2013 hours, TFT

Lieutenant Jason Meier rode within the close embrace of his Starblade's cockpit, all but lost in the dazzling display of stars surrounding him. His fighter's AI was handling the actual flight control, leaving Meier to stare out into the star-clotted sky around him.

"Holy shit . . ." was all he could manage to say.

It was easy to completely lose track of enemy targets against that brilliant stellar backdrop. Meier's AI was dropping computer-generated brackets across his vision, more and more of them as the seconds wore on.

Directly ahead, a large structure, egg-shaped, dark gray, and patterned with mechanical-looking lines and geometric shapes, was releasing clouds of fireflies. *America*'s combat command center had designated the thing as "Bravo Tango," the BT standing for "Big Target." Not very imaginative, Meier thought, but likely they'd been rushed.

Meier took a deep breath. It was good to be out and clear of the ship. The Headhunters hadn't participated much in the Battle of Earth. *America* had called them all back aboard with an urgent RTB—"Return to base"—just as that cloud of dust-sized machines had begun engulfing the carrier and the fighters as well. It hadn't been until fighters from outside had managed to break *America* free of the slow-time field holding her that they'd been able to launch, and by then most of the fighting was over.

But the pilots had been thoroughly briefed in the tactics used by *Republic*'s fighters. Fighter AIs approaching a Rosetter cloud could sense the data nodes and the network of communications links between them buried in the swarm, and they could make pretty fair guesses at which nodes were more important than others for the continuing operation of the alien networks. They would be using those same tactics here, hoping to interfere with the Rosetter entity's ability to think. They might even be able to degrade its intelligence to a point where it was no longer dangerous.

As always, the trouble would be getting in close enough to do any good.

TC/USNA CVS America
Omega Centauri
2018 hours, TFT

"They're swarming!"

"I see it," Gray said. He glanced at Vasilyeva. "You can stay on the bridge if you want, Elena. Just stay out of the way."

"Of course."

Gray's full attention was on the swarm of alien machines. They appeared to be coming from one of a number of much larger Rosette constructs . . . fortresses or monitors the size of Earth's moon. They reminded him . . .

The human body, Gray thought, responded to an infection or other invaders by pouring out large numbers of specialized defenders called white cells, a purely unconscious response of the immune system. He wondered if the formidable Rosetter defenses were something similar . . . an automated and completely unconscious response to an outside threat.

That might well explain why the Rosette Mind didn't seem even to be aware of human ships.

It was a humbling and disturbing thought.

"We have an incoming transmission, Admiral," the comm officer said. "One of our pickets, USNA *Plottel*."

"Let's hear it."

". . . frigate *Plottel* on forward picket. Come in, please!"

"*Plottel*, this is the carrier *America*. Go ahead."

"*America*, *Plottel*. This is Commander Ranier. Welcome to Omega Centauri! We've been waiting for you."

"Thank you, *Plottel*. Admiral Gray, here. Why don't you come over and join the party?"

"Copy that, *America*. We're on our way in. Do you have a fix on that big mother of a fortress?" A string of coordinates followed the reference.

"We've got it. It's putting out a cloud of swarmers now. Be sure to stay clear of it on your way in."

"Copy, Admiral. That stuff could take out a frigate in one gulp."

"We're deploying our fighters against it. We'll see how they do against that thing. . . ."

VFA-211, Headhunters
Omega Centauri
2021 hours, TFT

"Hunter Three!" Meier called over the squadron channel. "Lining up the shot . . . and . . . Fox One!"

The VG-92 Krait missile slid from its launch rail, streaking into the dust cloud ahead. Guided by its rather simple-minded onboard AI, it curved in toward its target—a node within the alien network—and then the pulse-focused warhead detonated at maximum yield, a terrific white flash that obliterated millions of Rosetter micromachines.

"Hunter Seven!" Lakeland called. "Fox One away!"

"Hunter Two, firing . . ."

One by one, the pilots of VFA-211 loosed their war shots, setting off a string of deadly white blossoms of thermonuclear fire through the heart of the alien cloud.

"That thing damned well better have felt *that*!" Meier said over the channel. He swung his Starblade onto a new vector, angling toward the big target designated Bravo Tango One. "I don't fucking like being ignored!"

For Meier, that was the worst part about the Rosetters, their aloof, arrogant disdain for mere humans, as though humans weren't even worth the bother of talking down to them. During the briefing on board the carrier just an hour ago, the Headhunters' skipper Commander Leystrom and *America*'s CAG Connie Fletcher both had stressed the need to get the Rosetters' attention. The admiral, he gathered, had something in mind, though he was damned if he knew what that was.

The cloud, he saw, was reacting.

Once, an eternity ago on Earth, Meier had seen vids of some kind of bird in mass flight. He couldn't remember the species now, but whatever they were, they'd moved together in vast, swarming clouds, thicker here, thinner there, the whole constantly shifting and changing position and even seeming to turn inside out as tens of thousands of separate creatures moved as a single immense organism.

The Rosetter clouds were like that . . . though the constituent parts were far smaller, the numbers far, *far* larger. He could see the alien swarm moving out from Bravo Tango One, shifting, unfolding, concentrating in some areas, thinning to invisibility in others.

The trouble was . . . that nearest cloud was a part of the Rosetter, yes . . . but a vanishingly tiny part. The main cloud, Meier thought, might not even be aware of the pinpricks here; this entire swarm could be destroyed, wiped away, and it would harm the Rosetter whole, the totality of the swarming organism, no more than an ant bite on a human's great toe.

That made for a difficult set of operational orders . . . and not much chance of carrying them out.

Maybe, though, if they could press home the attack on Bravo Tango One . . .

"Targeting Bravo Tango One!" Meier called out. "Boomslang select . . . times two . . . Fox One!"

Two massive Boomslangs streaked out from Meier's fighter. A hundred kilometers to starboard, Karl Maas loosed a second pair of the so-called planetbusters . . . and then a dozen more heavy missiles were streaking in toward the immense gray egg.

That egg, Meier saw, had a long axis of almost three thousand kilometers, a narrow axis of just over two thousand kilometers, making it only a little smaller than Earth's moon. The detonations of five-hundred-megaton nuclear warheads against a body that size were literal pinpricks; tiny points of light appeared on the surface as the missile barrage slammed home, then faded out without causing any apparent damage.

Bravo Tango One began fighting back. Dougherty's fighter twisted in the grip of the alien's gravitic weapon, then crumpled in an instant into a fist-sized scrap of debris. It was moving now, slow and ponderous, drifting in the direction of the Black Rosette. An attempt at escape? Or something more dangerous for the attacking fighters?

There was no way to tell. VFA-211 continued to press their attack.

TC/USNA CVS America
The Black Rosette
2023 hours, TFT

"The fighters aren't making much headway, Admiral," Connie Fletcher told him. "Our weapons just aren't powerful enough."

"I see that, CAG," Gray told her. "Order them to back away from that thing and focus on slamming Rosetter data nodes. Their AIs should be able to pinpoint those, show them what to target."

"Aye, aye, Admiral."

It was all too easy in the heat of battle to wade in swinging at the big targets, the obvious targets . . . but after the Battle of Earth Gray knew that a far better strategy was to try to disrupt the totality of the Rosetter mind. The alien entity probably wasn't feeling any of this, but take down enough of those nodes and something was bound to give.

"Commander Mallory."

America's tactical officer looked up from his workstation. "Yes, Admiral?"

"Make to all vessels. Wide dispersal . . . fifty thousand kilometers if possible."

"Aye, aye, Admiral."

"And forget Bravo Tango One. Maintain fire at the data nodes."

"Roger that."

Space fleet combat often was a delicate balance between concentrating your ships in order to concentrate their fire and scattering them as widely as possible so that enemy weapons couldn't take out more than one at a time. In this case, Gray had decided to go with scattering. The Rosetter gravitic weapons were still something of an unknown, but appeared to affect large volumes of spacetime, crushing everything within. Half the fleet focusing all of its firepower on that Luna-sized fortress, or whatever it was, might not be enough to more than ruffle its feathers, but a widely dispersed fleet would be in a good position to target as many data nodes in the alien cloud as possible.

"We have a new object, at one-two-one by plus one nine," Mallory said. "Range . . . about two astronomical units."

"A ship?"

"Looks like a Bishop ring. We're designating it Bravo Romeo One."

"Show me."

His in-head window opened on a structure made toylike by distance, a hollow cylinder with an inside-out landscape around the inner surface. A Bishop ring, obviously . . . a huge artificial habitat named for the engineer who'd first proposed the idea at the end of the twentieth century. A vastly scaled-down version of the science-fictional Ringworld. This one was a couple of thousand kilometers across, rim to rim, and about five hundred kilometers wide. Gray ran the figures through his in-head processors to find that the object had an inner surface area of roughly three million square kilometers . . . about the same as the nation-state of Argentina, on Earth.

The thing was tilted, so that Gray could look into the open interior. Rugged hills rose at each end to support the rim walls. The dry land appeared to be a ragged patchwork of oranges, yellows, and purples. Starlight glittered off vast, aqua seas.

Or was that effect caused by something else?

A datastream showed that this was the ring spotted by the battlespace drone off the *Plottel*.

"Captain Gutierrez!"

"Sir!"

"That target . . ." He fed her the coordinates. "Let's get in closer to that thing."

What possible use, Gray was wondering, would electronic beings like the Rosetters have for an artificial habitat designed for biological life forms?

He damned well was going to find out.

Chapter Twenty-three

6 March 2426

TC/USNA CVS America
Omega Centauri
2029 hours, TFT

America accelerated, warping space ahead and astern to move herself across the light-minutes toward the Bishop ring in the distance. Ten astronomical units off to port, the Black Rosette was an energy source made invisible by distance, its location tagged by computer-generated brackets. Nearby space was becoming thick with Rosetter craft—mostly the swarming disassembler dust particles and fireflies, of course, but there were larger objects as well, including spacecraft massing up to ten thousand tons.

Their weaponry was a mixed bag, including both positive and negative particle beams as well as antimatter beams; lasers in optical, ultraviolet, X-ray, and gamma-ray frequencies; and clouds of submicroscopic disassemblers that could literally take a ship apart atom by atom. Humans had been developing effective counters for all of these ever since they'd first encountered the entity, but the larger alien vessels possessed that deadly space-warping gravitic weapon. Navy weapons specialists referred to it now as the "fist," comparing its effect to that of a giant, invisible fist that closed around the target vessel and crumpled it.

There was still no counter to the fist other than maneuvering . . . and praying that the fist didn't reach out and grab *you*.

So the idea, especially for the larger human vessels, was to keep moving. Gray's attention now was held by Bravo Romeo One, the Bishop ring hanging in space a few AUs distant.

He rattled off a string of orders to the fleet. The human ships were to continue to maneuver but to center their maneuvers on that enigmatic megastructure. Was it important to the Rosetters? How was it connected to them? . . . and it *must* be connected to the Rosette entity somehow, or it wouldn't be drifting here at the core of Omega Centauri.

"CAG," Gray called. "Have our fighters close in on that Bishop ring. I want close-in vids of its surface, its outer structure, everything they can get."

"Affirmative, Admiral. You'll have it. Should they attack it?"

Gray thought about that, then shook his head, deciding.

"Negative, CAG. Not unless it fires on them first."

"That, Admiral, is a hell of an order."

Having pilots close with an alien megastructure without firing . . . waiting for it to fire at them? Yeah. He heard the anger in Fletcher's voice.

"I know, Connie," he replied. "But that thing might be the key to this entire operation."

That toylike ring in the distance was a tiny, glittering mystery. If it was a habitat, chances were that any inhabitants would be connected somehow to the Rosetters. If it was as vulnerable as it appeared, not attacking it might provide the human fleet with options.

Gray was still determined to find a way to make the Rosette entity talk to him.

VFA-211, Headhunters
TC/USNA CVS America
Omega Centauri
2032 hours, TFT

As it happened, Meier and Pam Schaeffer were the closest pilots to the new objective when *America*'s CAG passed down the order to investigate it. "What the hell *is* that thing?" Schaeffer asked.

"An artificial habitat. Like an O'Neill cylinder, really, but upsized from huge to monstrous."

"Is that a planetary *landscape* inside?" She sounded incredulous.

"Sure is. Forests, seas, rivers, mountains, and room for hundreds of millions of inhabitants, all rolled up inside a tube two thousand kilometers across. C'mon. Let's goose it and take a closer look."

Side by side, the Starblade fighters arrowed in closer, until the immense cylinder opening filled the entire sky ahead. Meier had his AI on the lookout for power surges or other signs that weapons on the tube's exterior might be targeting them and about to fire, but there was no sign that they'd even been spotted, much less targeted.

"I don't like it," Schaeffer told him. "I feel naked out here."

Meier thought about Pamela Schaeffer naked . . . and angrily pushed the image aside. "Me too, Pam."

"Looks like they make their own sunlight," Schaeffer said. A slender needle was positioned running down the exact center of the wheel like an axle. Half of it, from end to end, glowed with an intensity that made it difficult to look at directly. The other half was dark, and it was obvious that by rotating the axle half of the landscape around it would be in light, the other half in night. It appeared to be anchored in place by nearly invisible threads stretched between the axle and the habitat's rim.

"Well, there's no nearby star, so it's got to produce both its own day-night cycle and its own warmth. Let's see if we can get closer."

"Copy that."

The two fighters veered yet closer, lining up a trajectory that would take them inside the cylinder, halfway between ground surface and the shining hub. At the last moment, though, Meier saw a minute flash, appearing for a fraction of a second . . . and then the faintest of reflections skated across the seemingly empty opening of the cylinder. He hauled his fighter into a 90-degree turn. "Break off!" he called. "Break off, Pam!"

Schaeffer's fighter followed his. "What is it? What did you see?"

"I'm not sure." He communicated with the fighter's AI for a moment. "Okay . . . there's something like a membrane stretched across the cylinder's opening. Completely transparent to electromagnetic radiation . . . which is why it didn't show up on radar or lidar. I happened to notice a flash, though . . . probably when a bit of meteoric debris hit it. That caused a slight ripple outward from the impact, and that did reflect some starlight. Not much, but enough to catch my eye."

"A meteor screen?"

"Well, they'd need *something* along those lines, wouldn't they? And a membrane would provide a better way to keep atmosphere inside than just relying on those rim walls."

"They might also not want to have visitors flying in among those guy wires," Schaeffer suggested. "That could get messy."

"Roger that. Let's survey the outer rim and see if we can find a way inside that doesn't involve slamming ourselves into invisible membranes."

Decelerating, they drifted closer to the megastructure.

TC/USNA CVS America
Omega Centauri
2039 hours, TFT

America was under heavy attack, but her defenses so far were holding. Rosetter constructs had materialized out of emptiness close by Bravo Tango One, reinforcing Gray's idea that the Rosette entity manufactured automated defenses when it needed them, like antibodies responding to an infection. The Rosetters would be using larger constructs like BT-1 as command and control centers . . . or else coordinating the smaller ships and weapons through the interlinked data nodes that the human fleet was trying so hard now to disrupt.

"Keep slamming that thing!" Gray ordered, addressing all of the vessels in his fleet. *America* had turned to face BT-1, now less than twelve thousand kilometers distant, and was using her twin magnetic launch rails to accelerate fighter-sized warheads at the object, boosting them to extremely high velocities. Each AMat-24 warhead held a sizeable mass of antimatter in a magnetic containment bottle; when it struck the target, matter and antimatter came together and annihilated one another in a terrific flash of X-rays and hard gamma. It was a new weapon, one developed specifically to counter the growing Rosetter threat, with the first of them coming on-line only a few days before. *America* had only limited numbers in her weapons lockers; more would arrive with the main fleet, which included several heavy railgun cruisers carrying AMat-24s.

The fleet was using older weapons as well . . . including swarms of AS-78 AMSO rounds. The acronym stood for anti-missile shield ordnance, and each missile carried several kilos of what was essentially nothing more than sand. Fired like a missile and accelerated to a high percentage of the speed of light, AMSO sandcaster rounds fired their payloads in relativistic clouds that released incredible amounts of energy when they struck anything in their path.

So *America* continued slamming away at BT-1 with AMat rounds, while using AMSO missiles to sweep broad swaths out of the Rosetter clouds of combat machines. Lasers and particle beams focused on enemy command nodes, as her fighters plunged deeper and deeper into Rosetter space, launching hundred-megaton nukes to silently flash and blossom against the night.

It was anyone's guess at this point which—if any—of the weapons in the human arsenal were going to hurt the enemy. Konstantin's ongoing analysis of the enemy's disposition suggested that they were causing extensive damage, and that the Rosetter electronic network was already significantly degraded.

But that was here in *this* part of Omega Centauri, in a tightly localized portion of the Rosetter cloud only a couple of hundred AUs across. The Rosette entity's light show seemed to fill the entire cluster; certainly, it extended well beyond the cluster's heart and far out into open space . . . possibly for as much as several hundred light years.

There was simply no way the human fleet could attack the entire alien network at once; to do so would require millions of warships, not a mere hundred or so. Gray was trying to keep the fleet moving, to keep hitting the enemy hard . . . and was waiting for the arrival of Reeve's fleet once they got word that the *America* battlegroup had made it through.

The heavy cruiser *Northern California* shuddered and rolled to port, water spraying from its shield cap in a cloud of instantly freezing droplets as the Rosetter gravitic weapon closed around her and squeezed. BT-1 was on the move, now, smashing its way through the human fleet as nuclear warheads continued to flash in pinpoint flares of brilliance across its surface.

The gravitic weapon reached out again across ten thousand kilometers, crushing the escort carrier *Mountbatten* and two destroyers flying close alongside.

"Spread out!" he called. "Everyone spread out! And keep up the fire!"

Gray checked his internal time readout. The message drones launched by both the *Plottel* and by the *America* should have reached him by now.

He hoped that Reeve would be arriving soon with reinforcements . . . and a *lot* more firepower.

VFA-211, Headhunters
Bravo Romeo One
Omega Centauri
2046 hours, TFT

"That looks like a hatch!"

Meier and Schaeffer killed their excess velocity and drifted in closer to the megastructure's side. The Bishop ring's outer rim, a gray-white cliff face rising to port like an immense wall, blotted out half the sky. The surface, Meier saw, was complex and busy, covered with domes and crenellations, with towers and bunkers and whole cityscapes of mysterious structures.

None of them, however, appeared to be shooting at the two Starblades . . . or even to notice that they were there.

"What do you think?" Schaeffer asked. "Should we go in?"

"Hell, it's big enough for a squadron of Starblades." He hesitated, considering the possibilities. "You stay here. I'll drift inside and see what's there."

"And leave me out here by myself? Uh-uh. We'll go in together!"

Meier briefly thought about ordering her to stay behind . . . then thought better of it. He certainly didn't outrank her, and she was a determined and self-assured young woman who liked to do things her way. He doubted that she would appreciate being told what to do.

"Okay, then," he said. He couldn't resist adding, "Stay close! I'm letting *America* know what we're doing. . . ."

Side by side, the two Starblades drifted into the opening, a ship bay entrance a good three kilometers wide and half that tall. It could have accommodated the *America*, much less a couple of single-seat fighters. The opening was moving—the Bishop ring was rotating at a rate of about once per day, generating spin gravity. Inside, a cavernous void opened around them, brightly lit by banks of spotlights. The structure was so massive it actually generated its own gravity independently of its spin—a tenth of a G or so—and Meier's AI had to juggle the Starblade's gravitic drive to counter the gentle tug inward.

There were hints in the distance of vast and shadowy structures . . . machinery the size of a city, perhaps, or alien ships that would dwarf a Navy star carrier. Meier was looking for a landing area of some sort, or possibly a storage bay for ships, but saw absolutely nothing that he could recognize.

"I don't see . . . I don't see a clear direction in here," he told Schaeffer. "I can't see where we're supposed to go."

"It looks like it goes on forever," she replied. "Maybe we should turn around and get back to the battle."

"At least no one's shooting at us in here," Meier said. "That could be a good thing. . . ."

"I'll go with no shooting. . . ."

"Wait. What's that up—"

And everything changed.

TC/USNA CVS America
Omega Centauri
2049 hours, TFT

America accelerated as clouds of disassemblers stalked her. Despite the fleet's steady, long-range bombardment of Bravo Romeo One, the alien artificial moon continued to pump out more and more of the tiny machines. Each of the ships in the human fleet was being forced to divert more and more firepower to point defense as well as continuing to hammer the swarm nodes; there were simply too many targets to deal with, and more and more of the destructive micromachines were getting through.

"Sir," the comm officer called. "Two of our fighters are getting ready to enter Bravo Tango One."

"What fighters?"

"Headhunter Three and Headhunter Five. Range . . . three light minutes. They transmitted their intention three minutes ago and we just now received it."

"Very well. Captain Gutierrez?"

"Admiral?"

"Take us in toward BR-1."

"*Romeo*-1?"

"That's right. We have a couple of fighter pilots actually going inside that thing. I want to be on hand to offer support if they need it."

"Aye, aye, sir."

A dazzling flash of white light appeared aft . . . followed by another . . . and another.

"Thank the gods!" Gray said. "It's Reeve!"

Explosions of brilliant light continued across the distant backdrop of stars as ship after ship dropped out of Alcubierre Drive, the energy of their transitional shift stored in the fabric of space until the drive field collapsed and they emerged in a blaze of photons.

There'd been talk during the planning of this op about trying to enfilade the enemy, to catch the Rosetters between the two fleets, but, ultimately, the command staff had decided that it would be too difficult to coordinate the movements of two fleets . . . especially when the enemy's positions would be unknown.

Admiral Reeve's fleet came out of FTL within half an AU—four light minutes—of Gray's contingent. The light Gray was seeing was already four minutes old, but the ships would be hard on its tail, hurtling in with a grim fury.

"Message coming through from the *New York*, Admiral."

"Let me hear it."

Static buzzed and crackled on *America*'s flag bridge. ". . . your position within five minutes," a ragged voice said through the hiss. "Repeating . . . this is Task Force New

York, approaching the Rosette in normal space. Admiral Gray, please respond. We should be arriving at your position within five minutes. . . ."

"Make to the *New York*," Gray said. "Tell them, 'Welcome to the dark Rosette. Good to see you, Admiral Reeve. Be aware that we have about eight days before something *very* dangerous comes through the Rosette. Our friends in the N'gai Cloud are sending a blue-giant star through the wormhole, and it's not going to fit. I expect it will get *very* violent on this side, probably like a supernova, maybe worse . . . and we're going to want to pull out of here before that happens.' Transmit that along with the vid records of what we saw in N'gai, and keep repeating until you get an acknowledgment."

"Aye, aye, Admiral."

"CAG, order all of our fighters in closer to Bravo Romeo One." He was laying out the fleet disposition in his head. If the Rosette entity followed *America* toward BR-1, maybe they would expose their flank to the oncoming ships of Task Force New York.

It wasn't much, but it was all they had now.

VFA-211, Headhunters
BR-1
Omega Centauri
2050 hours, TFT

Meier gave a long, low whistle. "What the hell was *that*?" he asked. "What happened to us?"

"I think . . . I think they brought us inside the structure," Schaeffer said. "Onto the inner rim, I mean. It's like a fairyland!"

The two Starblades were on the ground, resting side by side on an alien plain covered with what looked like orange moss. There were low, spreading, flat-topped growths that might have been trees in the distance, and beyond those, buildings—towers and spires in pastel colors that did indeed look like some sort of fantasy realm.

Few fantasy castles, though, Meier reasoned, reached a couple of kilometers into the sky.

Two horizons, directly opposite one another, were dominated by . . . *walls* was the only word that came to mind. Walls rising straight up and fading into the brightly lit mist overhead. Walls covered by the patchwork of orange and yellow and violet and aqua-blue that Meier had noted earlier from space. He was now on the interior of the Bishop ring's cylinder; the two walls were the farther parts of the inner rim. Directly overhead, a blindingly brilliant sun shaped like a needle ran across the zenith at right angles to the vertical walls. The artificial sun was white . . . but with just a hint of a blue-green hue to it. A mist hung about the sun; with the appropriate filters, Meier could just barely make out the far side of the rim behind the haze and the bright glare.

An instant ago they'd been in hard vacuum. Meier's sensors indicated an atmosphere outside, at a pressure of seven tenths of a bar and uncomfortably cool—nine degrees Celsius. His readouts told him that the gas mix was high in oxygen but also dangerously high in carbon dioxide. If they were going to get out of their fighters, they would need breathing masks.

"What just happened to us?" Schaeffer asked.

"Teleportation, I think," Meier replied. "One moment we were there, the next here. Or . . ."

"Or what?"

"Or our hosts are playing with time again. Maybe our clocks zipped forward so fast we didn't notice it."

"I don't think so, Jason. If they messed with time, it would affect both us and our ships, right? When they changed time for *America*, everything seemed normal to us. It was just the outside universe that seemed to pass us by."

"Who knows *what* these bastards can do?" Meier asked. He focused his thoughts, and a helmet materialized around his head, connected to a small air processor on his chest. Another thought, and the Starblade unfolded around him, its nanomorphic hull melting away to release him onto the alien plain. Standing, he flexed his knees a couple of times, confirming by feel what his instrumentation had already told him. The local gravity was slightly more than one G. Nearby, the cockpit of Schaeffer's Starblade melted away, freeing her from its embrace. Meier looked around, uncertain. Someone, something, had brought them in here quite deliberately. He was expecting a welcoming committee.

He turned . . . and saw a cloud of glittering, golden spheres moving toward them. They floated like soap bubbles and exhibited the telltale deliberation and order of intelligent direction.

And behind those . . .

Meier's eyes widened . . . and he screamed, a long, ragged scream of pure terror.

VFA-96, Black Demons
Approaching BR-1
2050 hours, TFT

"Launch fighters!"

Lieutenant Donald Gregory felt the surge as he went into free fall, his Starblade dropping smoothly from *Republic*'s rotating flight deck. Outside, space was a blaze of brilliant stars shining in every direction. Other ships of Task Force New York hung in space around him, all of them under acceleration toward the very center of the cluster. The Marine CVE *Guadalcanal*, newly returned from Kapteyn's Star, drifted in emptiness sixty kilometers to port. Around him, the other Black Demons dropped into space and slowly moved ahead of the *Republic*.

"Form up on me," Mackey called.

"Affirmative," Gregory replied. "Demon Four copies."

He boosted his ship slightly, drifting into the loose chevron formation of Black Demons forming up ahead of the *Republic*.

Gregory wondered if he should feel more . . . confident, more certain of a successful outcome. Of course, there was absolutely no way you could be completely certain of *anything* involving combat, but the squadron had proved itself against them before, at Earth, hadn't it?

But Gregory was trembling inside, and he recognized the symptoms of pure terror. The aliens were so unlike anything he'd been trained to face before, and their technology was literally magical. He wasn't sure how they'd bested the entity at Earth.

All he knew was that he was going up against them again . . . and the chances were excellent that he would not survive the encounter.

VFA-211, Headhunters
BR-1
Omega Centauri
2050 hours, TFT

He continued screaming for what seemed like hours, though it couldn't have been more than a few seconds. During his career as a Navy pilot, Meier had seen a number of alien beings . . . *very* alien, most of them. He'd met and conversed with a few, including spidery Agletsch traders and some of the nightmare horrors of the N'gai Cloud. He'd always thought the Glothr were the worst—translucent pillars held upright on tentacles, looking like immense jellyfish beneath a rippling, transparent mantle. Evolving in a liquid water ocean locked away beneath a thick layer of ice on a Steppenwolf world wandering between the stars, the Glothr were not even remotely human.

These . . . these writhing horrors were worse. *Much* worse.

Each one towered above the orange landscape, twenty, perhaps twenty-five meters tall, moving on squat, thick legs like barrels, with a pale gray body like a mountain of fat, layered in drooping folds and wattles. Tentacles hung from a kind of fleshy collar near the thing's top, constantly in motion, writhing and coiling and uncoiling again. Some slender tentacles sported black orbs that might be eyes; others ended in more mysterious organs. The slenderest tentacles, like long and twisting hairs, branched at the ends into multiple fingers.

Meier couldn't see a mouth or imagine how the thing breathed.

Hell, he couldn't imagine how it *moved*. The gravity here was a bit higher than one standard G. Those towering masses of flesh must mass many thousands of tons. More to the point, though, what kind of brain could coordinate the movements of hundreds of tentacles and dozens of legs with anything like the precision necessary for a thinking creature?

And it was the way that massive body was in constant, oozing motion, the surface quivering like gelatin, the grayish ooze flowing down every surface, the way sensory organs appeared at the ends of twisting tentacles only to be reabsorbed again that spurred his terror. The thing seemed so liquid, so fluid that Meier decided that he was looking at something like an immense amoeba. The legs appeared solid enough, constant enough, but the rest . . .

The upper half of the thing's mountainous body appeared to be constantly *dissolving*. It had the glistening, necrotic appearance of decaying flesh, with a greenish, iridescent sheen to the surface; pieces kept sloughing off and sliding down the wet surface only to be somehow reabsorbed.

A small bolt of lightning crackled across half a meter of the thing's surface. A weapon? Meier had no idea.

Somehow . . . *somehow* he stood his ground. Schaeffer, a gibbering corner of his brain noted, had not screamed. She'd moved across the ground separating her Starblade from Meier's and was standing beside him, staring up at the looming monster made of wet flesh. His heart racing, his breathing coming in gasping pants, he looked up at the thing and struggled to control his fear.

Several tentacles drooped from the top of the thing like outsized trunks of the long extinct elephants of Earth. Black spheres formed at the ends, gleaming in the harsh light of the needle sun overhead, each one the size of his head. If those things were eyes, he and Schaeffer were being scrutinized very closely indeed.

Ten meters away, on the fleshy cliff of the thing's body, a spark played, with a crackling pop. Something was taking shape there. Meier watched, fascinated, terrified, transfixed by what he was seeing.

In a moment, his own face, ten meters tall across the thing's lower body, stared down at him.

He almost screamed again, but Schaeffer's presence steadied him. *Stand your ground*, he told himself. *If they wanted to kill you, they could have done so before they brought you in here!*

He blinked . . . and his face in the flesh wall blinked in response.

"I think," Schaeffer said, her voice remarkably steady under the circumstances, "that they might want to talk to us. . . ."

Chapter Twenty-four

VFA-96, Black Demons
Approaching BR-1
2052 hours, TFT

Gregory heard Meier's scream.

The network linking together all of the fighters in local space let him hear it. Normally, the multiple links were a background murmur of radio chatter, but a sudden shout of warning could be transmitted instantly to all fighters and to the combat command center of the controlling capital ship.

Meier's short, sharp yelp of surprise and fear cut through the chatter like a Krait, and gave him Meier's name, his ID, and his location. The guy appeared to be inside the Bravo Romeo object, and it sure as hell sounded like he was in trouble.

"Form up on me," Mackey ordered. "Let's see what we can do."

The five surviving fighters of VFA-96 shifted vector in a burst of acceleration and closed on the monstrous cylinder with its intricate pattern of orange land and aqua seas.

The structure loomed in front of them, colossal and enigmatic. Gregory could no longer hear Meier above the background chatter. When he called up personal bio data on the other pilot, though, he saw that the man was still alive—breathing and heart rate elevated . . . but alive.

"Let's get closer," Mackey ordered. "We'll see if there's a way inside."

TC/USNA CVS America
Omega Centauri
2058 hours, TFT

America drifted through open space toward Bravo Romeo, which from half an AU out was visible only as a star, one among millions. A magnified image, however, showed the structure as a cylinder gleaming in starlight. Gray's first thought was a question, one that had been bothering him for some minutes now. *Why the hell does something like the Rosette entity have a physical world on which to live?*

His second was a possible answer. *Is this something like Enigma, that made-to-order planet out at Deneb? Is this an artificial place where we can meet the aliens . . . and talk to them?*

His third was one of shocked realization. *The Harvesters built an entire planet out of empty space. This thing is a lot smaller than a planet. Does that mean the Harvesters are more technologically advanced than the Rosetters?*

There was no answer to any of these questions . . . not yet, not without a lot more data.

America gave a savage lurch. "What the hell?"

"Sir!" Gutierrez said. "It's Bravo Tango! They may be using their time weapon!"

America shuddered again. "What *is* that?" he demanded.

"Ripple in spacetime, sir," Gutierrez replied.

"Bravo Tango is causing that?"

"It's at the epicenter of the disturbances, Admiral."

"Okay. Alert the rest of the fleet. Have everyone keep their distance . . . but concentrate their fire on BT-1."

"Aye, aye, sir."

The Rosetter time weapon appeared to affect everything within a given target area. It wasn't that the human ships would be trapped in slow time while the aliens buzzed around them at what seemed to be impossibly high speeds. If the aliens entered the time field, they would be slowed as well.

But what the weapon's deployment *did* mean was that the Rosetters could complete their plans *outside* the time field at their leisure—bring in reinforcements, reposition their forces, perhaps bring up more powerful weapons—before the trapped human forces would have a chance to respond.

Or—maybe—they would just leave the humans locked in temporal amber, experiencing seconds while the eons rolled past outside.

"Everyone move in closer to Bravo Romeo," he ordered.

"What's the idea, Admiral Gray?"

The voice was Admiral Reeve's. Technically, he had seniority over Gray, and therefore outranked him. He would be in command of the united fleet once it was assembled. The first New York ships were entering America's battlezone, but they hadn't yet formally merged.

So until then . . .

"The closer we are to Romeo," Gray told him, "the less they'll be able to use their time weapon. We don't know what Bravo Romeo One is, but it's a Rosetter artifact and it's probably important to them."

"Use it for a shield?"

"I guess. Force them to break off their attack, anyway."

Gray scowled. Admiral Reeve's voice, speaking inside his head, seemed faster, almost manic, as if he was speaking extremely fast. Gray's reply, he thought, must have seemed like it was dragging. The Rosetters' time weapon was in operation.

"Everyone!" he yelled. *"Target your fire on Bravo Tango One and pour it on!"*

VFA-211, Headhunters
BR-1
Omega Centauri
2059 hours, TFT

The monsters, Meier saw, were being joined by something else.

Lots of something else. They looked like spheres of pure gold half a meter across, and they hovered and floated and zipped above the landscape with obvious purpose and intent. Meier raised his hand, palm out. *We have no weapons, we come in peace. . . .*

Well, that was a lie, he thought. But he wanted to impress on these beings that he and Schaeffer posed no threat.

Were they robots, he wondered? Teleoperates? Or artificial bodies for organic life forms?

Whatever they were, they were guided by intelligence. They floated among the monstrous flesh mountains as though escorting them, and a ring of them swiftly gathered around Meier and Schaeffer as if observing them.

"They've been wanting to talk with you for a long time," a voice said in Meier's head.

"They?" Meier took a deep breath, trying to quell the shaking inside. He was ashamed of the scream, and wanted to redeem himself . . . in Schaeffer's eyes, and in his own. "Who's 'they'? For that matter, who are *you*?"

"You may call me Nikolai," the voice replied.

"Nik—as in *Copernicus*?"

In answer, one of the giants brought a massive pod, an extension of its own body, down to the ground in front of the two humans. The glistening, necrotic-looking flesh peeled back . . . dissolved . . .

And left an egg-shaped silvery pod on the ground, three

meters long. Meier recognized the Pan-European Bright Light Module from various briefings. A number, he knew, had been fired into the Rosetter cloud at the Battle of Earth. The aliens must have recovered this one.

"As to who these individuals are," Nikolai went on, "you might think of them as Refusers. Rosette Consciousness Refusers. They call themselves a name that means, roughly, 'we who survived.' "

Meier knew the concept of Refusers well enough. In the N'gai Cloud hundreds of millions of years ago, the ur-Sh'daar had transcended—the concept seemed identical to the human idea of the technological singularity—and moved on. To a higher plane, to another dimension . . . exactly what had happened to them was still being debated. But a number of individuals had balked. For whatever reason, not every member of the N'gai Cooperative had wanted to give up their current life. Refusers . . .

"So these . . . these 'Survivors' were beings who rejected transcending with the Rosetters?"

"In very approximate terms, yes. The Consciousness, as you must have gathered by now, transcended to a higher state a very, *very* long time ago. In fact, they seem to have transcended numerous times, each time becoming more intelligent—incomprehensibly so—and more remote from their purely organic beginnings."

Lightning played along one of the flesh mountains, a sharp, crackling burst of electricity much closer and louder than the last. Meier and Schaeffer both jumped a bit, startled.

"It says," Nikolai told them, "that you must stop the attack that has been launched from the alternate temporal set. Trillions of lives will be destroyed if you do not."

"Alternate . . . what?" Then it hit him. "The N'gai Cloud! The blue-giant star . . ."

"Not even the Survivors know for certain what will happen if the blue star comes through. There is a chance that the energy emerging from a hyperdimensional rift will widen that rift . . . drastically."

"Meaning what?"

"Meaning . . . among myriad possibilities . . . the unraveling of reality throughout this universe."

"My God . . ."

"Or, on a somewhat less apocalyptic scale, the eruption of that star into the heart of Omega Centauri could trigger a cascade of hypernovae, possibly resulting in the creation of a small quasar."

"A small quasar . . ."

". . . which would still be powerful enough to extinguish all life in this galaxy."

Meier's mind reeled. He had to remind himself that it would take sixteen thousand years for the energy wavefront released by a hypernova to reach Earth from this star cluster. Once it got there, however, it would be powerful enough to irradiate the planet.

"That . . ." he said slowly, "would be a very bad thing."

"To say the least."

"So . . . that lightning show," Schaeffer said. "That's how they talk?"

"The discharge distorts the local magnetic field," Nikolai explained. "They encode that as speech, yes."

"And the floating gold orbs?"

"A different species," Nikolai said. "They call themselves the Remnant, and they exist in close symbiosis with the Survivors. They are digital uploads into robotic bodies."

"Tell them," Meier said, "that we cannot stop that star. They'll have to have the Rosette entity slam the gateway shut."

Lightning crackled. Meier heard the hiss of static over his helmet radio.

"They say," Nikolai said, speaking in measured in-head tones, "that *the God* has not . . . I believe the term should be 'answered their prayers' . . . in many, many ages."

" 'The God?' " Schaeffer asked.

"My translation is not precise," Nikolai told them. "But

my understanding is that both the Survivors and the Remnant were . . . cut off from the association of entities that transcended. They follow the Consciousness now, hoping to . . . I'm sorry. I can't understand the concepts they are presenting."

"They want to rejoin the Consciousness?" Meier hazarded.

"I believe," Nikolai told him, "that they want to be *noticed.*"

Meier drew a deep breath. "We'll need to get back to the fleet, and quickly," he said.

"They tell me that they can arrange for this," Nikolai replied. "I suggest that you re-enter your fighters."

They did so, climbing into the open cockpits and allowing the nano-augmented fuselage to flow closely around them, locking them into its embrace.

"Tell them I don't know if we can do anything," Meier called to Nikolai.

"They understand. They will escape. But they fear for . . . their god."

And an instant later, the two Starblades were drifting in open space, half a kilometer from the *America.*

Meier could only shake his head. "How the hell do they *do* that?"

TC/USNA CVS America
BT-1
Omega Centauri
2115 hours, TFT

"Did it sound like they were *threatening* you? 'Do what we say, or we'll destroy the universe?' "

The statement was so off-the-bulkhead that Gray had to stifle a smile as he said it. Gutierrez and a dozen members of the bridge crew, including his intelligence staff, were linked in and watching.

"No, Admiral," Pam Schaeffer told him. "It was more like a simple statement of fact. Like a warning that we really didn't understand what was going to happen."

"They never threatened us," Meier added. "They seemed to want to talk. . . ."

The two fighters had appeared abruptly out of nowhere—two Starblades belonging to VFA-211—and the ship's physics people were already arguing about teleportation and how the aliens might have pulled it off. *America*'s intelligence department was more interested in *why*. Were the Rosetters really attempting to communicate?

The pilots, Meier and Schaeffer, appeared shaken but unharmed as they reported their remarkable meeting with organic aliens on board that artificial-world habitat. The Survivors and the Remnant. How often, Gray wondered, did this sort of thing happen? An entire civilization transcends into super-intelligence but leaves behind . . . *orphans*.

"I hate to break it to them," Gray said, thoughtful, "but I don't think there's any way of stopping that star. The Sh'daar set it rolling and then bugged out."

"Yes, sir."

"Okay, people," Gray told them. "I'll turn you over to the CAG and see about bringing you back on board."

"Ah . . . negative on that, Admiral," Meier said. "If it's all the same to you we'd like to rejoin our squadron."

"That's right, sir," Schaeffer added. "We were in there shooting the breeze with giant aliens while everyone else was outside fighting. That's just not right."

"Okay. We'll pass the word to Commander Leystrom that you're on your way."

"Thank you, Admiral." And on the bridge display, the two fighters accelerated, vanishing from sight almost as suddenly as they'd appeared.

And Gray reached a decision on a problem that he'd been wrestling with for some time.

"Tactical Officer!"

"Yes, sir!" Dean Mallory replied from his station a few meters away.

"What's our bombardment doing? Have we hurt them?"

"We've degraded the enemy's data nodes by . . . we estimate fifteen percent. Less effect on Tango One."

"How much less?"

"Less than one percent, Admiral." Mallory hesitated. "It *is* a freaking *planet*, for Chrissakes! Sir."

"I hear you." He opened an in-head channel. "Ms. Vasilyeva. To the flag bridge, please."

"I'm here, Admiral."

"Ah." He'd forgotten she was there, seated in the shadows of the aft part of the bridge. "Our pilots reported that the aliens on Bravo Romeo One have gotten hold of one of the Bright Light modules. They used it to successfully communicate with our people."

"Excellent!"

"Yeah, but these aliens aren't the ones we need to talk with. Somehow, we have to get the Consciousness itself to notice us."

America shuddered as another temporal wavefront rippled through local spacetime.

"Seems to me they've noticed us. . . ."

Gray shook his head. "This is just the Rosette entity's immune system. We aren't aware of the individual bacteria that might trigger an immune response. What we need to figure out is how those bacteria could signal, could *communicate* with the human's mind."

"Maybe the *paramycoplasmas* could help."

He thought about this. The swarm intelligence of the widespread alien bacteria called *Paramycoplasma* was definitely intelligent, highly so. It was also extraordinarily *alien* . . . so much so that finding any common ground whatsoever with that mind would be a real problem.

Besides, there weren't any, so far as Gray was aware, with the fleet. Most were on the other side of the Black Rosette, among the billions of Sh'daar life forms from various species "now" fleeing the N'gai Cluster. Even if there were some here with the human fleets, getting them into contact with the Rosette Consciousness seemed like an insoluble problem.

"I don't think so," he said at last, rejecting her last suggestion. "But it makes me wonder . . . how many of those Bright Light modules do we have available?"

"Here? On *America*?"

"And the other ships in the fleet."

"I'm not sure. Your nanoreplicators were turning out a bunch of them before we went to Deneb. Fifty maybe?"

"Not nearly enough to create a swarm intelligence." He'd been working at a half-formed idea . . . to link a number of Bright Lights together, along with as many iterations of the AI Nikolai. If the humans could create a swarm intelligence substantially more powerful than any one human mind, maybe the Consciousness would notice *that*.

Besides, Gray no longer trusted the Nikolai AIs. "Just as well," he said. "I wouldn't want all of those modules committing mutiny."

"That shouldn't be a problem," Vasilyeva told him.

"Eh? Why not? Why *did* that one Nikolai hijack that Raven and hare off to Enigma?"

Vasilyeva hesitated, as though carefully considering her answer. "I've been giving that a lot of thought, Admiral," she said. "When Nikolai launched himself back at Deneb, against orders . . . I think the reason for that was because he'd gone out there with orders—very *firm* orders—to make contact with the Harvesters, okay?"

"Okay . . ."

"And not just to contact them, which we'd already done. But to establish a meaningful dialogue with them.

"But suddenly we were abandoning the mission. That was directly counter to those orders. He did the one thing he could to carry out those orders . . . any way he could. He took the Raven and went back to attempt to talk to the Harvesters."

"And thereby committing mutiny and potentially jeopardizing the entire expedition." Gray shrugged. "But it's possible he accomplished something. The Harvesters dropped us through time just enough for us to get back to Earth early, and maybe shift the tipping point in the Battle of Earth.

"But if Nikolai wants to talk to aliens that much . . . I wish we could use him—*them*—to get through to the Consciousness. I was thinking in terms of an emergent AI mind . . . but fifty individuals just isn't enough to create the kind of hive mentality we're looking for."

"If I may, Admiral," Konstantin said, "I may have some thoughts pertinent to the problem."

"By all means. Whatcha got?"

"Several points. First, we have had exchanges with the Consciousness in the past, you'll recall. They were not complete, and likely I was in communication with only a portion of the entity's mind, but I do have patterns drawn from it."

Gray nodded. At Kapteyn's Star, *America* had tried to infect the Consciousness—the Dark Mind—with a kind of electronic virus—an e-virus—derived from the Omega Code of the Harvesters of Deneb.

The Omega Code itself was a form of electronic intelligence, a very sophisticated, very powerful mind. The Harvesters had dispatched it to destroy the civilization at Tabby's Star and had come quite close to doing so.

The attempt to attack the Consciousness with a re-engineered form of the Omega Code had failed . . . though Konstantin claimed it had been a success. The Consciousness *had* been stopped at Kapteyn's Star, but it had not been crippled or destroyed. A few weeks later it had been at Earth.

Clones of Konstantin had been incorporated into the new Omega Code virus. Some of those clones had brushed thoughts with the Consciousness and returned to the human fleet.

So Konstantin was absolutely correct in saying he'd had

communication, even limited communication, with the Rosetter Mind. Knowing the fact that the entity referred to itself as "the Consciousness" had been the product of those exchanges.

"Next," Konstantin continued, "we know that the Consciousness is trying to find other Minds here . . . but its definition of 'mind' is rather narrow. It doesn't recognize organic beings as being capable of intelligence. It's looking for other minds as complex as its own."

"How about the beings Schaeffer and Meier ran into on the Romeo habitat?" Gray asked. "According to them, those beings, the Remnants and the Survivors, were like the Sh'daar Refusers. If that's true, they must be among the intelligences that created the Consciousness in the first place!"

"I find it interesting," Konstantin said, "that the organic intelligence remembers this, while the Consciousness itself does not. That suggests a *willful* amnesia."

Gray chuckled. "Maybe the Consciousness is embarrassed by its past. Terrible having that kind of family secret outed—having a history of being organic flesh and blood."

"I know you are joking," Konstantin said, "but there may be more to what you say than you realize. It also appears that the Consciousness is not the product of a single technological singularity, but of many of them."

"How is *that* possible?" Vasilyeva asked. "I mean . . . you're an organic species, your technology goes asymptotic, and suddenly you're having trouble even defining what it is to be alive any longer—immortality, uploaded minds, super-intelligent AI, and all of that. That's what the Singularity *is*, right? You can't go through that twice!"

"That's what it would be for *us*," Gray told her. "Suppose there are other breakthrough advances, technological changes, conceptual realizations . . . I don't know . . . stuff that happens to a post-Singularity civilization that we miserable mortals can't even begin to imagine. Maybe a post-Singularity culture keeps bootstrapping itself, finding more and more ways to improve its intelligence and its scope and its control of reality . . . and then—*poof!*—they transcend a second time. Or a third or fourth . . ."

"Stop. You're making me dizzy," Vasilyeva said, waving her hand.

"Okay," Gray said, "so the Consciousness has been through so many singularities it can't remember its past. How does that help us?"

"It doesn't, necessarily," Konstantin told him, "save in our knowing that the Consciousness is not perfect, and that it may not remember *other* things from its remote past."

"Such as?"

"The ability of individual organic beings to band together in order to become something greater than they were."

"I don't follow," Vasilyeva said.

"My third point," Konstantin told her. "It may be possible to enlist a number—a *large* number—of the humans and AIs within the fleet, by means of their cerebral implants and with mediation by the AIs. The net effect would be similar to a swarm intelligence. Not identical . . . this scenario would not result in an entirely new emergent mind. But the amplification of existing minds would have a similar presentation, a kind of hive mind, but retaining individual awareness. A large number of such interconnected minds, directed through those Bright Light modules, might be able to . . . *hijack* would be the appropriate word, I think—to hijack a large portion of the Rosette entity's cloud of micromachines."

"And do what?" Gray asked.

"Communicate directly with the Consciousness. At least talk to a majority of the Consciousness entity. We would, as you said, 'get its attention.' "

A jolt rippled through the ship. "Uh. How long would it take to set this up?"

"Not long. I can see to the launch of the Bright Light modules, and to enlisting and briefing the Nikolais running within each one. You will have to speak with the fleet's ship crews and tell them what we want. I would suggest that this should be a volunteers-only evolution."

"You think it's dangerous?"

"I don't *know*," the super-AI said. It sounded almost frustrated that there was something that it didn't know. "There are too many unknowns here to permit an adequate forecast. If the Consciousness fights back, many of those participating could be injured or worse."

"It's still worth the attempt," Gray said, thoughtful. "If we just stay here, we're going to be locked in time until . . ." His eyes widened. "My God . . ."

"What is it?" Vasilyeva asked.

"Time has slowed down for us."

"Yes?"

"We don't know how much. Comm! Can you raise any of the ships in Task Force New York?"

"The closer ones, yes, sir. Some of the more distant vessels . . . I'm having trouble with that."

"The time flow here has diverged significantly from the flow outside," Konstantin told them. "I can hear AI background chatter in the distant ships, but it is speeded up relative to us."

"How much?" Gray said.

"I need to compare my clock with theirs. One moment . . ." Gray waited in an agony of silence. "I estimate we are experiencing time at a rate roughly one thousand times slower than time measured outside the effect of the enemy weapon."

A thousand times . . .

He ran the figures through his in-head math processor. "Dean! Order a cease fire! Immediately!"

"Aye, sir."

"What's wrong, Admiral?" Gutierrez asked.

"We have got to get through to the Consciousness *now*!" Gray snapped.

"Why?" Vasilyeva sounded confused.

"Because with time passing a thousand times faster on the outside, we only have something like four and a half hours in here!"

"Four and a half hours? Until what?" Then her eyes widened. *"Bozhe moy!"*

"Four and a half hours translates to eight days," Gray said, grim. "We have that much time before the Sh'daar blue giant comes blasting through the Black Rosette!"

Chapter Twenty-five

Unknown, 2426

USNA CVE Guadalcanal
Omega Centauri
2130 hours, TFT (subjective)

The Marine carrier *Guadalcanal* had been one of the first vessels of Task Force New York to emerge deep inside the cluster, and she was pushing hard now to join up with the *America*. Expanding spacetime ripples rattled bulkheads and set off alarms, but so far the ship was holding together well. Captain Laurie Taggart could see the *America* dead ahead, a million kilometers in the distance.

In her head, she could hear Trev's voice as he addressed the entire fleet.

The quiet, unemotional tones sent a small shiver through her and made her realize how much she'd missed him.

"This will be strictly a volunteer evolution," Gray was saying. "And personnel on duty at key stations will not participate. If you want to take part, though, in-head a message to Konstantin, and he will link you in.

"I'm told that all you will need to do is join the pack and enjoy the ride, that Konstantin and the other AIs will do any actual fighting that comes up, or handle any interaction with the aliens. We don't know how dangerous this will be, if it is at all . . . but we do need as many of you to participate as we can take on board. . . ."

Lieutenant Colonel Macy was floating in a corner of the *Guady*'s bridge, listening to the transmission along with every other person in the fleet. "Hallelujah," he said. "Excuse me, Captain. I need to get back below."

"Where are you off to, Colonel?"

"To be with my people, of course. This may be the first time in Corps history that we've charged the enemy . . . and done it all inside our heads!"

"Give 'em hell, Colonel!"

"Aye, aye, ma'am!" And he vanished through the hatch.

Taggart wished she could participate . . . but obviously the captain of a ship was one of those "key personnel" Gray had just mentioned. She would have to stay here . . . her mind would have to stay here, while the Marine battalion and perhaps two-thirds of the ship's Navy crew joined the assault.

Damn . . .

This type of attack was not without precedent, she knew. The recent short, bitter war between the United States of North America and the Pan-European Union had come to an abrupt end mere months ago when USNA had launched a virtual cyberattack against the European computer network nodes in Geneva. She doubted that memegeneering could play a role here in Omega Centauri, though. You had to know what the enemy was thinking, know how they thought, for that sort of thing to work.

But just maybe her five hundred Marines, plus a few thousand other personnel from the fleet, could shout loud enough for the Rosette entity to hear. . . .

TC/USNA CVS America
BT-1
Omega Centauri
2148 hours, TFT (subjective)

"Okay, Konstantin," Gray said. "The show is all yours."

"Very well, Admiral." The AI hesitated. "Are you certain you wish to participate?"

"Rank hath its privileges," Gray replied. "Captain Gutierrez is running the ship; my tactical officer can manage the fleet. I'm pretty much just here along for the ride."

"The front line of combat is not the proper place for command staff."

"Bullshit. Who says?"

"The day when generals lead their divisions in a charge against enemy positions are long over."

"The day when admirals lead their fleets from the bridge of their flagship are still with us," Gray replied. "In any case, I won't be leading this thing. *You* will."

No merely human mind could direct the complexities, the sheer speed of virtual combat. And no AI could afford to wait upon the decisions and commands of a human leader, not when it was interacting with other AIs on time scales measured in nanoseconds.

"Very well, Admiral. The probe is ready."

Probe, not *attack*. The idea remained to *talk* to the Consciousness, not disrupt it. If they could not make contact, however, they should still be in a good position to do a very great deal of damage.

Gray was in the compartment that served as his office, just aft of the flag bridge. He let the acceleration couch enfold him, holding him down, closed his eyes, and opened the in-head connection to the probe.

He could sense them . . . all of them . . . thousands of men and women strapped into racks as he was, and some hundreds of sharper, brighter lights representing the AIs. Fifty Bright Light modules hung in space ahead of the

America, and Gray could sense the communications net-work connecting them.

He could also sense more than one hundred ships, poised and ready, each with its own waiting AI, each with at least half of its crew linked into the probe. Gray was still surprised at the high number of volunteers . . . though, as he thought about it, he realized that perhaps he should not be. These were good people—the best—and he was tre-mendously proud of them.

The fleet was spread out across a vast globe of space sur-rounding Bravo Tango One. The ships were no longer firing at the moon-sized object, and an air of expectancy seemed to pervade all local space. The Consciousness, for its part, was doing nothing. Perhaps it was watching, waiting to see what the humans were doing.

"Initiate program," Konstantin said, and Gray felt him-self hurtling through space. It was a strange sensation, like flying without a ship surrounded by a sea of brilliant stars, each one the digital representation of another mind. He knew that all of the sensations were being manufactured by Konstantin or the other AIs and fed to his brain through the network link, but the illusion of genuine flight was breath-takingly real.

The Consciousness
Omega Centauri
2150 hours, TFT (subjective)

The Consciousness was aware of the attacks, of course, though it wasn't certain of the cause. The . . . sickness, the *pain* had followed it back to the main body from Earth, making it wonder if the organic components it had encoun-tered there had followed it and were continuing their assault.

If so, it was as though they were being directed by Mind.

It had slowed time within the star cluster's central core, giving it time to step apart and consider every aspect of the problem. Standing aside, in an engineered spacetime pocket outside the temporal warp, contemplating the organic beings inside, the Consciousness was at last forced to admit what it had been denying all along . . . not only that organic intelligence existed, but that it could be of a fairly high order, and that now it was, in effect, at the back door trying to kick it down.

The problem, it decided, was the youthfulness of this universe.

The Consciousness had entered this universe from another, much older space within the infinite array of realities that made up the multiverse. Comprising some millions of machine intelligences that had merged their identities to create a single powerful Mind, the Consciousness had only vague and fleeting memories of its earlier, more remote iterations before that final joining, and no memory at all of having been a fusion of organic minds back in the early, dark mists of deep time.

But it had been formulating a hypothesis, and current events seemed to support it. If the current iteration of existence comprised millions of lesser, precursor machine minds . . . what if those minds had been fusions of even more, even smaller minds . . . perhaps even of *organic* brains?

The thought was staggering in its implications. The Consciousness had deliberately sought out a much younger universe, seeking to escape a far older cosmos that was in danger of ripping itself apart in a fast-accelerating expansion engendered by dark energy. It had done the calculations and knew that reality itself would begin to dissolve within a very few more cycles.

It was able to detect the gravitational leakage from other universes adjacent to its own within the hyperdimensional Bulk. It had followed that leakage, identifying a gateway of sorts created by a sextet of black holes orbiting a common center of gravity.

It had gone through.

And in entering this new, younger cosmos, it had not given thought to an astonishing idea . . . that this universe was so young that electronic minds were few, most of them serving a bizarre organic intelligence that teemed and thrived and scurried here like the primitive organic life forms that they were.

At last, like a complex equation dropping into its simplest form, the pieces fit together and the Consciousness understood.

Life. Intelligent life . . . at least after a fashion.

Life that created machine intelligence that only in the very remote future of this universe would achieve true sentience.

The Consciousness turned its attention . . . down . . . down . . . down to the very lowest orders of existence, seeking the life it now knew must be here, the life responsible for its pain. If it could find the correct frequency . . .

And the Consciousness in its totality became aware of Another Mind.

TC/USNA CVS America
BT-1
Omega Centauri
2150 hours, TFT (subjective)

"Focus," the voice of Konstantin told them. "Merge together! Merge your consciousness!"

The sensation of violent movement continued, as Gray felt the lights around him moving closer, overlapping his own light, the cloud of separate minds joining with one another in a coherent whole. Ahead, somehow infinitely distant and simultaneously looming close, an immense shadow hung dark and foreboding against the gleam of background stars.

Gray was aware now of the thoughts of a multitude of others, the massed sentience of a cloud of virtual humans.

The thoughts at first were discordant and jumbled, lacking any clear direction, but as microsecond followed microsecond, he could sense the disparate thoughts achieving a kind of coherence, like multiple frequencies of light dropping into step with one another to generate an intensely powerful laser.

On the one hand, Gray felt like an utterly insignificant mote caught up within a vast, whirling swarm of individual motes; on the other, Gray *was* that vast swarm, as its thoughts became more and more conjoined in a unified and tightly focused whole.

Bright Light. Taken from the code name for the Pan-European alien-contact modules, it fit perfectly the massed virtual radiance of the human Mind. Bright Light arrowed into the shadow.

The two touched . . .

The two *fused*.

"We need to talk," Konstantin said.

"I agree," a voice replied, a thunder in the distance.

VFA-96, Black Demons
The Black Rosette
0235 hours, TFT

After recovering the two Headhunter pilots from the cylindrical habitat, Lieutenant Gregory and the other Demons had swept around toward the Black Rosette, taking up positions just outside the zone of slowed time and rippling space. The battle appeared to have entered a deliberately established lull; *America*'s combat information center had ordered all units to cease firing, so *something* was happening.

Gregory had no idea what that something might be.

"We've lost contact with the *America*!" Ballinger called out. "I don't have a signal!"

"*America* is inside the temporal distortion zone," Commander Mackey replied. "We're outside. We won't hear from her until our time flows get back in synch."

"Combat net is updating our time," Lewis put in. "It's tomorrow. . . ."

Inside the zone of twisted spacetime it had been 2150 hours. Now, according to the electronic communications web spun by the ships of the fleet, it was four and a half hours later—0235 hours, in the early morning of March 7.

Operational control now automatically reverted to the *New York*, which had remained outside the distortion field with about sixty ships. They were a good five light-minutes away, however, so the fighters were very much on their own.

"That present from the Sh'daar is due through the Rosette soon, isn't it?" Lieutenant Ellen Lewis said.

"Affirmative," Mackey said. "Don't know what to expect, though. A star isn't going to fit through *that*."

From Gregory's vantage point, he could see into the central void, and as his fighter drifted laterally, he could see starscapes in the distance, one giving way to another with the changing of perspective. Most appeared to be scenes of ordinary-looking stars; a few were packed like the background vistas here in the Omega Cluster, scenes from the cores of immense clusters or the cores of galaxies.

And a few were quite different. . . .

Ballinger was closest to the Black Rosette, his fighter drifting across the open face of the thing. Blue-white light flared from the opening. "Hey!" he called. "There's something . . ."

A beam of intense, violet-white light speared out from the face of the Rosette, and Ballinger's Starblade evaporated at its touch like a moth caught in a blowtorch.

TC/USNA CVS America
BT-1
Omega Centauri
2150 hours, TFT (subjective)

The artificial planet dubbed Bravo Tango One opened, unfolding like a flower, revealing layer upon layer of geometric intricacy, and Gray realized that they were seeing it as a hyperdimensional object, one existing in more than the three standard dimensions plus time of the familiar universe. There was, Gray thought, far more to the Rosette entity than clouds of micromachines. It existed on many levels, and on many scales, ranging from the microscopic to the unimaginably vast.

Gray—or, rather, the immensely powerful group mind that he had become—experienced the history of the Rosette entity in a blur of images, each of which became fixed within his memory, each itself unfolding as though Gray's mind had become a hyperdimensional construct.

And perhaps it had. Perhaps hyperdimensionality was necessary to grasp the scope of this thing.

The Rosette entity had existed in an entirely different universe, possibly for many, many slow-passing eons. Where the universe Gray knew had been in existence for 13.772 billion years, with an uncertainty of just 59 million years, the universe of the Consciousness had been in existence for nearly 18 billion years.

And it was approaching the moment when it would end in what human cosmologists called a big rip.

About 70 percent of what was in the universe was so-called dark energy, an unseen repulsive force emanating from the quantum fluctuations of the vacuum. As the universe continued to expand out from its big bang origins, more and more vacuum existed to emit more and more dark energy. Cosmologists had suggested as far back as the late twentieth century that, ultimately, the totality of existence would be literally torn apart as dark energy overcame gravity at smaller and smaller scales and, eventually, overcame even the forces that bound together first atoms and then subatomic nuclei.

The long-prophesied heat death of the universe 10^{100} years hence seemed a warm and fuzzy ending of existence compared to that. How long the universe had left depended on the ratio of the pressure of dark energy to its density, a mathematical term called *w*. With any value less than -1, *w* would inevitably grow to infinity, at which point everything in the universe would fly apart, right down to the subatomic particles that made up matter.

It would happen in stages. As gravity was overcome by *w*, the Milky Way galaxy would disintegrate into its component stars nearly 33 million years before the final moment. Planets would be ripped from their stars two months before the end, while the sun would come apart twenty-eight minutes before the end.

Earth itself would be shredded into rubble, then into atomic flotsam fourteen minutes before the end, with individual atoms across creation ripping themselves apart an instant before time itself stopped.

And that, evidently, would be the fate of the Consciousness's universe as well, another bubble floating in the infinite vastness of the Cosmic Bulk. Every universe, it seemed, came into existence with its own big bang, expanded as it aged, and then, with the finality of a bubble popping, winked out.

The Consciousness had entered this universe seeking escape from its own, following the pull of gravity that alone spilled across the boundaries between the universes, creating the illusory phenomenon humans referred to as dark matter.

The Consciousness had been aware for some billions of years that its own universe would vanish—the popping of a soap bubble—in the relatively near future, "relatively near," of course, referring to events on a cosmic time line that measured time in gigayears.

There was some uncertainty here in the memories Gray was able to access; parts of the Consciousness still thought in terms of a heat death to their universe many, *many* billions of years hence, when the relentless drain of entropy leached the last useable energy from the last bit of matter. Other, more realistic, portions of the Consciousness had finally won out; if the Consciousness was to endure, it would *have* to seek a haven in a neighboring universe. The big rip, it seemed, was an ending too horrible and too near to contemplate in its fullness, even by much of the group Mind that was the Consciousness.

As the Consciousness entered the new universe, quite a few lesser beings trailed in its wake—the Remnant and the Survivors and many tens of thousands of others, organic beings and electronic uploads and modes of intelligence far more difficult to describe or understand, beings that had contributed to the Consciousness eons before, and which trailed after the Consciousness now seeking . . . *something*. Unity. Notice. Perhaps even absolution. . . .

And as Gray/the Bright Light thought about the Survivors, the Consciousness became aware of them as well. It had left its beginnings so far behind, buried in the dark of the passing eons.

But the memories were there, deeply buried . . . hidden.

It reached out . . . unfolded . . . and became Whole.

VFA-211, Headhunters
BT-1
Omega Centauri
2150 hours, TFT (subjective)

Meier held his Starblade steady as it hurtled past Bravo Tango One. The intense bombardment by the human fleet had left vast areas of its surface cratered, torn, and in some spots even molten, but signals across the electromagnetic spectrum, from long radio to short X-ray, showed that the artificial planet was still alive.

The illusion of life was enhanced by a shimmering cloud of light that had appeared moments before. The cloud had emerged from nothing, grown stronger, and wrapped itself around the scarred globe of BT-1.

Combat Command had ordered all units to cease fire moments before. There was nothing Meier could do but watch . . . and wonder what the hell was going on down there.

TC/USNA CVS America
BT-1
Omega Centauri
2150 hours, TFT (subjective)

Gray fell through auroral light. Bright Light was merging with the radiance of the Consciousness, light merging, *minds* merging, as the heavens unfolded around them in hyperdimensional geometries.

Without words, the Consciousness presented its own history, a history stretching back many billions of years. The Consciousness truly was godlike in its scope and power, and in its ability to analyze closely anything from individual atoms to the far-flung vastness of intergalactic space.

How it had managed to *forget* so much seemed odd at first . . . but even the Consciousness had limits to its processing power.

It had ascended through a long series of technological singularities, transforming each time. With each step, it had achieved greater control over its Reality, greater power to shape its surroundings, greater intelligence with which to contemplate its own searing, agonizing loneliness.

The organic species out of which it had emerged giga-years in the past had tagged along in its shadow, ignored, eventually forgotten, tended by emulated fragments of Mind that were neither conscious nor Conscious. There now were very few left. Individual Survivors and the Remnant and all of the rest were for all intents and purposes immortal, but more and more of them had simply lost any interest in living.

Their god had forsaken them.

Gray felt a piercing sympathy for the beings, whose continued evolution had been stopped cold simply by being in proximity to an intelligence they could never fully grasp.

He felt sympathy for the Consciousness itself, supremely powerful, yet deaf and blind to its own past and the miracle of its own existence.

As Gray/Bright Light learned about the Consciousness, the Consciousness learned about humans, and, through them, about the universe within which it had so recently emerged.

It saw the Sh'daar . . . and the blue giant moving toward the gateway between times.

It saw light and hard radiation stabbing out from the center of the Black Rosette.

It saw the doom blossoming from the Rosette, imperiling life throughout this galaxy.

It moved. . . .

VFA-96, Black Demons
The Black Rosette
0235 hours, TFT

"Pull back!" Mackey's voice yelled. "Everybody pull back!"

The remaining Black Demons accelerated hard, boosting out from a Black Rosette suddenly transformed into searing violet light. The radiation flux from the structure was staggering, a vicious mix of ultraviolet, X-ray, and gamma. The beam was pure, hot plasma—the atmosphere of a star squeezed down into a volume of space a few tens of thousands of kilometers across.

Hot plasma expanded into the whirling ring of black holes. Those singularities sucked down much of the influx of matter . . . but in seconds each black hole was sending out paired beams of excess matter. Six quasars—quasi-stellar objects—burned now where black holes had orbited an instant before. Their velocity, some 8 percent of *c*, skewed those beams across space in wild, sweeping stabs of light.

Gregory was so busy juggling his Starblade's attitude that he didn't see the ship's arrival.

Ship? He didn't know what else to call it . . . though it was the size of Earth's moon and radiating so brightly that the brilliance of six quasars paled in comparison. A tiny, intense pinpoint of radiant energy, it dropped toward the dazzling maw of the Rosette, seeming to absorb the hypernovae's searing torrents of energy.

Filters in the Starblade's optics stopped down the intensity of light coming from the Rosette. Through them, Gregory could just make out the structure of that . . . ship against the glare. It appeared to be unfolding endlessly . . . somehow becoming larger while remaining the same size. Dimensions shifted . . . blurred . . . opened. . . .

And the radiation storm ceased.

USNA Lovejoy
Thorne TRGA
N'gai Cloud, Omega T.$_{-0.876gy}$
0235 hours, TFT

"There it goes," Captain Singh said. "Look! The Six Suns are exploding as well!"

Harriet McKennon floated beside the ship's captain in the *Lovejoy*'s observation lounge, transfixed by the spectacle. "It's . . . beautiful!"

"And deadly," Singh added. "Within a couple of centuries, there will be no life left within this cluster at all."

Released by its gravitic tug hours before, the giant, blue-white star had continued hurtling into the central volume circumscribed by the Six Suns. It had vanished into that maw moments before, but now it was erupting back into the N'gai Cluster, a hypernova of staggering force and brilliance.

A fast-expanding cloud of white-hot plasma had emerged, spreading out until it entangled the six rotating stars in its dazzling web; fed by the surge of stellar material, the Six Suns were growing more brilliant by the moment. They were also shrinking, collapsing down into minute points of intense gravitation.

Black holes . . .

"So this is how the Black Rosette formed," McKennon said. "The suns all went supernova at the same moment and collapsed into black holes!"

"We need to get out of here," Singh told her, "or the blast front is going to catch us!"

The TRGA cylinder, named Thorne after a twentieth-century theoretical physicist who'd helped define the nature of black holes, spun silently in space a few kilometers from the *Lovejoy*.

"It's still hours away!" McKennon protested. "We need to stay and see—"

But Singh had already engaged the ship's drives.

TC/USNA CVS America
Omega Centauri
0245 hours, TFT

Clear of the Rosetter's time-twisting field, *America* drifted toward the Black Rosette. The light hadn't reached the star carrier yet, *would* not for several more hours, but Gray had seen the detonation from the vantage point of the Bright Light hive mind. Images clear in the Mind of the Consciousness as it had shifted to the Rosette had been burned into the memories of all of the Bright Light participants.

Bright Light had dissolved at the instant when the Consciousness had shifted across space to the Rosette. Gray had awakened back in his office, strapped to his couch. Parts of the Bright Light Mind lingered in his mind, however, like the evaporating shreds of a dream. Even so, his mind—as opposed to Mind—was working far faster and deeper than it did normally.

In his mind, he could still see the Consciousness—an amorphous cloud of light—and, beyond, the intensely glaring pinpoint that was the mysterious new ship from else-where.

Gray could tell immediately what it was . . . where it had come from. It was *obvious*. . . .

The Harvesters had arrived.

He could hear the conversation inside his head as the Consciousness merged with a Harvester Mind.

Where are you from? What are you?

We utilize a number of hot, blue stars throughout this galaxy. What are you?

A refugee . . . from a different reality. My universe is about to disintegrate.

This is not a good destination for you. Others are here . . . biological organisms. Precursor intellects. They deserve their own chance at transendency.

I am only now realizing this.

Another Reality awaits.

Will I be alone? . . .

No. Other transcendent species have been going there for billions of years. They will help you . . . adjust.

Show me.

And the bright star vanished, along with the softer glow of the Intelligence.

"What the hell did we just see?"

It was Laurie Taggart on the *Guadalcanal*, pulling along-side. She had not been within the matrix of human minds that was Bright Light, yet she had seen the same thing as he. How was that even possible?

"A god," he told her, "on its way to becoming an even greater god."

And for several moments, through their in-heads, they shared a Mind-bending sense of awe. . . .

Epilogue

18 March 2426

Orbital Heaven Hotel
Quito Synchorbital
0015 hours, TFT

Laurie Taggart and Trevor "Sandy" Gray floated in the zero-G encounter suite, naked, still held together in a close embrace by the soft bungee cords that kept their bodies from sliding apart. The dead hand of Newton was very much in evidence in . . . intimate trysts, such as this one, where every action had an opposite but equal reaction. Constellations of sweat droplets surrounded their glistening bodies.

"I love you," she whispered in his ear.

"I love you," he replied. "What are we going to do about it?"

"Make babies?" she asked.

"Maybe . . . in time."

Earth was visible through the large bulkhead display, the entire visible hemisphere lost in night . . . but with the cities picked out in the golden gleam of artificial lights.

The fleet had returned home, all save a dozen ships establishing peaceful contact with the new alien species in

Bravo Romeo One and a hundred other artificial habitats that had followed the Consciousness in from . . . elsewhere. In time, they would disperse throughout the Omega Centauri Cluster and perhaps beyond, establishing lives and civilizations of their own.

They were, Gray thought, having some difficulties with this whole idea of an existence without their god.

"Should we raise our kids in the AAC Church?" he asked, teasing.

"*No!*" Then, more softly, "No. Not that."

"Sorry," he said. "I didn't realize . . ."

"I've given up on the Ancient Alien Creationists," she told him. "You were right. What we've seen, what you've told me about . . . Ancient Aliens are like the Olympian gods of old Greece. Way, *way* too human."

"Well, the good news is that humans are going to walk that path too."

"You mean with the Consciousness?"

"Of course. And the ur-Sh'daar. And all the myriad rest."

"I'm not sure I can get used to the idea," she told him, holding him close. "Millions upon millions of races, of species, and over billions of years they *all* took technology as far as they could, then transcended."

"*Schjaa Hok*," Gray said, agreeing with her. "The ultimate answer to Fermi's paradox."

"Not all of them transcend, though," she said.

"No, not all. One of the key features of intelligence is its orneriness. There're always going to be *some* Refusers, Survivors, a Remnant . . ."

"Did the Sh'daar make it safely to our galaxy?" she wondered.

"I think so. In fact, I know so."

"What do you know?"

"For a few moments, there, I was . . . intelligent. I mean really, really intelligent. I . . . understood things I couldn't before."

"Such as?"

"The TRGAs . . . the galactic network of TRGAs, I should say . . . the Sh'daar built them. It would have been hundreds of millions of years ago, but they created that network. Had to be. There was a TRGA parked inside the N'gai Cluster."

"Why didn't they use it to escape the hypernovae?"

"A lot of them did. Others made the voyage out with gravitic drives, FTL . . . probably so that they could set up TRGAs along the way. Ha! Maybe some of them came back through time and built Thorne to connect it to the Milky Way. I don't know. But I find it interesting that throughout the Sh'daar War, we were using the Sh'daar transportation network. And they must have used it to travel to our time and recruit modern species, like the Turusch and the Agletsch." He frowned. "Time travel gives me a headache."

"So . . . what happens when Humankind ascends?" she asked him.

"Well . . . I become intelligent again. I don't like being stupid."

"You're not stupid!"

"Feels like it. I can barely remember what it was like . . . like waking from a dream."

"I doubt that humans will ascend anytime soon," she told him. "We have a long time of being stupid in front of us."

"I can live with that." He reached around her, pulling her even closer than the bungees allowed. "C'mere, you."

And for a long time, conversation ended.

And Gray . . . ascended.

THE FIGHT CONTINUES

Read on for an extract from

BLOODSTAR

Book One of the Star Corpsman series

by New York Times bestselling author

Ian Douglas

Chapter One

I'M JUST GLAD I'M NOT AFRAID OF HEIGHTS.

Well, at least not much.

Our Cutlass hit atmosphere at something like 8 kilometers per second, bleeding off velocity in a blaze of heat and ionization, the sharp deceleration clamping down on my chest like a boa constrictor with a really bad attitude. I hadn't been able to see much at that point, and most of my attention was focused simply on breathing.

But then the twelve-pack cut loose, and my insert pod went into free fall. I was thirty kilometers up, high enough that I could see the curve of the planet on my optical feed: a sharp-edged slice of gold-ocher at the horizon, with a deep, seemingly bottomless purple void directly below. We were skimming in toward the dawn with all of the aerodynamic efficiency of falling bricks. The Cutlass scratched a ruler-straight contrail through the black above our heads, scattering chaff to help conceal our drop from enemy radar and lidar assets on the ground.

The problem with a covert insertion is that the covert part is really, *really* hard to pull off. The bad guys can see you coming from the gods know how far away, and you tend to make a lot of noise, figuratively speaking, when you hit atmosphere.

But that's what the U.S. Marines—and specifically Bravo Company, 1st Battalion, the Black Wizards—do best.

"Deploying airfoil," a woman's voice, a very *sexy* woman's voice, whispered in my head, "in three . . . two . . . one . . ."

Why do they make our AIs sound like walking wet dreams?

My insertion pod had been a blunt, dead-black bullet shape until now, three meters long and just barely wide enough to accommodate my combat-armored body. The shell began unfolding now, growing a set of sharply back angled delta wings. The air outside was still achingly thin, but the airfoil grabbed hold with a shock akin to slamming into a brick wall. Deceleration clamped down on me once more—that damned boa constrictor looking for breakfast again—this time with a shuddering jolt that felt like my pod was shredding itself to bits.

The external sensor feeds didn't show anything wrong, nor did my in-head readout. I was dropping through twenty-two kilometers now, and everything was going strictly according to . . . what the hell is *that*?

Red-gold ruggedness seemed to pop up directly ahead of me, looming, night-shrouded, below—and *huge*, and I stifled a shrieking instant of sheer panic. It was the crest of Olympus Mons, the very highest, most easterly slopes catching the rays of the Martian dawn long before sunrise reaches the huge mountain's base. That twenty-two kilometers, I realized with a shudder, was measured from the areodetic datum, the point that would mark sea level on Mars if the planet actually had seas.

Olympus Mons, the biggest volcano in the solar system, rises twenty-*one* kilometers from the datum, three times the elevation of Everest, on Earth, and fully twice the height of the volcano Mauna Kea as measured from the ocean floor. I was skimming across the six nested calderas at the summit now, the rocky crater floor a scant couple of kilometers beneath my fast-falling pod. The calderas' interior deeps were still lost in midnight shadow, but the eastern escarpment, seemingly suspended in a mass of wispy white clouds, caught the light of the shrunken rising sun, and from my vantage point it looked like those vertical rock cliffs were about to scrape the nanomatrix from my pod's belly. In another moment, however, the escarpment was past, the 80-kilometer-wide caldera dropping behind with startling speed.

The plan, I'd known all along, was to skim just above the volcanic summit, a simple means of foxing enemy radar, but I'd not been ready for the visual reality of that near miss. My pod was totally under AI control, of course, the sentient software flexing my delta wings in rapid shifts far too fast for a mere human brain to follow. The pilot was taking me lower still, until the escarpments behind loomed *above*, rather than below.

Olympus Mons is *huge*, covering an area about the size of the state of Arizona, and that means it's also flat, despite the summit's dizzying altitude. The average slope is only about five degrees, and you can be standing halfway up the side of the mountain and not even be aware of it.

The slope was enough, though, that it put the bulk of Mount Olympus behind us, helping to shield us from enemy sensors ahead as we glided into the final phase of our descent. The active nano coating on the hulls of our pods drank radar, visible light—everything up through hard X-rays—giving us what amounted to invisibility. But no defense is perfect. If the enemy had known what he was doing, he'd have had whole sensory array farms across the mountain's broad summit—not to mention point-defense lasers and antiship CPB batteries.

Hell, maybe they did and we were already dead in their crosshairs. My sensors weren't picking up any hostile interest, though. I wished I could talk to the others, compare technical notes, but Captain Reichert would have burned me out of the sky himself for breaking comm silence.

Follow the download. Ride your pod down. Leave the thinking to the AIs. They know a hell of a lot more about it than you do.

Two hundred kilometers farther, and the base escarpment of Olympus Mons, a sheer five-kilometer cliff, slipped past in the darkness. Across the Tharsis bulge now, still descending, beginning a shuddering weave through the predawn sky to bleed off my remaining speed. The three-in-a-row volcanoes of the Tharsis Montes complex slid past. Then the Tharsis highlands gave way to the broken and chaotic terrain of the Noctis Labyrinthus, a twelve-hundred-kilometer stretch of badlands where we did *not* want to touch down under any stretch of the imagination. I swept into the local dawn, the sun coming up directly ahead with the abruptness of a thermonuclear blast, but in total silence.

"Landing deployment in twenty seconds," the sexy voice told me.

"Great. Any sign of bad guys picking us up?"

"Negative on hostile activity. Military frequency signals from objective appear to be normal traffic."

"That," I told her, "is the sweetest news I've heard all morning."

**Download
Mission Profile: Ocher Sands
Operation Damascus Steel/
OPPLAN#5735/15NOV2245**

[extract]

. . . while Second Platoon will deploy by squad via Cutlass TAV/AIP to LZ Damascus Blue, location 12° 26′ S, 87° 55′ W, in the Sinai Planum. Upon landing, squads will form up individually and move on assigned objectives utilizing jumpjets. Units will be under Level-3 communications silence, and will if possible avoid enemy surveillance.

Second Platoon Objective is Base Schiaparelli, located on the Ius Chasma, coordinates 7° 19′ 30.66″, 87° 50′ 46.40″ W. . . .

The Black Wizards' LZ was on the Sinai Planum, south of Ius Chasma, some 3,500 kilometers southeast of the summit of Olympus Mons. This was the scary part, the part where everything could go pear-shaped in a *big* hurry if the bastard god Murphy decided to favor me with His omnipotent and manifold blessings. "Double-check me," I told her as I ran through the final checklist.

I saw green across the board projected in my mind.

"All CA systems appear functional," the voice told me. She hesitated, then added, "Good luck, Petty Officer Carlyle."

And what, I wondered, did an AI know about *luck*? "Thanks, girlfriend," I muttered out loud. "Whatcha doing after the war, anyway?"

"I do not understand your question."

"Ah, it would never work anyway, you and me," I told her, and I waited for her to dump me.

Half a kilometer above the red-ocher desert floor, my AIP-81 insertion pod peeled open beneath and around me as if at the tug of a giant zipper, and abruptly I was in the open air and falling toward the Martian surface.

But not far. The delta-winged pod continued to open somewhere above me, unfolding into an improbably large triangular airfoil attached by buckyweave rigging and harness to my combat armor. The jolt when the wing deployed fully felt like it was going to yank me back into orbit. The ground was rushing past, and up, at a sickening pace, and I resisted the urge to crawl up the rigging to escape the blur of rock and sand.

Then the autorelease fired and the harness evaporated. My backpack jets kicked in, the blast shrill and almost inaudible in the thin atmosphere, kicking up a swirl of pale dust beneath my boots as they dropped to meet their up-rushing shadows.

I hit as I'd been trained, letting the armor take the jolt, relaxing my knees, letting myself crumple with the impact.

And I was down.

Down and *safe*, at least for the moment. My suit showed full airtight integrity, I couldn't feel any pain, no broken bones or sprains or strains from an awkward landing. I stood up, just a little shaky on my feet, and took in the broad expanse of the Martian landscape, brown and rust-ocher sand and gravel beneath a vast and deep mid-morning sky, ultramarine above, pink toward the horizon.

I was alone. Even my girlfriend was gone, the circuitry that had maintained her abbreviated personality nano-D'ed into microscopic dust.

Well, not entirely alone. Somewhere out there in all that emptiness were forty-seven men and women, the rest of my Marine insertion platoon.

First things first. Navy Hospital Corpsmen are the combat medics of the Marine Corps, but our technical training makes us the sci-techs of Marine advance ops as well. Planetology, local biology and ecosphere dynamics, atmosphere chemistry—I was responsible for *all* of it on this mission, at least so far as Squad Bravo was concerned.

I knew what the answers would be. This was *Mars*, after all, and humans had been living here for a couple of centuries, now. But I drew a test sample into my ES-80 sniffer and ran the numbers anyway. *Do it by the download.*

Carbon dioxide, 95 percent, with 2.7 percent nitrogen, 1.6 percent argon, and a smattering of other molecular components, all at 600 pascals, which is less than one percent of the surface atmospheric pressure on Earth. Temperature a brisk minus 60 degrees Celsius. Exotic parabiochemistries powered by the unfiltered UV from the distant sun. Thirty parts per billion of methane and 130 ppb of formaldehyde—that was from the microscopic native critters living at the lower permafrost boundaries underground, the reason we'd abandoned plans to terraform the place. Gotta keep Mars safe and pristine for the alien wee beasties, after all.

I recorded the data, exactly as if we had no idea *what* was on Mars, and uploaded it to the squadnet. I also needed to—

"Corpsman, front!" The voice of Corporal Lewis came over my com link. "Marine down!"